THE LUNAR WOLVES

K.E. DAVENPORT

**For The Spirits & Muses
who whisper strange tales at all hours
of the night.**

Dan laughed as Axel fell to the ground and disappeared. The white wolf locked his eyes on Mina, scared that Dan had finally done him in. He could see that Mina was terrified, and he tried to stay brave for her. But soon his whole body felt like it was engulfed in flames.

He roared in agony as he rose to his feet, determined to kill Dan. Mina screamed as Axel flew at Dan with his jaws wide open—ready to tear out the murderer's throat. But instead of striking Dan, Axel passed right through him like a ghost. Instantly, he realized what Dan had done to him. Years earlier, he had watched as Helen vanished into thin air right in front of Dan, and now he, too, was suffering the same fate.

Axel was incensed, but he took deep breaths to keep his wits about him. Thinking about what Dan had done to him would have to wait. Right now, he needed to stay focused on Helen and Mina. Everything he and Neriti had taught Helen was to prepare her for the moment at hand. Axel wouldn't give up and abandon her now. He had to find a way to help.

Dan grabbed Mina and set her on the floor of his large bathroom before wrapping his stubby fingers around her neck and shoving her down a long hallway. Axel looked back towards Roger, his nemesis. The large wolf was looking around the room, as though anxiously searching for something.

Axel moved to follow Dan and Mina out of the room when he heard Roger whisper to him from behind. "Despite what you believe, I did what I had to do. And even though I'm still furious over the choices *you* made, I won't allow you to stay here. Truly, Axel, you would suffer a terrible fate. Please understand that there's nothing you can do for Helen or the girl in your condition. You must go! *Now!*" he hissed.

Axel was stunned that Roger still had his voice, although it was just one more piece of evidence that the large lunar wolf couldn't be trusted. He'd betrayed their kind when he'd chosen to follow Dan. He and Axel might have been like brothers once, but that was long ago. Too much time had passed between then and now, and Axel no longer saw a brother when he looked at him. He only saw the wolf responsible for delivering the gas bombs that had silenced all the others.

Axel moved across the threshold into the hallway, but Roger spoke to him again, which caught Axel off guard. He wondered if Roger could see him. "Just so you know," Roger began, "I saved Helen once, years ago. After Dan changed her, she decided to look around the fort. If I hadn't intervened… well, let's just say it would've been bad for all of us. You don't understand what's happening here. You haven't seen the things I have. I swear on Neriti's soul, I'm telling the truth. You need to go now if you don't want to undo everything that Helen and the girl are trying to accomplish. If he captures you, I'll be forced to do things that I don't want to do."

"Is that a threat?" Axel asked angrily.

Roger shook his head. "No, it's me begging you to leave before something horrible happens."

There was desperation in Roger's voice, but Axel didn't care. He wouldn't leave Helen and Mina behind. Besides, Dan had made him invisible, which as far as he knew meant he couldn't be captured—not easily, anyhow. He ran down the hallway after Mina and Dan, but before he turned the corner, he looked back towards Dan's bathroom. Roger had disappeared, but Axel told himself it didn't matter. He had to keep going. He flew down the next hallway and the next until he reached Dan's chamber. He scanned the room and found the door that opened to the winding staircase.

Into the stairwell he leapt and up to the top of the tower. Axel jumped through the opening to the rooftop, and as he emerged, his breath caught in his throat. Just like he'd expected, he found Dan and Mina standing face-to-face atop the roof. However, lurking behind Dan was a monster made of black smoke unlike anything he'd ever seen. It was staring at Mina through two faceless, red orbs while whispering words into Dan's ear.

Axel took a step back, but the movement caught the monster's attention. The red beams that shone from its eyes shifted to him. Then, suddenly, the dark spirit's shapeless form began to expand in all directions, covering the rooftop like a blanket of dense, black fog. Axel was certain it intended to devour him. Quickly, he threw himself through the opening in the roof and down the stairs. But before he could make an escape, the dark spirit reached out and grabbed him, suspending him in mid-air above the first few steps.

Axel felt his lifeforce being ripped away. His energy was pulled out of him and stretched into a long glowing beam of light as it rotated towards the dark, menacing fog. It looked like the light from a star being spun apart by a blackhole. Sounds whooshed past Axel in all directions, but the loudest sound of all was a sharp whistle that seemed to echo inside his own head.

Axel felt the dark creature's energy merging with his own, and as the blending progressed, he understood what the creature was after. In an instant, Axel knew about the plan to destroy all life across the Moon's surface with the intention of creating new life that Dan would rule. Only this part wasn't true. The dark spirit intended to rule over the new creations. He was merely using Dan to do his bidding.

Axel was able to envision the giant tank of bubbling Shadow's Spine just beneath the stone roof, waiting to be released in the form of a toxic gas cloud that would kill everyone. The revelation was terrifying, and Axel could feel the dark spirit feasting off his terror.

All of a sudden, Axel heard the sound of shattering glass from the top of the tower. The dark spirit's attention turned towards the sound, though it continued to stretch and unravel Axel's energy while holding him firmly in his clutches. Axel hovered above the stairs, trying to think of a way to pull himself back together. But before he had time to formulate a plan, he heard a voice spinning around him inside the cyclone of dark smoke that was ripping him apart. It spoke softly at first but then grew louder so that he was able to understand it. A face appeared out of the smoke. It was Neriti.

"Axel, you have to go find the earth boy, Fred. The winged children were brought here for a purpose that hasn't been fulfilled yet. Take Fred to the ice tunnels, but first find Roger. He hasn't turned to evil the way you've been led to believe. He'll help you with the boy. The two of you must escort Fred to the ice tunnels immediately."

Axel was still reeling from having his energy stretched thin like a rubber band ready to pop. He tried to speak, but he couldn't form the words. Neriti seemed to sense what he was thinking, though. "I'll be okay. Stay brave, my dear Axel. Once Mina and Helen finish with Dan, the real work begins."

Neriti's face turned towards the rooftop as the dark energy continued to swirl around her. "You're about to be let go. Run as fast as you can and don't stop until you find the others!"

Neriti vanished, and Axel heard Dan scream from the rooftop. Then before Axel knew what was happening, his energy snapped back together, and the dark spirit flew out of sight. Axel seized on the moment and bolted down the stairs with Neriti's words still ringing in his ears. He ran back through the repeating hallways until he reached Dan's bathroom. His eyes darted around the large, tiled room, frantically searching for Roger. But he was gone.

Neriti had told Axel to find Fred *and* Roger, but unlike with Fred, Axel had no idea where Roger might be. And if he were being honest, he wasn't sure he was willing to find him. There'd been too much bad blood between the two. Searching for Roger would never be the hard part; it would be whatever came afterwards.

Without giving it any more thought, Axel sprinted through Dan's closet and down the long, frozen tunnel that led back to the subterranean trails deep below the glacier. He knew his pack's plan was to lead Fred to Bob's army. He just hoped the kid hadn't given them any trouble—or worse, given them the slip.

Axel made it to the bottom of the dark passageway and jumped into the narrow corridor where he and Mina had parted ways with his pack and Fred. Axel had always moved with ease through the dark tunnels below the glacier. He and the other wolves who'd survived Dan's massacre did everything they could to travel undetected through the interconnected web of tunnels below the Darkside, especially near Black Ice Fort. They knew that Dan had ways of getting to them. Roger had been one of those ways, in fact. So, they'd used their heightened senses and avoided using the crystals to light their way whenever possible.

But this was different. Axel had never been without a body while traveling through the tunnels, and it dawned on him that without his sense of smell, he was lost. As anxiety began to rear its ugly head, Axel hummed, hoping the crystals would respond to his voice, even though he couldn't make any audible sound. Much to his surprise, the crystals did begin to glow, lighting the tunnel walls in deep hues of red and orange.

Axel started along the path the others had taken towards Bob's army. But then, suddenly, he realized that something wasn't right. Instead of hearing his own guttural chant, Axel heard a low humming song echoing down the tunnel. Before he had time to locate the source, a high-pitched tone reverberated off the walls around him. As it bounced back and forth, the tone grew in frequency and pitch until Axel's head felt like it was going to explode.

He heard someone shouting over the deafening noise, but he didn't know what they were saying. The shrill ringing grew louder by the second. From out of nowhere, someone jumped on top of him, tackling him to the ground. It was another wolf. He felt their sharp claws digging into his back and their hot breath flooding his ear with warmth. The pain should've been excruciating, but the piercing sound was pounding through him so hard that it was all he could think about.

"I've walked into a trap," he thought. The breathing in his ear got heavier until he realized that what he was feeling wasn't breathing. It was shouting. Someone was screaming directly into his ear, but he couldn't hear them over the shrieking. Axel focused all his attention on the words being shouted at him, but it was nearly impossible to decipher any of it. The reverberating sounds were filling his head, and his eardrums were being ruled by the cacophony. Then, all at once, the voice broke through. "You're going to die…"

There was no longer any doubt in his mind. He'd been set up. Roger was on top of him, screaming in his ear and pushing him to his breaking point with the intense, painful sounds. Neriti hadn't come to him on top of the tower in his time of need. It was just another one of Dan's tricks. Clearly, the madman of Black Ice Fort had conjured something evil from one of his experiments—a dark formula he used to trick his victims into seeing whatever he wanted them to.

Axel knew he had to free himself, but the noise was too overpowering. He needed to escape the sound first. He kept humming, afraid to let the tunnel go dark or of not being able to see what Roger had in store for him.

Then, all of a sudden, Axel felt Roger's claws release. He attempted to stand, but before he was able to, Roger had him pinned again—this time on his back. Roger dug his claws into Axel's throat and began to strangle him. He struggled to breathe, but no breath came. As he began to black out, Axel stared into the face of his friend from long ago. Then the darkness took hold, and he floated away, leaving all the sounds behind.

CHAPTER 2

RUTH'S RESOLVE

Ruth sat slumped in her rocking chair sound asleep. It had been several days since their side had defeated Dan, which meant it had been several days since her own personal battle with Maude had begun.

She'd barely slept since their confrontation in the marketplace. Ruth had been well aware that revealing the truth to Maude would test their friendship—maybe even put an end to it. But knowing this ahead of time hadn't made it any easier to face the aftermath.

It had been painful to watch Maude lose her daughter all over again. Originally, Ruth had hoped that Helen's noble sacrifice might dull some of the anguish that it put her mother through, but Ruth realized how ridiculous that was now. The sacrifice Helen had made was something to be proud of certainly, but there was no pain suppressant in the entire world that could handle the torment of losing a child.

Within minutes of finding out about Helen, Maude had exiled Ruth from her former life. It had come as no surprise to Ruth that her friend was able to set aside her grief so fast. Maude had the strength of a warrior after the many hardships she had faced. Therefore, she was able to get herself through even the most difficult situations.

A few brief moments. That was all Maude had allowed herself to spend grieving for her lost daughter. Then she summoned every bit of strength she possessed and began to act —fueled by her anger at Ruth. First, she sent a silver bird to Bob to alert him to Dan and Helen's respective plans. Then she threw herself into making all necessary arrangements to end her friendship with Ruth. Permanently. She ordered the soldiers to sever their personal and professional ties with her petite, purple-haired ex-friend. From that moment forward, Ruth was to be shunned.

Ruth knew that Maude was well within her rights to do this, but she couldn't help feeling annoyed when she discovered how impossible it had become to even send a message. For years, she had relied on the carrier service she'd shared with Maude—incognito soldiers pretending to buy vegetables when, really, they were transferring correspondence on behalf of the two friends. Without access to the soldiers, Ruth was unable to send any kind of information to Maude.

And Ruth had a good reason for wanting to send information to Maude again, for she hadn't been given the chance to explain everything when she'd confronted her before. There was more to Helen's story, more to *all* of their stories. However, once Maude had stifled her sobs and regained her composure, she stood up and stormed across the marketplace. Ruth had shuffled along close behind her, trying to tell Maude about the *real* prophecy—the one she'd heard foretold with her own ears in Maude's very own living room. But Maude walked even faster, doing her best to ditch her betrayer.

Maude hadn't been able to shake her, though. What Ruth had to say was too important. She had to tell Maude everything before it was too late. Unfortunately, the second they came across one of the soldiers, Maude ordered the young man to escort Ruth back to her booth. "She's a danger to our mission," Maude had announced to the soldier—lying to get her way.

Ruth was hurt and frustrated. She hadn't expected to be shut out before she was able to reveal everything. Maude had always been quick to react, but she was also reasonable. At least under normal circumstances. "I guess I shoulda known better," Ruth scolded herself after the confrontation was over. "I shoulda made sure to put everything in that letter Helen forced me to write!"

It was true that she should've known better. After all, Ruth had spent her first year on the Moon watching Maude battle the demons inside of her, and she knew very well that Maude continued to battle these same demons every single day. Maude had never learned how to vanquish them; she'd just become expertly skilled at hiding them.

Ruth understood this better than anybody because she was the one who'd given Maude the tools to suppress this troubled part of herself. She had taught her friend how to compartmentalize her feelings—a technique that was meant to help Maude cope with the trauma of not knowing who she was or where she came from. But sometimes Ruth thought Maude had become a little too good at hiding her feelings. And certainly, Ruth was paying the price for this now as Maude went ahead and compartmentalized their friendship by forcing Ruth out of her life.

Ruth felt old. She'd been old when she arrived on the Moon, but that was a different kind of old than what she felt now. It wasn't the tiredness in her bones or the wrinkles across her skin. That sort of age had followed her from earth. This new kind of exhaustion was something different. She felt it in her heart. It told her that all the youth she'd stored away, all the big dreams she'd drawn energy from were all spent. A calm voice, more ancient than her own, whispered to her from the veil, telling her that her time was almost up. The only adventure left was one of surrender—to bravely leave behind the existence she knew and resign herself to the unknown.

Ruth had stewed over her failure to deliver the entirety of the message that had been entrusted to her. She'd stayed awake for days, thinking of ways she could pass along the information without causing Maude to shut her out even more. Eventually, however, Ruth's tired brain forced her to rest, not because she needed the sleep, but because her thoughts were churning around in circles and picking up momentum like a typhoon wreaking havoc on her mind.

Her eyes had been closed for a couple of hours when she emerged from a deep sleep and began to dream. She saw Helen as a little girl running across the gravelly field in front of her parents' workshop. She was barefoot and happy, just like she had often been when she was young. Her long, flowing hair bounced around her face, and she giggled when she spotted Ruth. Ruth waved, and the little girl began to run to her.

But as she drew near, Ruth saw something unusual in Helen's appearance. What she'd first perceived as a sparkle in Helen's youthful eyes, she now recognized as a silver flame burning inside each of her pupils. When Helen got within touching distance, Ruth began to feel the heat from the silver flames burning against her chest. It was warm at first, but once Helen was only a few inches away, the heat began to scorch the flesh right above Ruth's heart. She screamed, "No, Helen! Get back! Close your eyes!"

Ruth awoke to the sounds of her own muffled voice. What had sounded like yelling in her dream, now sounded like nothing more than hushed murmurs. Ruth knew right away she'd been asleep, only the skin above her heart still felt like it was on fire. She reached for the crystal that hung around her neck. It was scalding hot and glowing bright red like an ember.

"Helen?" she whispered aloud, but she knew the thought

was preposterous. Helen was gone. "No," she said. "This can't be Helen. It's gotta be something else. Another message, maybe. But what?" Then, suddenly, it struck her. "Oh my god! They've found a way to send Mina home!"

Fear and adrenaline awakened Ruth's senses. She knew she had to act fast. "But how?" she wondered. Maude had ostracized her. Nobody was going to help her, and she didn't have the mobility or stamina to run around searching for the girl or her old friends on her own. Ruth looked down the market row towards the other vegetable peddlers, the ones who'd stuck around to operate their booths even after they'd been freed from the twin's poison. For a second, she thought of asking them for help, but she quickly remembered that none of them were in any better shape than she was.

The crystal grew hotter, and Ruth had no choice but to remove it from around her neck. Holding the crystal by the leather straps it was attached to, she stood up and exited her wooden stand. Then as fast as she could, she made her way in the direction of Maude's booth, which was the only place she knew to look for the girl. She passed several soldiers as she walked along. A few of them knew her well, but when they saw her, they looked away nervously. "Chickens!" Ruth thought, although she knew they were just obeying orders.

By the time she made it halfway to Maude's, she'd run out of steam. She leaned against the nearest booth to rest for a moment while holding the glowing crystal away from her like the flaming hot jewel that it had become. Then just as she began to catch her breath, one of her favorite people came around the corner towards her. He was a soldier, but he was also a close friend. The two of them had arrived on the Moon close to the same time, and even though he'd lived nearly an entire lifetime since then, Ruth still liked to tease him about being a young man since that was exactly what he looked like.

"Max!" she called to him, pleading.

But Max turned the other direction and shook his head. "No, Ruth. I can't. Maude ordered—"

Ruth interrupted, "I know all about the orders Maude gave, Max. But I gotta find her and Bob—like *right now*. It's about the girl."

Everyone within earshot had stopped to stare at Ruth who was still holding the red-hot crystal out to her side. Max looked around sheepishly, clearly uncomfortable with the attention they were receiving. "Move along!" he ordered the crowd, but his voice sounded higher than usual. He cleared his throat and began again. "Move along, people. There's nothing to see here." Then under his breath, he muttered, "Just a crazy, old woman and her weird, glowing rock."

"I heard that!" Ruth snapped. "But you're right. I am feeling crazy. Crazy because Maude is punishing me for some truths that I *had* to school her on. But dang it if she didn't go and punish me too soon. And now I gotta get the rest of this information to her all snappy-like. It's a real matter of importance, you hear? And you know me, Max. Would I make this up? Haven't I always had Maude's back?"

Max nodded, but he couldn't seem to peel his eyes away from the glowing crystal, and suddenly, Ruth knew exactly what she had to do. To get her way, she was going to have to lie.

"Heavens! Look at this thing! If you don't take me to Maude right this instant, this dang rock, here, is likely to blow us up! And it's just one of lord knows how many! Dan went and planted 'em around the market in case he got beat. I've gone and figured out where most of 'em are, but only Maude can mix a formula to stop 'em from killing us. Take me to her now, Max, so we can get to setting this right!"

Max looked at Ruth skeptically. "But you said this was about the girl. What do the rocks have to do with her?"

Without missing a beat, Ruth replied, "She was with Dan

at the end, wasn't she? I'm sure she knows something about this too."

Max didn't seem convinced. "Alright, Ruth. But I'll go alone. Maude doesn't want to see you, and I'm not going to risk making her angry."

Ruth was already shaking her head. "No, Max. Look at this thing!" she said as she motioned towards the crystal dangling from her hand. We gotta move fast, or it's likely to blow!"

Max's skepticism shifted to worry. He hesitated a moment longer as he weighed his options. Then finally, he said, "Fine, Ruth. Let's go. But if this doesn't end well, you better take the fall for me."

Ruth nodded hurriedly. "Honey, if this don't end well, we are *all* likely to take a fall."

Max looked at the crystal again nervously and then turned to go, but Ruth shouted after him, "Where you going?"

He turned back with a look of confusion, but Ruth explained, "Didn't you hear me tell you we gotta fix this *fast?* You know I can't walk more than a snail's pace. You gonna have to carry me on your back. But don't go fretting now. I expect I don't weigh no more than a bunny slipper filled with brussels sprouts."

Max hung his head in defeat. He was fairly certain he was being duped, but he didn't feel like he could say "no" since there was at least a small chance that his friend was telling the truth. She seemed simple, but over the years Max had learned that there was far more to Ruth than she let on.

Max hunched down and let Ruth wrap her arms around his shoulders. Then he hoisted her up on his back and took off to find Maude. Ruth extended the blazing crystal out in front of Max. It was like a fiery carrot being hung in front of a stubborn mule to coax it along. Max sped past all the aisles towards Maude's booth, which was the last place he'd seen her. She and Bob had turned it into a temporary workstation a few days earlier. They'd asked the soldiers for privacy so they could work on a new, time-sensitive project. But everyone assumed it was really so they could be alone during these early days of mourning.

The two friends made good time, mostly because Max was mortified and wanted to put his piggy-backing days behind him as quickly as possible. Unfortunately, when they reached Maude's booth, it was empty. Ruth looked inside. In the middle of the booth was a work bench that offered a clue about where her friends might've gone. It was covered in little cut-up pieces of synthetic feathers which Ruth knew belonged to the wings Bob had created.

"Oh no!" she exclaimed. "I hope we're not too late. We gotta go, Max! If they're sending the girl off, they'll be somewhere outside the market. Head that way!" she ordered, waving the red-hot crystal towards the far end of the aisle.

Max didn't like being bossed around like he was Ruth's horse, but nevertheless, he followed her command and headed out of the market. Once they passed beyond the wall, they saw the shadowy figures of four people off in the distance. Ruth knew instantly it was Maude, Bob, and the girl, though she wasn't quite sure who the fourth person was.

"There!" she yelled in Max's ear. "We're not too late! Come on now! Hurry, Max!"

"Late for what?" asked Max.

"Never mind that," Ruth replied. "Just get us there as quick as you can. You'll understand soon enough."

Max charged ahead, but seconds later a giant burst of flame shot into the sky with what looked to be a human-shaped lump of clay right above it.

"Faster, Max! Faster!" Ruth yelled.

But Max was already going as fast as he could go, and by the time they got within shouting distance of the others, the ignited lump of clay was high above the Moon's surface.

. . .

Jacques watched as the petite mademoiselle was sent hurtling into outer space. His chest was swollen with pride, knowing he'd helped send the little heroine home to her family. With tears in his eyes, he took a few steps forward to stand below the tiny champion as she began her journey. "Au revoir!" he yelled as he waved goodbye and silently prayed for her safety.

Then, from out of nowhere, a strange sound caught the little chef's ear. At first, he didn't want to take his eyes off the young lady wrapped in his specially made cheese suit. She'd already grown so small, and Jacques worried he might lose sight of her altogether if he didn't stay focused. But soon the noise was too loud to ignore, and Jacques realized it was the sound of a woman shouting.

Jacques glanced over his shoulder to take a look at the source of the commotion. What he saw, however, was not at all what he had expected. "Zut alors! Bob! Take a look at this!" exclaimed Jacques.

Bob, who was holding the rocket-pack control tightly, replied, "Not now, Jacques! I have to keep Mina in view so that I know when it's time to turn the boosters on."

Jacques understood and tried again with Maude, who was standing nearby. "Maude, I know you want to see the little girl get home, but I think you need to take a quick look behind you."

But Maude ignored Jacques, except to shake her head, as though she were telling him she wasn't interested in what he was saying. He turned his vision again in the direction of the noise, trying to force himself to turn a blind eye to it like his friends. But finally, he exclaimed, "Non! Non! This is impossible to ignore! There is an insane, violet-haired woman riding a man, and they are headed this way! And the woman is whipping the man-horse across the chest with a very hot piece of coal that is tied to a tiny rope.

"I know this sounds strange, but I think you need to look, Bob. The violet lady seems to want something from you. She yells, 'Stop! Stop!' You hear this too. Non?"

Maude had started to shake her head emphatically. Through gritted teeth, she said, "Don't give in, Bob. She doesn't get a say in this. It's like you said, Mina has a family to return to. There can't be one good reason that blasted woman has for keeping her here a second longer."

But Bob couldn't help himself. He turned his head to see what Jacques was talking about. "Um, Maude. Sweetheart. Jacques is right. You need to see this. Ruth is riding Max towards us like a human rickshaw, and they both look pretty upset. I think we should bring Mina back down and find out what's going on. I can always reset the rocket-pack after we sort everything out."

Maude swung around. But instead of looking at Ruth, she looked directly at Bob. "Absolutely not! Ruth can't be trusted. Maybe you don't see it, but *I do!* And I'm not about to let her sabotage Mina the way she sabotaged Helen!"

Maude ripped the control out of Bob's hands and looked again towards the tiny speck of flame that was racing up, across the backdrop of space. She could hear Ruth pleading with her from behind. "No, honey! Don't do it! She *can't* go back!"

But Maude was a woman possessed by grief and fueled by rage. She began to work the knobs on the remote, even though she wasn't entirely sure what she was doing. Bob wrapped his arms around her, trying to take back control of the remote without hurting his frail wife. "Let me have it, Maude," he spoke softly but firmly in her ear. "You don't want to do some-thing that would hurt Mina."

Maude's eyes stayed glued to the flame as she fought back.

But then, suddenly, the tiny flame changed course, descending downward across the dark sky. Maude panicked. She knew Mina was tumbling back to the Moon, and it was all her fault. She let Bob take the remote. However, before he had control again, something terrible happened—Mina disappeared.

Maude gasped. "Where'd she go!?"

She turned to her husband, who was still looking down at the remote as he positioned his hands on the controls again. Bob glanced at Maude and then back up to outer space. He furrowed his brow and began scanning the different sections of sky where he knew Mina was most likely to be.

Maude grabbed Bob's arm. "Oh my god, Bob! Did the rockets go out? Is she still falling? We have to *do* something!"

Bob fiddled with a couple of knobs and pushed a button, but still there were no signs of the flames from the rocket-pack. "This doesn't make any sense," he said. "The radar on the remote isn't even registering the pack anymore. It's like…" Bob stopped and looked up at the dark sky. "It's like she vanished."

Maude felt weak. She held on to Bob's arm to steady herself and then turned to face her former friend—the woman she'd spent the last several days hoping to never see again. "What were you thinking, Max? You disobeyed my orders by bringing her here! I should have you court-martialed for this!"

Max looked uneasy. He lowered Ruth awkwardly to her feet, doing his best not to let the dangling crystal touch his skin. Its light had faded so that it looked like any ordinary crystal again, but it was obvious that Max didn't trust it.

"Ruth insisted she needed to speak to you right away. She told me that Dan hid a bunch of these tiny bombs around the market," he said, pointing to Ruth's crystal. "She said you would know how to neutralize them."

"And you believed that nonsense? That's not a bomb! It's her crystal necklace. Look at it! Can't you tell the difference between a necklace and a *bomb?*"

Max seemed embarrassed. He looked down at his feet. "Well, it didn't look like that before. It was glowing red, kind of like a bomb might do," he replied.

Ruth spoke up. "Maude, honey, I know you're angry and you got every right to be, but you didn't let me finish what I had to tell you the other day. And well, it may be too late now, but it's still mighty important that you let me do it."

Maude was fuming. She looked as if she wanted to slap Ruth, but instead she tightened her grip around Bob's arm. "There's nothing I want to hear from *you,*" she said sharply.

Bob, who was always the peacemaker, suggested, "Ruth, why don't you let Max take you back to the market. We've had it rough these last few days, and I think Maude needs some more time before the two of you patch things up."

Ruth shook her head dismissively and spoke directly to Maude, "I get now that I shoulda told you the truth a long time ago. I was trying to protect you the way I thought proper and the way I was told to do. But you gotta hear a few things before it's too late. I ain't trying to be dramatic or nothing, but I can feel my time slipping away. There's a cold hand laying claim to my heart."

"Don't be absurd!" Maude shot back. "You can't die! You're a Moon Traveler, just like the rest of us!"

Ruth glanced around at the others before setting her eyes on Bob. "Sugar, I think it would be best if you let me talk to Maude alone. I reckon it won't take too long, and you all don't need to go far. Just give us a little privacy, okay?"

Without another word, Max and Jacques began to walk out of earshot, back towards the market. Bob looked at Maude. "What do you say, sweetheart?" he asked.

Maude looked back at Bob and shook her head. "I don't want to. Besides, we've got to find Mina. What if something horrible has happened to her?"

But Ruth said, "Honey, Mina's what I've come to talk to

you about. I can clear a few things up for you. And I promise I ain't got nothing left to say that's gonna hurt you none. Not like what I told you last time. The rest of this is just some loose ends, but they're some important ones. I wish I'd been able to tell you before. It might've made this next part easier."

"What next part?" Maude asked.

"Well darling, if you want to know that, you're gonna have to listen to what I gotta say."

Slowly, Maude let go of Bob and nodded, giving him permission to leave her with Ruth. Bob squeezed Maude's shoulder and went to join Max and Jacques. Maude was trembling. Instinctively, Ruth reached out to comfort her friend, but Maude pulled away.

"*You* did this to me. You came out here to ruin everything the same way you did with Helen!" she said, lashing out.

Ruth looked at Maude with sad, knowing eyes. "No, Maude. I came out here to try and stop you from sending Mina back. To tell you why it wouldn't work. Mina ain't who you think she is. Ain't none of us are."

"Stop it, Ruth! You're talking crazy!"

"No, child. I wish it were crazy, but it's the truth. A truth told to me by your very own self nearly fifty years ago. I barely believed it to be honest, but I've had plenty of time to wrap my head around it. I guess as much as any mortal ever could, anyway."

"So, what are you saying, Ruth? If none of us are who we think we are, then who are we?"

Ruth worked to suppress a smile that raised the corners of her mouth. "Well now, honey, that's the whole meat and potatoes of it. I'm gonna tell you a story. You ought to remember some of it, at least. And when I'm through, if you still want me to, I'll leave you alone for good."

CHAPTER 3

THE VISION CRYSTAL, PART I

In the Early Days of the First Moon Travelers.

"Shah-sey, shah-sey, songue-shey, songue-shey…" Neriti heard herself singing alone. She glanced around the circle. The other healers had already transcended into their meditative forms. Something wasn't right. The group hadn't even finished their warm-up incantation, and normally it took dozens of these ancient songs to harness enough energy to connect to Theia.

Neriti looked up. The loose spirals of long, white energy strands had connected high above them in the center of the circle. Quickly, she closed her eyes. She knew she needed to ready herself, or she'd miss out on the vision.

Before she'd even had a second to calm her mind and slip into meditation, the way the lunar wolves had been taught to do in ancient times, Neriti connected to a vision. But it didn't flow into her like a stream passing through her mind's eye. It ripped through her like a raging current, determined to force its way. The feeling was so overpowering that Neriti had no option but to give in. It would've felt blasphemous to do otherwise, for it was evident that the Great Energy had something urgent to show them.

In her metaphysical state, Neriti saw the long neon bridge and the visitors walking across it. She saw tall, white columns that formed an entryway from the glowing bridge to the Moon's surface. The columns were made from the bundles of paper that The Moon Walkers had entrusted to the wolves before departing long ago. As they passed, the Moon Travelers stopped and picked the columns apart, one bundle at a time, before moving on. Neriti turned her head and saw several of the wolf leaders watching it all transpire. They nodded approvingly as the visitors entered the realm and took the bundles of paper.

Then the vision shifted, and Neriti was walking the streets of the human village, only it wasn't a village any longer. It was a large city filled with homes and buildings, a city square and parks. Neriti turned down a road that led through a neighborhood, looking back and forth at the houses as she went. In the front window of every home was an empty cradle, and though Neriti had never seen anything like this before, she understood it was where the humans laid their little ones to sleep.

The setting was eerie. Everything was silent and still. However, Neriti could feel electricity in the air which seemed like it was signaling the coming of some big event. When she reached the center of the neighborhood, she realized there was nobody on the street but her. A loud sound like a clap of thunder rolled across the sky, and a thick cloud of dust swept over the tops of the houses. The wind and grit blew across Neriti's face and fur, stinging her eyes and forcing its way inside her lungs. She shook her body in a futile attempt to rid herself of the pesky grains of dust that clung to her.

The rumbling in the sky shook the ground as it moved

closer. Neriti looked in the direction of the sound. A ray of sunlight was slicing through the heavy clouds above the rooftops. The ray grew brighter, and soon the entire cloud was bathed in radiating light. The dust spread apart, as though the light was repelling it. And once the air was clear again, Neriti saw that the source of the light was a small object hovering in the sky above her.

Neriti squinted, trying to see what the object was, but the light was too powerful and forced her to divert her gaze. She lowered her eyes but caught a glimpse of something moving in her peripheral vision. She turned her head towards the closest house and peered into the front window. There was nobody there, but the cradle inside had begun to rock back and forth on its own.

The floating object lowered closer to the ground. Neriti didn't dare look at it again, but she felt the intensity of its light growing stronger. She looked down the street at the other houses, and in every window she saw the same scene—a cradle rocking all on its own. As the object approached, the cradles began to rock faster and faster until the entire street had been illuminated in radiating white light.

Then just as the object's luminosity reached its pinnacle and began to soften, Neriti heard a noise that seemed familiar yet foreign to her. It sounded like the howls of a wolf pack in distress, but she knew that couldn't be because the noise was too guttural and whiny to belong to any wolf.

As the drifting object dimmed, the shrill, nasally cries became louder. Neriti turned her gaze once more to the floating object. She could see now that it was a small, opaque crystal descending slowly from the sky. The luminescent glow faded from the sparkling gem until the light inside of it had completely gone out. When the light was extinguished, the crystal fell the last few feet to the ground and landed softly.

One last thundering boom echoed across the sky, and all

the fussy cries were silenced, replaced by happy coos and gurgles. Neriti walked up and down the street, looking into all the windows. The cradles still rocked back and forth but remained empty. Then, suddenly, Neriti stopped as she caught sight of the first two visitors. The man and woman stood in a window across from her, and together they were holding three human young in their arms. They bobbed up and down and swayed back and forth, soothing the little ones with their rhythmic motions.

The vision brought warmth to Neriti's heart. The meaning behind it wasn't clear to her yet, but the love between these parents and their young was too sweet to ignore. It reminded Neriti of everything that had happened to her own family, and though the subject was painful, the sight of this family didn't cause Neriti to mourn for her lost grandchildren. Instead, it filled her with joy, as though the family represented some inexplicable promise of hope.

With this seed of promise firmly planted in her mind, Neriti awoke from the vision and found herself back in the circle with the others. Directly across from her, Neriti's close friend, Imgu, was the first to speak. "Okay, healers. Let's go around and share what we've seen, shall we?"

Each of the wolves took turns reciting the details of the vision they'd had—a practice that had been a part of the healers' ways for ages. They'd learned over many centuries that each wolf's vision contained different information. Therefore, it was important for everyone to share their experience in order to make sure they'd captured the full extent of whatever message the Great Energy was sending them.

Neriti listened carefully to the other healers but was surprised that none of them recounted a feeling of hope from what they'd seen. Instead, it sounded like the vision had made them wary. Tazi, a healer from another pack, summed up their thoughts well. "More visitors keep arriving across the bridge every day. And the more that come, the less likely it seems they'll ever leave. And now we have to worry about this too? If they build a great big city and start to reproduce, they'll surely try to take over all of Theia in a few generations!"

The other wolves nodded in agreement at this. Imgu, who'd been eyeing Neriti, asked, "And what do you say to this, Neriti? After all, it was your request to the Great Energy on behalf of the visitors which brought this vision about. Do you feel like you have an answer to take back to them now?"

Neriti looked around at the other faces in the circle. They seemed to be studying her, anticipating what she would say. She frowned. "Did none of you feel a sense of hope from this vision? Not from the knowledge that there might be more humans, of course, but something else. Something that was left unsaid. It was like Theia was making a promise of comfort and prosperity."

The healer named Yakuma snickered. "But whose comfort and prosperity is being promised?"

Neriti frowned. "I understand that these are hard times. The rest of you know I've suffered greatly, and hopefully none of you doubt my intentions. I'm not trying to create happiness for the visitors at our own expense. I'm only trying to understand them. There's little we can do to control whether they stay or go, but I fear that turning our backs on them will only make matters worse for us over time."

Imgu nodded. "No one here doubts your intentions, Neriti. We only worry that you've become too involved with the visitors' needs. We agreed not to share our knowledge and practices with them for good reason, yet you *have* shared some of this with them by acting on their behalf with the Great Energy. We all know you've suffered, and we worry it's clouded your judgement."

Neriti saw it as a betrayal to be spoken to this way in front of the entire group, especially since it was coming from one of her dearest friends. She decided to move quickly to disband their circle. "I'd like to break the vision circle so that I may reflect on this vision in private. I appreciate your cooperation and the fact that you stuck around after the pilgrimage despite your strong concerns over my judgement. I assure you all, though, that I am doing fine, and contrary to your fears, my mental acuity has never been better."

The other healers looked around at each other. It seemed as if they were expecting someone to respond, but it was obvious that no one wanted to challenge Neriti further. So, after a moment passed, Imgu sighed and said, "Okay. If there's nothing left to discuss, we'll go ahead and break the circle. Thank you and safe travels to you all."

The healers chanted their songs to disperse the energy they had harnessed while forming the circle. Then once the chanting was done, everyone said their goodbyes and left the circle except for Imgu and Neriti.

"You shouldn't have allowed your temper to ruin the circle, Neriti. Those healers were doing you a favor. I suspect they'll think twice about doing so again."

Neriti remained silent for a while. She had no interest in continuing the discussion with Imgu. Regardless of her anger, she *did* actually intend to sit and contemplate the vision for a while on her own. But Imgu—who was half the distance in age between Neriti's daughter and Neriti—still had a youthful spirit and was less inclined to let a good fight go.

"Aren't you going to say anything?" asked Imgu.

"What would you like me to say?" Neriti replied. "You seem to think you have this solved already. I'm an old wolf past my prime, too senile and overwhelmed by grief to realize I'm betraying my own kind."

Imgu retorted, "We never called you old or senile."

"No," replied Neriti. "But wouldn't I have to be if what you're saying about me is true? Not even heartbreak could cloud a wolf's judgement so much that they'd purposely betray other wolves."

Now it was Imgu's turn not to speak, and the two wolves sat silently for a long time. "So why *are* you helping them then?" Imgu asked finally.

"I'm not helping *them,*" replied Neriti. "I agreed to help one couple. *The first two Moon Travelers,* as they're known to the other visitors. They're smart, Imgu. Really smart. The others aren't stupid, but these two are capable of magic. Only they don't call it magic, they call it *science.* But whatever it is, they're able to create things with their knowledge. Big things.

"I know we have every reason to be fearful of the visitors, and I am. But these two are special. It's no wonder Theia brought them here first. Plus, they're kind. I can see it in them. And I'm not the only one, you know. Several of the pack leaders have taken a liking to them too."

Imgu looked away, as if these words pained her. "I know, Neriti. It's one of the reasons the other healers and I are so concerned. The visitors have barely been here for one full cycle, and the leaders are already letting their guard down. Just because the humans haven't killed us in our sleep yet doesn't mean they can be trusted."

"Yes, Imgu. But they're here, aren't they? We may have decided not to share our secrets with them, but unless we're planning to kill them in *their* sleep, we should probably try our best to understand them. And sometimes that will mean helping them like I'm trying to do now. It's the only way to keep our relationship with them on good terms."

Imgu nodded and began to walk towards her friend across the distance that had separated them in the healers' circle. "Well, you've gotten your vision. So, what do you plan to do—"

Imgu stopped and looked down. Then she lifted her right paw and gasped.

"What's wrong, Imgu?" Neriti asked. "Are you hurt?"

Imgu looked at her with a mixture of fear and awe. Neriti took several giant leaps towards her as Imgu looked down again. Neriti followed her gaze. Right below Imgu's raised paw was an opaque crystal the exact shape, size, and color as the crystal from the vision.

Neriti was speechless. Just like all the other healers, she'd been taught the lunar wolves' history in great detail. Yet never in all of their teachings had she heard of a vision manifesting into a physical object. The closest thing to it was when her little granddaughter, Mawd, had been transformed into the first Moon Traveler. But that had occurred during a healing ritual, not a vision.

"How is this possible?" asked Imgu. "And what are we supposed to do with it?"

Neriti took a second to think. Then she looked Imgu straight in the eye and said, "We give it to the humans. I think that's what Theia intends for us to do."

Imgu barely allowed Neriti to finish this thought she blurted out, "No way! There is no way we're giving the humans a crystal! Especially not a crystal from Crystal Crater! Are you completely out of your mind? If they figure out what kind of power it has, they'll use it against us."

Neriti replied calmly, "Technically, the crystal isn't from Crystal Crater. It came straight from Theia, which means if we disregard it or keep it for ourselves, we'll be ignoring Theia's wishes. Is that what you think we should do?"

Imgu shook her head like she was tossing the thought from her mind. "You don't know that's what Theia wants, Neriti. We didn't even get to discuss this as a council because you dismissed everyone so fast. There may be another interpretation of why the crystal was put here."

Neriti stared at her friend with a serious expression. "What other explanation can you think of, Imgu? In the vision, the crystal dropped to the center of the human village. You saw with your own mind's eye the impact the crystal had when it fell. You think a wolf is meant to possess this crystal? Really? Did the crystal create three wolf pups out of thin air with its magic? No, it put three newborn humans into their parents' arms. Are you really planning to stand in the way of this? If Theia wants the humans to have this crystal for something this big, are you really going to try and stop it from happening?"

Imgu hung her head and let out a loud grunt. Then she looked back up at Neriti. "Why is Theia doing this to us? Haven't we honored her *exactly* the way we were taught to? For millennia we've done *everything* we were supposed to do. Everything! Why are we being forsaken now?"

Neriti looked around a bit nervously. She and Imgu were the only ones left inside Crystal Crater. The wolves who'd stayed behind to journey home with Imgu and Neriti were waiting along the rim above the crater.

"I don't think it wise to question Theia, Imgu. The healers have been given visions of what's to come. I don't know if we can stop any of it from happening, but I do know that the best chance we have is to continue to trust the Great Energy. Trust that Theia will show us how to protect ourselves."

Imgu looked distraught, but nevertheless, she gave in. "Fine, Neriti. I won't stand in your way if you think this is what Theia wants. If you're going to do this, though, I strongly suggest you present the crystal to your friend, Ruth. If it must go to a human, it should go to her. She's the only visitor who's made any real effort to get to know us and understand our ways."

Neriti nodded. "Yes, Imgu. I think that's a wise decision. Ruth will be a good human to entrust the crystal to."

Imgu rolled her eyes. It was obvious she wanted her friend to know how unhappy she was. She turned away and began to walk up the path towards the crater's rim. Neriti picked up the crystal in her mouth, storing it against the inside of her cheek. Then she followed Imgu up the long trail. When they'd almost reached the top, Neriti spotted her son waiting for her with Imgu's partner, Wollavee, and sister, Molaye.

They walked in silence until they were almost out of the crater, at which point Imgu turned her head and said, "Your choice may be the correct one, Neriti. Everyone knows you're the strongest healer to come along in generations. Right or wrong, however, I've decided to disassociate myself from this vision and all it entails. Go and tell the pack leaders what we've seen, but do not use my name or the other healers to back your interpretation. You alone deserve all the credit or all the blame for what's to come."

Neriti didn't respond. Her eyes were locked on her son. She'd grown tired of Imgu's sanctimonious tone and was ready to move on. When they reached the top, Neriti nodded at Imgu's family. "Thank you for waiting for us," she said to them. "I'm sorry I kept her so long. Safe travels to you all."

Wollavee and Molaye bowed to Neriti. "Same to both of you," they replied to Neriti and her son. Imgu tried to shoot Neriti one last look, but Neriti refused to give her the satisfaction. "I understood your message perfectly well, Imgu. Consider yourself absolved from all credit or blame."

Then she turned from Imgu and began to walk alongside her son, back across the Darkside towards their valley home in the light.

CHAPTER 4

THE VISION CRYSTAL, PART II

Maude stared into the bubbling liquid, gripping her spoon, and doing her best to stay patient. She knew it was still too soon to stir the formula. She'd been trying to perfect the metal strengthener for days, but the liquid had lost its potency with each new rendering. She'd finally realized that it wasn't obtaining enough heat before she stirred in the last ingredient—a powdery mixture of silicon and magnesium.

A dark tan arm slipped around her waist and pulled her tight. A second later, she felt her husband push the side of his face against her own. It was warm, and for a moment she was able to relax.

Knock! Knock! Knock!

Maude looked across the kitchen and through the living room to the front door. The wool curtains were drawn so she couldn't see who it was, and she thought about not answering it. Bob stood up straight with his arm still wrapped around her waist. "Who do you think it is?" he asked.

Maude frowned. "How in the world would I know?" she replied. "This really can't go on. It has to be the tenth time someone's come calling today, and it's not even suppertime yet," she grumbled as she put down her mixing spoon and wiped her hands on her heavy apron.

Bob walked out of the kitchen and strode quickly across their tiny living room. "Don't worry," he said. "I'll tell whoever it is that they'll have to come back tomorrow."

He pulled the door open with a swift tug, and Maude heard him say, "I'm sorry, but you all will have to come back some other time. Maude and I have too much work to do tonight."

She tried to look around Bob's wiry frame to see who he was talking to, but within seconds she knew who it was by the sound of her voice.

"Oh, sugar, are you sure you can't spare a minute? Neriti and the others came all this way, hoping to discuss a matter of importance with you all."

Maude began taking off her apron. "Let them in, Bob," she called to her husband. "I'm probably not going to get this formula figured out tonight anyway. They can be our last visitors for the day, and then tomorrow we won't open the door at all."

Bob laughed at his tall, red-headed wife. "*Right*," he said sarcastically. Then turning back to their company, he explained, "She says that every night. Come on in, everyone, and make yourselves at home."

A petite, purple-haired woman with tan skin walked through the front door, followed by three white wolves. Maude made her way into the cozy living room to greet them, and Ruth smiled at her sweetly. "Sorry to barge in on you like this, hon. I know you get lots of interruptions, but these three traveled straight to Waldoff after returning to their homes from Crystal Crater last night. They've had a long journey."

Neriti, the smaller of the three wolves stepped closer to Maude. "Thank you for seeing us, Maude. I know you remember my apprentice, Axel, and my son, Ragher. We came to speak to you about the question you posed last time we met, though it might be better if we spoke alone."

Neriti looked at Bob who was standing behind Maude and then back at Axel and Ragher. "Could the males give us some privacy please?"

"Oh. Well…um…sure," Bob sputtered. "Here, fellas. You can follow me down the road, and I'll show you the work shed I've been building for Maude. I figure one day I might actually get to use our kitchen to cook some food without having to worry that the meal is contaminated with toxins." Bob and the two large wolves strolled out the back door together.

Ruth took a seat on the small sofa, and Neriti sat on the floor beside her. Maude didn't sit, though. Instead, she walked to the narrow, stone fireplace and placed both hands on the mantle above it, gripping it tight. "Would you like me to light a fire?" she asked. "Bob just got the fireplace to work after several redesigns. I know it's not cold, but the blue flames are kind of pretty…" She turned around to face her visitors. Her skin was flushed, and it was obvious from her expression that she felt nervous.

Ruth looked at Neriti like she was expecting her to respond to Maude's question, but when she didn't, Ruth said, "I think you ought to sit down, sugar. We don't need a fire right now. Let's just hear what Neriti has to say, alright?"

Maude nodded and sat down in a wooden armchair across from them. Once she was settled, Neriti began. "During the pilgrimage to Crystal Crater, I spoke with several of the top healers about the problem you and your partner are having producing a child. We decided to go on a vision quest on your behalf to consult the Great Energy. But the answer we received was most unexpected."

Maude looked skeptical. "The Great Energy? I thought you were planning to talk to the other medical experts you know, Neriti."

"Yes, well these medical experts you speak of are actually healers, like myself. And the way we look for answers to questions that seem difficult is by consulting the energy known as Theia. The practice was taught to us by the first beings who inhabited the Moon. They were known as the Moon Walkers."

"Moon Walkers? So, you're saying there were others here before the wolves?" Maude asked.

Neriti looked a bit reluctant to answer, but slowly she replied, "Yes. However, this is some of the information the pack leaders don't want your kind to know." Neriti motioned her head towards Ruth and said, "Your friend, here, has given us her word that you and your husband can be trusted, and I know you well enough to believe it to be so."

Maude seemed upset. "But I don't understand. Why are the pack leaders withholding information from us? Shouldn't we be working together to help each other?"

Neriti shook her head. "No, Maude. You need to think about it from the wolves' perspective. We've been here since ancient times, practicing the ways we were taught. The wolves believe that for the most part this has brought us prosperity and kept the existence we know in balance.

"To us, you Moon Travelers seem like newborn pups who are seeing the world for the first time. Everything is new to you. Therefore, you think it's okay to make it your own, to define it any way you please. *Unlike* newborn pups, though, your kind isn't malleable. You humans have come here set in your ways. It would be impossible to teach you as a whole to honor the Great Energy. It's not how you understand the world you live in."

Maude pushed back. "But it doesn't seem like you're even giving us a chance to prove you wrong. I mean, *I'm* not set in my ways, right? I don't even remember my life before I arrived here. And right now, the others are just trying to survive this foreign world without losing their minds. It's been a difficult adjustment for almost everyone. Maybe if the wolves offered some guidance to the Moon Travelers, it would help us bring our two worlds closer together."

"I understand your point, Maude. Really, I do. But the wolves don't see it this way. The healers have been given the gift of future visions by the Great Energy, and our most recent visions have convinced us that we're better off guarding our ancient secrets than sharing them."

"But Neriti—" Maude began.

However, Neriti cut her off. "Tell me, Maude. What do you make of the recent discovery of bones in the tunnels near the Darkside?"

Maude looked confused for a moment. She hadn't expected Neriti to change the subject so quickly. She took a minute to think about it, and while she did, Ruth said, "Neriti dear, don't you think you gals have strayed too far down the wrong path? After all, I thought the purpose of this visit was to tell Maude about what you found at Crystal Crater. Isn't that right?"

Both Neriti and Maude ignored Ruth, though. The beautiful, white lunar wolf sat patiently while staring with laser-like focus at the young human as she continued to search for an answer. Finally, Maude replied, "I don't know what to think of it just yet, but I do know it has nothing to do with me or where I came from. Those bones clearly belonged to some group of large beasts. Maybe you wolves know what they belonged to? Did the Moon Walkers tell you about them?"

Neriti smiled, as though she'd expected this answer. "But why do you feel the need to tell me that these bones have nothing to do with you? I can see plainly that you're a human and not a large, horned beast."

Maude replied, "Because Peter, the man who found the bones, told the other Moon Travelers that the bones belonged to my ancestors. He thinks that the beasts used to look like humans or human-like creatures and that they lived on the Moon before everyone else. He thinks they caught some horrible disease that turned them into the beasts but that, somehow, I managed to stay healthy and survive."

"And this theory seems unlikely to you?" asked Neriti.

Maude scoffed. "Yeah. It seems a bit far-fetched, I'd say."

"So, then the other Moon Travelers understand how ridiculous this assumption is? And they've set this man, *Peter*, straight. Yes?"

Maude looked away from Neriti towards the fireplace. "No," she said. "Not all of them." Then she looked back at Neriti. "But if the wolves know who the bones belonged to, *they* could set Peter and the others straight."

Neriti stared intently at Maude. "I want you to think about this seriously now, Maude. If Peter and the others have not used their own logic to conclude that these bones couldn't have belonged to humans, and they have not been persuaded by the other Moon Travelers who've tried to reason with them, then what would make you think that the wolves could convince them? Do you believe them to hold the wolves in higher regard than their fellow man?"

Maude shook her head. "No, I know they don't."

Neriti continued to push, even though Ruth had begun to show visible signs of anxiety—rotating between fidgeting with her skirt and shoving her hands deep into the sofa cushion.

"Then have they said anything about us that makes you think they'd believe the pack leaders' stories over their own concocted ones?"

Maude let out a deep sigh and bowed her head a little. "Okay, Neriti. I see your point."

Ruth looked relieved and said, "Alright, you two. Can we get back to business now?"

Maude looked up all of a sudden, as if she'd thought of

something important. "You said the healers received an unexpected answer from the Great Energy. What was it?"

Neriti nodded at Ruth, and Ruth held out her hand to reveal an opaque crystal.

"What's that?" Maude asked.

Neriti explained, "It's a special crystal. It manifested from the healers' vision after we called on the Great Energy to reveal to us whether you or any of the other visitors will be given the gift of raising your own young while stranded here on Theia. It's quite exceptional, Maude. Never before have we received a tangible item from any of our visions. For thousands of rotations around the Earth, we've practiced our rituals, but you and this crystal are the only physical manifestations that have ever appeared during any of our ceremonies."

Maude stared at the crystal in Ruth's outstretched hand. "I see. Well, what do you think it means?" she asked.

"I'm not entirely sure, but I suspect that the crystal might be intended as a type of charm for your kind. Possibly to help you bring about your dream of creating a family. There were two discernible messages in the vision. The first was that the humans are meant to have the papers that the Moon Walkers left behind. The writing and characters are foreign even to the lunar wolves, but if you can find a way to use the documents, then the pack leaders have agreed that they're all yours.

"The second message is more complex. I consulted with the pack leaders about what the other healers and I saw. The leaders have asked me to keep the details of the vision private. But they've agreed that the crystal should be possessed by a human. They've chosen Ruth."

Maude looked up at Ruth, who was smiling at her warmly. She turned quickly to Neriti. "But I don't understand. If the vision came about because of a question that *I* asked, then why does Ruth get to keep the crystal?"

Neriti answered, "This is what the leaders feel comfortable

with. They trust Ruth because she's the only human who has reciprocated the wolves' generosity from the beginning."

Maude seemed annoyed by this answer. She looked back at the crystal in Ruth's palm. The light in her living room was dim, yet somehow the crystal seemed to sparkle anyway. Maude asked, "May I at least hold it for a moment?"

Neriti nodded her head, and Maude carefully took the crystal from Ruth's hand. She drew it to her face, and suddenly all the light in the small house faded. And for a split second, the three were left in pitch dark. Then a moment later, powerful beams shot out of the crystal, lighting the living room once more. Ruth yelled with fright, "Drop the crystal, sugar!"

But Maude didn't respond. Her head fell back so that her face was pointed at the ceiling. Neriti stood up to try to help Maude, but before she could, a horrible symphony of thumping, banging, and clanging exploded out of the kitchen. The cabinets and drawers had begun to fling open and shut violently on their own, as if possessed by an angry poltergeist who was frantically searching for his spoons and spices.

Out of nowhere, a sparkling, blue fire ignited in the little fireplace, and Maude began to speak. Only, the words didn't belong to her. The voice that filled the room was loud and commanded attention. Neither male nor female, it was altogether otherworldly. It boomed and sang awkwardly but beautifully as it passed its message along in a medium that was quite noticeably foreign to the powerful voice.

Neriti and Ruth couldn't tell if it was using Maude's mouth, for the light around the young woman had grown so brilliant that neither of them could see her. However, it seemed that the voice was flowing from every particle of the light that encompassed her.

"Greetings I bid to you both. Listen now, for I have urgent messages to share. First, I speak to Neriti. The darkness that took Tahissi's pups is growing. It will come next for the travelers to achieve its end purpose. Stop it, or else all will be destroyed. Many tests lie ahead. Do not resist them.

"Three children will be born of the first travelers. Twin boys sent by the dark. Then a girl who will spring forth from the light. The darkness will manipulate the boys into doing dark deeds. But the girl will have power to restore balance to the Moon if she is taught well. Neriti, when you think it wise, you may tell the first Moon Travelers of this prophecy, but do not tell them where it came from.

"I speak now to Ruth. The wolves were smart to entrust the crystal to you. You must wear it at all times. Do not tell your human friend what has transpired, though. She will find out when the time is right. Too soon and the knowledge would ruin her.

"Many years from now, two angels will arrive. One boy and one girl. The girl must not be allowed to return from where she came. If she tries to leave—then and only then—you must stop her. This child's destiny is tied to the future of the Moon realm.

"The last message is for you both, yet it is too sacred to speak aloud. I will send it through a vision to you now."

Suddenly, one of the light beams that shone from the crystal rocketed towards the empty space between Neriti and Ruth, splitting into two as it went. The separate beams flew into their eyes, and for a brief spell, Ruth and Neriti's pupils glowed bright white before fading to black again.

The voice spoke once more. "This last message can never be shared. I must go, but my orders will be obeyed. So be it!"

And with this command, everything stopped. The terrible kitchen symphony ceased, the light shining from Maude disappeared, and the dancing, blue flames in the fireplace extinguished. As the light in the living room returned to normal, Ruth looked at Neriti in amazement. "Well, that's gotta be about the weirdest dang thing I ever saw!"

But Neriti shushed Ruth and gestured towards Maude.

Slowly, Maude's head lifted to an upright position. She looked as though she were awakening from a long slumber. With bleary eyes and a hoarse voice, she asked, "What happened? I feel like I was asleep, but weren't we just sitting here talking?"

Ruth glanced nervously at Neriti, but Neriti didn't give Ruth a chance to botch the lie. "That's right, Maude. You must not be feeling well. We were all just sitting here having a conversation when you fell asleep. That's okay, though. I just said to Ruth that I think it would be best if she held onto the crystal for now until we figure out its purpose."

Maude looked down at her hand which was still holding the crystal. "Oh, right," she said groggily, offering the crystal back to Ruth.

"Thanks, sugar," Ruth said sweetly. "And don't you go worrying anymore. While you were out, Neriti was telling me that she's certain you and Bob will have some kids of your own real soon. The Great Energy told her and the other wolves it was possible, and I reckon it's right."

Neriti looked annoyed. "Okay, Ruth. That's enough. Maude needs her rest."

Then to Maude, she said, "We'll leave you now. I'm going to go find Ragher and Axel. Hopefully, they and Bob have thought of a way to transport the bundles of paper to the human village."

Ruth and Neriti headed to the door, and Maude tried to follow them but found she could barely stand. "I think you're right," she said wearily. "I must be getting sick to feel this tired."

"It's okay, hon," said Ruth. "Just stay where you are and rest up until Bob gets home. Lord knows you need it with all the work you've been doing. I'll come check on you tomorrow."

Maude nodded her head at Ruth and Neriti as she watched them walk out the door. Once they were gone, she leaned back in her chair and looked around the room. She noticed a lump of soot in the fireplace. "That's strange," she said to herself, but then, suddenly, a thought popped into her head. "Blast it all!" she yelled as she remembered the formula she had been working on right before her guests showed up. She gathered her strength and forced herself to get up and turn around, feeling the urgency to check on what had become of her over-stewed concoction. Holding onto the wall, she took a few steps towards the kitchen but then stopped in her tracks.

"What in heaven's name did those two do while I was asleep?" she asked aloud. For scattered across the kitchen floor was a slew of metal cutlery and kitchen gadgets. Maude looked over her shoulder towards the front door, half expecting to find Neriti and Ruth standing there giggling about the joke they had played on her. But the house was empty. And with no other explanation for what could've caused such a massive purge of the kitchen drawers and cabinets, Maude just shook her head and carefully made her way to the stove.

"What in the name of all that's sacred was *that*, Neriti?!" Ruth could barely contain her excitement as they walked away from Maude's house. Neriti didn't respond, though. It was obvious she was deep in thought.

Ruth waited a little while but knew they were about to lose their chance to speak freely once they caught up to Bob and the male wolves. So, she broached the subject again while stepping around the front of Neriti to stop her. "Neriti, have you ever seen anything like that back there? Was that the Great Energy? Cause in all my years, I ain't never seen anything like that. I done nearly wet myself out of sheer fright!"

Neriti replied, "I would've said that I'd never seen anything like it several cycles ago. But there have been many strange happenings since the healers were first given visions regarding the arrival of your kind. I'll be honest, though. What happened back there frightened me too."

"So, what do you think it was?"

Neriti shook her head. "I don't know, Ruth. And I don't feel comfortable speculating without talking to the other healers first."

Ruth looked taken aback. She frowned. "No, honey. You can't tell the other healers. Didn't you hear what we was told? This information is top secret. If we go letting the cat outta the bag, we gonna surely make that thing mad. You understand?"

Neriti sat down, pausing for a moment to think. Then she said, "Yes, Ruth. You're right. This will have to be our secret, but there's something you should know."

Ruth tilted her head at Neriti quizzically, and Neriti explained, "The darkness that the voice spoke of is something the healers and pack leaders have known about since the beginning. We long suspected it was part of Theia—the part that ruled over terrible monsters. The very same monsters whose remains were found in the tunnels by that man, Peter, and the other travelers.

"I knew that this darkness would steal my daughter's family. I was given a vision of it beforehand. I happen to know, however, that the darkness is a separate entity than Theia. And I feel it's important that you now know this too because I think it's planning to target Theia next."

"Now, how in the world could you possibly know that?"

Neriti replied, "My family's path has been different than that of the other wolves. This path has been difficult, but it has also revealed more about this realm than the others are aware of."

"I see," said Ruth. "Well, I can tell you like your secrets, so I won't keep pushing, but I just gotta say that it feels like we could avoid a lot of heartache if everyone would just communicate better with one another."

"Hmm," Neriti moaned pensively. Then she spoke again. "It would seem we live in a time of transformation, Ruth. We wolves have adapted over many cycles in order to live comfortably and provide for the packs, but in many ways, we're set in our beliefs, just like the travelers. However, I can see that this may no longer be an option. It feels as if we're standing on the precipice of a great change. I don't know what it will mean, but I guess for now, we'll have to trust the messages the voice has given us."

Ruth nodded, "That's the truth, sugar. And I think we better follow them messages to a tee too, cause I ain't never wanna be on the bad side of that big, shiny voice-light. It may be about the strangest thing I ever done saw, but I reckon it means business."

Neriti's heart felt burdened by the seriousness of their situation as she tried to make sense of it all. Yet even so, she couldn't help but smile at Ruth's unusual way of speaking. "Yes, Ruth. I reckon it means business too. So that's the way it shall be."

CHAPTER 5

CONVINCING

Present Day on The Moon.

Axel opened his eyes to nothing. It was dark and silent, and for a split second, he wondered if he were dead. This thought faded fast, though, as the throbbing pain in his throat and stinging wounds from Roger's claws reminded him that he was very much alive. He moved around to get his bearings and realized he was still on his back, likely where Roger had left him.

He sat up slowly, unsure of how much damage the evil lunar wolf had done. Besides his sore neck and the cuts on his body, Axel's head felt as if an entire steam engine worth of pressure had built up inside his skull. He noticed that even the slightest movement caused his head to hurt more, and there was a ringing in his ears that seemed to be related to his feelings of nausea. Axel sat perfectly still for a moment, not knowing what to do next. He hoped if he gave himself a few minutes, an idea might magically pop into his head.

Returning to the fortress wasn't an option, but the thought of having to sing again was too much. Nevertheless, Axel understood he couldn't rely on his sense of touch alone. He needed to get to the army quickly and find a way to warn the others about what he'd seen on top of the tower.

He stood up, readying himself to sing to the crystals once more, but a deep voice called to him from a few feet away. "Don't!" the voice ordered. "If you sing, it will start all over again. You're not a wolf anymore. Or at least the crystals don't recognize you as one. Theia made sure that only the wolves could use the crystal's magic. Anyone else who tries to use it experiences what you did. I yelled at you to stop singing, but when you couldn't hear me, I was forced to go to extreme measures. To be fair, though, if you hadn't stopped, we'd both be deaf by now. Or worse."

Axel's head was pounding. He'd assumed that Roger had run off, thinking he was dead. It hadn't occurred to him that he might be waiting there, hiding nearby in the darkness. He tried to make sense of it. He was certain that Roger had intended to kill him, but if that were true, then why hadn't he finished the job? He could've done it so easily, yet here they were. So, what did Roger want from him? He knew he needed to find out.

"I don't believe you," he replied. "I doubt the crystals can even hear me in the state I'm in. You probably made them do that!"

"I didn't. But if you want to test your theory, go ahead and sing. I'll be happy to choke you again."

Axel knew Roger might not be telling the truth, but he didn't want to take the chance. His body ached all over, and he couldn't afford to have a repeat of what he'd just been through.

Roger spoke again. "I'm guessing you saw Neriti? Up on the tower?"

"Yes...I did," Axel said surprised. "How did you know? Or

was that all a trick? Part of whatever evil plan you have brewing."

"It wasn't a trick, Axel. And we need to get going to find the boy. It's urgent. I know you don't trust me, but hopefully you can at least acknowledge that I could've killed you earlier and didn't."

Axel retorted, "That may be true, Roger. But—"

Roger stopped him. "My name isn't Roger. You *know* that. I'm no longer bound to Dan, and I want to hear my actual name again."

"I thought you said we were in a hurry," Axel snapped at him.

"We are. You were saying?"

Axel took a second but then continued, "That may be true, but not killing me doesn't excuse the fact you betrayed your own kind. You even betrayed Neriti, for crying out loud! Your own mother!"

"I didn't betray my own kind or Neriti."

"Really?" Axel asked sarcastically. "Then what the hell do you call skulking off to work for Dan? Aiding in the torment of the other wolves? Even carrying it out!? And don't you dare pretend like you didn't tell Dan how to find Neriti. Where to go so he could murder her with his own hands! I know it was you, *Roger!* I know it was!" Axel screamed into the darkness where Ragher stood.

"Enough!" Ragher shouted. "You don't know what you're talking about! I didn't betray Neriti. I loved her more than you could possibly imagine, which is why I did everything she ever asked me to do. It's even why I went to work for Dan—to protect her and *you!*"

"What do you mean protect us? You didn't protect us from anything!"

"Yes, I did. It's what I'm trying to tell you. Neriti and I knew someone needed to go to Black Ice Glacier to keep Dan in check. We even knew we'd probably never see each other again once I left, but I still went to keep you both safe. That's how important my mission was. Neriti and I were well aware that the spirit controlling Dan was dangerous. Somebody had to keep a watch on him, and I'm the only one who can see the spirit. Or at least that was true until you and Helen were changed."

Axel snarled. "You're lying!"

"No, Axel. I'm not. It nearly tore you apart, right? It's what the dark spirit does. Do you really think if Dan had that kind of power this whole time, he wouldn't have used it? It's not a trick at all. It's much, much worse than that."

Feeling a bit more convinced, Axel asked, "So you're saying that thing…that *dark spirit* is real?"

"Yes, he's real, and Neriti knew about him long before she died. The spirit wants to destroy all the creatures on the Moon. He tricked Dan into carrying out his plan, and he won't rest until he succeeds. Killing Dan won't stop him. Honestly, I don't know if anything will. He can manipulate and even steal energy if the circumstances are right. It would have stolen Helen's lifeforce after Dan changed her, but I convinced her to leave before it was too late."

Axel didn't know what to do. Ragher's story seemed convincing, but he couldn't be certain that any of it was true. Axel knew Ragher could be lying to lure him to his side. He'd believed the worst of Ragher for a long time, and it was impossible for Axel to overlook all the wrongs he had committed against their kind.

Plus, if what Ragher said was true, Neriti had gone to her death purposely deceiving Axel over what had become of her only son, his former best friend. This idea broke Axel's heart. He had loved Neriti like she was his own mother, and so it pained him to think she hadn't trusted him—at least, not entirely.

"How are you able to see me? Or Helen?" Axel finally asked.

Ragher replied, "Not yet. We have to get to the boy. The dark spirit will be looking for him soon. It's crucial we find Fred before *he* does. I'll try to explain more along the way."

"But how are we supposed to make it through this tunnel in the dark? I'm assuming you still refuse to sing to the crystals on account of your terrible voice?"

Ragher laughed. "That's not why I didn't sing to the crystals before. But no, I still don't sing to them. I can navigate us through the tunnels without their light, though. Just follow the sound of my voice."

Axel didn't like the idea of following Ragher blindly through the tunnels. However, he felt it would be best to get away from Black Ice Fort and out of the sub-glacier tunnel system as quickly as possible. "Fine," he said, agreeing to go along with Ragher. "But don't try anything funny."

As they began to walk, a question came to Axel. "You know of these ice tunnels Neriti spoke of? This place I'm supposed to take the boy. I've lived a long time, but I've never heard of any such tunnels."

"Yes," Ragher responded in a somber tone. "I know them well, but there's no reason you would've heard of them before. The wolves don't know they exist."

Axel snorted. "Oh really? Then how do you know about them?"

Ragher replied, "Neriti learned many secrets before her death. Ancient secrets that the lunar wolves weren't meant to know. Now that you've been changed, I imagine you'll learn many secrets too. More than you'll care to know, perhaps."

Axel didn't understand what Ragher was talking about and wondered if he was being vague because he didn't have a good answer. It wouldn't be until years later that Axel would remember Ragher's words and realize he hadn't meant to be vague. In truth, Ragher had been trying to warn him.

THE BEAM from Fred's flashlight sliced through the thick, black curtain that enveloped the Darkside. He'd been wandering across the lunar terrain for several hours, following the map that one of the soldiers had given him before he left to explore on his own.

Fred and the wolves had reached the army right as the news broke that Dan was dead. The army's fight was over before it really ever began. The sensation of relief and gratitude was palpable amongst the soldiers. They'd been told to expect anything—including horrific chemical attacks that could kill or wound them in excruciatingly painful ways. At the very least, the soldiers were certain that Dan would unleash some form of return fire. So, the fact that everyone had stayed alive and in one piece felt like a miracle.

Fred had been a bit dumbfounded at the news. He hadn't expected Mina to survive her encounter with Dan, and at first he didn't believe he'd heard the soldiers correctly. There was no way a little thing like Mina could defeat someone as evil as Dan. It didn't make any sense, yet apparently it was true.

Fred decided to be happy for her. He assumed she'd get to go home, just like she wanted. As for him, he had more important things to think about, like coming up with a way to monetize the crystals he planned to mine. The first step, he thought, was to map the underground tunnels. Doing so would give him a good estimate of how many crystals there were, which would help him to calculate how much profit he could make.

It had all seemed like a great idea when he set out to find the tunnels, but as he became more and more certain he was lost, he started to doubt himself. *What did that soldier say again? Something about going slow and matching the natural landmarks to the map?* Fred hadn't felt like going slow. He thought he could aim his flashlight around as he sped along. He'd been sure he'd at least spot the big landmarks without getting dangerously off course. Now, however, he wished he'd spent more time paying attention to where he was going since nothing his flashlight shone on seemed to match the map at all.

After closely examining the various points on the map, Fred began to spin around in an attempt to find anything that looked familiar. But soon, he caught sight of something unsettling in his beam of light—a blurry, white object on the horizon, moving towards him at a fast speed. Fred hesitated for a moment to determine whether his eyes were deceiving him. However, once he blinked a few times and moved his flashlight back and forth, he became confident there really *was* something approaching, and judging by its speed, he knew it would be hard to outrun.

Immediately, he turned and began to sprint away. He crumpled the map in his hand and gripped his flashlight so that it didn't slip from his fingers. He knew it might be better to turn it off and hide in the dark, but he didn't have the courage to try.

The bright beam of light bobbed up and down in front of him, which caused Fred to feel disoriented like he was in a dream. He wondered if he was outrunning the creature, but just as this thought entered his mind, he heard a voice from close behind ordering him to stop. It was deep and grumbly, and Fred pictured a large, middle-aged man calling to him. This image didn't match the fast, white object he'd seen before, but Fred decided that the man must be using some other means of transportation to have caught up to him so quickly.

He realized he'd been beat, but he didn't feel as afraid now that he knew his pursuer was human. He turned around to face the man but was aghast to find that it wasn't a man at all. It was a large, white wolf. And not just any wolf, but *Dan's* wolf.

"Thank you for your cooperation. I've come to deliver a message," said Ragher.

Without hesitating, Fred kicked dirt into Ragher's face and took off running again. Ragher yelped as gravel flew into his eyes, but he didn't wait to recover before chasing after the kid. It only took him two seconds to catch Fred again, and when he did, he jumped on top of him, pinning him down. "You stupid kid! I'm trying to save you!"

"Let go of me!" screamed Fred.

Ragher turned his head to the side, panting. Looking into the dark, he said, "I know that! But it doesn't seem like he's going to cooperate *without* force either!"

"Who the hell are you talking to?" asked Fred.

"Fine! But you're not the one who just had dirt kicked in your eyes." Ragher grunted.

Addressing Fred again, Ragher said, "I'm going to get up now, but don't try to run, or I'll have to knock you down again."

Then, Ragher shouted, "That's not true, Axel! I had you pinned at least half of the time during that fight." Ragher paused and then seemingly to no one, he replied, "Yes! *Half!*"

"My god! You're completely insane!" Fred exclaimed, unable to hide the fear in his voice.

Ragher laughed as he backed away from the young man. "No. Not completely insane. Not yet anyway. Axel is here too. Dan transformed him so he's invisible now. But look, we've got to get you down to the ice tunnels quickly. There's something very evil out there looking for you."

"No way!" Fred yelled. "I'm not going anywhere with you! I'm not stupid. I know you're Dan's wolf."

"I'm not Dan's wolf. Upon his death, I was released from the vow I made to serve him. It was given so that he would keep me close. I was a spy, you see. It was necessary that someone stay on the inside to keep things under control. I've sacrificed decades of my life to keep others safe. Including *your* kind."

"You call what happened back there keeping everyone safe?"

"Yes. I do. It's regrettable how far it all went, but I believed in Helen. I knew she and the girl would come one day, so I waited and steered Dan away from doing any large-scale damage in the meantime."

Ragher spoke to Axel again, "I know that! Do you really think I don't know that? I mourned the wolves too, but unlike you, I didn't get to grieve. I had to stick to the plan! Anyway, we can't do this here. You two don't seem to get the urgency of what we're up against.

"There's no time to waste, Fred. We have to get you to the ice tunnels now. With Dan gone, the dark spirit is coming for you. I'm certain he's already out there somewhere, scouring every inch of the Darkside, searching for you. The poison Dan fed you still runs through your veins, which makes you an easy target. The dark spirit is seeking to control you the way he controlled Dan, and he *will* succeed if given the chance."

Fred replied, "Fine, say you're right, and this thing is looking all over the Darkside for me. Why, then, should I go hide in some freezing cold tunnels? Why not just go back to the Dayside where it's not even looking?"

"No," Ragher said firmly. "You still don't get it. This spirit has incredible power. If you're weak, he can get into your head and control you. And there's no reason to think he won't find a way to reach you on the Dayside. I lived with him for decades, and even I'm still surprised by the amount of power he has. The only place we can be sure he won't find you is the ice tunnels. But look. If it will get things moving faster, I'll make you a deal. Come with us to the ice tunnels now and stay there while I explain everything. Then if you think I've been unreasonable, you can leave. I won't stop you. And at least you'll stay hidden for a little while."

Fred looked skeptical. "How do I know this isn't a trick?"

Ragher shook his head. "You don't," he said in frustration. "But if you choose to keep wandering around like this in the dark, you're going to find out soon enough. He'll turn you into a full-blown monster. He's done it to many others besides you. Are you willing to take that chance?"

Fred thought about it for a moment while pointing his flashlight around like he was looking for something in the distance. "Okay. I'll come with you. But you promise I can leave whenever I want? You won't try to stop me?"

Ragher agreed, "Yes, I promise I won't try to stop you."

Fred nodded.

"Okay, let's get going," said Ragher. "I'll let you set the pace, kid. But I suggest you run at the fastest clip you can manage. And for god's sake, turn that flashlight off. The dark spirit might be partly omniscient, but let's not make this any easier for him, shall we?"

Fred, Ragher, and Axel took off into the dark. Ragher spoke the whole time, giving directions so that the other two could follow along without much trouble. Fred could feel the temperature dropping as they went, which was surprising because it was the first time he remembered being truly cold since arriving on the Moon.

After a while, Ragher told them to rest. "We've made it to our first stop."

"What do you mean *our first stop?*" asked Fred.

"I thought we were going straight to the ice tunnels, Ragher. What are you playing at?" demanded Axel.

"We're nearly there, but it won't do any good to go all the way to the ice tunnels without making this stop beforehand."

Then to Fred, Ragher ordered, "Turn that flashlight on, kid, and shine it to your right."

Fred did as Ragher directed and pointed his flashlight over to his right. Ragher followed the beam of light until he reached the edge of a small rock pile. He stopped and began to dig on an angle. After he'd dug several inches down beneath the rocks, he lowered his snout into the hole and grabbed hold of something in his mouth. Fred continued to shine the light on Ragher, and soon it became clear what he'd dug up. The light glistened off a tiny jar that Ragher was holding between his teeth.

"What's that?" asked Axel.

Ragher walked towards Fred and set the jar down at his feet.

"This is the only way that Fred will be able to enter the ice tunnels."

"What does that mean?" Axel asked suspiciously.

Ragher explained, "There's a reason the wolves don't know about the tunnels, Axel. They've never come close to seeing them before. There's an entrance to the tunnels right in between the two discs that the Moon Walkers built—only the Moon Walkers *didn't* build the discs. That part of the ancient knowledge was fabricated by the wolves—by the first healers to be exact.

"Whatever *did* create the discs made it so that the entrance to the ice tunnels couldn't be seen by lesser creatures. That includes all the beings who came after the Moon Walkers. It seems that whoever put the tunnels here didn't want them to be tampered with. It's how they've stayed hidden all this time."

Axel asked, "So then, if the tunnels are hidden to everyone who came after the Moon Walkers, does that mean the dark spirit is a newer creature too? Is that why he can't find us there? And, how am *I* going to see the tunnels if I'm still a wolf? I'm guessing you've already drank some of this formula, but what about me?"

Ragher let out a sigh. "Too many questions, Axel. We need to hurry still. We're close, but we're not there yet. Fred, go ahead and drink what's in the vial there." Ragher motioned his head at the little cylinder by Fred's feet.

Fred looked nervous. "What's it going to do to me?"

Axel laughed. "That's funny. He ate bunches of Dan's apples, yet now he's nervous about a little thimbleful of liquid." Then Axel paused and thought for a second before asking, "But really, what's it going to do to him?"

Ragher replied, "Well for starters it will help you get to safety a lot faster than standing here talking about what it's going to do. But in addition to that, it will change you until you're halfway to the state Axel's in now."

"Wait! *Invisible!?* No way! I'm not going to be turned into another one of your imaginary friends."

Axel snapped, "We're not friends." Even though he knew Fred couldn't hear him.

"My god! The way the two of you are acting, you'd think that facing the dark spirit was a better fate than letting me help you!"

Fred scoffed. "Yeah, well your so-called 'help' erases me from existence. So, no thank you!"

Ragher barked, "It doesn't. I told you already. It takes you *halfway* to Axel's state. It's a much smaller dose of the formula that Dan used on Axel. It will change you to the point of being able to see the entrance to the tunnel, but you'll still be in a solid state. Now drink the damn liquid!"

Fred griped, "I think I liked you better when you were submissive." But he picked up the small jar and unscrewed the lid. He shivered a little and looked around again with his flashlight. "I can't believe I'm doing this," he said. Then without further ado, he knocked back the tiny concoction.

"Eww!" he whined like a toddler being forced to drink his medicine.

Ragher rolled his eyes. "You'll live. At least if you hurry that is. Now, turn off your light. We won't need it in a few minutes."

Ragher spoke as the three continued on their way. "Axel, you'll see the tunnel when we arrive because you're not a wolf anymore. I'm sorry to tell you, but you'll never truly be a wolf again after what Dan did to you. And to answer your question, I've never had a drop of the formula Fred drank. I don't need it. I've always been able to see the tunnels' entrance.

"As far as the dark spirit is concerned, he was here even before the Moon Walkers. I don't know how he came to exist, but I'm pretty sure he wasn't put here by Theia."

Axel slowed down for a second, falling behind. Then, suddenly, he sprinted to catch up. "My god, Ragher!" he yelled. "I think I've figured it out. But it can't be true, can it?"

"Holy crap! Who's that?!" gasped Fred. He shivered as the three jogged through the dark. "Where'd that voice come from, wolf?"

Ragher replied, "That's Axel. I told you I wasn't completely insane."

Axel asked Ragher, "So, he can hear me now?"

But before either Ragher or Fred had a chance to answer, they moved out of the darkness and into the light. The transition happened quite suddenly. One second, they were on the Darkside, and the next they were standing inside a large space that was as bright as day. The light, however, wasn't like it was on the Dayside. It was sterile and white, and it was confined to one large section of land.

It took their eyes a moment to adjust, but once they had, they could see that they were standing a short distance away from a curved white dome with a darkened, rectangular entryway carved into its front. It appeared that the dome was made of something akin to white concrete, and Axel thought it looked like the top half of a giant eyeball sticking out of the ground.

Fred and Axel stood with their mouths open for a moment. Then Axel asked seriously, "That's the entrance to the ice tunnels?"

Ragher nodded. "Yes, that's the entrance to the ice tunnels."

Axel continued, "And you're a Moon Walker?"

Ragher nodded again. "Yes, Axel. And I'm a Moon Walker."

IT TOOK the army several days to tear down and pack up their valley base camp near Black Ice Glacier. The soldiers departed in over a dozen different waves. The first wave was led by Bob, who felt pressed to return home to Maude with his first-hand account of what had happened to Helen—the only casualty of the operation they'd waged against Dan.

As different sections of the camp were disassembled, the soldiers formed groups and carried the equipment back to the Dayside. Using the salvageable parts from their camp, the soldiers were planning to build a new camp that would serve soldiers and civilians on the Dayside until more suitable quarters could be established.

Lt. General Goodman had appointed himself to be the last person to leave the valley. The tall, muscular soldier with a long face knew that he'd be the most meticulous of all the higher-ranking officers at seeing that not so much as a scrap was left behind. He wouldn't allow the soldiers to disrespect the dark valley that had been their home for so long by leaving it littered with trash. Once every manmade odd and end was accounted for, he ordered the remaining soldiers to move out and follow the most direct path back to Waldoff Market. Goodman's plan was to make a quick sweep of the valley to ensure that nothing had been overlooked. Then once he was finished, he would jog at a brisk pace until he caught up to his unit.

The stretch of land that the camp had covered was by no means small, but Goodman had confidence that his high-powered flashlight would easily illuminate any scraps or waste that had been forgotten. When he reached the edge of the former campsite, he felt good about the work the soldiers had done to leave no trace of themselves. One last walkthrough on his way out, and he'd know for sure that his orders had been followed to the letter.

He turned to go but heard a strange noise over his left shoulder. *Clink, clink, clink!* Goodman's breath caught in his chest. He knew he was alone but couldn't imagine what would be making this sort of sound all the way out in Glacier Valley. He spun back around with his flashlight pointed in front of him like a weapon.

There was nothing there. His body felt tense, and it took him a moment to steel himself so he could explore further. He moved his light over the ground a few yards out to see if he could identify where the noise had come from. At first, he saw only a scattering of gray rocks, but then the beam ricocheted off of something dark, yet shiny. "Now what could that be," Goodman wondered. He moved closer to it and knelt down. It appeared to be some sort of black, diamond-shaped jewel nestled amongst the other stones.

He shined his flashlight right above the black crystal and marveled as a shimmer of blue electricity spread over its surface. "Hmm," he thought. "That's not like any moon crystal I've ever seen." He didn't like the idea of taking anything from the valley that belonged there as he always stuck to the philosophy that natural habitats should be preserved. However, something about this crystal spoke to him; it felt like its oddness was luring him in. "Well, I suppose it wouldn't hurt to hold on to it for a little while in the name of science. I can show it to Maude and Bob and then return it to its home when I'm passing this way again."

But even as Goodman had this thought, a voice whispered in his ear that the crystal belonged to him now. A gift from the valley for all his *unappreciated,* hard work. Goodman didn't hear the voice exactly, but the seed was planted just the same. He put the crystal in his pocket for safe keeping and departed the valley for good.

By the time he arrived back on the Dayside, Goodman had forgotten all about his intention to show the crystal to Maude and Bob. During his travels, he'd thought long and hard about his role in the army over the last couple of years while repainting his memories in a different shade and convincing himself that too often he'd played second fiddle to Bob. As the crystal sunk its hooks into him, Goodman made up his mind that he'd always been the one who'd shown *true* leadership skills. Bob was a hack, a science geek who thought he could make himself into a leader just because he knew how to invent a few doohickeys. Helpful gadgets, maybe, but nothing that was truly special.

Goodman saw now that *he* was the one who had sacrificed the most to help the soldiers deal with their worries and fears. He'd kept them brave and mentally strong during all their wasted days, waiting for Bob to give the order to fight. An order that took way too long to come because Bob was too chicken to face his own son in battle. An order that took too long because Bob was weak-minded and thought it better to wait on the manifestation of a silly prophecy rather than using strategy and skill to fight an intelligent battle.

By the time Goodman met up again with the soldiers, he'd not only decided to keep the crystal for himself, but he also had begun to formulate the beginnings of a devilish plan. The soldiers couldn't know it yet, but the stormy winds of war hadn't subsided upon Dan's demise. They had only damped down. Eventually, a new war would begin to brew, and this time the Moon Travelers would be forced to fight it on their own turf.

CHAPTER 6

THE ICE TUNNELS

"How is it possible?" Axel looked at Ragher in astonishment.

"What are you two talking about? How is *what* possible?" Fred grumbled, feeling rather ill from the concoction he'd consumed. He stared at Axel who was blurring in and out of focus. "Stop it!" he hiccupped. "Why aren't you holding still?"

"Hey, kid," Ragher spoke to Fred. "You better not get sick on us."

Then to Axel he said, "Come on, Ax. We've come this far. Let's get the boy inside. I'll explain everything once we do."

"Don't call me that!" Axel snapped at him. "I'm not *Ax* anymore. But fine, let's get on with it."

Ragher and Axel moved towards the white dome as Fred followed behind them weakly. Inside the entrance to the dome there was a tunnel that sloped downward. They couldn't see where it led to, although it wasn't dark inside, for a blue tinted glow illuminated the icy, white walls. Fred shivered at the thought of walking into what looked like a long, refrigerated tube.

"You'd better go first, Axel. Then the kid. Then me."

Axel gave Ragher an annoyed look but went ahead anyway. Fred didn't follow him, though. "Your turn, Fred. Follow Axel," said Ragher, addressing Fred like a child.

But Fred continued to stand there staring into the tunnel and shivering. Ragher told him, "You know you're not actually cold. You just think you're cold because of your past experiences."

Fred rolled his eyes, even though it made him feel nauseous to do so. "What is it with this place? Everyone's always telling me that my feelings aren't *really* my feelings. That I shouldn't feel the way I do. Well, maybe I want to feel cold…or hungry…or…" But before Fred could finish his thought, he threw up.

Ragher jumped back to avoid getting any of it on him. He said, "Well, kid, I guess you showed me. Anyway, if you're better now, go on in. I'll follow right behind you."

Fred stumbled forward as directed. He had descended several yards down, when out of nowhere, Axel appeared right in front of him. "Turn around! It's a trap!" Axel yelled as he tried to push past Fred.

Fred hesitated, but when he noticed that the tunnel dead-ended a few feet behind Axel, he understood what he meant. He spun on his heels, but it was too late. A thick sheet of ice, taller than Fred, broke away from the wall and blocked the exit. "Damn it!" cursed Axel. "I can't believe I fell for this! *RAGHER!* I know you're up there! Let us out of here!" he yelled at the ice blockade.

Axel didn't have to wait long to talk to Ragher, though, because a moment later the ice moved to a different side of the wall, and Ragher appeared in front of them. Axel rushed towards the opening, but a split second later another large sheet of ice broke apart from the tunnel wall and replaced the first sheet of ice, thwarting his escape.

"That won't work," said Ragher calmly.

"Oh really? Why not?" asked Axel. "I'm sure If I just get the timing right—."

"You'll never get the timing right—" began Ragher, but before he could finish, the walls of ice around them started to move as they broke apart into separate, moving ice sheets. And soon, Ragher, Axel, and Fred were being pushed to the side of the exit. The moving ice sounded like metal gears clicking together in unison. The sound was so loud it was almost deafening. Within seconds, the moving walls had pushed the trio several yards sideways, and the little section of tunnel that they'd been trapped inside was sealed off. Fred groaned uneasily as a section of ice behind him shoved him forward into another ice partition that was moving more slowly. "Don't worry, kid," Ragher shouted. "They rearrange themselves all the time, but they won't hurt you, as long as you don't try to fight them."

Axel yelled at Ragher, "Why the hell did you bring us here?"

But before Ragher could respond, the sounds of the metal gears suddenly ground to a halt as the sheets of ice pushed themselves back together. A long, icy tunnel had opened up in front of them. The walls were bright white and so shiny that they looked as if they'd been coated in water.

"What's going on, Ragher?" Axel asked angrily. His ears were still humming from the loud, metallic sounds.

Ragher explained. "The tunnels are a moving labyrinth between the two metal discs. They store the memories of everything that's happened on the Moon from a certain point in time."

"What do you mean? How is that possible?" Axel demanded.

Ragher nodded. "You'll see soon enough. Though eventually, I think you'll agree that the *how* is less important than the *why*. These tunnels were designed this way for a reason, but I've never been able to figure out why they were built."

"How did you find out about them?" Fred asked.

Ragher glanced at the young man like he'd almost forgotten he was standing right next to him. "I don't know," he replied, shaking his head. "My very first memories are of the ice tunnels," he answered. "I was trapped inside of them for a long time. But I don't remember how I got here. I just know that by then, I was the only Moon Walker left on the Moon."

Suddenly, there was a loud whirring sound, and the tunnel walls lit up with moving scenes like there were a bunch of invisible movie projectors being pointed along different sections of the icy corridor. Seconds later, the soundtrack that matched each moving scene came to life, and the entire tunnel was flooded with noise. It sounded like chaos. There was too much sound to make sense of anything that was happening. Fred covered his ears in protest, and Axel looked around in a panic. Ragher was the only one who didn't seem fazed at all.

"How do you make it stop!?" Fred screamed.

Ragher shook his head. "You can't!" he yelled back. "But it's really not that bad! Pick a spot on the wall to focus your attention on! Soon, you'll only be able to hear the sounds that go along with what you're watching!"

Axel looked at Ragher, as though he were talking nonsense, but Fred was willing to try anything. He locked his eyes on the closest scene. Two large wolf packs were traveling across the Dayside while many miles away, a large group of horned monsters occupied a small area of land along the border of the Darkside. The beasts stood in dirt pits fighting each other. As soon as Fred began to watch, the focus of the scene zoomed in on the beasts, and Fred watched the monsters brawl—kicking and punching, goring and biting. After a few minutes, he turned back to Ragher. "What in god's name is this?"

It was Axel who responded. "Those are the bryobane," he

said in a tone that almost sounded like reverence. He looked mesmerized by the moving images of the beasts grunting and snorting as they impaled each other with their massive horns. "Not even in my worst nightmares did I ever come close to imagining how terrifying they were."

"Hmm," Ragher moaned. "Well, you'll see a lot more of them while we're here. A lot more of everything, I should say. The way it works, or at least the way it worked for me when I was down here all those years, is that your energy draws memories to you. For instance, if you're feeling sad you might get one set of memories that play over and over until you begin to feel more hopeful. You get used to it after a while. I got to the point where I could call up almost anything I wanted to by changing my emotions."

Axel asked, "How long were you down here for?"

Ragher paused to think. "I don't know," he said finally. "But I suspect it was a few thousand years."

Fred looked away from the bryobane scene. "A few thousand *years?!*"

Ragher nodded sadly. "I couldn't escape. Once you're in the ice tunnels, you're at their mercy. There's no way out until they let you out."

Fred was furious. He faced Ragher while behind him a scene of a giant bryobane feasting on a smaller one played out. "You damned wolf!" cried Fred. "You lied! You said I could leave whenever I wanted to."

Ragher nodded. "I did what I had to in order to get you here, but what I said about not trying to stop you from leaving is true. It's just that it won't make any difference now that you're here. I imagine you'll be here until you've seen what you're supposed to."

It was Axel's turn to yell at Ragher. "You told us that 'lesser' creatures can't see the entrance to the ice tunnels.

Clearly, this place isn't meant for us. So, what makes you so sure we're supposed to be here at all?"

Ragher looked down the long ice tunnel. "The walls are about to shift again. Both of you, follow me and stare at the moving scenes as we go. It will make it easier to hear me, if you're only picking up the sound from one scene at a time."

Fred, who was still fuming, was about to object when the rotating metal gears began ticking away again. Immediately, the ice sheets pulled apart, sliding around each other in their coordinated dance. Ragher ran down the hall to avoid getting trapped between moving walls of ice, and Axel and Fred ran after him. "I learned it's best to get as far down the tunnels as you can before they change. The less tunnel you explore, the less you're given the next time. I've been trapped in some pretty tight spaces in the labyrinth after refusing to go any further than the ice sheets forced me to."

Axel yelled over all the noise, "Are you saying that the ice tunnels are aware of our presence?"

Ragher seemed to shrug at the question with his tone. "I don't know if it's consciousness, artificial intelligence, or what. But most definitely they were designed to react to whoever's inside."

The group had almost reached the end of the long tunnel when they were shoved to the side by a tall block of ice. The other walls glided around them until they formed a new tunnel about three quarters the length of the previous one. Right away, the scenes appeared across the tunnel walls. "Keep walking until we reach the end!" shouted Ragher.

Axel and Fred focused on the scenes as they passed them. There were visions of lunar wolves moving through tunnels of bright crystals, singing the ancient songs; visions of healers gathered around the sick and hurt; visions of the earliest Moon Travelers arriving on the Moon from across the neon bridge.

"To answer your question, Axel, the reason I know you two

are meant to be here is the same reason I was freed from these tunnels so many years ago. The history of the Moon lives inside of the labyrinth's tunnels, but there are also other passageways—ones that contain *visions*. These passageways move across different parts of the labyrinth and are revealed less frequently. They're much more difficult to navigate than the tunnels, but they're important. The last one I went through nearly broke me, but eventually it led me out of the labyrinth. During my time inside that passageway, I had a vision that showed me I would have to return someday with you two."

"That's the stupidest thing I've ever heard!" shouted Fred. "You expect us to believe that a mechanical tunnel told you the future?"

"Ragher, the kid has a point," said Axel. "You were just a pup when I met you, barely older than myself. None of this makes sense. How could you have been a Moon Walker that lived inside a moving labyrinth for thousands of years if you were Neriti's son?"

Ragher nodded. "I understand your doubts, but it's not my job to persuade you in any direction. I completed my mission by bringing you here. The rest is up to you to learn."

The ice sheets shifted again, this time forcing the three to move to the side and forward. As the walls around them transformed, the scenes across the ice changed too. When the gears had come to a halt, and the ice sheets had formed solid walls around them once more, Axel saw something that left him stunned.

It was a vision of a glowing ball of white light moving through the darkness. Suddenly, there was a loud *"pop"* like a firecracker, and the ball of light changed into a glowing, white wolf. It spoke to itself. "Concentrate. You have to concentrate. It will find you if you don't hold your shape." The shapeshifter looked down at his feet. "Damn it! Stop glowing! You can't glow, remember? You practiced this. My god did you ever practice this. Come on, Ragher! Hold it together. You can do this. You just have to find her."

"This was you?" Axel asked. "But…*how?*"

Ragher tilted his head towards another scene, a few feet from where they stood. They moved over to it. The scene was of a little wolf pup playing at the edge of Crystal Crater on the Darkside. The pup seemed to be chasing something that wasn't there while off in the distance, the pilgrimage chants could be heard echoing from the bottom of the crater.

Suddenly the little, white wolf froze. She lowered herself down slowly on her stomach, staring ahead at the dirt a few feet away. A few seconds passed. Then like a tiger stalking its prey, she pounced on the dirt, grabbing her invisible prey between her paws. She giggled but then looked over her shoulder towards the crater, worried that someone might have heard her laughter.

Fred began to speak loudly, pulling Ragher and Axel's attention away from the little wolf. "This is pointless! I'm *not* going down memory lane with you wolves. I refuse to be kept in tight quarters, breathing the same air as you two filthy creatures for one more second! I want out of here. *Now!*"

Fred pointed at Ragher. "You! The non-blurry one! I know you're lying! Show me the way out, or I swear I'll make you sorry."

Ragher turned his head away from Fred and back to the wall where the scene they'd been watching continued. "There's nothing you could ever do to me, kid, that would make me any sorrier than I already am. Feel free to stop breathing, though, if you wish."

Fred walked towards the wall where the scene of the little wolf was playing. Without moving his head, Ragher growled— warning Fred not to interrupt the scene further. Fred stopped in his tracks but began to hum quietly to himself, as though he'd never had any intention of causing more trouble.

Ragher and Axel watched the playful pup hop around at the top of the colorful, glowing crater. Judging from her size, Axel guessed she was about three years old.

The soft chanting that echoed out of the crater poured over their senses, as if it were reaching into the fabric of their deepest consciousness, gently tugging on its seams

Suddenly, a large, white wolf appeared out of the darkness, startling the little wolf. "Where did you come from, wolf?" the pup asked, struggling to put on a brave show.

The large wolf didn't respond. It walked to where the little pup stood, stopping in front of her to stare down.

"Oh, I see," said the pup. "You're not a wolf at all, are you?"

There was a loud popping sound, and the large wolf changed into a green bulbous form that might've resembled a snowman if there'd ever been a snowman made of radioactive ooze before.

The little pup looked again towards the rim of the crater. "Quick! You better get out of sight. Someone will have heard you."

Again, there was a loud popping sound, but this time Ragher transformed into a little, white wolf, the same as the pup. "Neriti! Where are you? You better not be getting into trouble up here!" someone called from just below the crater's edge.

The little girl pup looked at Ragher and whispered, "Don't say anything! Let me do the talking. And *don't* go turning into something else, okay?" Ragher didn't say anything. He just nodded.

An adult wolf with beautiful, soft fur and shimmering, silver streaks woven throughout her mane appeared over the top of the rim. "There you are, Neriti. You had me worried again. You should be down there with the other pups, learning the chants."

Neriti's mother looked past her at Ragher. "Who's this?" she asked.

Neriti glanced back at Ragher nervously. Then she turned to her mother again with a look of relief. "This is a new friend I've made. He's from another pack."

"Oh, another troublemaker, I see," said her mother jokingly. "Well, the two of you better get back down to the pilgrimage. You won't learn all the ancient lunar wolf teachings by playing around up here."

Neriti objected. "But *Mom*, I already know all the songs. And it's boring down there. Please let me stay up here a little while longer. My friend and I just want to get some of our play spirit out before we have to sit again for a long time."

Neriti's mom looked at Ragher. "What did you say your friend's name was?" she asked her daughter.

Neriti spun around and looked at Ragher with a face that suggested she was expecting him to do something. But Ragher was still obeying her orders to remain silent. Realizing that he wasn't going to be of any help, Neriti blurted out the first thing that popped into her head. "His name is Luumi."

"Luumi?" her mom questioned as she eyed Ragher. "As in Luumi, the son of the Rawali Pack leader?"

Neriti nodded. Then she looked back at Ragher and again at her mother. "He doesn't like to talk a lot."

"I can see that," said her mother. "Okay, you two can get your play spirit out for a little while longer. I'll stay a few feet down from the top of the crater while you run around, but I'll be back up to grab you both in just a few minutes."

"Thanks, Mom!" Neriti shouted happily, jumping up high in a show of excitement.

The white and silver wolf nodded kindly at her daughter and then turned to walk back down the path into Crystal Crater. When she was out of sight, Neriti turned back to

Ragher. "Good job holding your shape! Was that hard for you?"

Ragher nodded. "Yes," he said in a pup voice. "But I think I have it now. I seem to be able to hold my form best when I don't think about it too much. In fact, it would probably be better if we change the subject." Ragher paused and then continued, "I didn't expect you to be so little."

Neriti laughed. "What do you mean? You don't even know me. Why would you have expected me to be anything at all?"

Ragher shook his head. "I know you very well, actually. You're Neriti, the most gifted healer the lunar wolves have ever known. Except, I guess that hasn't happened yet."

Neriti smiled at Ragher. "I like you. What's your name, spirit?" she asked.

"My name's Ragher," he responded, "but I'm not a spirit. I'm a Moon Walker. I've come to take care of you."

Neriti laughed again. "Oh, really?" she asked. "Who sent you to take care of me? Don't they realize I already have a mother and father who take care of me?"

"No, you don't understand," said Ragher. "Your parents aren't going to live much longer. In a few more years they'll be gone, and you'll be all alone."

All the playfulness suddenly drained from Neriti's face. "How dare you!" she yelled at Ragher. "Why would you say such a thing to me? You're a bad spirit, aren't you? You shouldn't have come here! Go now! Go back to wherever it is you came from!" Then she turned around and ran to the rim of the crater, disappearing over the edge.

Ragher started to run after her. "Wait!" he called, but before he'd gone very far, there was a loud "*pop!*" as he turned into something that looked halfway between a hairy troll and a warty toad.

Ragher looked down at himself to see what he'd become. Then he looked away from the crater into the darkness. "You can't be here like this. The dark spirit will find you and eat you!" he scolded himself in a croaky voice. "Change back to a wolf. Change back to a wolf!"

Nothing happened, though. "You have to get to the Dayside, Ragher. Concentrate. Think wolf. Think wolf. Be the wolf. Don't make any noise. Don't draw attention. Just flow into the change."

He heard Neriti's mother getting closer while calling for the little wolf pup she thought her daughter had left behind. "Luumi? I don't know what happened with Neriti, but you need to come back inside the crater now. It's not safe for you out here on your own."

Ragher took a deep breath, and then came a deafening "*Pop! Pop! Pop!*" as he changed from a troll-toad into a green blob, then back into a shining ball of light, and finally into a glowing, adult wolf again. He looked down at his large paws. "No!" he yelled as Neriti's mother reached the top of the crater.

"Oh!" she gasped, startled to see the glowing, white wolf standing before her. Ragher looked back at her in a panic. Not sure what to do or say, he galloped off into the darkness. "Wait!" Neriti's mother called after him. "It's okay. I'm a healer!"

But Ragher kept on running, too afraid to let everyone know what he was. He worried that if they found out, his nightmare would come true—the dark spirit would come after him and devour him, just like he'd seen happen before.

"Tick...tick...tick." The metal discs began to rotate, and the spell the vision had cast over the trio was broken as the ice sheets pulled apart once again.

Fred looked at Ragher, "This whole time you've been able to change into different forms, but you stayed a wolf? *Why?*"

Axel spoke to Ragher too, ignoring the question Fred had posed. "So, if you aren't actually Neriti's son, then why did you pretend to be?" he asked as the fragmented ice shoved them even deeper into the underground lair, into a new ice tunnel that was slowly pulling itself together in front of them.

"You'll see, Axel. Before you leave here, you'll know as much as I do and probably more."

"But why? You still haven't explained anything. Why are we here if the kid and I aren't like you? If we're only 'lesser' creatures like you spoke of before?"

"Because you aren't 'lesser' creatures anymore. To fulfill your destiny, you had to be transformed."

"What do you mean 'transformed?'" asked Fred.

"You've both transcended. You're Moon Walkers now. It was the only way."

Fred's voice sounded more agitated than ever. "The only way to *what*?" he asked.

Ragher replied, "The only way for you to save your former kinds. The only way to ensure that the Moon realm lives on."

Axel shook his head in frustration. "But that was Helen's job. She already made sure that Dan didn't destroy Theia. She and the girl saved the Moon realm."

Ragher stomped his foot. "No. You saw it with your own eyes, Axel. Helen wasn't saving the Moon realm from Dan. She was saving it from the dark spirit. Dan was just a pawn, and he was defeated. But the dark spirit isn't mortal. He's ancient. He was here long before any of the rest of the creatures, just like Theia."

Axel asked, "Are you saying the dark spirit is a god, Ragher?"

Ragher looked at the vision that was playing on the wall closest to them. It was a scene from when Helen was little, no more than five or six. She was riding on Axel's back, holding tight to the fur around his neck and giggling with excitement. She looked up at the dark expanse above them and smiled, enjoying the sensation of the wind on her face as they raced across the lunar plain with the rest of the wolf pack.

"Yes, Axel. That's what I'm saying. But as I told you before, I completed my mission by bringing you here. It's time, now, for the two of you to see for yourselves."

CHAPTER 7

THE AWAKENING

Mina sat at her grandfather's bedside, holding his warm, frail hand with both of hers. He'd been in a coma for a couple of weeks, but every so often he would stir, giving her hope that he might still awaken. She rested her head on the side of his bed and let out a deep sigh.

A little over two years had passed since she'd returned from her adventure to the Moon realm, and since her return it seemed as though her grandfather's general disposition and memory had grown stronger. Or at least they had until recently when he'd taken a sudden and sharp turn for the worse.

The doctor who'd examined him said that her grandfather had suffered a serious stroke and would likely only hang on for a few more days. The best they could do was to bring in hospice workers to take care of him and prepare to say good-bye. But that had been two weeks earlier, and still he hung on.

Her grandfather had not been conscious at all during this time, but Mina watched as he fought to stay with her. Whenever he stirred, he seemed to be struggling against some unseen force—battling an invisible foe to fight his way back to the waking world. Sometimes, Mina wondered if there was something important he needed to do before he could let go.

"Come back to me, Grandfather," Mina whispered. "I'm right here. I can help you with whatever you need."

"Mina?" her father spoke to her from the doorway of her grandfather's bedroom. She sat up straight and looked at her dad. "Your mother and I would like to speak with you in the kitchen for a moment before we leave for work. The nurse will come in while you're gone so your grandfather won't be alone."

Mina looked at the date on her watch. She hadn't realized it was Sunday, the day her parents worked the overnight shift at the hospital. Time had become blurred since her grandfather had fallen ill. She'd been allowed to stay home from school to be with him before he passed, although she wasn't sure if that would continue now that he was holding on so much longer than everyone had expected.

Mina gently squeezed her grandfather's bony hand. Then she stood and followed her father into the kitchen where she found her mother sitting at the table. Her mom smiled at her, but Mina could tell that she was nervous.

"Take a seat." Her dad gestured to the chair opposite her mother, and Mina sat down. Her father took the chair at the head of the table and looked at his wife, as if he was expecting her to say something. However, she continued to silently stare at Mina.

So, he began. "As you know, honey, your mother and I have wanted to practice medicine overseas for a while now. It's our desire to help people who don't have access to the kind of healthcare we enjoy in this country."

Her mother chimed in suddenly, "In some of the poorest and most remote countries, there is *no* healthcare system to speak of."

Her father looked at Mina's mother and nodded. "Right.

Some places have hardly any healthcare system at all. And there are many villages that don't have any doctors or nurses for hundreds of miles."

Mina looked at her parents. As much as she tried, she couldn't recall having heard them mention a desire to offer medical care overseas before, and she didn't understand why they were talking about it now.

"I don't get it. What are you saying?"

Her mother spoke, "Well, honey, we waited as long as we could, but this has been a work in progress since even before you disappeared. Then, once you were back, we thought it best to monitor you for a while, so we put our plans on hold indefinitely.

"We know it's bad timing with your grandfather in the condition he's in, but right before he had his stroke, we committed to a two-year medical trip to Africa. We would've told you sooner, but we wanted to wait until after the funeral. Unfortunately, we can't wait any longer. We leave in two weeks."

Mina felt dumbfounded. She was well aware that her parents were more aloof than other kids' parents due to their overzealous commitment to their work, but this level of disregard for her feelings was completely unexpected.

"So, you waited for the only person in the world who's ever shown me genuine love and care to go into a coma before you took your trip? Because you thought *that* would be good timing?!"

"Don't be so dramatic, sweetheart. Like your mother said, we already made these plans before your grandfather fell ill. Of course, we'd hoped he'd be around while we were gone, but you still have Bonkers. Plus, you'll be away at school in a couple of years, and we think now is a good time for you to get used to being on your own. It will be excellent practice. You'll just need to be careful not to tell people that you're all by yourself here.

It's doubtful anyone would ever suspect it, but it's better to play it safe, you know? Also, your mom and I would prefer it if you don't answer the door to strangers. Understand?"

Mina couldn't believe it. "This is a joke, right? A sick and twisted joke?" she asked.

Her parents looked at each other, and Mina knew in that instant that it was true. "This is ridiculous! Do you know why nobody would ever suspect that I was alone in this house? Because *normal* parents don't abandon their children and leave the country for two years! Being at the hospital all the time wasn't enough negligent parenting for you? You have to take it to the extreme and move to an entirely different continent?" Mina shouted as tears poured down her face.

Her mother sighed. "We thought this might be difficult for you, but I hope you realize that our trip will do a lot of good. We'll be helping adults and children who don't live the sort of lives we do. These are people who've never experienced the miracle of modern medicine or enjoyed any of the medical conveniences we take for granted. You understand why this is important. Don't you, darling?"

Mina felt helpless. With this one statement, her mother had taken away Mina's ability to make any argument without sounding selfish. But Mina thought her parents were really the ones being selfish, for never choosing her. She knew it was probably childish, but she couldn't help wondering why they'd even bothered having her in the first place when they had no real interest in her life.

Her father looked at the clock on the wall. "We have to go, Marion. We're already late." Then to Mina, he said, "Take some time to think it over. We can talk more tomorrow after we get home from the hospital—once you've had time to process this."

Mina understood now why her parents had picked this

moment to tell her about their trip. They knew they'd have an easy exit if it didn't go well. She didn't say anything. What was there to say? Nothing she did or said would change anything. It never had with them.

Her parents got ready to go, and Mina walked back into her grandfather's room. The nurse smiled brightly at her when she came in. "He's still sleeping soundly," she said, as if to reassure Mina that her argument with her parents hadn't disturbed him. The nurse put a hand on Mina's shoulder as she walked past her and out of the room.

Mina sat down by the bed again. She listened to the slow, methodical sounds of the medical equipment that had been brought in to monitor her grandfather's vital signs and to help him breathe. The little mechanical noises brought her a sense of peace, and she realized how ironic it was that her grandfather's medical equipment managed to comfort her more than her own parents.

"Please come back, Grandfather," she whispered again.

His chest rose up and down in a gentle rhythm that made Mina sleepy. As she watched him breathe slowly through the tubes in his nose, she began to think over all the time that had passed since she'd returned from the Moon. She tried hard to recall the time she had spent with her parents during the last two years, but their faces weren't the ones that came to mind as she searched through her memories.

Of course, her mom and dad had been relieved, even grateful, to have her home. Her mother hadn't stopped hugging her for what felt like an entire day. It was the first time in her entire life she could remember her parents taking some time off from work just to be with her.

However, once the flood of emotions had subsided, they did return to work, and it seemed like they'd barely stopped working since. Neither her mother nor father had ever been the doting type, and so once everything felt normal again, they quickly carried on as if it were.

For Mina, however, nothing felt normal anymore. From the moment she returned, she lived in two different worlds. Her body was present on Earth, but it felt like she'd left the rest of herself behind on the Moon. The only time she ever felt like her former self was when she spent time with her grandfather and Bonkers. The rest of the time she walked around like an empty shell, completely unconnected to anything or anyone around her.

Of course, nobody except for her grandfather knew her secret. She couldn't tell anyone else what had happened. She knew they'd think she'd gone mad. So, she made up a story about being washed out to sea and getting stranded on an unfamiliar shore with a terrible leg injury that had made it impossible to get home quickly. The tale satisfied her parents, but she could tell that her friends and classmates didn't believe her. At least not entirely.

It was evident that she had become the dominant topic of conversation while she was gone. And unfortunately, she'd committed the grave sin of showing up *alive* again without an intriguing enough explanation. Therefore, her classmates had been forced to use their own imaginations to fill in the missing details.

In the meantime, Mina became a social pariah. To her peers, she was the embodiment of every lurid tale that had been concocted about her disappearance—alien abductee, runaway circus clown, child bride, pirate hostage, etc. And although there were some who didn't believe any of this ridiculous gossip, Mina was too weighed down by the burden of guarding her real story to seek solace in their friendship.

A few hours passed. Mina was reading a story out loud to her grandfather when the nurse came in and interrupted her. "Will you be alright, love, if I leave before Edgar gets here?"

Edgar was the nurse who pulled the overnight shifts. Mina nodded. "Sure, Deb. He's been quiet all day. I guess he might really be nearing the end now," she said, trying to put on a brave face, even though she felt broken inside.

Nurse Deb smiled sympathetically. "Well, not to give you any false hope, but it's been my experience that you can't predict cases like your grandfather's. Every day can be different. I wouldn't draw too much meaning from a day of quiet. A mind in a coma doesn't run on a clock or follow a calendar the way it does when it's awake."

Mina smiled. She liked the idea of her grandfather's mind being free from the confounds of time. At least, it was something.

"Well, goodnight, dear. See you tomorrow," she said as she turned and left.

Setting the book down on Grandfather's nightstand, Mina stood up and stretched her arms. She looked out the window and was surprised to see little beads of water sliding down the glass. Apparently, it had begun to sprinkle outside. Bonkers, who'd been curled up at her feet, snoring all afternoon, stood up and did some stretches of his own. Mina knew these stretches well. It was Bonkers' way of telling her he was ready for dinner. "Alright, boy. What will it be tonight? Boeuf bourguignon or chicken confit?"

Those were the names of Bonkers' canned dogfood, although it was really just a fancy way for people to figure out whether they were serving their canine friend beef gruel or chicken gruel. Mina thought it hardly made a difference which one it was, though. Bonkers drooled the same amount, no matter which gruel he was being served.

She started to move into the hallway when she heard her grandfather let out a slight moan. She stopped without turning around. Waiting. It wasn't the first time he'd made a sound, and Mina knew it could be another one-off. When a few seconds passed in silence, Mina continued on to the kitchen.

She made Bonkers dinner and then walked to her bedroom to grab a couple of books that she was supposed to be reading during her absence from school. She figured her grandfather would be just as happy to hear about the wonderful world of geometry proofs as he was to hear the stories she'd been reading to him. After all, the doctor had said he was likely too far gone to hear any of it. Yet even so, Mina refused to give up. "Maybe, I can bore him so badly with math that he'll wake up just so he can tell me to stop," she thought.

But when Mina walked back into her grandfather's room, his eyes were wide open, and he was muttering something under his breath. She was stunned. A mixture of elation and fear washed over her. She was relieved to see her grandfather awake, but she could tell right away that he was distressed.

Dropping her books, she ran to his side. "Mina, I have to tell you this now, and you must listen," he said softly to her, though his eyes were fixated on the ceiling instead of her.

Mina squeezed his hand to let him know she was right there next to him. Her grandfather slowly turned his head towards her, and his clouded eyes sparkled with the love and affection he'd always shown her. "I'm so happy you're awake," she said. "I've been so worried. The doctors, they said…well, never mind. I'm, I'm just so thankful."

Her grandfather nodded and squeezed her hand too. "Help me get into a seated position. I have to tell you this now," he repeated. "There should be a couple of pillows in my closet right there. Be quick and fetch them for me, will you?"

Mina turned and opened the closet to retrieve her grandfather's pillows. The rain had picked up outside. The wind rocked the trees back and forth, and she could hear branches squeaking against the windows on all sides of the little cottage.

Mina said to her grandfather, "You seem so much more

alert. You've been asleep for two weeks, and yet you seem sharper than ever."

"Well, the mind and body are amazing inventions, Mina. They don't always do what's expected of them, and yet sometimes they do more." He put his arms to his sides and began to lift himself up on his own.

"No, please. Let me help you," she said, grabbing ahold of his arm and pulling him forward as she positioned the pillows behind his back.

Then once he was propped up on the bed comfortably, she asked, "Now, what is it you wanted to tell me?"

"Hmm, where to begin exactly. I guess first, I should explain that whatever it is you think I've suffered from, whatever malady the doctors told you I'd fallen ill with, isn't what really happened."

Mina was confused and began to worry that her grandfather wasn't as well as he seemed. "The doctors checked you over, Papa. They said you've had a—"

"No, listen to me. I'm telling you that's not what happened. They're trying to deceive you, little one. The man who watches me at night and the woman during the day, they aren't nurses, Mina. They're guards. And your parents, they're not who we thought either. It's important that you accept this, so you can move on. Go forward. You have no future here. I didn't understand it before because my memories were being suppressed, but you were taken away to the Moon for a reason, and now you must go back."

Mina was terrified by what her grandfather was saying. Her logical mind felt panicked. It told her that her dear, sweet grandfather was beyond repair. The stroke that had put him into a coma had scrambled his brain so that he no longer lived in reality. Her heart felt even more panicked, however, because it sensed that what he was saying might be true. She wasn't sure that it was a good idea to encourage him, but she had to know. "What do you mean that my parents aren't who we thought?"

Her grandfather continued, "My wife. Cate. She wasn't human, Mina. She was magical. I didn't remember it from before, but now I do. She's the one who put me into that deep sleep and told me all these things. I'd completely forgotten how beautiful and smart she was. It was impossible not to fall in love with her. I believe she's a true enchantress."

"But grandmother is dead, Papa. Are you saying she came back as a ghost to tell you that your nurses are guards and that her daughter and son-in-law aren't who they say they are?"

"Yes, Mina. But Cate's not a ghost. I'm not even sure she's able to die. She's more like a deity than a mortal life form. But there's another part to all of this that's just as important. She's not your grandmother, Mina. She's your mother, and I'm your father.

"Your whole life, my memories were so jumbled. I believed what I was told—what we were both told all these years—that your mother was my daughter and your father her husband. But that wasn't right. They were strangers to us. It was a lie to keep us trapped in the world they wanted us to live in.

"Right now, your real mother is out there wreaking havoc by creating this storm. And in doing so, she's created this moment for us. She's keeping the night guard at bay so that you can finally know the truth and know what's at stake."

Outside, greenish-blue electricity lit up the sky followed by a rolling clap of thunder that rattled every windowpane in the cottage.

Mina was skeptical. It all seemed extraordinarily far-fetched, but she knew that wasn't entirely fair since her grandfather had never doubted *her* wild story. She decided to give him a chance to explain. She asked, "But then, who are the people pretending to be my parents? And why would anyone try to trap us here on Earth when this is where we're from?"

Her grandfather smiled. "I know you have many questions, my girl, and you'll have many more. Searching for the answers is what will lead you to your future. I'm sorry I don't have more for you. Your mother wouldn't tell me everything, but she wants you to know that she's upset over how you've been treated. You should never have been allowed to return from the Moon. You still have an important role to play there."

"But I *had* to come home," Mina insisted. "Or I never would've seen you and Bonkers again."

He smiled at her. "Yes, well, I didn't say *I* was outraged. You've made my life worth living, my sweet Mina. I only wish I could've been a father to you instead of a befuddled, old man."

Mina clasped his hand tightly. "Don't, Papa. You've been wonderful, and there's still time. You're awake now and better than ever. We can do all the things we've always done, except now you'll get to enjoy them more. It'll be like a whole new life." A loud clap of thunder crashed above the cottage. The lights flickered, and Mina jumped halfway out of her chair as Bonkers tried to crawl under the bed.

"It's going to be okay, my little darling. I'm very sorry to have to ask this of you because you already have such a big secret to keep. But it's important. You cannot tell anyone what I've told you, for I fear it might put you in danger. It's true that you have a powerful mother, but I suspect she isn't able to protect you the way she would like to. Understand?"

Tears had begun to fill Mina's eyes, but she nodded, trying not to blink. She could tell he was leaving her behind again— only for good this time. "Please, Papa. I don't want to be here without you. *Please* don't go."

All the energy that had enlivened the old man suddenly drained from him all at once. Mina wiped away her tears as she watched her grandfather sink into his pillows, looking even older and more tired than ever before. "Don't cry, my beautiful Mina. You have many more big adventures out there waiting for you. Carry me in your heart, and I will be there for them all."

Mina looked down at his hand, holding it tight. She could hear light rain falling on the leaves and grass outside the cottage. When she raised her eyes a few seconds later, he was gone.

THE FUNERAL WAS HELD two days later on a beautiful, clear day. Mina's parents had already planned everything a week earlier. And though it pained her to think about it, Mina sensed they'd been waiting a little too eagerly for her grandfather's corpse to hurry up and manifest so that they could get on with it.

The graveside ceremony was small. Her grandfather had lost track of his friends during the years that he'd struggled with his memory. Or at least that's what Mina's parents told the minister who presided over the service. Mina wondered if that were true, though, or if he'd been kept from seeing other people after his wife had died. Or left. Or disappeared. Mina wasn't sure which it was anymore.

She'd barely slept since the night her grandfather died. She couldn't stop thinking about everything he'd told her. She wrote it all down in a journal to prevent any part of it from slipping away, partly because she knew it might be important but also because she didn't want to forget anything about her last moments with him.

She stayed up and thought through the whole exchange again and again, dissecting parts of her childhood that supported his claims and others that didn't. There was the fact that she had barely seen her grandfather when she was little. Her parents had taken better care of her then. Her mother had sung to her almost every night before bed, and her father had read stories to her. It was hard to imagine imposter parents showing her that kind of love.

But on the other hand, her parents had spent an enormous amount of time away from her since she was five. They were always at the hospital or catching up on their sleep. Plus, she'd never been allowed to visit them while they were at work. Whenever she'd asked if she could come, they always put her off. They told her the hospital was no place for kids, even though she knew other kids who got to visit their parents while they worked at the hospital.

There were also some memories that strongly supported her grandfather's outrageous claims. Like the ones in which her grandfather consistently mistook Mina for his own daughter. Excuses were always given to explain it away. *Her grandfather was becoming forgetful, and Mina bore a strong resemblance to her mother at the same age.* But had her grandfather actually been remembering correctly? Mina wondered now.

She was torn. Doubting that her mother and father were her real parents seemed like madness, but doubting her grandfather felt wrong. Of course, it was more logical to assume that he might've woken up with some degree of brain damage that caused him to imagine all his preposterous assertions. Yet for the short amount of time he'd been awake, he'd seemed even more lucid than ever.

"How did Grandmother Cate die?" Mina blurted out suddenly as her grandfather's coffin was lowered into the ground. She stared at her grandmother's tombstone. *Here lies our beloved mother and wife. May you always rest in peace.* Mina thought it was interesting that the date of death carved into the stone was a full year before Mina had been born. This certainly didn't correspond to her grandfather's story. However, she still felt suspicious.

"Don't you remember, sugarplum?" Mina's father asked. "I'm sure we've told you this before. She had cancer. It all happened very fast."

Mina continued her questioning. "And what about your parents, Dad? How did they die?"

"Come on, kiddo. You know this story. My parents were gone long before you were born. They died in a terrible accident. An explosion at the factory where they worked."

"And where are their gravestones? Why don't you ever go see them?"

"They're buried in the small town I grew up in. Hundreds of miles from here. What's with all the questions? We're here to honor your grandfather, you know?"

Mina thought for a second and then said, "I'd like to see pictures of the family, especially you and Grandmother Cate, Mom. I'd like to see what you looked like when you were little and what she looked like. See if I can spot the family resemblance."

Mina's mother and father looked at each other, but Mina couldn't tell if there was a secret meaning to the exchange. "Is there something wrong with that?" she pushed.

"No, dear," her mother replied. "I'm sure we have some old photo albums put away somewhere. Give me time to look for them. We're going to be busy the next few days, getting ready to go. But I'll try to find them before we leave."

Mina nodded and looked back at the rectangular hole in front of her. This was it, she thought. It was time to grow up. Every person she'd ever cared for was leaving her behind, whether by choice or not. She still didn't know if she believed all the crazy things her grandfather had told her, but considering the circumstances, it didn't really matter if she did or didn't. What had become clear was that she needed to find a way to contact the people she had left behind. She needed to contact her friends on the Moon.

CHAPTER 8

NEW WALDOFF

Years had passed since the Moon Travelers had first begun to build a new city, although by the looks of their large village, one might've assumed that it had existed for a few hundred years. The homes, shops, and restaurants were built out of stone and mortar, and cobbled together so that there was no obvious separation between the units on the exterior. The one and two-story buildings lined both sides of the streets. And the streets were laid out in a complicated spiderweb pattern which was intended to make it difficult for trespassers to find their way in or out of the city.

As people's memories resurfaced of the destruction Dan had done to the first lunar city, it became a common belief that the Moon Travelers needed to do a better job of protecting themselves and their property against outside threats. Never mind that the previous threat had come from within their own community, or that the people who wanted the new city to be fortified were the same ones who'd allowed—if not downright encouraged—the events that led to the ruin of their past city.

However, before the consensus to build the fortified city was reached, the citizens formed committees to draft up different proposals for the overall design and construction of New Waldoff. Maude, in her last role as a public servant, served on one of these committees with Bob and several of their allies. Their committee proposed a more modernized and high-tech city, similar to the suburban-type neighborhoods in the original Waldoff, except even more energy efficient and adaptable to new technology.

Maude and Bob's committee presented their proposal first. Before they started, Bob rigged up a microphone and speaker system from some of the old army equipment, realizing there would likely be a huge turnout to hear the proposals. After all, every single Moon Traveler had a vested interest in learning about their options for the new city. And it turned out Bob was right. Thousands of citizens showed up and surrounded the wooden platform that had been erected to serve as a stage.

In terms of ingenuity and volume of ideas, Maude and Bob's committee set the bar so high that the next several presentations paled in comparison. Each committee had one or two original ideas of their own, but it was nothing that couldn't have been easily added to the swell of technological advancements and efficiencies that the first committee had proposed.

The last committee to go was comprised of several former army officers who'd served under Bob, including Lt. General Goodman. In addition to the officers, a large group of ex-soldiers dressed in uniform stood on stage in the background during the presentation. None of them had been assigned to the committee, but it appeared that they were there to lend their support.

From the start, Goodman made it clear he was in charge. While the other officers remained stationary, Goodman roamed around the stage, looking around at the audience with an expression that seemed practically sinister at times. To begin, he announced, "The threat has been neutralized." Then, he paused. "That's what we were all told, right? That without spilling one drop of blood, the enemy was defeated. Did you feel grateful that day? Maybe even lucky?"

The audience didn't respond. It seemed like they were waiting to see where Goodman was going with his questioning. "How many times since arriving on the Moon have you had your lives turned upside down?" Goodman seemed like he was trying to smile sympathetically, but it came across more like conceit. "I'd say the majority of you would need more than one hand to count the number of times your normal lives have been tampered with." He strode back and forth across the stage, pausing often so his words had time to sink in.

"Well, what if I told you that now is our moment to change all that? With some due respect, these other presentations you heard today were okay if you want to live in a city full of gimmicks. But what you *should* be asking yourselves is this—will my new city keep me safe? Will it prevent me from having to suffer more hardship whenever we're attacked again?"

By this point, people in the crowd had begun loudly whispering to each other. But Goodman continued, "And I know some of you might be thinking that those days are in the past. Because after all, *the threat has been neutralized.* Right?

"But let's face it. The reality of our situation is that we've quite possibly become immortals. Gods, if you will." A few people gasped at this suggestion, but Goodman explained, "Oh, I'm not saying we *are* gods, but therein lies the problem. It would seem we've obtained infinite life, and yet we can barely protect ourselves during this endless time period. If we don't do something now to strengthen our position against those who seek to destroy us, we will continue to face these kinds of problems on and on, forever and ever."

"So, what do you propose?" shouted a man from the middle of the audience.

Goodman smiled. "I'm glad you asked," he replied smugly, "because it gives me the chance to throw the question right back to you. My fellow officers and I have drawn up a general outline based on what we know from our military experience. We've added in various fortifications and tactical designs that we're confident will keep our city safe. But we want to hear your ideas too. We know that all of you have your own personal concerns about your safety, and we want to address them. So go ahead. Start tossing some ideas at us!"

The crowd glanced around at each other silently until a man at the back shouted, "I want an alarm system in my own home, to make sure my neighbors ain't trying to rob me in my sleep!" A few people in the audience laughed at this, but then another man yelled, "I think we need a police force to keep the peace, now that the army is disbanding and all." Then a few more chimed in, "A wall to keep the bad guys out!" "Guards to man the wall!" "An old-timey village with secret passageways, an alligator moat, and giant catapults to hurl rotten vegetables at our enemies!" Nobody was sure whether this last suggestion was a joke or not, but nevertheless, it was written down on a giant chalk board, just like all the other suggestions.

The rest of Goodman's presentation became an audience brainstorming session regarding what lengths they wanted to go to protect themselves. Nobody on the committee ever made a cohesive argument for *why* they needed such heavy fortification for their new city. It seemed, instead, that everyone was perfectly fine working under the assumption that, someday, they just would.

The audience spent several hours coming up with one grandiose idea after another, which at times sounded like a competition to see who could come up with the most elaborate idea of all. But the end result was that the audience had helped envision what the ideal version of an ultra-protected city should look like. It was to be a secured, old-timey village that could guard and weaponize its citizens against all the unidentified adversaries that the audience commonly referred to as "them" and "they."

Right away, Bob and Maude recognized they'd been beat. Goodman had succeeded at winning over the crowd by not only promising them a city that would protect them, but also by giving them a say in its design. In the days that followed, Bob sought a meeting with Goodman to congratulate him on his popular vision and offer his assistance with inventing additional features that would help the city prosper. However, the meeting never occurred.

It was strange. The assistant that Goodman had hired to do his scheduling never seemed to pencil Bob in. So, whenever Bob arrived at Goodman's makeshift office inside one of the army's large tents, there was never any record of the appointment. It seemed his old lieutenant general had become popular, too, because every time Bob dropped by, Goodman was either away on business or engaged in another appointment. After several attempts, Bob took the hint, and the two never spoke again from then on.

Bob often wondered why Goodman had treated him so dismissively. From Bob's perspective, they'd had a nice professional relationship when working together on the Darkside. On several occasions, they'd even spent time discussing their lives and families to pass the endless wait before the battle began. Bob had no clue what had gone wrong between them or why his former top-ranking officer had decided not to come to him when he was recruiting the other officers to serve together on a committee—at least as a courtesy, anyway.

He supposed it might have something to do with Goodman wanting to get out from underneath his shadow, but this didn't seem like the Goodman Bob knew. And so, he continued to think about the situation from time to time, as though it were a mechanical problem he couldn't quite solve.

Soon, Bob threw his energy back into designing new ways

to create energy saving technologies that could be integrated into their *new* old-style village. Yet almost right away, a man showed up at Maude and Bob's temporary tent quarters, demanding a meeting. He introduced himself as Mr. Burles, but Maude and Bob were already familiar with him. He was a shifty fellow who'd been a loyal follower of the twins and one of the first volunteers to drink Dan's poison.

Mr. Burles explained that he'd recently been appointed as the Elegance and Taste Commissioner of New Waldoff, which made Maude laugh. "Elegance and Taste Commissioner? What sort of absurd title is that?"

Mr. Burles didn't like being teased, however, judging by the sour expression across his face. And Bob nudged Maude to get her to ease up.

"Yes, well, I suppose we can't all sit around playing *magic* all day. Some of us have to live in the real world and handle grown-up responsibilities," he retorted.

Maude put her hand over her heart. "Oh, pumpkin, you think that's a grown-up job title? When no one would ever be able to guess what it even means? Something to do with making sure that we all wear matching socks and use our silverware correctly, I suppose?"

Bob didn't like the back-and-forth bickering that had begun. So, he interjected, "Mr. Burles, I'm assuming you didn't come here just to announce your new position. Is there something you were wanting to discuss with us?"

Mr. Burles focused his attention on Bob. "Yes, in fact, there is. I've been sent here to inform you that you needn't bother submitting any more plans for the betterment of the city's energy or technology use."

"And why is that?" Maude asked annoyed.

Mr. Burles smiled spitefully. "Because Minister Goodman has decided that the city should stick to the older technologies. Less *difficulty* that way, you see."

"Minister Goodman?" Maude snorted. "I didn't realize that Goodman had become a clergyman."

Mr. Burles laughed condescendingly. "Oh, no. Not that kind of minister. He's the Prime Minister. The Dual Council just elected him this morning."

Maude and Bob looked at each other with stunned expressions. "What council are you referring to?" asked Bob.

"The soldiers' council," Burles answered. "I mean, they're not called that, of course, but essentially that's what they are since both sides are made up entirely of former soldiers." Burles paused and then continued, "Hmm, I would've thought they'd have asked you to join them. Oh well. I guess they already had everyone they needed." Burles bit his bottom lip and mimicked a sad face to taunt Maude.

"Well, if that's all you came for," said Maude, gesturing her arm towards the exit.

Burles stuck his nose in the air. "Yes, well this won't be the last time you hear from me. I've been asked to oversee all the building plans while the town is under construction. The council wants to ensure that the 'old-style village' look is correctly implemented. The Prime Minister wants all of it to be quite uniform, you know."

Maude nodded her head dismissively as Burles spoke, like she wasn't listening to a word he was saying. "Okay, great," she said as she pushed him towards the exit. "Just make sure you let us know you're coming next time, and we'll whip you up a real *magical* treat. Something so elegant and full of taste you'll practically choke on it!"

Mr. Burles had just walked past the raised tent flap when he turned back to Maude like he was going to say something. But before he could, Maude pulled on a rope to the side of her head, and the tent flap fell with a sweeping thud right in Burles' face. Maude turned back to Bob, and the two looked at each other anxiously for a moment before either one spoke.

Finally, Maude said what they both were thinking, "Is this really happening again? Is Charles Goodman really planning to usurp power the same way our boys did? Has nobody learned anything from the last three decades!?"

Bob shrugged his shoulders. "It would seem not, but I'll tell you something, dear, I would never have thought Goodman capable of this. Even after he snubbed me all those times, I thought he was just trying to make a go of it on his own. Get out from underneath my coattails, as the expression goes. This just isn't like him, Maude. He was a good soldier—a rule follower and obedient. It's why I made him my second in command."

"Yes, well, this is a great deal more than trying to get out from underneath your coattails. Goodman seems to think he's been given carte blanche to lord over every aspect of New Waldoff, just because the people chose his city proposal. And now he's even putting himself in charge of it! The nerve of this guy, Bob! What in the world are we going to do to stop him?"

Bob looked stumped. "Well, I'd like to go talk to him, but we know he won't see me."

Maude shook her head. "If he's already crowning himself emperor of the land, I think it's likely he's beyond reason. We can't let this get out of control like last time, though. We turned a blind eye to the twins and look at where *that* got us!"

Bob hesitated before he continued cautiously, "I know you're worried because of what happened before, Maude, but surely this can't be as bad as that. At least Goodman has been trying to give people a say in how things are built. Plus, he has a council, and it sounds like he's appointing some commissioners, although I still don't understand what that man Burles is supposed to be doing."

Maude said, "Oh, darling. You've always seen the best in everyone. Honestly, it's one of the things I love most about you.

In fact, it's this side of you that inspired me to repair my friendship with Ruth before she died.

"But, Bob, we have to try to do something about all of this before it's too late. Think about it. Helen sacrificed herself so that all those people out there could live freely. And you promised her you'd spend the rest of your life making sure that wasn't for nothing. Are you really going to gamble it all away on the hope that Goodman is still the best version of himself deep down inside?

"What if we give him the benefit of the doubt just like we did the twins, and we're wrong again? I'm too old for this, Bob. I can't…" But Maude stopped. Tears were beginning to stream down her face, and her words caught in her throat.

Bob wrapped his arms around her and held her against his chest. "It's going to be okay. You're right, sweetheart. I know I can't get to Goodman, but I can still talk to the rest of the soldiers. I'll begin scheduling some meetings right away. I'll make Max my first stop. Maybe I can get through to some of them—remind them of what we were prepared to fight and die for not too long ago."

Maude nodded weakly against Bob's chest. She was tired. The same kind of tired Ruth had spoken of right before she'd decided to pass on. Maude wasn't sure she had the strength to do battle anymore. Fighting for their world the one time had caused her more heartache than she thought any one person should ever have to endure, and she didn't think she wanted to go through it all again.

However, Maude wouldn't let herself dwell on this now. Secretly, she knew she had work to do before leaving—a mystery to solve that might finally bring her some peace regarding her past, and even more importantly, an understanding of what had really happened to her sweet Helen.

Bᴏʙ's ᴅᴇᴛᴇʀᴍɪɴᴀᴛɪᴏɴ ᴛᴏ appeal to the soldiers' better nature went nowhere. From Max, he found out who the council members were and then met separately with the seven whom he'd considered friends. The response he received from each of them was the same, however. In fact, the conversations went so similarly that Bob was certain the officers had gotten together beforehand to plan what they were going to say when they met with him individually.

Bob pleaded with each soldier to consider disbanding the legislative and executive bodies of government so that the people could vote for the members they wanted to serve on the council, as well as choose their own prime minister. The push-back he received, though, was that the council believed they'd made the right decision and felt no need to alter their plans. Again and again, Bob was told that the people had already cast their vote when they overwhelmingly voted for the fortified version of New Waldoff. This was evidence—the former officers explained—that the Moon Travelers wished for protection. And who better to provide it than a council made up of trained soldiers?

In regard to Goodman's ascension, each soldier tried to alleviate Bob's concerns over the former lieutenant general's power grab by assuring him that Goodman was still the dutiful soldier he'd always been. The exact words they used were, "He's a gifted and compassionate listener and the most skillful problem solver of us all. Truly, he was the obvious choice for prime minister." Upon the third time hearing it, Bob began to wonder if Goodman himself had told the soldiers to say this, and by the seventh time, he was convinced that he had. Bob could tell it had been crafted as a snub towards his own decades worth of service that had often gone unacknowledged.

At the end of each meeting, the officers promised Bob that plenty of checks and balances would be created to make sure the new government operated above board and in the best interest of its citizens. But when Bob pressed the issue, not one of the soldiers came anywhere close to giving a satisfactory response that explained what these checks and balances would look like or how they would work.

By the time Bob met with the last few of his trusted ex-officers, he was even more disheartened than Maude. He knew something would have to be done, but he felt like his hands were tied. If he spoke publicly against Goodman and the council, he was certain he would come across as being bitter about not having been appointed to one of the city's leadership positions. Plus, with no checks and balances, he wasn't sure what might happen if Goodman or the council had him arrested for speaking out.

Maude and Bob worked together to think of how to tackle the problem, but the best they could come up with was to start talking to their private circle of friends—the ones they knew they could still trust. The consensus among their circle, though, was that they'd have to wait on Goodman and the council to reveal more about how their government would operate. Most felt that it was too soon to stand up to the beast when they weren't even sure what kind of beast they were fighting yet.

So, Bob threw himself into his inventions again. Despite Burles' order, Bob refused to give up on the work he was so fond of. He might not be allowed to build inventions for the betterment of New Waldoff, but he could surely modernize the interior of his own newly constructed home with a few gadgets. Plus, he thought that if his own inventions became popular enough, other people might hire him to help modernize their homes, as well. And then what would the council do? Deprive people of products that could improve their lives? "Well, they might," thought Bob. But if so, at least it would alert everyone to how the new government planned to do business.

Unfortunately for Bob, right after he and Maude moved into their new home, their friends and neighbors began showing up at all hours, seeking the couple's advice and guidance, just like in the old days. This time, however, Maude made it clear from the beginning that she had no interest in returning to her former role as one of the town's go-to problem solvers. She explained to Bob and the others that she was too old and tired to be of any use. But Bob knew this wasn't true. Maude was just as sharp as when they'd first met. It was possible she was more easily exhausted, but her mind was still capable of running full laps around everyone else's.

Bob knew the real reason Maude didn't want to take on other people's problems was because she had started a project —one that was based on the information Ruth had given her the day that Mina left. Maude had been guarded about the details Ruth had shared. But Bob understood that because of this confrontation, his wife was now on a hunt for ancient knowledge that would help her learn about her past and what had happened to their daughter, Helen, after she disappeared.

Maude's first steps had been to track down and collect all the papers that the lunar wolves had given to the Moon Travelers decades earlier. Originally, the papers had belonged to the Moon Walkers and had been covered in symbols that didn't make any sense to the Moon's current inhabitants, but Maude had invented a formula that nearly erased all of these markings. Dulling the markings had made it possible for the travelers to use the papers for their own record keeping, design work, and letter writing.

Maude had worried that erasing the Moon Walkers' writings was a mistake, and now she absolutely hated herself for having gone through with it. When Ruth finally told her the truth about what happened in Maude's tiny living room all those years ago, something inside of Maude changed forever. The booming voice and its secretive predictions, along with Neriti's vision and the crystal it manifested—all of this had seemed like a faded memory when she heard Ruth describe it. In addition to the spark of memory Ruth had stirred in Maude, Ruth had also recounted everything she'd learned about her crystal over the last few decades. And from what Ruth told her, Maude became convinced that the Moon Walkers' papers held the key to how the Moon realm actually worked and where her daughter had ended up after she vanished for good.

So, with Maude completely immersed in her mission to restore and decipher the Moon Walkers' writings, Bob was forced to give up his own work in order to help the Moon Travelers who kept showing up on their doorstep. Briefly, he considered making his own excuse so that he'd be able to carry on with his inventions instead, but Bob had too much of a servant's heart to say "no" when he felt needed.

Later on, once New Waldoff was fully operational, Prime Minister Goodman announced that the city would establish a court system. Maude and Bob were cautiously optimistic that the system might serve as a check on the council and Prime Minister's powers. However, their hope never came to fruition.

When Goodman revealed more details about the judicial system, it became evident that the courts would have no authority over the government's dealings. Instead, the system was being created, according to Goodman, "So that citizens won't have to depend on unqualified agents to help them solve their problems. And so that they might take their concerns before an unbiased party of peers to help them settle disputes fairly."

Again, Bob took this as a personal insult, since from the beginning, he and Maude had acted as the Moon Travelers go-to "fixers" and "problem solvers." Yet even so, Bob hoped that this new system might free him up to work on his inventions full-time. But again, it wasn't to be. For soon enough, people were coming to Bob in distress after finding out they'd been sued by neighbors, or friends, or sometimes even family members. It turned out the courts had no limits as to what types of cases they would hear, which left everyone free to use the judicial system to solve any kind of problem at all.

Soon enough, Bob was cajoled into becoming a defense attorney. The very first case he agreed to take was to represent Terry, the son of his friend, Martin. A lawsuit had been filed against Terry, alleging that he'd purposely caused a dog named Mizer to attack him while walking home from the store one evening.

Bob had trouble refusing the case because of how backwards the plaintiff's complaint seemed to be. Terry had been the one who had suffered terrible lacerations up and down his legs from the bites he'd received. In fact, the dog attack had been so vicious that Terry had been forced to seek professional medical attention to stop the bleeding and stitch his wounds.

Terry denied doing anything to provoke the dog and said he believed it was the scent of the dried meat he was snacking on that had caused the dog to follow and eventually maul him. By all accounts, the dog had been in an aggressive state when he was captured. Once examined, Mizer was diagnosed with a canine mental disorder that causes dogs to prey on humans. The solution was to order the dog's owners to keep Mizer indoors permanently. But this hadn't sat well with Mizer's owners, Mr. and Mrs. Tazzity, so they sued Terry in an effort to restore Mizer's reputation as a respectable canine.

Bob had thought the whole thing was ludicrous. It was obvious that the dog was unfit to be out in public. Yet somehow the Tazzity's had painted themselves as the victims instead of doing the responsible thing by compensating the real victim in the whole ordeal—Terry.

Bob had used every logical argument he could think of to get Terry acquitted, but the jury had been persuaded by the prosecutor's compelling closing statement. "Only Mizer and Terry know what happened on the street that evening, and one of them can't talk. Is it fair to assume that Mizer attacked the kid without provocation when it's just as likely—if not more so —that Terry egged Mizer on? Should we punish all animals for their animal-like instinct to defend themselves?"

The questions were ridiculous, of course. But it didn't help that the prosecutor was allowed to keep an adorable stuffed animal, made in the likeness of Mizer, in a seat at the plaintiff's table. As the counselor gave her closing statement, she continually looked at the stuffed toy while referring to her actual client. She even stopped to pet it a few times. And judging by the way the jurors eyed the large, plush animal, one might have thought they believed it to be the *real* Mizer sitting at the table with a goofy grin stitched to his face.

Eventually, the jury found Terry guilty of creating the circumstances that led to the attack against him. Luckily, he wasn't fined, but Mizer was, thenceforth, allowed to roam the streets again, and within a week's time he'd attacked another boy, whose injuries were far more severe than Terry's.

Bob hoped that his willingness to help out his friend's son might go unnoticed, especially considering how poorly it all went. But the people who still sought his help didn't care about the outcome of the Tazzity case. They were just relieved to have someone sensible in their corner.

So, the floodgates opened, and soon Bob was officially appointed as New Waldoff's defense attorney—a position he'd never wanted and was surprised to get, considering how little Goodman seemed to care for him. He could have tried to decline the appointment, but in typical Bob fashion, he refused to say no when he knew he could be of service.

It was the end of another long workday, and Bob was finally headed home, winding his way up and down the cobblestone streets. It was late, and shadows blanketed the narrow lanes. The days and nights in the old-style village were similar to ones back on Earth. In fact, picking a location that closely mimicked Earth's equatorial cycle between light and dark had been one of Goodman's main requirements when he and his followers were choosing a location to build New Waldoff.

After a long walk home through the maze of streets, Bob walked up the steps to the front door of the two-story, one bedroom home he and Maude shared. Just like all the other houses and buildings in New Waldoff, their home was part of a long row of connected units that stretched across an entire city block.

A cyakine gas lantern hung on both sides of the door, each with an orange flame that burned dimly within. Bob was horrified when he'd learned that the council had settled on cyakine gas for the city's main source of heat and light energy. He and Maude were the ones who'd discovered the volatile gas during their early days on the Moon while they were exploring the deep caves on the Darkside. They had been searching for elements they could use to create new formulas and inventions. However, they quickly realized that cyakine gas was unstable when it interacted with certain oils, especially baskar's oil—an oil Maude had derived from the edible frey-frey bush that was one of the lunar wolves' main food sources.

If Bob had been given prior knowledge regarding the council's intention to use the gas, he would've strongly objected over safety concerns and offered to put together a proposal on the stable options they could consider instead. But just like every decision the Dual Council made, he and the other citizens were kept out of the loop.

"I'm home," Bob called as he walked through the door.

"Oh good," he heard his wife's frail voice call back to him from their bedroom upstairs. "Come on up. I've got some news."

Bob hung his hat and coat on the hook by the door and climbed the wooden steps to the second floor. "How did your cases go today?" Maude asked as he entered their cozy, loft-style bedroom that was set up with a full-sized bed, a small wardrobe, a leather armchair, and a metal desk and chair. Maude sat behind the desk, leaning over a pile of papers that were scattered across the top.

She looked up and smiled at Bob as he walked across the room and bent over to kiss her cheek. "It was a good day. I won one of the cases in the morning, and the afternoon case was dismissed before it went to the jury."

"Oh, really?" Maude asked. "Was it due to mistaken identity again? Or did another plaintiff get their lies all mixed up?"

Bob laughed. "No, neither this time. The case was brought by a man who decided to sue his best friend when he caught the friend sleeping with his wife. I'm certain the verdict would've gone the way of the plaintiff, but during a recess, two of the jury members met with the judge to confess that they'd also been having relations with the man's wife."

"So, the judge declared a mistrial?"

"Not exactly. Judge Moffit left it up to the accuser but told him he might want to consider that the problem had less to do with his best friend and more to do with his wife. And after some thought, the man decided to drop the case. I assume I'll be defending the wife soon enough. So, what news do you have for me, dear?"

Maude bit her bottom lip, and Bob groaned. There was only one person in the world who ever caused Maude to bite her lip. There used to be two. "What has Dale done now?" asked Bob.

Maude shook her head. "Maybe nothing. The guards reported that several of the animals have taken ill with a mysterious stomach illness. The council would like you to go out and talk to Dale. See if you can find out whether he might have something to do with it."

"Why don't they get one of the veterinarians to go out there first?" asked Bob. "It could just be some farm animal flu, you know? I really don't see how Dale could be poisoning the animals from inside his cell."

Maude laughed. "Of course, dear. But they did all of that already, and like I said, it seems to be a mysterious illness. At least, nobody qualified has any idea what's causing it."

Bob knew there was no point in trying to argue further. It wasn't Maude asking him to go; it was the council. Even after Goodman and the soldiers took over everything, they had still expected Bob and Maude to continue handling Dale's imprisonment. The only change they'd made was that all the correspondence between the guards and the two of them now had to run through the council first.

Dale had been given half of the Sheep Spa to live in, just like Maude had promised. The other half of the old factory was used as offices and living quarters for the guards who took turns watching Dale around the clock while also tending to the upkeep of the farm animals.

Bob sat on the end of the bed and took off his shoes and socks. "I'll go, but it will have to wait one more day. Cary's trial starts in the morning. It's scheduled to last all day, but hopefully we'll wrap it up quickly so it doesn't spill into the next one."

Maude nodded. "Do you think you'll be able to get him a win?"

Bob sighed. "Who knows. The juries are too unpredictable, and this new judge is a piece of work. I don't think he's familiar with any system of law in the entire galaxy. Plus, he's a real 'shoot from the hip' type of guy and isn't too keen on letting me make my usual arguments, or at least any that are centered around facts and reason."

Maude smiled. "Maybe there's another way to persuade the jury, then? Heaven knows you and I are zero for a million when it comes to winning reason-based arguments in this place. Haven't we learned over and over again that most of the travelers make their decisions based on their emotions and pay little mind to logic?"

Bob looked pensive for a moment. "You know, Maude. I think you might have something there. Maybe I should try using another approach to make some headway. I mean, I can't give up on logic entirely, of course."

Maude shook her head. "No, of course not, dear," she agreed.

Bob went on, "But maybe there's another way to go about it. I'll give it some serious thought before I fall asleep. How's your work coming?"

Maude looked back at the huge pile of papers covering her desk. "Well, I've managed to restore almost all of the markings, but I'm still quite a ways from figuring out what it all means."

Bob reached out and took Maude's hand in his. "I wonder if you should take a break from this for a little while. I know you've been working hard. Maybe it would help if you had some time to clear your head. I know I could certainly use a break from all the courtroom madness. Let me put some of my upcoming cases on hold, and we'll take a vacation. We can go camping near one of the old caves, just like in the old days."

Maude looked at her husband sadly. "I'm sorry, Bob, but I can't leave my work right now. It's too important. I know there are answers right in front of my face. Answers about what happened to Helen. And what happened to me too—how I got here without any memories from before."

"But, darling, don't you worry that without some sort of key, you might never decipher the Moon Walker's language?"

Maude looked at the papers and shrugged. "I suppose I worry about that a little. But before Ruth died, she told me she'd always known that once I was given the truth about the crystal, I'd figure out the answers to all my questions. She said it was the feeling she had the day the spirit spoke to her and Neriti through me. She said it was like the spirit was telling her I would know the whole truth once I was ready for it. And I'm ready now, Bob. I want to know what happened to me, and I want to know where Helen is. Even if it's not an answer I'll be happy with, I still want to know."

Bob nodded at Maude. He wanted to know about their daughter too. Helen had revealed so much before she vanished, yet there were still many unanswered questions about what had happened to her. Unlike Maude, however, Bob was happy to go on living without these answers. He didn't feel any sense of urgency to uncover the mystery behind her disappearance. It wasn't that he didn't care; it was that he sensed it was something he wasn't meant to know in this lifetime. Plus, Helen had made it clear that she didn't want him and Maude to try to find her, and he wanted to respect her last wishes.

Maude's obsession to find out what had happened to Helen and to discover the truth about herself worried Bob some. He sensed she was preparing herself for more than just the truth— for a time when the two of them would no longer be together. The thought of this made Bob want to jump up and light all of Maude's papers on fire. Yet he knew how important it was to her to find the truth. Thus, he wouldn't stop her, even though it broke his heart to watch her drift further and further away from him.

"Okay, sweetheart. I understand," he said. His eyes shined weakly like those of a young boy trying to find his courage.

"But come to bed now, won't you? I'd like to hold you for a little while. That is, if you aren't feeling too restless."

"No, that would be nice," Maude granted him. "I might not want a vacation, but my eyes sure could use a rest."

The two lay on their sides with Bob's arm draped across Maude, holding her against his body. He wanted to ask her what she'd do when she found all the answers she'd been searching for, but he suspected he already knew. Therefore, instead of talking, Bob held his wife tight, doing his best to surrender to the moment while secretly tucking the memory away so that one day when he was all alone, he could relive these seconds and remember what it was like to feel the closeness of Maude's body against his own.

CHAPTER 9

FRED'S PASSAGEWAY

Mina awoke gasping for breath. It was the middle of the night, and the light from the Moon spilled through the window, illuminating her bed in a silvery white glow. She sat up and looked across the room. Bonkers was standing with his front paws on the windowsill, wagging his tail and whining like he wanted Mina to open the window so he could jump out.

Slowly, Mina climbed out of bed to see what Bonkers was looking at. But as she drew close, she could tell something was different. Instead of a forest stretching out along the horizon, Mina could see the night's sky dotted with hundreds of twinkling stars. When she reached the window, she looked towards what should have been the little clearing that surrounded her cottage, but the clearing had been replaced by a sandy beach. And beyond the sandy beach was a vast, dark sea.

"What on Earth, Bonkers? What happened to all the grass? And the water? Shouldn't it be on the other side of the cottage below the cliffs?"

Mina was about to turn around to check the windows at the front of the house when she noticed the beach begin to move. The ground looked as if it were spinning in a wide circle. Then, suddenly, the sandy beach began to slip away into a gigantic sinkhole that was forming next to her cottage. Bonkers growled, and Mina looked down at him in surprise, having never heard her best friend make such a deep sound before. Bonkers turned his nose towards her, but it wasn't Bonkers' face staring back at her. It was Axel's.

Mina took a step backwards. "Oh my! Axel, you're alive!" Mina exclaimed in astonishment. "I'm so happy to see you, but what have you done with Bonkers' head?"

The lunar wolf didn't respond. He just looked at her sadly for a moment before turning his gaze back to the sinking sand outside her window. The hole had grown so large that the entire beach had nearly disappeared, and in its place, a giant metal wheel ascended until it was level with the ground.

"Tick, tick, tick." The wheel turned slowly, one click at a time. Behind it, the ocean lunged forward, pushing big waves across the beach that crashed over the side of the wheel, into the gaping hole beneath it. As the wheel turned, Mina saw something rising from its center. She leaned forward so that her nose almost touched the windowpane, trying her hardest to see what was emerging from the sinkhole.

"Oh my god! It's Fred!" she yelled, shocked to see her friend at the center of the wheel. His back was turned to her, but once he had made it to the surface, she was certain it was him. His body was fully illuminated under the Moon's radiant light, so much so that Mina thought Fred looked like he was glowing.

She ran from the cottage with Axel's head and Bonkers' body following her. When they reached the giant metal disc, Mina began to run along the outside, hurrying to face Fred. "Fred! Don't move! I'll find a way to help you across!" she called to him.

But as she made her way to the front of Fred's body, she

saw that his jaw was frozen solid by a block of ice that covered the lower half of his face. Fred clawed at the ice, struggling to pull it off, and Mina watched for a moment in horror as Fred tried speaking to her through the barrier. He sounded frantic, but his words were too muffled to understand. It was an awful sight, and Mina knew she had to act fast to help her friend. She twisted around to see if there was something she could throw to him to help him pry the ice from his jaw, but just as she turned, a giant wave slammed down on top of her.

Mina sat up in bed, gasping for air. She looked around. Her room sparkled in the moonlight, just like in her dream. She stood carefully, trying her best not to disturb Bonkers, who was snoring loudly on the edge of the bed. As she moved towards the window, she let out a sigh of relief. The trees and clearing were right where they should be. Mina looked back at her bed. She had been having this same dream frequently during the last several weeks, and she was beginning to wonder if it was more than just a dream.

She'd been alone for almost a year and had settled into her school, shopping, and home routines months earlier. She'd done a perfect job of keeping her solitude a secret. It was just another part of herself that she couldn't share with the rest of the world. However, she kept this part of her life hidden, not because of her parents' insistence, but because of something her grandfather had told her before he died. It was the part about Mina's grandmother, or possibly mother. "I suspect she isn't able to protect you the way she would like to."

Mina had thought about these words many times, wondering what they meant. Why would her grandmother—*or mother*—need to protect her? Was it the same reason that she and her grandfather—*or father*—had been lied to? Mina didn't feel like she was any closer to answering these questions than she had been a year ago. Yet having lived by herself for so long with few other people to talk to, she'd become much more willing to accept all the things her grandfather had tried to convince her of. His absence had made them even more meaningful. The journal where she'd recorded his final words became her most prized possession—the last sacred moments of her favorite person's life captured within its pages.

As she climbed back into bed, Mina thought of Fred trying to call to her in her sleep. She wondered what he'd say to her if his lips hadn't been frozen shut every time she saw him. Had he discovered something that could help her solve the puzzle her life had become? Probably not, she thought. After all, what would Fred know about her Earth life all the way back on the Moon?

Mina felt drowsy and cuddled up next to Bonkers. As sleep took hold and all the fragments of waking consciousness faded away, Mina heard a voice, possibly her own, whisper inside her head, *Come and find me, Fred. I'm ready to go home.*

MANY DAYS and weeks had passed since Ragher, Axel, and Fred had begun to wander the ice tunnels together. Of course, there was no way of knowing how long it had been, but if forced to answer, Ragher would've guessed a year or so. Watching the scenes play out across the ice sheets had caused their minds to grow numb. Their self-awareness dimmed as their focus and attention blended into the different timelines that appeared and disappeared across the tunnel walls.

This anesthetized existence was better than acknowledging the harsh reality of their situation—that they were caught in some kind of sentient labyrinth that determined what they saw, when they saw it, and worst of all—whether they continued to be held captive by it.

"Tick…tick…tick." The three companions barely heard

the sound of the wheels in motion anymore. It had become only another part of how they lived, no more than a yawn telling them they were tired or a heart flutter reminding them to their own excitement. The sounds of the wheels merely told them it was time to move. The tunnel was ready to recalibrate itself and push them farther along.

Axel had watched countless hours of his own life. At first, he'd found it thrilling to relive some of his best moments. But other, less impressive scenes eventually followed. And when these scenes began to repeat on a loop, the novelty wore off, and Axel began to long for an escape. Apparently, the labyrinth sensed this too because the worse Axel suffered while watching certain scenes, the more often these scenes replayed.

After the twentieth time of watching his parents and sister lose their battle to Darkside poisoning, Axel felt like he might go mad. He even thought about bashing his head against the ice to make it all go away. "Tick…tick…tick." Right as Axel reached his lowest point, the first passageway appeared in the middle of the tunnel's icy walls like a portal to another dimension. The dark void mesmerized Fred and Axel.

"What is it?" Axel asked.

"It's one of the passageways I told you about before," explained Ragher. "I think it might be meant for you," he told Axel.

Axel and Fred gazed into the dark tunnel. Not even the glowing white light from the ice seemed to penetrate its depths. "Well, there's no way *I'm* going in there," said Fred defiantly.

Ragher rolled his eyes. "That's not helpful, kid, and eventually you *will* have to go through one of these passageways. Probably lots of them even."

"Ha! Make me!" Fred retorted.

But Ragher just gave him a little nod, as though they'd come to an agreement.

"I'd like to see you try," Fred muttered under his breath, but Ragher had turned his attention back to Axel.

"There's no point in putting it off," Ragher told him. "I tried to avoid the passageways many times when they appeared, but it was never any use."

Axel didn't acknowledge Ragher, though. He was looking into the darkness, as if he were staring at something far away. But Ragher sensed what was really going on—Axel was afraid. "Look at me, Axel," he said. But Axel continued to stare into the passageway as though stupefied. Ragher shouted, "Look at me!"

Startled by Ragher's sudden outburst, Axel turned his head to look at him. "You'll be alright," Ragher reassured him calmly. "It's true that the passageways test you, but they don't cause any physical harm. Besides, you'll get a break from the labyrinth for a while."

"But where will I end up?" Axel asked nervously.

Ragher shook his head. "I don't know. Possibly outside the tunnels, although I doubt it. Not yet anyway."

Axel looked back into the void that awaited him. "Okay," he said with brave uncertainty as he crept forward into the passage. Then, "Tick...tick...tick." The ice sheets rotated quickly, and Axel was swallowed whole.

"What the hell was that?" Fred stammered. "Did the labyrinth just murder the blurry wolf?"

It was obvious that Fred was unsettled by what he'd just witnessed. His face was pale, and he didn't move from his spot against the wall as a new ice tunnel began to open up to the side of them.

Ragher laughed, however. He couldn't help it. "No, Axel will be fine. Like I said, the passageways don't do any physical harm. They're the whole point of why we're here. They're designed to help you see your true path—to identify what's important. You'll see what I mean when we meet up with Axel again. He will seem like he's changed a little."

Fred snickered. "Hopefully, he's less blurry. It hurts my eyes to look at him."

"He's not blurry, Fred," Ragher corrected him as they walked together down the long ice tunnel. "I just didn't give you a strong dose of that formula when I changed you into a Moon Walker. It's why you can't see him very well."

"Then how am I able to see *you?* Aren't you a Moon Walker?" asked Fred.

"Yes, but never mind that right now."

Fred could tell Ragher was hiding something, though, which suddenly made him interested. "Well, wait a minute now. I want to know about this. Why didn't you give me a bigger dose of formula? Am I really a Moon Walker or not?"

"Yes, Fred. Well, sort of. You have some Moon Walker traits now. But I didn't give you a full dose because that formula also causes invisibility, and I happen to know that you still have an important job ahead of you. I don't know how long you'll be here, but eventually you'll rejoin the Moon Travelers on the Dayside. And it won't do any good if they can't see you. Understand?" Ragher asked, trying his best to hide his disdain for the young man.

Fred shrugged it off. "Fine. Whatever you say."

Ragher could tell that Fred didn't believe anything he'd told him, but that's what Ragher had been counting on. He understood that it wasn't his job to show Fred his path. In fact, he'd been given strict orders not to reveal anything important to Fred, or Axel either for that matter.

"Tick…tick…tick." Fred and Ragher continued to follow the tunnels through the labyrinth, neither saying a word. Now that Axel was gone, the scenes that showed up belonged mostly to Fred and the experiences he'd had since arriving on the Moon.

After a while, however, the scenes began to shift to moments from Fred's past, moments from when he'd lived on Earth. This troubled Ragher, although he didn't say so right away.

"Are you starting to remember your past?" he asked numerous times. "Does *this* scene seem familiar to you?" he pressed Fred rather seriously as they watched a young version of him sitting on a man's knee. It seemed like the man might be Fred's father, but Fred shook his head.

"I have no idea who that is. I don't even remember ever looking like that kid. Are you sure that's me?" Fred asked.

Ragher laughed. "Well, it's certainly not me."

Watching the scenes from his childhood made him feel empty inside. Fred knew he should be able to recognize people's faces, especially the people who took care of him. From what he could tell, they had been sensitive and kind, and he clearly loved them. Yet there was nothing inside of him that felt like a connection to them in any way. No twinge of love, or longing, or even a tiny hint of recognition.

Finally, after they'd walked through miles of scenes from Fred's life, Ragher said to him in a slightly elevated tone, "Think, Fred. Can't you remember *any of this*?"

Fred shot back, "Do you think I want to be completely oblivious to my own memories? Dan poisoned me! Don't you remember that? I mean, you were his helper, right? Or maybe it's *you* who'd rather forget."

Ragher hung his head. "I'm not trying to give you a hard time, kid. It's just that this doesn't make any sense. I don't know how the labyrinth could capture memories from Earth. From everything I've ever understood about the ice tunnels, they only store memories from this realm, which means we shouldn't be able to see any of this."

"Hmm. Well couldn't it be possible that it's tapping into my memories? I mean, we watched about a billion rounds of that blurry dog's memories before he got eaten by the dark tunnel."

Ragher sighed. "You know his name is Axel and that he's a wolf, Fred."

"I thought he was a Moon Walker."

"Right," replied Ragher wearily. "Anyway, those memories were already stored in here. The closest thing I can think of to liken the ice tunnels to is a time capsule for the Moon's entire existence."

"Well, you must be wrong. Because how else could we be watching any of this?"

Ragher shook his head. "I don't know, kid. It's way beyond me."

After that, the two didn't speak again until a short time later when Fred's own dark passageway opened up. Fred put up a fight, just as he'd threatened to do, but Ragher did what needed to be done.

Later, when Axel reappeared from behind a bright sheet of ice and asked what had happened to Fred, Ragher simply said, "It took some convincing, but the kid finally made it into his own passageway."

Then without speaking, Axel and Ragher walked side by side through the ice labyrinth until they stopped to watch a scene from Ragher's life. "You alright?" Ragher asked before Axel became too engrossed in the story in front of them. Axel nodded.

This was enough for Ragher. He understood all too well what it was like to live through something you didn't think you could survive. He'd been through it hundreds of times before, and it had never gotten any easier.

"Let me out!" Fred screamed over and over into the darkness. He had fought Ragher as hard as he could, but the lunar wolf had been much more determined and stronger than he was expecting. Fred was frightened to be alone again in the dark with no way out. In fact, the idea terrified him.

"You damned wolf! Get me out of here!" Fred shrieked, but it was completely silent in the dark passageway. Fred didn't understand how it was possible, but the space he occupied absorbed all sound. There wasn't even the slightest hint of an echo to his screams. It was as if he'd wandered into a sound desert. The air around him soaked up every last vocal vibration before it had the chance to linger. Fred fell to his knees and sobbed. He couldn't believe this was happening to him again, that Dan's stupid wolf had come to finish him off. And worst of all, that he'd fallen for it.

When Fred was finished crying, he sat for a long while without any sense of time or space. His throbbing head was the only thing he was fully aware of, and he would've given anything to put an end to his suffering. He was no stranger to the pain of isolation. The months or years he'd spent inside the deep glacier well had taken a toll on him that he was certain he'd never recover from. He had learned hopelessness during that period. There'd been no likelihood of escape, and he hadn't possessed any memories to fill the endless amount of time with. Therefore, he'd made the decision early on to give up and wait for the end to come.

Fred lay on his side in the passageway like a sad, neglected dog. Even as colors and images began to float around in his line of vision, Fred remained motionless. He had no intention of being lured out of his depression by a bunch of meaningless hallucinations.

But then, suddenly, Fred's whole body felt like it was being ripped in half as he was jerked into an upright position and pulled through space at breakneck speed. When the motion stopped, Fred was sitting tied to a chair, staring into Dan's black eyes. Instantly, he recognized the scene. He was back at

Dan's fort, being interrogated right before he was thrown into the well. Fred smelled something burning. He looked to his side and saw that the feathers on his wings were on fire.

Dan laughed maniacally. "You aren't good for much, you dumb brat. I don't know why they sent such a useless spy. Makes me think you aren't really a spy at all. Just a decoy." Dan looked at Ragher who was standing in the corner, watching. "What do you say, Rog? Think he'll last very long down in the well?" The large lunar wolf lowered his head and shook it side to side.

Dan turned back to Fred with a wicked grin. "Yeah, me neither."

Fred felt his body starting to be ripped away from the scene, but before he lost sight of the room, something came into focus that he knew hadn't been there before. It looked like a thick, black fog hovering right behind Dan. He might not have thought anything about it, except that the black, swirling smoke had giant, red eyes that were staring right at him as he was pulled from the memory.

Fred shuddered at what he'd just seen. Back in the void, he felt even more afraid than before. He wondered if the dark spirit was hiding there in the pitch black. Moments passed but nothing happened. Fred thought about lying back down when suddenly his body tingled again, and he knew he was about to be torn out of the darkness once more. His insides screamed in pain as he felt himself being pushed across time and space. He jerked to a stop and found himself back in the well, only it wasn't dark like it should've been. Light from the crystals bathed the vertical tunnel in bright light.

Fred looked up to see Mina floating gently towards the ground with her wings spread out behind her, just like before. But there was more to the scene than the first time. A bluish haze surrounded Mina, similar to the black haze Fred had seen around Dan, except there were no frightening eyes peering out of it. Once Mina reached the ground, the swirling smoke that enveloped her quickly flew straight up and out of sight.

The light in the well faded, and Fred heard someone speak. It took him a second to realize it was his own voice. "Who are you?" he heard his former self ask.

Mina replied, "I'm Mina, from Earth." However, what happened next was nothing like his memory. Mina's voice disappeared, and a deep, loud voice cried, "I came here to save you!"

The walls around Fred began to shake as the words ricocheted off of them. Fred could hear the crystals above him breaking free and smashing together as they fell. Seconds later, the walls began crumbling, disintegrating into tiny pieces. He felt the dirt pouring down on top of him like an avalanche and the ground underneath him sinking away.

Fred heard a horrible scratching noise below him which he recognized as the same sound he'd heard when the wolves had dug a tunnel underneath the well to rescue him and Mina. Fred hoped they'd come to save him again, but he quickly changed his mind when he felt giant claws grabbing ahold of his body from out of the darkness. The sharp nails sunk into him and pulled him headfirst, deeper into the sinking dirt and sand.

Fred slid down, down, down into what felt like an endless ocean of sand. As he fell, giant wolf heads pushed their way through the sand, biting and growling at him. Fred tried to pull away, but there was nowhere to go. Then a voice began to zoom past him, like a car racing back and forth. It sounded like Dan. "She's gone! She saved you, but you let her go! Stupid kid! He doesn't know anything! What a worthless brat!"

A few moments later, the sand disappeared, but Fred continued to fall through the darkness until he heard a loud "Tick...tick...tick." He looked down and saw that he was falling towards a giant metal wheel. It was turning slowly beneath him in the shadows. Then all of a sudden, sand started to rise up from beneath the wheel like a huge waterspout. Tons of grit and grain flew past him while he continued to plunge headfirst towards the giant disc below. Blinded by the sand, he closed his eyes and kept them shut until he no longer felt the particles against his skin.

When he opened his eyes, he realized he was standing at the center of the metal wheel, facing a stormy sea. Slowly, the giant disc turned around him. "Tick…tick…tick." Fred was certain he was going to be sick. The jerky movements had left him queasy, and his head was pounding even harder than before. He started to lean forward, but then out of nowhere, he heard Mina's voice calling to him from behind. Too sick to turn around, he tried to yell back but found that his jaw was paralyzed.

Mina appeared in his peripheral vision, taller than he remembered but with the same long, dark hair. She told him to wait there while she found a way to help. Fred tried to tell her that he would solve the problem on his own, but he still wasn't able to move his mouth.

He brought his hands to his face and discovered a block of ice covering the lower part of his head. He pulled at it, desperate to free himself, but the ice was frozen solid—too thick to break apart. Mina looked scared. Fred wanted to tell her it was going to be okay, but suddenly a giant wave rose straight up in the air behind her. "Mina! Look out!" he tried to yell, but she couldn't hear him. She turned around to face the wave, and Fred lunged forward. But before he had the chance to save her, he was ripped from the scene and dropped into the dark passageway. All alone.

Once everything was still and quiet again, Fred brought his hands to his jaw. Just like he'd expected, the ice was no longer there. It had all been a dream, perhaps, or possibly a hallucination. Fred sat on his heels and leaned over the ground. His whole body shook as the hopelessness he knew so well tried to take hold. This time, though, instead of laying down and accepting his fate, Fred concentrated on the memory of Mina's face.

Had she really been there trying to help him, he wondered. Part of him hoped so, although he knew it would mean she'd risked herself to save him again when it seemed as though she, too, was in need of saving. Fred stared into the darkness, but he didn't see the all-consuming void in front of him. He'd begun to replay memories of Mina in his mind's eye. And when he was finished, the first selfless thought he'd had since being poisoned by Dan popped into his head. *Tell me where you are, Mina, and I'll come find you.*

CHAPTER 10

THE CASE OF THE FADED KNIT HAT

ob arrived at the courthouse early the next morning. It was situated at the heart of the walled-off stone village inside a large one-story structure that served as the city's only judicial building. The courthouse boasted three courtrooms—one for civil cases, one for criminal, and the third for small claims. It hadn't been necessary to build three courtrooms, considering the same two lawyers and judge worked every single case. But Goodman had insisted on it, and so it was done.

Bob had been awake most of the night, thinking of ways he could handle the new judge. It wasn't the easiest problem to solve, however. Before taking over for the previous judge, Judge Moffit had been one of the most opinionated and outspoken members of the council. And before becoming a council member, Moffit had reported to Lt. Gen. Goodman as Colonel Moffit on the Darkside.

Bob wasn't sure whether the two men had gotten along during their army days, but he imagined that Moffit's loud-mouthed personality was responsible for his new assignment to the courtroom. The former judge, Judge Jerry, had been assigned to the brand-new position of Land Ambassador, making room for Moffit to take his place. Like many of the ambassador positions, Bob had no idea what a Land Ambassador was supposed to do, or if the role was considered a step up from being a judge. But nevertheless, this was how it played out. Judge Jerry was sent off to new pastures while Judge Moffit picked up the reins in the courtroom.

Playing judge all day was clearly something Moffit was excited to do. Unfortunately, from the moment the new judge arrived in court, it became evident that he lacked the ability to be impartial, and hardly a minute ever went by without him giving his opinion on whichever part of the case they were hearing.

On his first day on the job, Moffit had begun by making fun of Bob's tweed suit. Then later in the trial, he'd interrupted Bob to inform him he didn't care for Bob's style of litigation or the look of the defendant. To be fair, though, Moffit also told Margie, the prosecutor, that her lilac pant suit was too masculine-looking.

The case should've been a slam-dunk for the defense. Bob's client, Gunter, had been accused of stealing a wheelbarrow. But besides having a mostly solid alibi that involved being at home with his family during the theft, there was also the fact that Gunter had a rare case of scoliosis. He could barely walk, much less push a wheelbarrow across town in the middle of the night.

Gunter might have gotten the verdict he was expecting without any trouble, but when Bob objected to Moffit's comments about Margie's wardrobe, Moffit made it clear he had it out for the defense attorney. Without being requested to do so by the opposing counsel, the judge ordered Gunter to stand up and walk the width of the room. Bob objected to the request on the grounds of unprecedented courtroom procedure, but Moffit just laughed at him.

Gunter had strained to make his way across the front of the courtroom, grabbing onto tables and chairs for support, but after he was finished, Moffit announced, "Seems like the man can walk just fine when he's got something to hold onto!"

Again, Bob objected. "Your Honor, Gunter doesn't have the sort of balance that would allow him to keep a wheelbarrow from dragging on the ground. Surely, the jury can see how he struggles to keep himself from falling over."

Moffit looked directly at the jury and told them to disregard Bob's objection. Then to the whole courtroom he said, "Never trust a man in tweed, ladies and gents! A man who dresses in tweed is a shady man, indeed!"

Bob was furious. It was frustrating enough that the juries were difficult to reason with, but now Bob had the added burden of a judge who enjoyed tainting the trials. He knew that the best way to beat Moffit at his own game would be to outsmart him. The only problem was that if Moffit figured out what Bob was doing, he'd retaliate.

That was the reason Maude's suggestion to focus on the jury had resonated with Bob. If he couldn't beat Moffit, maybe he could at least find a way to win over the jurors. So, after stewing on the problem all night, Bob came up with a few ideas that he hoped would work during the next trial—Dome vs. Dome.

The case was an odd one. The plaintiff, Rita Dome, had filed a lawsuit against her son, Cary, stating that the raggedy hat Cary wore was financially devastating to their family. She alleged that their family's clothing business had suffered from lost revenue due to her son's hat driving away customers.

The legal filing that Margie wrote on behalf of her client, Rita, stated, "My son cares more about his hat than his family's own livelihood. My husband, daughter, and I have encouraged Cary, the defendant, to wear a proper hat or go hatless, but he refuses. If he can't be bothered to dress the part of a respectable clothier, then we have no choice but to seek to reclaim his share of our company. And we ask that Cary be ordered to give us fair compensation so that we may recoup the earnings we would've made if not for our lost sales."

Twenty minutes after Bob entered the vacant courtroom, Cary and his family arrived together. Bob greeted them at the back of the room and then escorted Cary to the front, showing him where to sit. Cary was a large young man with a hard expression. When he spoke, though, his facial features softened, and he looked like a gentle giant.

After they were seated, Bob asked quietly, "How're you and your folks getting along? Have they tried to talk to you about the case?"

Cary shook his head. "No, we don't talk about it at home. They told me their lawyer said we weren't allowed to."

Bob nodded. "Right. It's for the best. It's too bad it had to come to this, but hopefully we can get it settled justly and send you all home feeling as though the problem was solved to everyone's liking."

Cary frowned. "Don't think that's possible, Bob. Is it okay if I call you that?

"Sure," said Bob.

"Like I told you when we met last time, my parents and sister really hate this hat. They said they won't be happy until it's burned to ashes, but there's no way I'm ever gonna let that happen."

Bob stared at Cary's faded knit cap which was pulled down over his ears. It was mostly pink with white zig zags worked into the design. Light blue, braided strings of yarn hung down at the front of the hat on both sides and knitted, white stars were sewn onto the strings. It wasn't the nicest looking hat Bob had ever seen, but it certainly wasn't the worst either.

During their initial meeting, Cary had told Bob that he understood his hat wasn't conventionally stylish but that he had a deep emotional attachment to it—the way a child sometimes feels about a blankie or stuffed bear. He told Bob that the hat made him feel connected to his past because his great grand-mother, Amelia, had knitted it, and his grandmother, Erica, had sewn the stars on later.

Bob nodded. "No, I doubt you'll be forced to burn your hat, but we're going to have to appeal to the jury's sense of nostalgia to win the case. I think it would help if you testified. Tell the jury about your hat's connection to family history and what it means to you."

Cary was already shaking his head, though. "I can't do that, Bob. I get real nervous talking in front of a crowd. There's gotta be another way to tell the jury how important my hat is without me making a spectacle of myself."

Bob sighed. "Hmm. Well, I'll do my best to explain it to them, but I think it would drive the point home if it came from you. You don't have to put on a show or shove your feelings in their faces, but it would help the jury see that you're a real person who's being bullied by his family."

But Cary continued to shake his head vigorously while Bob spoke. "Okay," Bob said, letting the matter drop.

Right then, Judge Moffit, a balding, middle-aged man in a long, black robe, threw open the door at the front of the court-room and came storming in like a bull charging into an arena. He had a sour look on his face that seemed slightly cartoonish due in part to his rubbery-looking skin. It appeared as though Moffit had spent too much time in the sun despite his years of service on the Darkside.

"All rise!" shouted the court bailiff as she hurried into the courtroom late. Everyone stood up, including Cary's family and the eight courtroom visitors who were divided equally between the two sides.

By the time the room had risen to their feet, Judge Moffit had already taken his seat behind the bench. Without looking up from the metal papers he was sorting through, he motioned for everyone to sit back down.

"A hat this time?" Moffit asked, though he spoke to no one in particular. "Well, alright. This should be good. Or at least entertaining. A squabble between a family who sells clothes, but they don't like their son's headwear. Seems like a waste of time to bring your grievances to court when you could simply steal your son's hat. But please, don't let me stop you from embarrassing yourselves." Moffit snickered but then continued, "Now, before the bailiff brings in the jury, I want to remind the counselors that there will be no funny business in my courtroom." Moffit glared at Bob. "What I say goes, and I don't want you undermining my authority. Got it?"

Both Bob and Margie nodded, even though it was obvious that Moffit was focusing his attention only on Bob. He didn't care, however, about Moffit's attempt to scold him. Instead, he was relieved that the judge had decided to reprimand him *before* bringing in the jury this time.

"Alright, bailiff. Tell the jurors to get their butts in here!" Moffit ordered.

The bailiff opened the door at the front of the courtroom and ten jurors—four men and six women—entered the room and sat down inside the jury box. As they got situated, the judge began to speak to them. "Members of the jury, you've been chosen to hear a case brought by a mother against her son."

Several of the jurors gasped at this, but Moffit kept going, "I imagine for those of you who are mothers, some of this will be difficult to hear. But hear it you must. The decision you make will forever change the course of this family's fate. Therefore, I implore you to listen carefully to the details of the case so that you may determine the best outcome."

Moffit paused for dramatic effect and made a point to look each juror in the eye before speaking again. "Today in this civil courtroom, we will listen to the case of Rita C.C. Dome vs. Cary C. Dome. The lovely Margie in her less than flattering, pea-green skirt will be your prosecutor today while the dark tan bloke over there will bore you with legal jargon and mindless detail. Capiche?"

Bob had thought for a moment that Moffit might have turned a corner. His instructions to the jury were more coherent and serious than usual. But he soon realized that it was all part of the show Moffit liked to put on. The judge had just altered his script.

Margie stood and began giving her opening statement while strolling back and forth in front of the jury box. She described a distraught mother whose only interest was the welfare of her family, a mother who had painstakingly taught her children the family business for many years, a mother who would never do anything to hurt her children's physical or mental well-being, and who only asked that her children do their best to help run the family's clothing store.

Then she described Cary as a selfish son who cared more about his silly hat than his family's livelihood. Margie told of how Rita had asked Cary to choose another hat many times over when she realized that her son's hat was negatively impacting their sales. But Cary had refused.

"It gives a mother no pleasure to have to go to such lengths to correct a child's naughty behavior, but Rita has become gravely concerned over the future of their clothing store. She knows that if Cary doesn't lose the hat, they will surely lose their business," Margie spoke dramatically to the jury.

Borrowing a page from Moffit's script, Margie walked slowly in front of the jurors while taking the time to look each of them in the eye. "All this mother wants is for you fine folks to give her the chance to save her family business. A chance that not even her own son is willing to grant her. On behalf of my client, I beg of you to order Cary Dome to destroy his hat and give up his shares of the business so that he can no longer prevent his family from gaining financial prosperity."

Margie sat down as Bob stood to take his turn. But before he could begin his opening statement, Rita leaned over to Margie and whispered loudly, "That was all real swell, but we don't want *both* those things to happen. If Cary gives up the hat, we'd be perfectly happy for him to keep working with us."

Bob smiled. He didn't hear what Margie whispered in response, but he was sure it was something about asking for the most extreme outcome in hopes that they might get the jury to agree to half of it. "Ladies and gentlemen," he began, "where does it end? Today Cary's mother is asking him to get rid of the hat she disapproves of—a hat that means a great deal to my client, on account of the family history that is tied to it. Yet that isn't really the point. Is it?

"Let's pretend that Rita succeeds at winning her case because you all agree that Cary's fashion sense is somehow damaging his family's clothing business. Well then, who's to say that tomorrow my wife won't file a lawsuit to keep me from wearing the tweed suits I love so much?"

Moffit interrupted Bob, just like Bob had planned. "Well, she certainly should. Those suits are a disgrace to fine apparel."

Bob nodded. "See, there you have it. Maybe Judge Moffit and my dear wife will even gang up against me. They'll say that I can't win cases wearing my tweed suits. My wife might argue that I'll get fired if I continue to wear my suits, which will prevent me from providing for our household. Whereas the honorable Judge Moffit might claim that my suits are making a mockery of his courtroom because he thinks they're too distracting."

Moffit grumbled, "Don't give me any ideas, Counselor."

Bob laughed in a friendly tone and continued. "So then, I ask you again. Where does it end? What if I don't agree with the way my neighbors dress their children? I could claim that the clothes their kids wear make my kids' clothes look shabby. Does that mean my neighbors should have to choose different clothes for their kids? Or buy new ones for mine?"

Moffit interjected, "You're losing them, Bob. Everyone knows your kids are dead or in jail."

Bob could've slugged Moffit over this remark, but he steadied himself and kept his composure. "What if you don't like the way I wear my hair? Say I'm not keeping up with the latest trend or that suddenly it's popular to be bald. Should it be okay for the court to order me to shave my head? Truly, I ask you good people. Where does it end if we allow our courts to rule over our personal choices and tastes?

"Now, the prosecution will try to tell you that my client's hat is somehow harming the family business. But who among you has ever left a clothing store because you didn't like what the shopkeeper was wearing?"

A juror in the front row with oddly shiny skin, a big head, and an even bigger bleached blonde hairdo raised her hand. Moffit laughed, and the woman looked at the judge with perky, self-satisfaction—the same way a golden retriever looks at its owner after performing a trick.

Bob ignored the interruption. "Well, I'd hazard to guess that most of you don't base your clothing decisions on what the salesperson is wearing but on the actual clothing that the store has in stock." A few of the jurors in the back nodded in agreement. This apparently annoyed Moffit, who overreacted by banging his gavel against the bench and ordering, "The jury will control themselves!"

Bob went on, "The notion that a shopkeeper's poor taste in hats could affect whether a shopper purchases clothes from said store is so preposterous that it borders on being infantile. Doesn't it seem more likely that the Dome's haven't bothered to take an honest look at what's been causing their declining sales? That instead they picked an easy scapegoat in the form of their son's hat?"

Several of the jurors began to laugh. Bob looked at them and saw that they were staring at Moffit. When he turned, he found that the judge had made a sailor's hat out of a metal sheet of paper and stuck it on his head. In addition, he wore a Cheshire Cat grin and was mockingly nodding his head along to Bob's speech. When he saw Bob looking at him, he placed his finger over his lips horizontally and began flapping it up and down in front of his mouth while blowing loudly.

Bob had prepared himself for this sort of behavior, however. "Please, everyone, give your attention to our one-of-a-kind Judge Moffit, who is demonstrating my point perfectly. Does the judge's hat detract from the decorum of the courtroom? Well, perhaps. But should the judge be forced to remove his hat if it's doing no real harm? Of course not."

Bob knew that Moffit's hat *was* doing harm—at least to his case—but he absolutely refused to let the judge have the upper hand. He had decided to incorporate Moffit's antics into his argument rather than allow the distractions to unnerve him.

But Moffit refused to allow Bob to get away with this for long. "Alright, sport. I think we've heard enough of your long-winded argument. Take a seat so someone else can have a turn," he said while giving the big hairdo lady a little wink.

Bob wanted to throw his hands in the air, but he kept his cool and returned to his seat next to Cary. "Okay, whose turn is it next?" Moffit barked, as though he were completely unfamiliar with courtroom procedure.

"It's my turn, Your Honor," Margie responded as she rose to her feet.

"My god! This is going to be really dull if we have to listen to you two numbskulls go back and forth all day. Why don't either of you stuffed shirts ever give anyone else a turn?"

Bob stood up to explain how the trial was supposed to go,

but before he had the chance, Moffit began to bang his gavel against the bench repeatedly. "No! No! No! Sit back down, Counselor! I know what'll happen if I let you open that damned yapper of yours! We'll all be dead before you get to shutting it again!"

Bob scowled but didn't respond.

"Alright, Margie in the puke-green skirt, you can go again if it means I don't have to listen to that ham for a while."

Margie spoke, "Sir, I'd like to call Mr. Dome Sr. to the stand."

"You Mr. Dome?" Moffit asked while gesturing at the red-faced man who was sitting right behind Rita Dome in the visitor's section. The man nodded. "Alright, well what are you waiting for? Come on up here and let this little lady in her putrid outfit ask you some questions."

Mr. Dome stood and walked to the front of the courtroom, taking a seat on the witness stand. "Mr. Dome, how many years has—" Margie began.

But Bob stood up and said, "Objection, Your Honor. The witness hasn't been sworn in by the bailiff."

Judge Moffit rolled his eyes before pretending to bang his head against his desk. Then he jerked back up and said to Cary's father, "This guy over here in the tweed thinks you're a liar. Are you a liar, sir?"

Mr. Dome shook his head nervously while glancing in Bob's direction. "Good for you!" said Moffit. Then directing his focus back to Margie, he said, "Okay, you can finish your question, split pea soup!"

Margie nodded. "Mr. Dome, do you love your son?"

Mr. Dome stared at Margie questioningly, like he was waiting for her to tell him what to say. But Margie just nodded at Cary's father, as if to reassure him that it was okay for him to speak his mind.

"Yes, I love Cary very much."

"And would you do anything for him?" Margie asked.

Mr. Dome looked over at his son, "Why yes, I think so. He's always been a good boy, so I don't think he'd ever ask me to murder no one. I probably wouldn't do that for him. Is that alright to say?"

Bob stood up again. "Objection, Your Honor! How is this relevant to the case?"

Judge Moffit scowled at Bob. "This case is about an ugly ass hat! If I sustain every time you object on account of relevancy, we aren't going to get very far. So, do us all a favor and stick your objections up your—."

That was it. Bob couldn't take it anymore. "I'm just doing my job, Your Honor," he interrupted. "It would be helpful if you would try and do yours!"

A hushed silence fell over the courtroom, except for one of the jurors who let out a taunting "ooh!"

Moffit didn't even pretend to pause to weigh his options. Immediately, he picked up his gavel and hurled it across the front of the courtroom at Bob. Luckily, Moffit hadn't taken the time to aim properly, and the judicial hammer smashed into the front of the defense table instead of striking Bob. The top of the gavel broke apart from its handle, and both ends went flying across the floor in opposite directions.

Moffit leapt up and leaned over his bench with a demented look on his face. "I want to see you in my chambers now, Counselor! Everybody else, we'll break until after lunch!"

"After lunch?" Margie asked. "But that's hours from now!"

Moffit stared daggers in Margie's direction—still fuming over what had just occurred. "Right! After lunch it is!" Margie exclaimed, hoping to avoid angering the judge further.

Moffit stormed down from his bench and shoved his way in front of the line of jurors, who were already following the bailiff out of the room. Bob grabbed ahold of his satchel with one hand and began scooping up his metal sheets with the other.

"What should I do while you're meeting with the judge?" Cary asked.

Bob shook his head, thinking about the encounter he was about to have in Moffit's chambers. "I guess you can go across the street and see if the tavern is open for lunch…"

Suddenly, Bob straightened up, as though he'd thought of something. He reached into his bag and pulled out a small metal sheet and a pen. Then he etched something down quickly across the scrap metal and shoved the little piece into Cary's hand. He looked over his shoulder to make sure no one was listening, and when he turned back to Cary, he said, "Take this across the street and give it to John. He's an old friend and an army buddy of mine. He'll want to ask you some questions. Make sure you tell him all about your case and what's happened in the trial so far. Got it?"

Cary nodded but asked, "What's John going to do?"

Bob grabbed his bag and began heading towards the door at the front of the room. "Hopefully, he's going to help us win our case. I'll see you back here after lunch!"

Bob disappeared behind the door, and Cary looked down at the note Bob had handed him. "Rally the troops!" was all it said.

"Don't you ever address me like that in my courtroom again!" Moffit yelled at Bob as he entered his chambers. Bob had never been invited into the judge's office before and was surprised by how elegant it was. There were dark hardwood floors, an ornate wooden desk with decorative engravings, and heavy, green drapes that hung in front of plated glass windows. It reminded Bob of the president's office at the university he'd taught at for a short while.

Moffit continued, "You think just because you were the general of the army that you can still force your way around here? Please! You were a joke then, and you're a joke now! Thank god Goodman finally showed us what an imposter you are—a louse riding his coattails, using his strong leadership to try and bolster your own. How pathetic! Well, *Bob!* We all see who you are now. If you had half the smarts as our dear Prime Minister, you wouldn't have gotten yourself stuck in the situation you're in.

"Haven't you wondered why none of your former officers have come to *your* defense? Ironic, isn't it? You've been turned into a court jester—a silly clown, defending other silly clowns. And yet nobody has stepped forward to take *your* side. Nobody's said, 'Hey maybe we should show the general a little more respect. Give him a dignified role in our new town.'

"Please, tell me you stay up late every night, thinking about what you've become. Or were you already so painfully aware of how weak you are that you just decided not to fight it? Decided you might as well go ahead and accept yourself as the dope that you are?"

Bob was blindsided. He'd expected to be chewed out about what had happened in the courtroom, not to have his entire character brought into question. He was having a difficult time wrapping his head around what the judge had just said. It had never occurred to him that his former officers might think he was a washed-up joke, and he wondered if it could actually be true. "What in the world did Goodman tell you?" Bob asked.

Moffit laughed. "He told us everything! He told us how you used to cry like a ninny every night, worried about what the other soldiers thought about you, worried about when the war would start, worried about what would happen to your ruthless sons after it was all over. He told us how you never gave any of your own orders or solved any problems and how you relied on him to do it all for you."

Bob was taken aback. In one fell swoop, Moffit had nailed almost every single one of Bob's insecurities during his time as general. Of course, the rest of it was absurd lies. Bob had given all his own orders and had never once cried in his tent. And as far as solving problems, he couldn't think of any problems he hadn't at least had a major role in solving. It seemed that Goodman had taken it upon himself to rewrite the history of their time together on the Darkside, but Bob wasn't quite sure why, unless it was because Goodman saw him as a serious threat.

He asked, "Didn't it ever occur to you that Goodman might have made all of that up so that none of the officers would question why he was taking the top leadership role over me?"

"Please! What have you ever done to deserve a leadership role?" Moffit asked incredulously.

Bob scoffed. "I was the general of the whole army!"

Moffit rolled his eyes. "Yeah, but we all knew you were a lousy one even before Goodman told us all that other stuff. You think we enjoyed waiting around for some little girl to show up so we could get the party started? It was demoralizing!"

Bob looked stunned, and Moffit snickered. "You didn't think we knew about that, huh? See, this is just what I mean! You had no idea what was going on right under your very nose. A lot of us wanted to oust you so we could attack Dan on our own, but no matter how many times we tried to form a coup, Goodman always stopped us. He told us we had to be patient, and we listened because he was more sensible than you.

"I guess he was happy to be free from your nonsense, though, because once he was no longer under your command, he sure changed his tune about you fast." Moffit grinned at Bob smugly from behind his desk, clearly taking great pleasure in cutting him down.

"Okay. I get it," said Bob. "Goodman has it out for me. I'm

glad you told me because now it all makes sense—why he didn't take my meetings or ask me to join the council. Honestly, though, it's not a big deal. I don't have any ill will towards Goodman even if he doesn't feel the same way about me. And despite your point of view about how things went on the Darkside, there were still plenty of good soldiers who were happy to serve under my command, which I know because I still speak to them regularly.

"But now that you've gotten that off your chest, what *I* would like to discuss is why we can't get through a single trial without you interrupting the proceedings and corrupting the jury. You understand that it's not me you're hurting, right? The only damage you're doing is to the defendant's chances of getting a fair trial."

"See, there you go clowning around again, Bob. Or do you really believe that you're making a difference here? I mean, you can see how ridiculous these cases are. Who cares about some dumb guy's ugly hat, or a cripple who likes to steal wheelbarrows on the sly? It's just theater. A way for the simple folk to spice up their meaningless lives as they live out eternity in otherwise boredom."

Bob laughed mockingly. "Oh, you're one of *those* people. Huh, Moffit? You think our existence here is eternal, even though several of the travelers have already passed on?"

"Ha!" countered Moffit. "They didn't pass on. They gave up! Which just goes to show how pointless this all is. Hell! We might be back here in a hundred years, trying these same damn cases because everyone's forgotten we already tried them!" Moffit yelled, slamming his fist down on his desk. "But at least during this go around, Bob, I'm going to need you to stop riding my ass about procedure and what not. You're spoiling my entertainment and sucking all the fun out of this job!"

Bob shook his head. "No. I won't do it. You may think all

this extra time we have makes our lives meaningless, but that's only true if we don't continue to evolve. The only scenario in which nothing we do matters is if we stop trying to create a better existence for ourselves. And part of the way we create a better existence is by setting boundaries and helping each other to resolve conflict so that we can continue to push forward. That's one of the things we can accomplish in the courtroom. But not with *theater*, as you call it. We do it by following the rules and giving each case the same unbiased attention and consideration.

"It's similar to what Maude and I did to help the Moon Travelers for many years. We helped people find solutions to their problems, and over and over again we got to see how doing so breathed new life into the people we were helping. It made it easier for them to continue with their journeys while freeing them up to explore new ideas and projects, instead of wasting time on what wasn't working. You may not see the value in that, but I do. So, you can either fire me or accept that this is the way I'm going to carry on—fighting to help others forever."

Moffit rolled his eyes at Bob and grumbled, "Can't fire you. This is where you're supposed to be."

"What does that mean?" Bob asked suspiciously.

"Goodman wants you in the courtroom," Moffit responded. "Thinks it'll keep you tied up and minding your own business. Guess he's right. You seem to have a real passion for all this garbage."

Bob stared at the edge of Moffit's desk for a minute. He understood he'd been manipulated, but he wasn't sure it really mattered. After all, someone needed to handle the cases. If Maude had been able to help him with the workload, he might have walked out right then and gone back to helping people from the comfort of his own living room. But he knew that wasn't an option.

Plus, the impression Bob got from the private conversations he and Maude were having with their close friends was that something had begun to stir in many of the citizens of New Waldoff. He and Maude weren't the only ones who understood that Goodman's government was rotten. It had become obvious to anyone paying attention that the people had no real say in their governing. All they had was the ridiculous court system that served more as a distraction than anything else.

"Okay. So, how do you want to handle this then? I take it you aren't planning to leave either?" Bob asked.

Moffit scowled. "Nope. Goodman wants me here too. Said he needs someone with gravitas to run the show. Not like that last dope."

"Right. Well, if we're stuck with each other, then can we try to act civilly during the trials at least?"

Moffit shook his head. "No. We'll do things *my* way, since it's *my* courtroom."

Bob sighed in exasperation. He knew he was never going to get anywhere with Moffit. Never in a million years were they going to see eye-to-eye. "Fine. May I be excused, then?" he asked.

"Yes, but not before this one last thing. You can go ahead and wind yourself up all day long with your logic and your yappy speeches, objecting to this and arguing that. But if you don't learn to follow my lead like a good, little dance partner, I'm going to do everything I can to make your time here a living hell. Capiche, hombre?"

Bob's face flushed with anger. He turned around and grabbed the doorknob, squeezing it hard to release some of his frustration. "Right. See you after lunch," Bob said curtly as he exited Moffit's chambers and headed back to the courtroom.

"No more mister nice guy," Bob thought. He was done trying to keep the peace with Moffit. "Let the jackass play dirty if he wants. I'll win my cases on the high ground or burn out trying. And in the meantime, I'll expose Moffit for what he really is—a slick cowboy who thinks he's important just because he can fit into a robe."

Bob's new resolve helped him feel better, even though he wasn't sure how he was going to execute his plan yet. Little did he know that none of it would matter, for his days in the courtroom were already numbered.

CHAPTER 11

BOTH SIDES OF A MASSACRE

I t was cold in the darkness—the kind of cold that crawls so deep, it feels like the chill is coming from within. Axel still hadn't grown used to it, even though it was his tenth, thirtieth, or maybe even hundredth journey through one of the dark passageways. If Axel had correctly estimated how much time they'd spent in the ice tunnels, it had been years since the earliest days of their captivity.

Axel stared into the darkness, longing for warmth. The cold that ran through him made him feel empty. He walked forward a few steps and jerked his head to the right. He thought he'd caught a glimpse of something, possibly the beginning of another scene. But there was nothing there. It was only a phantom vision, or a hiccup in his brain—a coping mechanism to make up for the lack of input he was receiving.

The passageways weren't like the ice tunnels; they didn't seem to have any solid space or defined measurement. There was never a moment he walked into a wall or brushed against any type of barrier. On the other hand, the endless space didn't prevent him from feeling claustrophobic. On the contrary, he felt smothered by the experiences the passageways forced him to endure.

Whenever a dark passage was ready to receive Axel or one of the other two, a hole in the ice labyrinth opened up, and either Axel, Fred, or Ragher would feel it beckoning. They always sensed which one of them was being drawn into the void, and they were never able to resist it for long. Of course, at one time or another, each of them had tried.

Most of the time, there seemed to be little rhyme or reason to what they were put through. However, they always emerged a different version of themselves. More beaten down, perhaps, but also more enlightened.

Axel's first experiences in the passageways had been horribly traumatizing. He'd had to live through the murder of every last wolf who'd been slaughtered by Dan and the other psychopaths who'd carried out the massacres. Sometimes he was the wolf being murdered. Other times he was the murderer. He felt the emotions of both sides. There was the senseless hatred and cowardice of each human who partook in the murders and the fear, sadness, and stoicism of each wolf who was killed.

Thump, thump. Thump, thump. These were the sounds Axel heard echoing again and again. They were the sounds of the wolves' paws beating against the lunar surface. Sometimes the sounds were deafening—entire packs moving as one as they fled the mobs of humans attacking them. Other times the sounds of the wolves' paws were faint—a small family or lone wolf breaking away from the protection of the group, choosing to hide on their own.

Thump, thump! This was also the wild beating of the predators' hearts—racing against time and reason to exterminate the wolves. Thump, thump! Packs are ambushed and divided up, making it easier for the blood-thirsty hunters to kill the adults and elders and children with their swords and pitch-forks and crossbows.

Thump, thump! The solo wolves and the families who venture off on their own are drawn out from their hiding spots and smoked out of their holes before being beaten and butchered.

Axel didn't know how many incarnations he was forced to live through or how long the visions lasted, but each one felt like an eternity. He was stabbed. He was beaten. He was sliced and shot. He stabbed, he beat, he sliced, and he shot. The horror was all encompassing, not just because it was horrifying to watch thousands of innocent lives wasted, but because of the glee and satisfaction it brought to the murderers. The humans who slaughtered the wolves feasted off their violent acts of hatred, laughing as they bathed in the blood of their prey while enjoying every drop of carnage they inflicted.

Of course, all of this was in the past now. Axel had already lived through it in real life. At the time, he'd been a sort of conveyor of wolves. He was a protector of his kind, ushering as many families as he could to the safety of the tunnels under-neath the surface of the Darkside.

Working to save these last wolves was something he'd been proud of up until now. For years, he'd unwittingly lied to himself, believing he'd done all he could to preserve the wolves by keeping them from going extinct. But after living through the terror over and over again from each player's perspective, he finally understood that his own role had been that of a coward. He'd risked his safety to travel back and forth, sure. But by not facing their tormentor or doing anything to stop the evil, Axel and the others had allowed it to prevail. He'd helped their kind survive, but they were no longer free—only alive.

Watching the wolf massacre so many times had filled Axel's heart with hatred. Yet as the thousands of stories continued to play out, the hatred subsided, replaced by a deep connection to each life lost and a determination to right the wrongs that had been committed against them.

Axel became certain that his time in the labyrinth was coming to an end as his sense of purpose grew. He thought he finally had it all figured out—the dark passageways were helping him understand who he was meant to be. They had broken him down so that he could rebuild himself into a braver, stronger wolf.

He felt ready now, and he began to think of the "tick… tick…tick" of the giant metal wheel as a countdown signaling his impending release. It was something tangible to connect to in the ever-shifting ice tunnels. It kept him moving, which was good, for the truth was much bleaker. If Axel had only realized how much further he had to go—how many more trips through the dark passageways he would still have to make—it would've broken his spirit. But that was the blessing of the ice tunnels. Only the past and present could haunt them there. The future was still unknown.

"Grab the nets, Jay, and start passing 'em out! We're gonna take our men and flank the bastards on the west side!" yelled a man with a round face and large gut.

Fred cringed as he watched the scene unfold through the eyes of this man called Jay. He'd already witnessed the same scene many times over, and he hoped this would be his last time trapped inside the body of one of the travelers who had taken part in the wolf murders.

Unlike Axel, Fred had only seen the massacre through human eyes. The passageways had taken him backwards through time. He had begun in the body of the man who'd committed the last wolf murder and was now watching, again, as the events of the very first massacre played out.

Jay, a man of about thirty with stringy, yellow hair and a medium build, looked down into the canyon where a few hundred wolves were trapped, though they weren't aware of it yet.

"Well, heck Boris. Which side's the west?" Jay asked.

Boris shook his head. "Don't you got any sense in that thick skull of yours? Look at the sun, dummy! Sun sets in the west!"

Jay looked up at the huge black sky above them to locate the sun. "Shoot, Boris. I don't know that you can tell which direction is west on the Moon like you can back home. Hasn't anyone ever told you before that we're riding on top of some big 'ole metal discs buried underneath the ground? Hell, the sun don't even ever set here!"

Boris looked agitated. "The sun does set where we're at right now, Jay, and that *there* is a setting sun," Boris said, pointing at the sun.

Jay frowned. "I still don't think it works the same here."

"Oh, for Pete's sake! Just hand out them nets like I done told you to!" Boris ordered.

Jay grumbled a little, but he went and opened the large, metal chest that was packed full of folded-up nets made of rope. He grabbed a stack and started passing them out to the dozens of bearded men who were standing around, looking irritable, like they had a terrible thirst with no water in sight.

From atop a rock near the edge of the canyon, Boris gave them instructions. "Alright, everybody, the time you've been waiting for has come! Everyone with a net, grab a partner to help you spread it out. We're going to work our way along the path that leads to the bottom of the canyon, and when we get there, we're going to charge the beasts.

"Right now, our counterparts on the other side of the canyon are keeping the wolves from escaping. They're down there surrounding them while pretending like they want to make peace. But when they see us coming, they're gonna go on the attack. Those of you without nets, make sure you got your weapons ready. We take no prisoners and leave no survivors!"

Jay had already gone back for all the nets and was passing out the last one when he added, "Except for the pups and females!"

Boris glared at the back of Jay's head. "No, men. Those ain't our orders. Dan said no survivors!"

Jay whipped around to face Boris and said, "Well, I'm sure that's not what he meant. Nobody would give the order to kill a bunch of innocent pups!"

One especially scruffy-looking man, a few feet to Jay's left shouted, "They wolves, ain't they? Young or old, male or female, there ain't nothing innocent about no wolves!"

Then a man holding a crossbow in one hand and a net in the other yelled, "They're all liars! We know they poisoned and killed all the first moon visitors! They ain't got no problem killing us, so I ain't got no problem killing them. Every last one!"

The crowd began to whoop in agreement, and Jay suddenly felt sick to his stomach. He hadn't realized that the battle plan they were following involved killing innocents. Whenever they'd talked about taking no survivors, he'd assumed they were talking about the male wolves. It had never occurred to him that they were going to kill everyone.

After the men settled down, Boris pumped his fist in the air and yelled, "Move out, soldiers! Let's go! Let's go! Let's go! Our battle awaits!"

Dozens of men armed with crossbows and metal bats hurried towards the switchback path that led to the bottom of the canyon where the large group of wolves was gathered. Jay didn't move, though. He knew he couldn't go through with it now. Even if he wasn't the one killing the female wolves and pups, he didn't have the stomach to be near it.

One of the guys at the back of the group called to him. "Ain't you coming, man?"

"Of course!" Jay lied. "I'll be right there. I just gotta grab some arrows before heading down." Then he made a show of opening the trunks that held the crossbows and arrows.

The guy grunted and continued following the group. Soon, the men at the front of the line began making loud war cries as they picked up the path to the bottom of the canyon. Jay knew the plan. They were trying to surprise the wolves so that they had a better chance of closing in on them fast.

After the last of the men disappeared into the giant chasm, Jay inched towards the side of the cliff to watch the scene unfold from above.

"Seriously?" thought Fred, who had no choice but to see what the man saw. "You don't have the stomach to partake, but you have no problem watching this?"

Before Boris' group of men had even reached the bottom of the gorge, the men who'd been talking to the wolves held up their weapons and attacked. Fred tried to close his eyes, even though he knew it was impossible. He'd already been in hundreds of bodies and watched this same bloodbath dozens of times. There was no way to shut out the visual atrocities. But he always tried. The only thing he could do to ease some of the terror was to hum loudly. It didn't do much, but sometimes it helped to drown out the blood curdling screams.

Of all the massacres, Fred hated this one the most. He knew it by heart, having lived it so many times. The so-called peacemakers began the attack by maiming the front line of wolves with their blunt weapons. They went for the wolves' knees with the intention of wounding the adult males so they couldn't escape. Then as the other group of men joined the slaughter, they pushed their way through the injured and finished them off.

The men, however, didn't go completely unscathed. Several of the attackers were killed immediately when the larger wolves, who were acting in self-defense, went for the men's throats. Quickly, the other men surrounded these wolves and shot them with their arrows until they lay dead on the ground.

From his elevated vantage point, Fred watched as many of the pups and smaller wolves—the females and elders—tried to make their escape by climbing the steep wall behind the pack. At first, most of the men were too preoccupied to notice that these wolves were getting away, but Fred knew from personal experience that this wouldn't last long. As the first of these wolves reached the top of the canyon, some of the men who'd made it to the middle of the pack noticed there were less wolves than there should be.

"Look up!" one of them yelled, pointing the others' attention to the tens of wolves climbing the steep canyon wall. Then the leader of this particular group of men shouted, "Miller, Gresham, Sullivan, and Stephens, go after those beasts! We don't want 'em running off to warn the other packs!"

Of course, Fred didn't need to go after these wolves to know what would happen next. He'd already gone after these wolves several times over inside the bodies of Miller, Gresham, Sullivan, Stephens, and the twenty or so men who joined their posse. Some of these men stood guard above the steep wall, shooting arrows into any wolf who got close to the top. Others rode their horses for several miles before locating the first sets of wolves who'd escaped the horrors inside the canyon. They were executed on the spot—mothers, pups, and old, frail wolves.

By the time Fred witnessed these merciless acts of cruelty, Dan's poison was nearly out of his system. However, it wasn't until the first time he watched what came next that the final drops of poison fizzled away for good.

"Come out, come out, wherever you are!" called the deep, sing-song voice of one of the dark-haired, bearded men who had rode after the fleeing wolves.

All of the escapees had been accounted for except for a few of the pups whose mothers had hidden them in a narrow ravine underneath the low hanging branches of a large chansasa shrub. The mothers had made a last-second, gut-wrenching decision to hide the pups after realizing the evil men were bearing down on them. They knew there was no chance that their own lives would be spared, but they hoped that their hidden pups might go undetected and eventually find their way to the safety of another pack.

"If you come on out now, 'lil pups, we promise we won't hurt you!"

Fred's heart ignited in a fiery rage every time he heard this phrase. Even the first time he'd heard it, he knew it was a lie, but he'd also known that the wolf pups would believe it. They were young and trusting and had no reason to doubt the men's honor—a quality so revered among the wolves that every single one of their stories touched on the virtue.

What happened next would stay with Fred for the rest of his days. The memory had been seared into his mind. Six pups peeked over the ravine's ridgeline. Then one by one, they hopped over the side and walked shyly towards the men. But they never stood a chance. The moment all six were in view, the man with the deep voice gave the order, and the pups were relieved of their lunar lives, marking the complete extermination of their once mighty pack.

When Fred had arrived on the Moon, he hated the wolves.

The intelligent, silent creatures had seemed unnatural, and he believed they couldn't be trusted. His mind had been so concrete on the matter that he never would've believed his feelings for them could change. Yet after repeatedly living through the demise of almost every single lunar wolf and watching them suffer at the hands of these truly ignorant and evil humans, Fred couldn't help but revisit his initial feelings of hate towards the wolves.

He compared his own behavior to that of the twisted people he was forced to possess. Unlike Dan's followers, Fred had never considered murdering the wolves, but he certainly hadn't treated them well either. He'd talked down to them and violently resisted their help, even going so far as to kick several of them when they hadn't kept their distance.

Fred felt ashamed now. He wished he could blame his behavior on Dan's poison or some obvious misunderstanding, but the truth was that he, too, had acted ignorantly when he first met them. After some soul searching, Fred realized he'd been afraid of the wolves, and that instead of addressing his fear, he'd allowed it to create hate inside of him. This hate had prevented Fred from trying to know or understand the wolves, and therefore, it had blinded him to the wolves' true nature.

As Dan's poison wore off, Fred began to look to Ragher as a sort of guide who could help him make sense of what he was experiencing inside the passageways. He sensed that Ragher knew more about how the ice tunnels and passages worked than he often said, especially since he'd already spent so many centuries trapped inside of them before. Whenever Axel wasn't around, Fred spoke to Ragher about the visions he was having in the passageways. And after a while, the pair became close as they formed a teacher-student bond.

"Why do the passageways continue to force me into the bodies of all those brutal murderers? Watching it happen so many times isn't having any sort of new effect on me. I already know I'll be haunted forever by what I've seen. These visions have permanently changed my mind—how I view the humans and the wolves too. I'm never going to forget what I've learned here."

Ragher listened carefully as Fred posed his question and took a moment before answering. "I believe you will be haunted by what you've seen, but what you don't realize yet is that you *will* forget most of what you've experienced here, eventually. The mind is sneaky in this way. It keeps us moving along our path, but in order to do so, it must dull our memories, especially the traumatic ones. It filters them out to keep our thoughts healthy. Just like our livers filter out toxins to keep our bodies healthy.

"Over time, your mind will erase or mute most of the trauma you've lived through here, which is good. Our minds *should* be healthy. The darkness isn't expecting your brain to remember everything it's being shown. That would be impossible. The passages are forcing you to live these tragic events time and time again in an attempt to change your heart. Because once your heart has changed, it won't matter whether you remember what you've been shown. You'll forever feel differently and therefore *act* differently. Kind wolves don't face difficult situations with just their heads. They face them with their hearts also. Kind humans are no different."

Fred nodded. "I think I understand, but I still don't really get what it all has to do with me. I mean, I wasn't even on the Moon when the wolves were killed, and obviously it's too late to fix any of it now."

"You're wrong about that, Fred. If anything, it's too *early* to fix it."

Fred stared at Ragher confused. "What are you saying?"

Ragher's eyes smiled at him. "Haven't you wondered why you're down here learning the Moon's history?"

Fred scoffed—a habit left over from when he was still

consumed by Dan's poison. "So, you think I'm going to be able to fix things? Between the wolves and the humans?"

Ragher nodded. "I think you're going to try. That's why she brought you here. But not just you. The girl too."

"*Who* brought us here?" Fred pleaded.

Ragher stared at Fred for a minute, as though he wanted to say more. But finally, he said, "I wish I could tell you, kid. But you're going to have to wait a little longer. You'll know when she's ready."

A SHORT TIME LATER, Ragher found himself inside his own dark passageway. He had journeyed through so many voids during his long life that the darkness felt like another kind of home to him. Ragher no longer had access to his earliest memories, but during the centuries he'd found comfort in watching the Moon's stories play out across the walls of the ice labyrinth.

Just like Axel and Fred were journeying through the dark passageways to find their purpose, Ragher had discovered his own purpose when he fell in love with Neriti. He had spent decades living by her side within the visions that the darkness pushed on him. In these visions, Ragher had lived as a disembodied spirit watching Neriti as she made her every move, clueless to his presence. Or at least, that's the way it had seemed.

Now that Ragher had actually lived by Neriti's side as her partner in real life, he wondered what these visions of Neriti from long-ago had really been. He'd never suspected he was being shown the future, which is why he was shocked that Neriti was only a pup when they first met.

After this encounter, Ragher believed he'd been given special access to the future. However, the scenes that he lived through in the passageways never manifested. In the visions he was shown, Neriti never had children, and therefore she never suffered the great losses that she and Ragher eventually experienced. In these visions, Ragher had watched Neriti grow extraordinarily powerful. She became a healing ambassador who oversaw the medical and spiritual needs of all the wolf packs. Ragher had believed it was something she'd been born to do. It lit her up, and she thrived in the role as she solved the most difficult problems of her time.

But this version of Neriti never came to pass, and Ragher wondered if it was his interference in her life that had caused Neriti's fate to deviate from what he'd seen. However, the thought that this could be true was devastating, and Ragher felt bitter whenever he spent too much time considering the possibility.

Ragher spoke into the darkness. "The kid has grown much wiser. The poison is gone, and he's becoming curious about his purpose."

A female voice spoke to Ragher from out of the void. It was loud and crisp with not even the slightest reverberation. "And what have you told him?" she asked.

"Nothing, just as you commanded. I wonder though…" Ragher paused.

"Yes?" the voice questioned him.

Ragher thought over what to say next. What he *wanted* to say was that he believed Fred should go free. That he no longer wanted to be a part of whatever plans the woman in the void had created. That he didn't want to be involved in setting the boy up to be a stooge the way he had been.

After a few moments had passed, he simply said, "Nothing. The boy has learned much from what you've shown him. I think he's ready for his mission."

"This is good news, Ragher. You have done well. Only a little while longer before he and Axel will be released. Theia will return soon, and once she does, there will be many changes."

Ragher asked, "Will you allow me to go to Neriti then?"

"We shall see, Ragher," said the voice. "For now, lay your head down and rest. I'll reward you with a dreamless sleep for all your hard work. Enjoy it while you can, for there is still a long journey ahead."

THE HUNG JURY

Bob didn't eat lunch that day. He'd become too lost in thought. After his meeting with Moffit, he had sat at the defense table, brainstorming ways he could appeal to the jury's feelings *and* common sense. He could have gone home or across the street to the tavern for some company, but he wasn't ready to discuss his meeting with Moffit yet. He still needed time to process it, but at the moment, all he wanted to do was focus on the case at hand.

Sometime just before noon, Bob was pulled from his deep thoughts by the sound of a crowd outside the courthouse. Quickly, he strode to the windows to see what was happening, but his view was from the side of the building, and all he saw was a small group of protestors heading towards the front of the courthouse, holding signs.

A few seconds later, Cary walked in with a smile across his face. "Hey, Bob!" he said. "John told me to ask you whether you want to let the troops in or if you'd prefer them to wait outside."

Bob laughed excitedly, realizing the request he'd sent John

had actually come to fruition. "How many people did he get?" Bob asked.

Cary replied, "He sent out a few of his regulars to spread the word, but a lot of folks are just beginning to show up. Don't know how many yet. Unfortunately, I think the other lawyer figured out what we were doing. I heard her talking to a bunch of people outside John's tavern after your friends started telling everyone what we were up to, and it sounded like they might be planning to copy us."

"Hmm," Bob said pensively as he moved to the back of the courtroom where Cary stood. "Well, that's okay, I suppose. They're entitled to have their own protest. Let's just hope ours is bigger."

Bob rested his hand on Cary's back and checked his watch. "We still have a few minutes before the trial gets underway again. What do you say we peek our heads outside to see how things are shaping up?"

"Sounds good," Cary replied, and the two men headed through the large, arched corridor that led to the front of the courthouse. As they got closer, Bob could hear a large crowd of people right outside the front doors. It sounded like they were all trying to chant at once, but none of them were chanting the same thing, which made it impossible to understand any of their words.

Bob felt nervous over what he was about to find on the other side of the doors. He nudged one open a crack and peeked out. From what he could tell, it looked as if there might be over a hundred people gathered in front of the courthouse. He shoved the door open wide to get a better look, and right away he saw that there was a clear divide between the people who were flooding the courthouse lawn and steps.

On one side there were people wearing fancy, formal clothing and holding up signs that read: "I wasn't born to suffer your poor fashion!" and "Throw ugly hat guy in jail!"

On the other side there were people wearing all sorts of hats—cowboy, bowler, cloche, top, boater, floppy, and even one or two beanies, fezzes, and turbans. These people were hoisting signs that read "My fashion won't be dictated by your taste!" and "Free the ugly hat guy!"

Bob looked at Cary. "The hats are on our side I take it?"

Cary nodded, and Bob asked, "Do you have any idea where these people got the idea that this is a criminal case?"

Cary shrugged his shoulders. "I told John that my family was trying to take away my rights by denying me the freedom to be a hat-loving man. But I guess maybe the message got wonky somewhere along the line. Kinda like that game of telephone we all played as kids. It would start with somethin' innocent like: "My uncle gave ten giblets to his steer." But then it always ended up sounding somethin' like: "My monkey pulled a gerbil from its rear."

"I see," said Bob with a hint of concern. "Well, the crowd's a bit rowdier than I'd like. I think it's best if we leave them out —" But before Bob could finish his sentence, he caught sight of Margie making her way down the center of the fancy-clothed mob. For a second, the two locked eyes, and Bob knew what he had to do.

Both attorneys leapt into action. Margie began yelling at her group to follow her to the courthouse as she hurried into the building. Bob made a V-shape with his pointer and middle fingers. Then he stuck them between his lips before letting out a high-pitched whistle to get his side's attention. "Hey, hats! Are you going to let these fashionistas steal all the good seats? Follow me inside if you want to support Cary!"

Dozens of men and women wearing hats cheered in response and began to rush the courtroom steps, pushing and shoving their way inside. However, Bob heard a few of them ask, "Who's Cary?"

Bob and Margie ran in front of the large crowd, down the

corridor to the backdoors of the courtroom, right behind where the audience sat. They reached the doors at the same time. Always a polite gentleman, Bob opened the door for Margie but said in a sly tone, "After you, Counselor."

Margie nodded her head and said smugly, "Oh, well thank you." But as she entered the room, she waved to her group to follow her in, preventing the hat-wearing folks from taking a turn to enter. Bob wasn't having it, though. He elbowed his way past a woman wearing a black, satin ball-gown and matching gloves, who was speaking rudely to a woman in a frilly, orange sunhat. "Come on in, ma'am! Don't be afraid to step on a few toes if you have to," he said to the woman in the sunhat. Then to the others behind her, he called, "This way if you want to support your freedom to wear hats! Got a head, right? Might as well dress it up any way you see fit!"

Even as Bob said the words out loud, he could barely believe they were coming from his own mouth. Yet he was tired of being defeated. He knew how ridiculous this particular fight was, but after the way Moffit had acted in court and spoken to him in his chambers that morning, Bob just couldn't stand the thought of losing. Not again. Not today.

Shortly after Margie and Bob took their seats next to their clients, the door at the front of the courtroom swung open, and in walked Judge Moffit. But when he saw all the people packed noisily into the courtroom, he slowed his pace. He climbed up to his bench and yelled towards the door. "Bailiff! The presence of your ass is requested in my courtroom. *Now!*"

Afterwards, the judge glanced at Bob to see if he'd gotten a rise out of him with his distasteful comment, but Bob didn't give him the satisfaction. He kept his eyes glued on the door, watching as the bailiff came sprinting into the room while tucking her shirt in. Bob shook his head in disbelief, for it was obvious that the bailiff had been finishing up in the bathroom and hadn't been given any warning that the judge was ready to start the trial again.

"Bailiff, I'm going to need you to control the audience. Explain to these folks that there will be order in my courtroom if they don't want their butts to wind up in a jail cell."

"Yes, sir!" said the bailiff as she checked the zipper of her pants.

Then she looked up at the audience and yelled, "Here ye! Here ye! The honorable Judge Moffit's court is now in session! Find a seat right this instant or turn around and exit the same way you came in at the back of the courtroom. Those of you who don't got a seat can stand outside the courthouse and listen to the hearing on the speakers at the front of the building."

The thirty or so people standing at the back of the courtroom began to shuffle out, except for a young couple wearing fancy, matching tracksuits, who tried to pop a squat on the floor in the aisle. This upset the bailiff, and she began to wave her arms at the couple as they situated themselves in a cross-legged position. "No sirree, you two! A seat means a *chair*. This courtroom ain't a playpen! You better get your sweet cheeks off the ground and hightail it out of here pronto!"

The couple scowled at the bailiff but followed her orders. Moffit picked up his gavel which looked as though it had been duct-taped back together and banged it against the table in front of him. "Come to order! It seems we have a few new faces in the court since we adjourned. I don't know what could've possibly drawn you all here today, but hopefully nobody tricked or bribed you into coming. Everyone here knows this is a case about some idiot guy and a hat, right?"

At the front of the audience, Cary's sister jumped to her feet and yelled, "My brother's not an idiot! His hat may be ugly and smell like head sweat, but at least he's got manners!"

The young woman's father grabbed ahold of his daughter's

arm and tried to pull her back down, but it was too late. Moffit yelled, "Bailiff! Get this uppity, young woman out of my sight! Now!"

The bailiff approached Cary's sister and pulled her forcibly past the other seated guests towards the door at the front of the courtroom. The young woman refused to be silenced, though, and continued to shout as she was dragged away. "We should never have come here! I support my brother! Tell them about the family vote, Cary! *Tell them!*"

The door at the front of the room slammed shut, and Moffit yelled, "Let this be a warning to the rest of you! I have no patience for any kind of disrespect in my courtroom. Get out of line, and I'll send you to the slammer!"

Bob had to stifle a laugh over Moffit's blatant hypocrisy. However, he knew what the judge really meant. Moffit didn't care about respect; he just didn't want anyone disobeying his authority.

Moments later, the bailiff returned alone. Cary leaned over to Bob and whispered, "What did she do with C.C.?"

Bob whispered back, "Technically your sister has been held in contempt of court. She'll probably have to sit at the police station until the trial is over and then pay a fine. But, Cary, what did C.C. mean when she said, 'tell them about the family vote?'"

Before Cary could explain, though, Moffit began to speak again. "I'm not thrilled about all you folks being here today. It feels like you're making a mockery of things with your stupid headwear and self-important smocks. And seeing as such, I've decided to change things up a bit."

Bob didn't like the sound of this. He held his breath and waited for the other shoe to drop. The judge continued, "We're going to skip over that part where you two clowns get to come up here and chit chat away with whoever you feel like. Go ahead and take your turns making your case."

Moffit looked at Bob. "But try to make it snappy, hammy! These folks might think they're all hot and bothered over some dumb hat now, but you'll lose 'em quick if you give 'em some long spiel about outerwear freedoms."

Bob ignored Moffit and passed a sheet of metal to Cary, signaling with his etching pen that Cary should write down his explanation about the family vote. Moffit waved his hand up and down at Margie's outfit as she stood up. "I see you've really dug in your heels on this hideous skirt-suit, Counselor. I was pretty sure you'd make a wardrobe change during that long break I gave you. Or does it take more than a few hours for that? I know how you women are about picking out clothes."

Margie replied, "No, I just happen to like the color green, Your Honor."

"Even in that 'rotting corpse' shade?" Moffit asked.

Margie nodded and smiled. "Yes, although I prefer to think of it as the shade of 'spring leaves.'"

Moffit snickered. "Well, I guess one man's spring leaves is another man's grassy diarrhea. Anyway, you may proceed."

Margie nodded at the judge and began her oral argument. "Ladies and gentlemen of the jury..." She looked over her shoulder at the crowd wearing their Sunday best before returning her focus to the jurors. "If I worked as a vet, wouldn't it be my responsibility to take care of sick animals? If I were a plumber, shouldn't I do my best to repair my client's leaky pipes? If I were a cook, shouldn't I taste my own butternut sasquatch recipe before serving it in my restaurant?"

Bob couldn't help himself. He stood up and yelled, "Objection! The prosecution is being unclear. The defense would like to know what a butternut sasquatch is."

Moffit rolled his eyes. "Overruled, because no one cares."

"But, Your Honor! Don't you want to know if there's some legendary, buttery-nut, ape-man delicacy we're missing out on?"

The judge started banging his gavel on the bench as Bob spoke. "That's enough out of you, quacky! Consider this your first warning!"

"Quacky?" Bob whispered to himself as Margie continued.

"And if I worked as a clothing store clerk, shouldn't I wear tasteful and elegant clothing that will entice more customers to shop at my boutique?"

She walked slowly in front of the jury box, staring down each juror as she passed. Then finally, she said, "If you listen closely, I think you can hear your hearts telling you the answer." Margie cupped her hands over her mouth, and in a tiny voice, she proceeded to imitate a beating heart. "He's guilty, he's guilty. Bump-bump. Bump-bump. He's guilty, he's guilty. Bump-bump. Bump-bump." Then she paused, rested both hands on the edge of the jury box, and said, "I rest my case."

Bob was completely shocked and appalled, not only because Margie's argument had been ridiculous, but also because it was obvious that the jurors had lapped it up. He looked at Margie as she took her place beside Rita. She seemed confident in the performance she'd just given, and for a moment Bob wondered if he needed to rethink his strategy. However, before he could decide, he felt Cary push something against his elbow. He looked down and saw that it was the metal sheet he'd given Cary to write his explanation on. Quickly, he read what it said.

Moffit turned to Bob. "Alright, Daffy. It's your turn. Short and sweet is the name of the game. Go!"

Bob stood and walked towards the jury, trying to shake the sudden feeling he had that he was walking into an extremely important moment that he had no control over. It was like he was the engineer of a passenger train that was headed off a cliff, and he had just discovered there were no brakes. He took a deep breath to dismiss the feeling and began to address the jurors, "Where does it end—"

"It ends when you finish your babbling," Moffit quipped.

Bob held back his anger. "With all due respect, Your Honor, you haven't even given me the chance to begin my argument yet."

"Ha! That's the problem, sport! We all know that once *you* begin, it never ends!"

The entire courtroom broke into laughter, and Bob decided he would have to ignore the judge's outbursts if he was going to make his case before the decision was handed over to the jury.

"If you find my client guilty, do you think it will end with hat suppression? I don't. I think we'll have created a dangerous precedent, and it will only get worse from here. If we tell a man he isn't free to wear any hat he chooses, what other personal choices might be taken away next? I'll tell you which ones. The ones that are dearest to us. The ones that are so personal that they shouldn't be —"

Bob was interrupted again, but this time by Cary. "Ow!" he shouted as people in the audience began to giggle. Bob looked over and saw that Moffit was casually throwing little pieces of metal writing scraps at his client. In addition, Moffit had placed his leather dress shoes on top of the bench and had hung his socks from his ears, presumably to make fun of the tassels that were hanging from Cary's hat.

"Damnit!" Bob exclaimed, suddenly aware that he didn't have much time left to finish his argument before the judge's erratic behavior completely derailed the trial. He began to talk fast. "We cannot allow our tastes and choices to be dictated by anyone besides ourselves, or we lose all hope of holding on to our bigger freedoms, like picking our own leaders or the way in which we're governed. Only those freedoms may already be gone."

"Stop it!" Cary yelled. Bob turned around again and saw that Moffit had chucked one of his shoes at Cary and was getting ready to throw the other. Bob knew he couldn't engage, or he'd lose the floor. He spun back around to face the jury. "We need a governing body that serves the interest of its people. One that allows us to keep our freedoms and make our personal decisions privately, regardless of what other citizens think or believe. The Dome family is a perfect example of this."

"That hit my tooth!" Cary whined, but Bob didn't let it distract him.

"The Dome family took a vote on whether Cary should be allowed to wear his hat while working in the store. The result was three to one in favor of prohibiting Cary from wearing his hat in the store. But then they took another vote."

Out of the corner of his eye, Bob could see Rita whispering to Margie, but he kept going. "This vote was whether Cary should be forced to remove his hat permanently and give up his shares in the family business—"

"Objection!" Margie shouted, interrupting Bob.

Bob didn't look around. He held onto the side of the jury box and waited for Moffit to sustain. But nothing happened. Bob turned towards the judge and realized that Moffit was bent over, doing something behind the bench. Bob seized on the opportunity to finish his argument. "This time the vote was three to one in favor of not only letting Cary keep his shares of the business, but also letting him wear his hat outside of the store. This should've been the end of it, but Rita was angry that the second vote didn't go her way. So, she made a big stink about it and took her son to court."

"Here it is!" yelled Moffit, and suddenly the terrible sound of metal crashing against tile rang out from the middle of the courtroom. Bob's heart jumped into his throat, and he nearly fell into the jury box as he leapt away from the noise. Timidly, he looked to the middle of the floor and saw that Moffit had tried to toss a large metal book at Cary. However, he hadn't been able to throw it very far, and so it had landed many feet short of the defense table.

There was a stunned silence across the courtroom. Bob glanced at Moffit, but the judge was looking around his bench, as if searching for something else he could throw. Bob used the moment to declare, "I ask for the Dome family's votes to be upheld, and I rest my case!"

Judge Moffit, who still had socks dangling from his ears, said, "Oh good. I guess you *can* be quick when properly motivated." Then turning his attention to the jury, he asked, "Alright, what do you all say? Is this guy guilty or not?"

Some of the fancy dressers in the guest section began chanting, "Guilty! Guilty!" And a few more shouted, "Lock him up! Lock him up!" While several others yelled, "Burn the hat! Burn the hat!" This prompted the hat donners to chant, "Innocent! Innocent!" and "Save the hat! Save the hat!"

The judge went mad over all the noise. He turned bright red in the face and screamed, "BAAAILIFF! Get these people out of here! NOW!"

The bailiff strode across the front of the courtroom, and in her loudest voice, she shouted, "Alright, everyone! Stand up and make your way to the back exit! You got two minutes to skedaddle before I start hauling you off to the jailhouse!"

Several of the people who'd heard the bailiff stood and exited the room, taking the others with them. But the chanting didn't die down. In fact, it seemed to grow louder the farther away the crowd got, and by the time all the guests were gone, the chants had begun to echo around the outside of the building. Bob knew this meant there had to be hundreds of people out there, gathered around the courthouse, waiting on the verdict.

Moffit tapped his fingers on the top of the bench impatiently and asked the jury. "Have you decided yet?"

The jurors had turned in their seats to face each other and discuss the case. Of course, the normal procedure was for the jurors to meet behind closed doors to decide the outcome of the trial. But nothing about this trial had been normal, and Bob knew there was no point in objecting since Moffit was determined to have his way.

After a couple minutes of whispering, a male juror in a plaid, flannel shirt stood up and declared, "We're ready, Your Honor!"

Moffit nodded and motioned at the man to spit it out. "Good. What're we having?"

The man looked confused by the question but continued, "We find the guy in the ugly hat guilty and not guilty."

Again, the judge picked up his gavel and banged it against the bench over and over again, but this time it was out of frustration with the jury. "That's not how this works, flapjack!" he yelled at the juror. "Ugly hat guy can only be guilty or not guilty. He can't be both!"

The man in plaid shrugged. "Well, that's how we voted. Some of us think he should burn the hat, and the rest of us don't care."

"Sit down, champ," Moffit ordered the juror. Then to the entire jury he asked, "How many of you think this man right here is guilty?"

Five hands shot up, including the woman with the big hair. "Well, I'll be!" Moffit exclaimed. "I've never had a tie in my court before. Ladies and gentlemen, we have ourselves a hung jury! Case dismissed!"

Margie stood up to protest. "But, Your Honor, how are our clients supposed to handle their domestic affair without a verdict? Shouldn't we have a do over trial with new jurors?"

Moffit, who was already standing up and collecting his

things, shook his head, which made the socks on his ears swing back and forth. "No way, sweetheart! You aren't going to make me sit through *this* case all over again. That family can figure it out on their own like they should've done in the first place."

Bob thought this might've been the first reasonable thing he'd heard Moffit say since becoming the judge. Just then, the noise from the crowd grew louder, and Bob realized that they'd heard the jury's deadlocked decision over the speaker system. Yet judging by the chant that was quickly gaining steam, Bob wondered if they'd misunderstood what had happened in the courtroom.

"Hang the jury! Hang the jury!" The phrase reverberated all around the building.

Moffit smirked at the jurors as he exited the courtroom. "You all might want to wait around until that crowd dies down. Sounds like they aren't too pleased with your *non-verdict*. Instead of disappointing one side, you've gone and pissed everyone off!" Moffit said as he gave a taunting wave goodbye and laughed his way out the door.

Margie and Bob walked to the windows to observe the scene outside. Bob remarked, "It looks like they're on the move. Maybe they're taking their protest to the streets."

But suddenly everyone's attention moved towards the back of the courtroom. A huge clamor had erupted inside the courthouse and was echoing down the long corridor that led to the courtroom. It was obvious from the noise that the doors to the courthouse had been flung open and there were people pouring into the large entryway at the front of the building.

Bob knew this was bad. He turned around to face the jurors, many of whom looked frightened. "We've got to get you out of here," he stated firmly.

He motioned to the bailiff. "Take the jurors out the back of the building as quickly as you can! If there's a large crowd behind the courthouse, keep the door locked and wait until their gone. Otherwise, let the jurors leave one at a time so as not to draw any attention."

To the jury he said, "If anyone questions you, tell them you're a court assistant and that the jury went out the front of the building. Hopefully, that'll throw them off your scent."

The juror with the big hair was whimpering, and black streaks of mascara ran down her face. Again, Bob spoke to the bailiff. "Make sure this one doesn't exit the building until she's gotten cleaned up. Otherwise, she's likely to give them all away."

The bailiff nodded at Bob. "Come on, all of you!" she shouted at the jury, trying to snap them out of their shock. "We're going to get you out of here safely, but you gotta follow my instructions. Now, let's move!"

The jurors stepped out of the jury box and followed the bailiff out of the courtroom. Once they were gone Bob said to Margie, "I'm going to take Cary out the side entrance to try and draw off some of the mob. How do you feel about taking Mr. and Mrs. Dome to your office until this all blows over?"

Margie said, "Yeah, I can do that. But, Bob, do you think this is going to get violent? They're not really going to try and kill us over a stupid hat, are they?"

Bob shook his head. "I hope not, but I think this is about more than just a hat, Margie."

Margie looked at Bob questioningly, but he pointed towards the exit to show her it was time to go. Margie went ahead and guided Cary's parents into the hallway that led towards the court offices at the back of the building, away from the crowd. Bob and Cary tailed close behind. They could hear the rowdy mob approaching the doors on the other side of the courtroom. "Drag 'em out of there!" someone shouted as Bob followed Cary and the others into the quiet hallway and closed the door behind them.

"Go with Margie and your parents," Bob directed Cary. "I'll be there in a second."

Then Bob ran into the nearby custodian closet and grabbed a metal screwdriver. When he got back to the courtroom door, he shoved the screwdriver between the door and the doorframe on an angle, wedging it underneath the door handle so that the handle was stuck in place. Bob hoped the makeshift lock would prevent the crowd from gaining access to this part of the courthouse. He listened for a moment to see if he could hear what was happening behind the door. There were several people yelling back and forth to each other. "We've got to find the jury and get them to overturn the verdict! That hat guy belongs in jail!"

Another person shouted, "Forget about jail! Let's hang him *and* the jury!" Then a chorus of "Hang the jury!" mixed with "Hang the hat guy!" broke out.

Bob took off in the direction of Margie's office. When he caught up to the others, Mrs. Dome was crying hysterically. "You can't take my baby out there! They're gonna kill him!"

Bob looked at Margie, but Margie shook her head as though she wasn't sure what to do either. "Mrs. Dome, you've got to get ahold of yourself and keep quiet. I'll be frank with you. Those people in the courtroom right now are the ones we should be worried about. The crowd on the outside of the courthouse isn't as likely to be hostile. If Cary and I go out there and talk to them, we might be able to persuade some of them to go home, which would help the police get things under control."

Mrs. Dome grabbed her son tightly. "I'm so sorry, Cary," she said sobbing. "I wish I'd just left you alone about your ugly hat. It should have been your decision whether you wore it or not. I just worried you might not find a girlfriend or ever get married if you didn't take it off."

Mr. Dome gasped. "Rita! Is that what this was all about? You told us that our sales had gone down!"

Mrs. Dome sniffled. "Well, they did go down for a while after we moved to the new location. But lately they've been up again since the smoothie place opened next door."

Mr. Dome shook his head disapprovingly, but Bob didn't wait for the couple to work it out. "Margie, you all need to hide in your office. You know to barricade the door, right?"

Margie nodded. "Yeah, I got this. You two go on. See if you can talk some sense into those jokers out there."

Bob smiled and said, "Alright. We'll try." Then he and Cary took off, but not before the large man in the faded knit hat gave his mother a tight squeeze and his father a firm hand-shake goodbye.

Bob and Cary rushed through several hallways, winding their way towards the building's side exit. As they hurried, Bob filled Cary in on his plan. "When we walk outside, we're going to head in the direction of John's tavern. Once the crowd sees your hat, they're going to want to talk to you, but let me speak on your behalf. I'm going to try and take the tone of the conversation down a few notches. Okay?"

Cary nodded, but Bob could tell his client was anxious. He placed his hand on Cary's shoulder. "We're going to be alright. If things get out of control, we'll make a beeline for the tavern. Ready?"

But before Cary could answer, Bob pushed the door open and stepped out onto the cobbled walkway that ran along the side of the courthouse. Cary followed a bit reluctantly, scanning the area as though he were looking to see if there was any trouble lurking nearby. After a moment, he seemed satisfied with the situation, and he and Bob began to walk through the crowd, surprisingly unnoticed.

When they made it to the frontside of the building, they could see the tavern on the other side of the courthouse square. Bob looked around to get a sense of how many people had come to protest, and from his quick count, he estimated there were at least a thousand protestors surrounding the courthouse. He was curious, however, why nobody seemed to notice Cary. But as he scanned the crowd, he suddenly found his answer.

There were big groups of men and women moving through the streets, wearing knit hats just like Cary's. Bob wondered how they had made these knock-off versions so fast, but then as one of the protestors passed close by, he realized that their hats weren't the same. It seemed as though someone had taken a pink and blue marker and colored a bunch of white hats that were similar to Cary's. The guy who passed them wearing the copycat hat nodded at Cary and said, "Cool, man! Your hat looks authentic! Great job!"

Cary looked at Bob like he had suddenly found himself among space aliens. "What's going on? Why are all these people wearing hats like mine?"

Bob didn't know what to say. Evidently, Cary's case had sparked some kind of movement, but Bob had no idea what the movement was about. So, he replied, "Only one way to find out!" And he took off towards a rough-looking group of men and women who were standing around, wearing hats like Cary's.

"Wait!" Cary shouted after him. "What are you doing?"

Bob didn't wait, though. Something inside of him had snapped. He didn't know what had caused it exactly—whether it was Moffit, or Goodman, or the fact that he felt like he had no control over the awful things that were happening around him *again*. But regardless of what had caused it, Bob recognized that he'd sat around too long waiting to see what shape this government was going to take. It was time to take action, and he was going to start by getting to the bottom of the protest.

"Hey, all of you!" he called over to the rough-looking group. Only a few of the women, who were standing on the edge of the small crowd, looked at Bob to see what he wanted. Bob walked up to them with Cary trailing behind and said, "Hello, folks. My client and I would like to know what your hats represent."

A petite woman with dirty blonde hair and sunburned skin laughed at Bob and yelled to a big guy with a frizzy, black beard. "Yo, Skip! This lanky dude wants to know about our hats."

The tough guy named Skip, who Bob recognized as one of his sons' followers, stared at Bob menacingly, and Bob realized he'd made a mistake by approaching this particular crowd. However, when Skip's eyes shifted to Cary, his gaze softened. "Hey, Beck. Don't you recognize your own leader when he's staring you right in the face? That's ugly hat dude, Cary Dome!"

"Whoa!" said the woman named Beck. "You're Cary Dome? Bro, you're, like, my new hero! We all just heard what you did to your folks! That's hardcore, man! Sounds like they had it coming, though!"

Cary looked confused. "Wait, what I did to my folks?"

"Yeah, dude! Telling them to shove their rigged vote where the sun don't shine and then burning their clothing store to the ground? That's crazy! I wish I had the courage to do stuff like that!"

"What do you mean?" asked Cary. "My family's clothing store didn't burn to the ground."

Another bearded man with a round middle chimed in, "Oh, yes it did! But we hear ya, man! Gotta play dumb in front of the stiffs. Like this guy in the suit. What's his deal?" he asked, pointing at Bob.

But instead of responding, Cary said, "Wait! My family's store *really* burned down?"

Bob felt bad for Cary. But he knew it was better for their safety if Cary played along with the role these people had thrust upon him, so he took over. "What my client means is that he had nothing to do with that fire as far as any court of law is concerned." Then to Cary, he said, "Ready to go for that drink now?"

Before Cary could answer, the man named Skip said, "Well, ooh-ee! That's some of the fanciest pants lawyer-speak I've ever heard. Say, you look a lot like a man who used to lead a renegade army, but you can't be him because no general I've ever known would wear such a sissy-looking outfit."

Bob understood the man was trying to bait him, but he didn't care. "You must have me confused with someone else," he replied to Skip in a firm tone. "But just so you all know, the Prime Minister favors heavy-handed rule. It's likely he'll be sending the police to break up this protest soon. It would be better if you all went home before that happens."

Several of the men and women in the group looked at each other and began to laugh, like they were in on some kind of joke. The woman named Beck explained, "Who do you think told us to come here today? Goodman and the council gave everyone permission to take the day off and stir up some trouble. Hell! I saw half the council protesting right out front a few minutes ago!"

Bob didn't understand at first, but then suddenly he realized what was going on. Goodman was playing the role of the "cool parent" in an attempt to undermine anyone who claimed he'd established an authoritarian regime. Bob was irritated, but he couldn't deny that this was actually a pretty clever plan on Goodman's part. Essentially, he was giving the people a chance to blow off some steam so that they wouldn't join together to revolt against him.

"I see," said Bob. "Well, try not to do too much damage, or else you'll have to deal with me and my sissy outfit representing you in court one day soon. Come on, Cary. Let's go get that drink."

Skip laughed. "Damn, Cary! Your lawyer sure is lame. No wonder his sons never wanted anything to do with him. You know you don't have to listen to him? He don't own you. You're free to do what you want. Stay with us, and we'll show you around to some of the others. You've become a legend to a lot of the people around here."

Bob looked at Cary's face, trying to gauge what he wanted to do, but Cary was looking back at him with an uneasy expression that told Bob he had no interest in accepting Skip's offer. "I'm sure my client appreciates your invitation and would be happy to be treated like a legend some other time. However, the two of us currently have some legal matters to discuss. You'll have to excuse us."

Bob said to Cary, "Let's go."

Before they could leave, however, the man with the round middle stepped in front of Bob and got right up in his face. "He ain't going with you, scumbag."

Cary tried to intervene on Bob's behalf, but before he could say anything, the man pulled his arm back and then punched Bob across the jaw. Bob went down hard. His head slammed against the cobblestone. Bob saw Cary leaning over him, but he was too stunned to move and too discombobulated to understand what was happening. A circle of people had gathered around and were yelling "Fight! Fight! Fight!"

In a daze, Bob stared back up at his attacker. The oily-faced ruffian looked like he'd gone mad. His eyes were wide, and his jaw was clenched. Bob thought he looked like a rabid dog, waiting to tear him apart.

More people crowded around them, shouting. But then, strangely, Bob felt himself beginning to float back to his feet. Someone was lifting him up from behind. A familiar voice with an Irish accent shouted over his shoulder. "Rufus, if you ever want to be served a drink in this town again, you better back away from my friend right now." Bob recognized the voice as John's.

The insane-looking man named Rufus was visibly annoyed, but he lowered his fists and took a couple of steps back. John pushed Bob away from the rowdy crowd, in the direction of his tavern. Bob was puzzled by what was happening, but even in his state of confusion, he sensed there was something he was forgetting. Suddenly, it came to him. "Cary!" he shouted.

"It's okay," John said reassuringly. "Cary's right here behind you, although I imagine he's not too thrilled with you at the moment. You shouldn't have been messing around with that crowd back there, Bob. The two of you could've been killed."

Bob didn't say anything. In his current state, he couldn't make heads or tails of what was happening. If he'd been in his right mind, however, he would've known that what John said was true. If he'd been in his right mind, he would have admitted to himself that he'd recognized more than just the one guy named Skip. Those men and women had been some of the twins' most faithful followers. They were the ones who'd gone after the wolves many years earlier, leaving a giant stain on the travelers' history. More than a stain—a giant, infectious wound.

Bob had been so desperate to do something that he'd thrown all caution aside. He'd wanted to get a win. But not just a win for Cary. A win for himself. He needed to feel like what he was doing mattered again. What Moffit had said to Bob in his chambers about being a joke had affected him more than he cared to admit. If Bob hadn't been so dazed, he might've been able to see that his bruised ego had been responsible for his carelessness. However, none of this meant anything to Bob at the moment since his brain was on a sabbatical from reality.

When they reached the tavern, Cary walked ahead and

held one of the doors for them. Inside, John escorted Bob over to a dark wooden booth and sat him down. Then he spoke to the servers behind the bar, who were his two grown sons. "Samuel, Egan. We're shutting down. Show everyone out and then lock the doors and pull the blinds. We don't need any of those hooligans coming in for a drink so that they can pour more fuel on this senseless fire."

The young men did as they were told, and John turned back to Bob, who looked woozy. "You okay there, pal?" he asked.

Bob nodded his head a couple of times and said, "I think a dog might've punched me in my mouth."

John smiled. "Oh, yes indeed, Bob. He clocked you pretty good, I'd say."

John turned to Cary and said, "You two can wait out the chaos here. I've got some work to do around the place while it settles down out there. I'll come back and check on you in a while but mind that our friend doesn't lose consciousness. He's surely got a concussion. I don't know how those work on the Moon, but if they're anything like Earth concussions, then we might lose him if he falls asleep."

"Lose me where?" Bob asked goofily.

"Oh boy," said John. "You okay to watch him?" he asked Cary.

Cary nodded, and John said, "Good lad." Then he disappeared into the back of the tavern and out of sight.

CHAPTER 13

THE NIGHTMARE

"Mina, I'm home!" her grandfather called from the back door. Mina knew it was him even before she heard the door open. Bonkers had been sitting in the kitchen, facing the back garden, and whining excitedly while Mina got ready for school.

"Hello, Papa!" she called from her bedroom. "Would you mind taking Bonkers outside? I think he needs to go."

"Of course!" her grandfather responded. "That's why I'm here. To take Bonkers on a long walk. Isn't that right, Bonkers?" he asked in a silly voice.

"Thanks, Papa. Let me grab his leash for you." Mina looked down at her vanity table and grabbed Bonkers' long, blue leash, but when she looked back up at the mirror, she realized she'd dressed herself in the wrong clothes. Instead of her school uniform, she was wearing a sweater and pants that looked just like the sparkly, purple sweater and star print leggings she'd worn in middle school. "Wow!" she thought to herself. "I can't believe these still fit."

"Hold on, Papa!" she shouted. "I have to change real fast if I don't want to be late."

Mina's grandfather called back to her, "Don't worry, dear. Bonkers and I will be fine. When you're ready, come and meet us by the sea."

Mina heard the door slam shut. She looked back in the mirror and saw that she was wearing her school uniform, after all. Except, it was all black and not the navy and gray plaid she was supposed to be wearing. She looked across her room at the clock on her nightstand, but it didn't seem to be working. The glowing, blue numbers had changed into unrecognizable symbols that were much dimmer than usual.

"I better hurry," Mina thought distractedly. "I can't miss more school. I already missed so much when Papa died."

"Oh my god!" she exclaimed. "Grandfather is dead!"

A cold chill ran through her, and immediately she began to panic, frightened that Bonkers had been stolen. Yet what was even more terrifying was she sensed that whoever had taken him wasn't a person at all, but some supernatural, dark force.

Mina looked down at her hands where Bonkers' leash should've been, but it was gone. She raced to the back door, her heart pounding in her chest. She reached for the doorknob, but just as she did, a huge gust of wind blew into the kitchen, throwing the door wide open and pushing Mina back against the kitchen table.

Unwilling to yield, Mina leaned into the wind and fought her way out the door. Once she was in the clearing by the side of the cottage, the wind died down. However, it had grown dark out. Green storm clouds swirled above her in the most threatening looking sky she'd ever seen. She didn't stop to think about it, though. She had to find Bonkers and bring him home.

Mina looked to the tall trees that stood high above the seashore. A woman's voice whipped around her, as if it were bouncing from one gust of wind to the next. "When you're ready, when you're ready, when you're ready," repeated the woman again and again as the wind pulled at Mina's hair and clothes. Then a booming voice dropped out of the sky. "WHEN YOU'RE READY, COME AND MEET US BY THE SEA!"

The sound of the voice sent shivers down Mina's spine. She was almost too scared to move, but her desire to save Bonkers rekindled her bravery. She ran towards the tall trees—the giant, steadfast soldiers who guarded her cottage.

Yellow lightning bolts leapt from the sky and struck the earth around her. Clumps of dirt and grass exploded into the air. Debris rained down everywhere, and Mina cried out in horror as she threw her arms over her head for protection. Before she reached the trees, a thick bolt of lightning appeared high above. It curved around on itself and struck the tops of several trees like a fiery scorpion tail reaching beyond the heavens to attack Mina's earthly guards. Huge branches hurtled to the ground, and Mina had to dive out of their way to keep from being crushed.

Once she made it through the trees to the top of the cliffs, the dark clouds suddenly cleared. Mina searched back and forth, hoping to find Bonkers, but the beach was empty. She ran down the dunes towards the water to look for any sign of her beloved hound. She knew this is where he was supposed to be. It's where the unseen man had told her they'd be, not to mention the voice in the sky.

Mina swept her eyes over the sand. When her gaze reached the lapping waves, she caught sight of something glistening beneath the water. A little sliver of light was reflecting off an object that was poking out of the sand. She ran into the shallow water and knelt down in front of the reflection, scooping her hand into the rolling waves to retrieve the item.

She grasped something that felt like a rope and pulled it out of the sand. It was Bonkers' leash. Mina's heart sank, worried she'd lost her best friend forever. She looked out across the ocean. A shadow was approaching, and as it swam into view, she realized it was a monster wave headed for shore. She screamed as loud as she could, but then suddenly she realized she was back inside her little cottage, tangled in her sheets.

Bonkers lifted his head an inch off the bed with a semi-comatose expression. It was clear he wasn't too concerned over whatever was going on. He didn't even fully open his eyes, and a second later he lowered his head and fell right back to sleep. Mina slowed her heart rate by taking several deep breaths. Her skin felt cold and clammy, so she pulled her blanket down on top of her tight.

She'd had lots of recurring nightmares since her parents left, and it was times like these that she wished she wasn't on her own. When she didn't fall right back to sleep, she got out of bed and wrapped a blanket around her. Then she went to the window and stared into the night. "When you're ready, come and meet us by the sea." This was the phrase her grandfather's voice always said to her in the dream. "But ready for what?" she wondered.

She looked into the sky to see if she could catch a glimpse of the Moon. Her heart longed to see it, even though she knew it wouldn't be there. Lately, Mina had been keeping track of its phases, and tonight marked the beginning of a new Moon. "Even the Moon has abandoned me," she thought.

Mina felt anger boiling up inside of her over everything her parents had put her through. After they'd left, she'd fallen into a deep depression, something she'd never experienced before in her young life. If she hadn't had Bonkers there to take care of, she wasn't sure she could've carried on. Whenever she wasn't at school, she stayed in bed and replayed memories of her entire childhood—the good and the bad. None of it made her feel any better, though. Her heart was crushed. The reality of her situation was that she was unwanted and unloved.

It was the journal in which Mina had written down her grandfather's final moments that finally managed to pull her out of her funk. She began to fixate on every detail of what he'd said before he'd died, analyzing everything to the nth degree and imagining what it might mean. Clearly, her real mother possessed magical powers if what her grandfather had told her was true. And Mina wondered if this meant that she, too, had some kind of magical abilities. It might make sense, she thought, after everything that had happened to her.

She stared at the spot in the sky where she knew the Moon *was*, even though she couldn't see it. She focused her attention and tried to concentrate on sending a message to her friends. "Bob and Maude, it's Mina. Please figure out a way to get in touch. I need to talk to you as soon as possible."

It wasn't the first time Mina had tried to send some variation of this message to the Moon. She knew it might just be wishful thinking, but for now, it was the only way she could think of to contact her friends. And even if it was silly, it was better than doing nothing.

Feeling tired again, Mina climbed back into bed and draped her arm over Bonkers. She listened to his deep, loud breathing, and soon she was fast asleep once more.

CHAPTER 14

AXEL'S PASSAGEWAY

For years, Axel, Fred, and Ragher shuffled through the tunnels, watching the Moon's memories play across the walls. Their movements were choreographed by the gliding sheets of ice as they were ushered here and there through the ever-changing labyrinth. Then every so often, the sheets of ice would part, and an unknown force would call on one of them to surrender himself into the void.

As the metal wheels ticked along, Axel became obsessed with breaking free from it all. For many months he'd been longing to reunite with the other wolves and tell them what he'd learned. Plus, it had been ages since he'd embraced his purpose—the one the visions had helped him discover. Therefore, he didn't understand why he was still being held captive when he knew he was ready to become the wolf leader he was meant to be. The kind who would stand up to his enemies.

"Tick, tick, tick." Axel walked alone. The others had been called away, possibly days ago, into their own dark passageways. He saw the walls move apart and reveal a dark void. He expected to see one of his friends emerge, but instead the passageway summoned him.

Axel entered into the darkness and sat down. He waited patiently, hoping to show the void that he was ready for any test it could give him. After experiencing every second of the massacre, he knew he could handle whatever the darkness might show him. Nothing could undo him after everything he'd already been through.

It was silent for a long time, and Axel wondered if the void might be deciding what to do with him. Then finally, after a long period of sensory deprivation, Axel felt himself ripped away from the darkness and flung into a new reality.

Just like always, his body ached as it snapped into place. Axel looked around and realized he was on the Darkside of the Moon. It wouldn't have seemed any different than the passageway except that there was a faint glow radiating all around him. He looked down and saw paws. They were moving fast across the terrain. He could feel a twinge of fear growing inside his chest, only the fear didn't belong to him. It belonged to the wolf he was inhabiting.

Axel quieted his mind. He'd learned during his previous incarnations not to push his own will. It never worked. It just became a fight and delayed the vision he was supposed to be having. As he surrendered to his new embodiment, he wondered if he was about to experience yet another part of the wolf massacre. However, the glowing made him suspect otherwise.

A memory resurfaced at the back of Axel's mind. During his first days in the ice tunnels, he had watched the earliest scene between Neriti and Ragher play out multiple times. It was the one where a shapeshifting Ragher approached a young Neriti at the edge of Crystal Crater. However, the timing had seemed all wrong. Ragher had brought Neriti a prophetic message that she would be orphaned soon, and the upsetting news had caused her to banish Ragher before she'd learned his purpose for being there. Then after shifting a few more times,

Ragher had fled into the dark in the form of a glowing, adult wolf.

Axel silenced his own thoughts, hoping to learn whether he had indeed ended up inside Ragher's body. He felt the panic pounding within the wolf's chest cavity, the tension in his muscles as they strained to run at full speed. He sensed he was trying to hide from something. *But what?* Could it really be that the dark spirit was after him?

The running continued for a long time over dimly lit rock and dirt. Axel could hear the wolf's heavy panting. When he began to slow his pace, Axel assumed it was because he was tired. But then he felt a flash of curiosity inside the wolf's head. Suddenly, Axel realized there was a light glowing dimly nearby in the shape of a white orb. It bobbed up and down like a spherical buoy rising and falling in a pitch-black sea. "What the devil," whispered the wolf, and his voice confirmed to Axel that it was Ragher he possessed.

Axel sensed his old friend was too afraid to investigate the little light and was certain that at any second he would run off in a different direction to avoid facing the orb. But he was wrong. Ragher found his courage and began to creep towards the bobbing light, and as he got closer, the orb brightened and began to float to the side. Ragher stopped in his tracks, and the orb stopped too. Evidently, Ragher didn't know what to make of this because he continued to stand motionless for a long while. Then finally, he began to walk slowly towards the light again, and again the glowing orb moved to the side.

Axel thought it seemed like the light was being playful, but something about it felt wrong. Apparently, Ragher thought so too because he turned from it to go in the opposite direction. But before he'd taken two steps, a deep voice called to him from out of the darkness. "What a handsome, little toy you are. Come with me, and my master will give you everything you've ever dreamed of."

The words sent a wave of fear through Axel. Ragher turned to face the voice but found only darkness. However, the shining orb had moved much closer to where he was standing. Ragher said in a raised tone, "I know who you are, and I have no interest in doing business with your master. My loyalty lies elsewhere."

The deep voice laughed wickedly. "Oh! You truly are a precious plaything! No wonder my master wants you for his own."

"Laugh all you want, but it's I who feel pity for *you*. I know why you hide in the darkness. I've seen your story and what he did to you. Return to your master and tell him I'm no one's *plaything.* And if you're brave enough, you can go ahead and tell him to do his own dirty work from now on."

The ground around Ragher suddenly trembled, and there was a loud *"pop!"* A second later, a monstrous being with spiky teeth emerged from under the cloak of darkness. Its body was illuminated by the glowing, white orb that hung from an antenna on the side of its face. On the other side, another identical antenna framed its head, though this one was capped by a darkened orb. Axel gasped loudly inside Ragher's body, and Ragher flinched as though he'd heard Axel's cry.

The monster's baritone voice rattled its spear-like teeth, but its jaw never moved. It was like its words flowed from somewhere deep inside its repulsive body. "I hid myself in darkness to keep from frightening you. It was a courtesy that I see was unnecessary. You must be very brave if you know of my master and yet you still order me to deliver such a message. I doubt, however, you'd be brave enough to deliver that same message yourself. You may think you know him from those little scenes you've watched in the safety of your icy fortress in the off-lands, but I assure you that watching his cruelty isn't the same as experiencing it firsthand."

Ragher nodded at the grotesque creature. "I don't doubt

what you say, but if your master is planning to eat me, then he should come after me himself. I won't be led to my death by you."

"Death? No, no. You're mistaken. He doesn't want to eat you. He wants to free you."

Ragher scoffed. "Oh, really? From whom?"

The rubber-faced ghoul blinked beneath the white film that covered its eyes—the only movement it had made since revealing itself. "From your own master, of course."

"Well, it seems that you're the one who's mistaken then, because I have no master. My only loyalty is to the wolves."

Again, the ghoul laughed wickedly. "You've been fooled so easily. No master? *Really?* Who do you think imprisoned you in those icy tunnels for all those centuries? Didn't you ever question why you had no memory of how you got there? It's because *she* didn't want you to know what she'd done to you. *That's* who you're being loyal to whether you realize it or not. She was your jailor. Not your friend. A master who locked you away inside a labyrinth so that you could spend all your days watching other's lives while having no life of your own. *That's* the kind of master you've chosen to serve."

Ragher hesitated. Axel could feel him struggling over what to make of the monster's accusations. Eventually though, he shoved his mental calculus aside and fired back, "She didn't imprison me! I just had to find my own way out of the ice tunnels. But even if what you say is true, the cruelty that has been done to me is no match for what your master has put you through. I take it that you're clever enough to know you're an abomination? The spirit created you for his own dark purposes with no concern for your well-being, or the fact that your very existence goes against nature."

The deep voice hissed, "What is this 'nature' you speak of? Is it another master? One that disapproves of *my* existence yet honors a shapeless idiot such as you? Stop kidding yourself, *shifter*. You and I are not so different. There are parts of us that are exactly the same, even. The only real difference is whose bidding we do. But that will change one day. Mark my words!" The monster exhaled a thick, green gas which caused Ragher to gag and cough. Then it let out one last howling laugh as it disappeared.

Suddenly, Axel was pulled from this scene and launched into another. His mind, however, was still thinking about what he'd just seen. He thought he knew everything about the Moon realm and what lived there, yet he'd never heard mention of a monster such as this before. He had believed that all the monsters were exterminated when the bryobane were killed off. But this thing that Ragher had talked to was in some ways even more terrifying than the legendary bryobane, for it showed a level of intelligence that the bryobane had been known to lack.

Axel wanted to be released from the passageway so he could find Ragher and ask him more about it, but the darkness wasn't through with him yet. He looked around and realized he was inside one of the wolf dens. He stood staring at a wall that was lit by the flames of a simmering, blue fire. It took him only a matter of seconds to realize he was still inside of Ragher's body when he heard a sweet, tired voice speak to him from behind. "Ragher, darling, come to bed. I'm getting cold and need you to warm me."

Ragher turned to his side and looked down at a very pregnant Neriti who was looking up at him lovingly. Immediately, Axel felt his stomach churn and his heart begin to quicken. He didn't understand exactly what he was seeing, but he suddenly felt ill. Neriti had been a mother-figure to Axel *and* to Ragher. In fact, Axel had grown up believing that Neriti *was* Ragher's mother. Therefore, the scene in front of him didn't make any sense.

Ragher dropped down next to Neriti and pushed his body

against hers. He nuzzled the top of his brow against her neck, and she giggled. "I know you're feeling restless again, Ragh. You've barely slept the last few days. Is it the twins? Are you nervous about them being born? Because you know you're married to the best healer there ever was," she said to him teasingly. "We're going to be fine. *All* of us."

But when Ragher didn't reply, Neriti became concerned. "What's really troubling you, Ragher? Come on. Don't keep secrets."

Ragher pulled his head away from Neriti's neck and stared into her eyes while they lay on their sides. "That *thing* has been hanging around again recently. I noticed it was stalking me right after we learned about the twins. I ignored it for as long as I could, and eventually it left me alone. But then it appeared again a few days ago. It keeps following me everywhere I go."

Neriti rose slowly to a seated position, clearly straining from the extra weight of the pups she was carrying. She looked nervous but stayed calm. "Why didn't you tell me this earlier?"

Ragher sat up too. "I didn't think it was something to worry about at first, Riti. The dark spirit has been sending that thing to spy on me ever since I left the ice tunnels years ago. He wants me to know he's always watching. That he's not going to forget about me. It's never been anything I couldn't handle, though."

"And now?" Neriti asked with a furrowed brow.

"He's taken it up a notch. He's figured out he can apply more pressure because we're expecting."

"What exactly did that thing say to you, Ragher?" Neriti asked hotly.

"It made a promise. It said if I don't travel to Black Ice Glacier to meet the dark spirit in person, he'll come for the pups after they're born."

"What the hell, Ragher? *Come for the pups?* He knows they won't be like you, right?"

Ragher shook his head. "I don't think it matters, Riti. It's a threat. He's trying to force me to go over there after all these years of refusing him. And it's worked because I'm going."

Neriti looked alarmed. "No, Ragher! You can't! He'll kill you! Or turn you into whatever that thing is that follows you. You said so yourself!"

"I know what I said, but I don't have a choice now. Can't you see? The dark spirit is smart. He waited until I'd built a life with you to make his move. He knew it would be impossible for me to resist his threats once I had something to protect."

Neriti was shaking her head. "No, Ragher. I won't let you do this. You were sent here for a reason, and I'm not going to let you sacrifice yourself to that horrible monster and his pet ghoul. There has to be another way."

Ragher spoke sullenly. "I wish that were true, Riti. But *this* is the way. I was sent here to protect you and that means protecting our pups too. If sacrificing myself is what I have to do to keep the three of you safe, then that's what I'm going to do."

Neriti began to cry desperate tears. "No, Ragher! How could you possibly think sacrificing yourself would protect us? What if this monster decides he wants me next? Or what if once he's finished devouring your energy, he decides that maybe our pups have inherited your Moon Walker powers, and he decides to go after them too? What then? Don't you see that sacrificing yourself won't end this for us?"

Ragher hung his head. He loved Neriti with all his heart. He had desired her from the moment he first saw her in the ice tunnels centuries earlier, centuries before she was even born. It was a desire that was as real to him as his need for air. But it was dangerous, too, because this intense love he had for her made it nearly impossible to say no, even when every part of him was telling him he should.

"What do you suggest we do then, Neriti?" he asked.

Neriti slowly paced across the floor of their den, thinking over the dilemma and weighing their options. Ragher sat patiently, feeling as though his wings had been clipped. He wanted to do what he knew was right and give himself over to the evil spirit so that it would leave his family alone.

As far as Ragher knew, there was no reason the dark spirit would want the pups unless he believed they possessed the same level of power as Ragher. Even if the twin pups were half Moon Walker, it wouldn't matter as long as they looked and acted like wolves. Ragher had seen the wolves' history, and he knew from what he'd witnessed that the dark spirit wasn't allowed to go after wolves, even if that hadn't stopped him from tormenting them at times. What the dark spirit was really after was Moon Walker energy—*his* energy.

Practically the entire night passed before Neriti spoke again. Ragher rested on the ground while his wife alternated between pacing and sitting. Once she was through, she looked as though she'd aged half a lifetime. Her hair seemed thinner, and her eyes were sunken. "Okay, Ragher," she said. "I'm ready."

"Have you thought of a plan, my love?" he asked her.

She nodded, although she looked defeated, and Ragher wondered if she planned to give in. "Yes," she replied, "although it's not what I really want."

"What is it?" he asked.

"I've thought through every scenario I could possibly imagine that would keep our family safe, but the only one that makes any sense is for you to leave us."

"So, you agree then? I should face him?"

Neriti shook her head. "No. I don't want you to face him. I want you to run away, only I don't want you to do that either, really. We'll just make it *look* like you've run away. When the pups are born, we'll give one of them to my best friend, Lizel, and her husband, Rothel. As you know, Lizel is due about the same time as me, but the dark spirit won't know that she isn't expecting twins like we are. She and Rothel can take our pup and raise it with their own."

Ragher was horrified. "What are you talking about, Neriti? Why in the world would we give away one of our pups?!"

"Please, Ragher. Stay calm. We aren't going to give away one of our pups exactly. We'll still be able to watch over him or her, and in the meantime, you'll take the place of our pup. I know you swore you'd never shift again, but I think this is the only way to keep us all together."

"But the dark spirit *knows* I can shift! He'll figure out what we've done and come after us. It's not safe!"

"Do you really think the dark spirit would believe you've chosen to give up one of your pups so you could take its place? Or that he'll risk meddling in wolf business when he knows he's not allowed to come near us?" Neriti asked with a raised eyebrow, hoping she could force Ragher to seriously consider her questions.

"No! I guess I don't. But only because the plan is a coward's way out!"

"Right, and he knows you're not a coward."

Ragher began to say something else to Neriti, but Axel didn't hear the rest. He was in too much shock from what he'd just learned. Rothel and Lizel had been Axel's parents, and he'd had a twin sister, too, named Nemii. He could barely remember any of them now because they had died when he was very young.

Axel had always believed his parents and sister had died from Darkside poisoning after getting separated from the pack during one of the pilgrimages. He'd watched the scenes surrounding their deaths over and over again in the ice tunnels. He'd heard his mother and father shouting odd phrases while laughing gleefully, as though they'd become enchanted by their terrible sickness. "Follow the white light,

Lizel!" "Run faster, Rothel!" "Something amazing lies ahead! I can feel it!"

But now Axel understood that these wolves weren't his parents. Not his real ones, anyway. Neriti had stepped in after the tragedy to take care of him like a mother, but it turned out that she had been his real mother all along. And Ragher, his childhood friend who'd been like a brother to him, had really been his father. Axel went over it again and again until it felt like he was drowning. His mind spun out of control as he tried to make sense of information that made no sense at all.

Axel's thoughts turned to Tahissi next—his real sister—and suddenly the spinning stopped. *Oh my god!* Had she known the whole time? Axel screamed at the top of his lungs, and a giant, invisible lasso cinched around his waist and catapulted him across time and space until he was back inside a scene he'd already lived through—one of the most miserable of his entire life.

Axel recalled that the episode had occurred about a year after the triplets and Tegelro died. For the year leading up to it, Tahissi had been in a constant state of mourning. She didn't sleep or eat much, and she never spoke to anyone except for Neriti, Ragher, and Axel.

She had ignored her family's pleas to return to her child-hood den, and instead decided to continue living inside the den that she'd shared with Tegelro and the pups. Axel had joined her there soon after the tragedy in order to help look after her. After all, she was the twin-sister of his best friend—or so he'd believed—and the daughter of Neriti, his mother-figure and mentor. Therefore, by extension, Axel had considered Tahissi family too.

Ragher was gone often during this time period, always on some sort of business that he and Neriti were secretive about. Axel wished he could go back in time and see for himself what Ragher had been doing. But even more so, he wished he hadn't spent so many days alone with Tahissi in her den. He had thought he was doing the right thing by offering himself to her as a healer and a friend—someone who could help her gently mend the threads of her torn-apart life.

Before Tahissi's devastating loss, Axel had never cared for someone so tenderly. He and Tahissi had still been relatively young at the time of her family's murder, and even though he had spent several years training as a healer, he hadn't had the chance to practice on his own yet. Consequently, he wasn't prepared for the powerful bond that Tahissi's need for compassion and his unconditional empathy would create between them.

In the early days, Tahissi sat and stared at the walls of her den, as though she were watching her own memories play out across them. At the time, there was a lot of fuss being made over the earthling called Maude who'd appeared out of a beam of light that had fallen from the sky. Neriti was caught up in the panic over what to do about the unsettling miracle, and even though she tried to be there for her daughter, she was often pulled away for long periods of time.

This was the space that Axel filled. He sat with Tahissi and stared at the wall too. He knew there were no words or healing rituals that could ease Tahissi's pain. The best thing he could do to help his friend was to be there with her—to act as a boulder she could reach for whenever the ocean of grief she was swimming through threatened to pull her under.

The first few weeks went by with very few words, and then one day, Neriti convinced Axel to take a break from watching over Tahissi. She told him she wanted him to pay a visit to her friend, Imgu, the head healer of a pack that lived a day's journey away. She said that Imgu had offered to let Axel shadow her while she made her daily rounds healing the sick. Neriti said she thought it would benefit him to observe a different interpretation of their practices. But really, she had grown concerned over how much time Axel was spending by Tahissi's side.

Following Neriti's instructions, Axel departed and was gone for over a week. Tahissi, who hadn't been informed of Axel's trip, didn't take his absence well. She spent every day wailing for Tegelro and her lost pups. Neriti tried to comfort her daughter the best she could, but Tahissi pushed her mother away. From an early age, Tahissi had known her parents' secret and was well aware that Ragher was her father and Axel her brother. And in the privacy of their own den, Tahissi and her parents had acted the way they always would have if they hadn't been burdened by their secret.

Tahissi knew that her mother had seen visions of the darkness taking the triplets before the horrible event had occurred, and she suspected the secret they'd kept all those years had played a major part in their deaths. Therefore, Tahissi decided she was through pretending. She knew she couldn't go so far as to tell Axel the truth, for she worried it would endanger his life as her parents had often suggested. However, she wanted Axel by her side now and only him. She drew comfort from their bond as twins, and she hoped that Axel might awaken to the truth on his own if given enough time to recognize their special connection for what it was.

Unfortunately, Axel *had* come to recognize their deep connection. But without the truth to provide context, he misunderstood it as feelings of romance instead of the unique bond between close siblings. Once Axel returned from his time with the other pack, Tahissi revealed that she'd felt heartbroken while he was away. She told him that his presence made her braver, and that whenever he was around, she knew she could get through the day feeling a little less broken.

The revelation was enough for Axel. For months, he didn't leave Tahissi's side for more than a few hours at a time. He decided it was his responsibility to make sure Tahissi healed properly. After all, he was training to be a healer, and what better initiation into the practice than to help a close friend overcome a tragedy.

Every night, the two slept cuddled together for warmth and comfort. If Tahissi hadn't been so consumed by her grief, she might've realized how she was setting her brother up to misunderstand her affection towards him. But her heart had been terribly wounded by her loss, and in some unchecked part of her brain, she assumed Axel would know she was too damaged to be interested in romantic love again.

However, Neriti understood well the effect that her children's time together was having on Axel, and at one point, she cautiously confronted him. "You know that Tahissi has suffered a great loss, one that will prevent her from ever loving again freely. Right, Axel?"

Axel couldn't possibly decipher the true meaning of what Neriti was saying, though. And by that point, he'd fallen so madly in love with Tahissi that he only heard what he wanted to. He believed the time they'd shared together had given him special insight into her soul, and he wouldn't write her off as easily as Neriti seemed willing to do. He believed Tahissi would one day be able to love again because he wanted it to be true. He wanted her to love *him*.

Eventually, Axel worked up the courage to tell Tahissi his feelings. He knew she might need more time to heal, but he didn't care how long it took. He just wanted to be with her—to continue taking care of her for the rest of their lives. However, he had no plan or strategy for how to broach the subject. So, one night as they lay next to each other, drifting off to sleep, Axel decided he should just go ahead and tell her. And it was this precise moment that the passageway had brought him back to, forcing him to revisit one of the most painful memories of his life. In the flesh.

Axel felt the original excitement run through his younger

body along with the hesitation and fear over telling Tahissi the truth. The older Axel wanted to stop himself. He would've done anything to prevent this younger version from revealing his feelings. But he knew he had no control over the past.

As he watched Tahissi next to him—her eyelids fluttering as she fell into a dream—he felt his youthful heart start to swell with so much love that he thought it might burst. Suddenly, he blurted out, "I love you, Tahissi!"

Tahissi's eyes shot wide open, and she stared at Axel, as though he'd just shouted that they were being attacked by an army of zombie bryobane. Axel held his breath, waiting to see what would happen next. His heart beat out of control, and Tahissi continued to stare at him in shock for another moment before relaxing her expression and sitting up. Axel mirrored her by sitting up too.

In a cool, detached voice, Tahissi said, "I love you too, Axel. You've always been like a brother to me, and I don't think I could've gotten through the last year without you."

Feeling undeterred, Axel confessed, "Taking care of you during the last year has been eye-opening for me, Tahissi. I know it was absolutely the worst situation ever that brought us together, and I swear I'd change all of it for you if I could. I'd bring back the pups and Tegelro and make everything perfect for you again because that's how much I love you. I would do anything to make you happy."

As Axel spoke, Tahissi's face changed from cool and relaxed to full-on distress and mortification. "No, Axel. This isn't *right*. These feelings you have are sweet and kind, but they're not meant for me."

"Of course they're meant for you," Axel insisted. "Look, I know that everything you've gone through has left you feeling empty. I know that part of you wishes it could be over so you could be done with the pain. But I still see so much left for you in this world. I think you can be happy again. That *we* can be happy together. It might not be the same as before, but don't you think it's worth a shot? Don't you think your family would have wanted for you to find happiness again?"

Tahissi closed her mouth tightly. She wanted to tell him the truth about why his love for her could never be, but she was too scared of what might happen if she did. "Axel, you're a good wolf with the most amazing heart, and you *should* live the kind of happy life you speak of, but it has to be with someone else. I'm no longer interested in that kind of love.

For the first time since declaring his feelings, Axel looked hurt. "Tahissi, you shouldn't punish yourself—"

She shook her head and interrupted, "I'm not punishing myself. I promise. If I were capable of loving like that again, I would allow it to happen. But my heart has forever changed. All I want for the rest of my days is to be surrounded by the platonic love and support of my family and pack."

Axel began to argue again. "I think you feel this way now, Tahissi, because your pain is still raw. I sense, though, that your heart will change one day, and when it does, I want you to know that I'll be waiting for you."

Tahissi grew visibly frustrated. She didn't know what more to say to her brother to discourage him without telling him a truth that would cut him to the core. Many times, her parents had ordered her never to tell Axel the truth, not just because it could put him in danger, but because they knew it would hurt him to learn they'd given him away.

Keeping Axel in the dark was the agreement their parents had made. It was the only part of Neriti's plan that Ragher had gotten his way on. Ragher had told Tahissi it was to keep from hurting her brother, but secretly it was because of the shame Ragher felt over taking his son's place to protect himself.

"Axel, you have to listen to me," Tahissi begged. "My heart will *never* change about this. You've become a dear friend to me, but I will never love you the way you think you love me. You're going to have to accept this. I couldn't bear it to know I'd kept you from living a happy life with a family of your own. One of us should have that, and it can no longer be me. So, please! Promise me you'll forget all of this and think of me only as a sister. Nothing more."

Axel didn't say anything for a moment, but then he sighed deeply. "I don't want anyone but you, Tahissi, and I'm prepared to wait my whole life. If you don't want me, then I'll be fine never experiencing that sort of happiness either. I only want what you want. My fate is forever tied to yours."

Tahissi groaned. "You don't know what you're saying. You don't—"

But Axel cut her off. "I *do* know what I'm saying, and nothing will change my heart. But I can see that it's no longer right for me to stay here, now that you know how I feel. It would be too challenging for both of us, so I'll say goodnight."

For the first time since the death of her pups, Tahissi felt a different kind of pain. It was pain over the suffering she'd caused someone else. Suffering she'd created because she'd been too careless with her brother's feelings. She wanted to ignore it and tell herself it didn't matter, that he'd get over it and find someone else. But she knew that without being able to tell him the truth, he might never move on, and certainly things would never be the same between them until he did.

Hastily, she called after him. "I love you, Axel, but you're right. Being around each other, now that we both know your true feelings, *would* be too challenging. I don't think you should come around again for a while. I think it would be good for you if you took some time away from here. Maybe go and visit some of the other packs. Consider choosing somewhere else to begin your healing practice."

Axel turned back to look at her. His eyes reflected the depth of the torment he felt. "Tahissi, I don't *want* to leave you. I want us to be together when you're ready."

Again, she shook her head. "You aren't hearing me. I will *never* be ready for that. If you really love me like you say, then you need to trust me and do as I ask. It's the only way you can ever make me happy."

Axel felt anger growing in the pit of his stomach. "No, Tahissi! I know you have feelings for me! You can't just kick me out of your life. I've spent a year taking care of you. You need me. We need each other!"

Tahissi stayed strong and kept her tone firm, if not a bit cold. "The love I have for you is nothing like what I felt for Tegelro, and it never could be. You may be right, Axel. I may open my heart up again one day. But if that day ever comes, even if you've waited your entire life for me, I still won't choose you. I swear it."

Tahissi's words pierced Axel like a blow from a dagger. He'd never been hurt so badly, and his initial reaction was to growl at Tahissi, which caught them both by surprise. Then once he got ahold of himself, he began to cry angry tears. He shouted, "I will never forgive you for hurting me like this! You could have dangled my love on a string the rest of our lives, and it would have been far less cruel than what you just said to me. I hope you do find love again someday, Tahissi, but I hope it's only as great as the guilt you feel over breaking my heart!"

The older Axel cringed at these words as his younger self turned and stormed out of Tahissi's den. The Axel who'd been forced to relive this scene knew that he and Tahissi would never reconcile. Axel married soon after for the convenience of having a partner, but he never allowed himself to fall in love again.

He stayed with his pack, and Neriti continued to be his mentor, but he barely ever spoke to Tahissi. They'd see each other occasionally in passing, and Tahissi would greet Axel with the same warmth she'd always shown him. But Axel would act prickly and distant in an obvious attempt to prove that her affection no longer mattered to him. Axel's spitefulness towards Tahissi kept his heart bruised and tender. But in a way, this was an intentional choice. For somewhere inside, he knew that allowing his heart to heal was equivalent to letting go of his love for Tahissi. Yet staying angry meant he could continue to secretly love her with the hope that one day she would change her mind.

The vision flashed forward, dropping Axel outside of the home he'd shared with his wife. About two years had passed since that fateful night in Tahissi's den, when Ragher showed up at the entrance to Axel's lair one morning, looking as broken as he'd ever seen a wolf look before. "Tahissi's gone, Axel. We think she was suffering from survivor's guilt. It's a difficult thing to overcome when the tragedy is as large as the one our family has had to face. The amount of trauma an event like that leaves in its wake——" Ragher's voice caught in his throat, and he quickly gasped for air, as though he were trying to prevent himself from crying.

"It's like a landslide that lasts for years. If you don't keep digging yourself out steadily, it piles up until one day you realize you're never going to beat it. That you're never going to find your way back to the surface. So, you decide to stop digging for good." Ragher could barely finish this last sentence as his tears began to flow. "I think that's what happened to Tahissi," he said weeping. "I think she decided she'd done enough digging for one lifetime."

Ragher hung his head and sobbed. Axel sat beside his friend in silence, the same way he'd sat beside Tahissi and stared at her den wall. After a while, Ragher's tears subsided, and he looked over at Axel. "She loved you, you know? You were a wonderful brother to her. You helped her enormously after she lost Tegelro and the pups just by being there for her. Honestly, I'm not sure she would've survived that first year if it weren't for you."

Axel shook his head. "No, Ragher. *You* were her brother. I was just doing what any healer would've done." Ragher smiled at Axel, and the two continued to sit for a while until Ragher felt strong enough to return home to Neriti.

After that day, Axel's heart was heavy with guilt. He knew that what had happened between Tahissi and him had nothing to do with her death. Yet he couldn't stop thinking about how she might have found the courage to live if he had stayed by her side. Soon, these thoughts began to torture him, but he felt like there was no one he could share them with—no one to help him deal with the guilt he felt. Even if he'd been brave enough to talk to Neriti about his love for Tahissi, she was Tahissi's mother. And Axel was too scared that she might blame him for playing a role in her daughter's death.

Thus began a self-destructive period of Axel's life. He left his wife and his job as an assistant healer and took off on his own. He wandered across the Moon, trying to find meaning in what had happened. But he never could.

He thought often about joining Tahissi. His heart ached to see her again, to tell her he was sorry that he hadn't been there for her despite the rejection he'd suffered. He climbed mountains and slept out in the open, praying for some sort of divine revelation that would make him feel whole again. When nothing inside of him changed, though, Axel became angry. He screamed his fury into the wind and howled his pain into the velvety black sky. He hoped that if Tahissi were out there amongst the stars, she might hear him and know how sorry he was.

After a year of living alone, Axel decided to rejoin the pack. Neriti was grateful for his return, but not Ragher. Neriti had known all along about the rift between her children once Axel had confessed his love for Tahissi. But Neriti had kept Ragher in the dark, knowing how much it would upset him to find out that the lies they told had led to more heartbreak.

However, when Axel left the pack, Ragher nearly went mad with anger. He was outraged that his son had abandoned his wife and shirked his responsibilities as a healer. Ragher threatened to go after Axel and drag him back, but Neriti prevented him from doing so. She explained why Axel was so upset, hoping that Ragher would be able to see it from their son's point of view. But the truth only angered Ragher more. Once again, the lie he'd been cajoled into all those years earlier had come back to haunt them. He'd lost his daughter and grandchildren by not doing what he knew was right and facing the dark spirit. And now the big lie was threatening to ruin his son's life too.

Ragher pulled away from Neriti and began to spend more time on the Darkside, angry at her for not allowing him to sacrifice himself years earlier and angry at himself for not having stood up to her. He was also furious with Axel for not living up to the expectations he had. Because deep down inside, Ragher believed Axel was a better wolf than himself. And up until the moment that Axel abandoned the pack, Ragher had clung to this belief like it was a lifeboat full of redemption for all the lies he and Neriti had told.

From the beginning, Ragher had carefully crafted his relationship with Axel in an attempt to play a formative role in his son's life. Over and over again, he had told Axel that he would always be there for him and that there was nothing that could come between them. He had hoped it would be enough for his fatherless son to know he at least had one true friend in the world to confide in. But it had turned out that it *wasn't* enough because clearly Axel hadn't felt like he could talk to Ragher about his feelings for Tahissi.

Back in the dark passageway, Axel thought about how Ragher had treated him when he returned from his year away. For weeks, Ragher had avoided him and given him the cold shoulder until, finally, Axel confronted him. "Stop acting like you don't know me! If I've upset you, then tell me what I did! You're acting like a child!"

Ragher lashed out angrily, "I *don't* know you! Or at least you aren't the wolf I thought you were. You abandoned your wife and your practice. And for what? To take a vacation from your pain? You think you get a free pass because you had to deal with a secret heartbreak? What about Neriti and me? It wasn't easy for us either! But we didn't run off and ditch our responsibilities!"

Axel had known of course that it wasn't right to leave his wife the way he had, but he hadn't expected Ragher to be so upset with him about it. "You don't understand, Ragher. Something inside of me died with your sister, and I couldn't just pretend like it didn't. I needed time to figure out why."

"Yeah, I get it, Axel! You loved Tahissi. We all did. But you chose to let her death become an excuse for causing others pain. That's something I can never forgive. Instead of honoring Tahissi, you darkened her memory when you left everything behind. I thought I knew you better than that. I thought you *were* better than that."

For years those words had stung Axel. Even after he thought that Ragher had betrayed their kind, Axel continued to replay this conversation over in his mind. He'd let it drive him to do better and motivate him to be stronger. But now— now he saw Ragher's words in a different light. These hadn't been the words of a grieving brother who'd lost his only sister. They were the words of a grieving father who'd lost his only daughter. Except Ragher was *his* father too, and instead of trying to make amends for all the damage the lies had done to their family, Ragher had chosen to get his anger out by shaming his only son.

Finally, Axel could see that he'd slipped off the right path because he hadn't understood the true ramifications of his feelings and actions. The lies his parents had told had impacted their family to the point of ruin, and as he pondered this, Axel began to feel anger rising up inside of him from deep within, replacing his shame with rage.

Light trickled into the dark void. The edge of two ice walls turned towards Axel like a doorway opening up to him, welcoming him back into the memory labyrinth. The darkness faded, which should have been a cause for relief, but Axel had already become fixated on his newfound fury. It was time to face Ragher. It was time to seek revenge for the past.

CHAPTER 15

THE TAVERN

Bob sat in a booth at the back of John's tavern, holding a cold steak to the side of his face. Slowly, he was regaining his ability to function as a reasoning adult. For a while, he had been enjoying the relaxation that manifested at the height of his concussion. The short-lived moment had occurred right as Bob became reacquainted with his own existence but was still too injured to process what was going on in the world around him.

Cary sat across from Bob in the dark booth and sipped on his ale while tapping nervously on the metal fork in front of him. "Feeling any better?" he asked, noticing that the lights in his lawyer's eyes had turned back on.

Bob nodded his head but then suddenly became aware of the cold meat pressed to his face. He lowered it to the plate in front of him. "Yeah, I think I'm doing better," he replied. "How did we get here? I remember talking to some circus bears, and then…did one of them try to maul me?" Bob smiled to show Cary he was joking.

Cary smiled back. "Yeah, that guy, Rufus, really didn't care much for your face. In fact, I'm not sure any of those circus bears out there want to be friends with you. Sorry to have to be the one to break the news."

Bob took a sip from the pint of dark liquid he found sitting in front of him and laughed. "You didn't break the news. Rufus' fist did."

Cary chuckled, but then he became serious. "You know that was a bad decision you made, trying to talk to those guys, right? Didn't you recognize them after we got close?"

Bob looked embarrassed. "To be honest, it took me a minute. It's been a lot of years since the massacre. I think I've done my best to forget about it as much as possible. It was a horrible time for my wife and daughter, and I still feel guilty that I didn't do more to stop it."

"Do you think there's more you could've done?" Cary asked.

"Maybe," said Bob. "At least early on. Before things got out of control. We knew that many of the travelers were prejudiced towards the wolves. If I'd encouraged better relations between the two sides from the start, maybe it would've helped. I just never really thought that people's prejudices amounted to that much. It didn't dawn on me that there was real hate behind them. And I certainly never imagined that all the tension would come to a head due to the actions of my own sons. I knew the boys were mischievous—capable of serious vandalism, even—but I had no idea how truly deranged they were. Especially, Dan."

"You didn't want to see it," Cary stated bluntly with a knowing look. "It happens in families a lot. We overlook the flaws of the ones we love to make it easier to love 'em."

Bob nodded. "Yeah, I guess so. The irony is that I've seen what damage my silence has done, and yet I've continued to stay silent. By not standing up to Goodman in the beginning, I allowed him to take absolute control of New Waldoff. He told lies about me and degraded my character to the point of making me seem like a complete buffoon to anyone who would listen. And even worse, he set up a government that's completely dependent on his rule.

"It's why I wanted to go out there and meet people in the streets today. I thought maybe I could use my voice and your case to help take back the narrative Goodman's created and inspire a few of those groups to start questioning what's going on behind the scenes. I thought I might be able to help them see that Goodman's way of doing things isn't any better than Dale and Dan's."

Cary responded, "I don't think those people that showed up today are the ones you're going to reach. They seemed more interested in causing mayhem than talking all sensible like. But I have a question. What's the Prime Minister telling lies about you for? What good does it do him?"

Bob thought about it for a second and said, "Because when someone morally misguided, like Goodman, sees you as a threat, they'll try to defame you any way they can think of. They'll call you a loser, an idiot, and a traitor. They'll tell everyone you're out of touch. The examples they give might even contradict each other, but the kind of people who take part in this nonsense don't care. Like Goodman, they do it to distract from their own shortcomings and devious intentions.

"Dan and Dale did it with the wolves. They created falsehoods about them and turned the wolves into a common enemy for the travelers to unite against, with Dan and Dale leading the charge. In Goodman's case, he's made me the common enemy.

"Humans enjoy feeling like they're a part of a team. It's actually pretty frightening how simple it is to bring people together over something they hate. Nothing stirs emotions more than thinking you've joined a crusade against something you believe is wrong.

"In Dan and Dale's case, once they had their base, they

drew a line in the sand—it was them against the wolves. In most cases, once that line is drawn, it's impossible to reason with people. Emotion reigns supreme, and the choice is made a million times over to deride facts and knowledge in order to uphold your side's point of view. It's sort of insane to watch so many otherwise knowledgeable people look truth in the eye and spit at it because it doesn't correspond with the way they *want* things to be. But there you go."

Cary took a long drink of his ale. "So, why didn't you and Maude ever try to lead? You know, before the twins came to power?"

"Maude and I were never interested in being rulers despite the fact that we were encouraged to form a government and lead early on. Apparently, we were naïve. We wanted our anonymity as much as we could have it. But I see now that by not serving as leaders, we've continued to leave the doors wide open for the power hungry. At the very least we should have been out promoting leaders that we knew would be fair-minded.

"Of course, when it was my own family wreaking havoc, it became too personal, and I overlooked some important lessons. And now, because of that, it's all happening again."

Cary spoke softly, as if he were telling Bob a secret, "You know, me and my family were some of the folks poisoned by your sons."

Bob nodded. "I know," he said. "I'm sorry about that. From what I remember, your parents were some of the first to drink the poison. Is that right?"

Cary looked down at his ale. "Yeah, that's right. I knew it was a bad idea, but I couldn't stop 'em. They were so dang sure it was gonna solve all their problems."

Bob asked, "But if you knew it was a bad idea, then why did *you* decide to drink it?"

Cary shrugged. "Sometimes you get pulled into weird situations on account of your family. I know *you* can relate. After most of my friends and family drank the poison, life got pretty lonesome. Then once I saw that maniac, Dan…oh, sorry. No offense, Bob."

Bob flicked his hand to dismiss Cary's concern. "It's okay," he reassured him.

"Well, after Dan burned down our city, and everything I knew was gone, I figured I might as well join 'em. I guess I'm just the type of guy who goes wherever my people go. Metaphorically speaking, of course."

Bob took another big swig from his pint, rocking back and forth in his seat a little. "You know, Cary," he said in an almost jovial tone, "I can respect that. But if you ever feel like you're between a rock and a hard place again, Maude and I'd be happy to help you find a better solution. You just give us a buzz, alright?"

Cary smiled and said, "Thanks for the offer, Bob. But after what went down today, I suspect we might all be looking for a better solution soon. You and Maude too."

Right then, John called to Bob and Cary from the front windows of the tavern where he was assessing the scene outside. It was nearly dark, and when Bob turned, he saw that the gas street lanterns had already come on. "I'm opening the place up again, just so you know," said John. "But don't worry. The crowd has mostly died down. I promise I'm not feeding you to the wolves."

Bob flinched at the remark, which John noticed. "Oh, sorry. I forget not to use that expression anymore." Then John called to his son, Egan. "Go grab your brother and tell him it's time to serve again. You two can unlock the doors. But don't make a show of it. We aren't looking to drum up any business from the remainder of *this* lot."

John came and sat down next to Cary in the booth. In a

hushed tone he asked, "Speaking of wolves, Bob. Have you heard anything more from Axel's pack since he vanished?"

Bob shook his head. "No, but from your tone, I think you already know why."

John nodded. "Yup, Goodman hasn't exactly been friendly towards the wolves since taking over. I sure feel bad about the way they've been treated. We've made it pretty miserable for them since we got here. So much for having them help us get rid of Dan. We just went and replaced him with *a new* Dan."

Bob added, "We've made it more than miserable for the wolves, John! Hell, we almost exterminated them. I'm surprised they're still willing to come anywhere near us. If the shoe were on the other foot…Well, we know how that would go. Any excuse for violence. Isn't that right, ladies and gentley men of the jury?" Bob had begun to slur his words, and John reached for his drink to pull it away.

"I should probably not have given you the strong stuff after taking a hit like that, Bob. You might need a bit more time to recover before you go drinking again," said John.

Feeling emboldened by the blow to the head and the liquid courage coursing through him, Bob grabbed at the pint glass John was pulling away and chugged the last quarter of ale inside. Then he slammed the glass down on the table and declared, "You can't cut me off! I was a general! Who else here had the courage to lead an army against their own blood?"

"Take it easy there, Bob," said John, trying to calm his friend. "I don't think you want to go drawing any more attention to yourself today. Why don't you let Cary, here, walk you home?"

"Walk me home!? What do I look like? A child? Or a dog? That's what everyone thinks of me now that Goodman's had his say, isn't it? I bet they call me 'General Crybaby' and 'General Dog Brains' behind my back! What did they ever have to do that was so brave?! Hell! More than half of them can't even remember what happened because they were fried out of their gourds. By their own choosing, no less! Walking around that damned market like a pack of idiot zombies!"

Bob looked at Cary for a split second like he realized he might've offended him. But then he seemed to forget again and continued, "Where's *my* respect for serving all those years? And I don't just mean as general!" Bob's voice was growing louder as he spoke. "Where's Maude's recognition for working night and day to make this place better for everyone? Or for us having to give up our own daughter to protect you all? Huh!?" Bob banged his fist on the table but accidentally hit the side of the steak plate, which flew into the air with the steak before shattering on the floor.

"Great work, Bob! Look at what you've done now," John said as he bent over to pick up the raw steak and the plate shards.

Bob looked at Cary through squinted eyes. If he'd been able to see clearly, he might've noticed that Cary looked upset.

The young man said, "Maybe if you and Maude had spent more time keeping tabs on your own family, you wouldn't have had to sacrifice so much."

Bob suddenly sobered up a little. "What did you just say to me?" he asked in a dangerous tone.

Right at that moment, Maude walked through the doors of the tavern, and John looked up at her like she was an angel of mercy. "Oh, thank god you're here! Your tall mess of a man has had a terrible day, and now he's hell bent on making a mess of my tavern!"

Maude smiled. "Good to see you too, John. Why, hello there, Cary. I hear you boys had a busy day." Cary gave Maude a half-smile and nod, though he still looked sore from before.

Maude addressed John, "I was told you're getting a delicious shipment of lamb any day now. When can we expect you to make your famous stew?"

"Aww, yes. You heard right. I bet you it will be ready by tomorrow evening if you'd like to stop by for a bowl."

Bob flung his head to look up at Maude and John who were standing face-to-face. "What in the heavens are you two talking about!? Maude! Are you having an affair with John?" Bob asked incredulously.

Maude burst out laughing. "No, my dear. But I can see now that John was right about you. You do look quite the mess," she said, looking down at his bruised face and dirt-stained suit. "Can I take you home, darling? I think you may have had all the fun you can stand for one day. You may look like you're twenty-something, but you know you have the soul of an octogenarian."

Bob smiled at his wife goofily and said, "You may look like an octo-jerry-airy-in, but you're is just as beautiful as the first day we met!"

Maude laughed. "I think that was meant to be sweet. A bit garbled, but sweet. Let's go, my love, before you get too tired to walk home on those clodhopper feet of yours." Then to John she said, "Help me get him up, will you?"

"Of course, Maude. I already lifted the devil once today. Move aside, and I'll get him for you." John scooted the table out of the booth and grabbed ahold of Bob under his shoulders, hoisting him to his feet with a firm grip. Bob looked a bit wobbly, but Maude was ready with a glass of cold water which she threw in his face.

"Hey! What'd you do that for?" he asked, shaking his head like a wet dog.

"Are you awake yet? Can we go home now?" Maude asked seriously.

Bob looked at her and grinned. "Only if you carry me."

"Ha! Looks like he's staying with you tonight, John!"

John laughed. "I appreciate the offer, Maude, but Bob's not the kind of company I prefer to keep in the wee hours."

"Well, suit yourself," Maude said playfully. Then to Bob, she said, "I guess you're coming with me, after all." Slowly, the two began to walk towards the doors, hand-in-hand.

With her other hand, Maude turned and waved to Cary and John. "Thanks for watching him today, gentlemen!"

John waved back. "Be careful going home, you two! Will I see you back here tomorrow night for some stew?"

Maude nodded. "That sounds lovely, John. Goodnight!" Then she and Bob made their way out of the tavern.

"What was all that business about stew?" Bob asked after sobering up on their walk home. He and Maude were sitting on their living room sofa, taking off their shoes.

"There's going to be a get together tomorrow night at John's place above the tavern. I think the old band is looking to play some new music."

Bob frowned. "Maude, I'm feeling too old and beaten down to make sense of what you're saying. Can't you just tell me what's going on?"

Maude leaned over to Bob and stared at the scrapes and bruises on his face. "I'm sorry, dear. That awful man really did a number on you. I think you better let me put some ointment on those scratches before you lay down for the night."

Bob grabbed Maude lovingly around the waist. "Not until you explain about the stew. You're starting to worry me."

Maude looked nervous. She leaned away from him and glanced around the apartment, as though she expected to see someone standing there listening to them. Quietly, she said, "A friend came by to visit during all the chaos today. There's talk that something big is about to happen. So, a few of the folks from the old crew are getting together to discuss the matter."

Bob looked around the same way his wife had just done and then asked loudly, "Do you think our place is bugged?"

Maude stared at Bob like she couldn't believe how obtuse he was being. "Of course not!" she exclaimed, though her expression said otherwise.

"So, I take it we're talking about the same crew from the old days in the market?" Bob asked.

Maude sighed but nodded. She realized her effort to speak in code had been pointless.

"Goodman was part of that crew, you know?"

Maude scowled. "Well, he's not part of it now. I can promise you that! You know, I was really worried about you today, Bob. I didn't know what that mob was going to do."

"How did you find out about it?" Bob asked.

"I told you already. A friend stopped by."

"Okay," said Bob, clearly annoyed that Maude was still acting mysterious.

"You should go to bed soon," Maude told him. "You remember you have to go to the Sheep Spa in the morning?"

Bob hung his head and groaned. "No, but that's the upside of having sustained head trauma, right? You get a free pass to forget whatever you want?"

Maude looked at him sternly. "You really want to tell the council you can't go? After what happened today in that courtroom?"

Bob pushed back. "You act like I had something to do with that, Maude! I was just doing my job."

"Oh, really? Was it your job to tell John to 'rally the troops?'" she asked. "Didn't you realize that the other side was going to figure out what you were doing? You know there aren't any secrets in this town. There weren't any secrets in Waldoff either for god's sake! And *that* city wasn't even built for the purpose of spying on its citizens, like this one!"

Now it was Bob's turn to look nervous. He hated fighting with Maude, but even worse than fighting with her was thinking that she might be in some kind of danger. With all her talk of spying and code speak, it was finally beginning to dawn on him that their place might *actually* be bugged. Bob already knew he had a bullseye on his own back when it came to Goodman, but he worried that if Goodman had people spying on them, then Maude might become a target too.

"I'm sorry, Maude. I didn't mean to frighten you today. I just wanted to try something different like we discussed. I'm tired of being pushed around all the time. I mean, I've been doing all I can to help people my entire life for god's sake! But by the way some people treat me, you'd think I was a villain!" he exclaimed.

Maude leaned over and wrapped her arms around him tightly. "I know, darling. I know. The problem isn't you, though. It's that a lot of these people don't really seem to know what's good for them. They support the leader who talks the loudest, not the one with the most sensibility. Anyway, we can discuss it more at the meeting tomorrow night. You know we're not the only ones who feel this way."

"Yeah, I know," Bob replied. "I'll get up early and head to the spa. Hopefully, I can finish with Dale fast enough to make it back in time for some stew."

Bob leaned back on the sofa and pulled Maude with him. They began to kiss. A second later, he leaned his head away and said with a mischievous smile, "Hey, I've got an idea. Let's *really* give those bugs something to listen to." Then, he wrapped his arms around Maude tightly and began to kiss her neck as she melted into him and let out a blissful sigh.

CHAPTER 16

BY THE SEA

"Tick, tick, tick." Mina listened to the classroom clock counting off the seconds until it was time to go home. It was her junior year of high school and her second year on her own. Her classes had become an escape from the harsh reality of her life. During the last two years, Mina had spent as much time as she could at school—going in early and staying late. The library was her sanctuary, a place where she went to be physically close to others without feeling the pressure to talk to them. After all, there was barely anything Mina could discuss about her life without having to lie.

On the weekends, when school was closed, she walked across town to the public library. She brought Bonkers along, towing him in her little, red wagon. Mina left Bonkers tied to an old oak tree next to the library while she checked out books. However, she always hurried back to him with her arms full of stories that she then proceeded to read aloud.

Bonkers enjoyed this part of their outing the most. He lay by Mina's side, resting his head in her lap as she leaned against the large oak. Then he'd fall asleep with his best friend's voice gently flowing through his long ears. In the evenings, as dusk settled in, Mina would steer Bonkers home with all their newly borrowed books stacked around him inside the wagon.

"Tick, tick, tick." Mina looked at the clock as she fought back tears. The last couple of years, she had stared at the classroom clocks, willing time to move slower. But not today. Today, she had to run home to Bonkers the second the bell rang, just like she had done every school day for the last several weeks.

Bonkers had begun to show serious signs of old age and had grown weaker and more detached from Mina over the last month. All the white hairs that had slowly snuck their way into his black and tan fur had been a warning sign that Mina refused to acknowledge. Part of her had hoped that if she ignored the obvious signs that Bonkers was aging, then it would stop being true. And she wouldn't have to face losing someone else she loved. But Mina understood it was more than just the thought of losing someone else, for even if her grandfather had been alive, or her parents had been around, Mina knew in her heart it wouldn't have made any difference. Nothing would ever make it easier to accept the thought of losing her best friend, the sweet, hairy angel who'd watched over her since she was born, in the form of a sausage-shaped hound dog.

Before she left Bonkers that morning, Mina had tried to feed him his breakfast, but he wasn't interested in food. He had barely eaten over the course of the last week. When she'd said goodbye to him, he'd been lying on her bed. She had leaned over him and kissed the top of his head softly, but he didn't move except to angle his big brown eyes towards her.

She knew that none of this was good, but she had told herself he just needed to rest and would be better when she returned that afternoon. She kissed the top of his nose, caressed his ears, and then slowly made her way out the door. All day, she'd tried to stay positive, tried to push away the thought that she'd possibly left her best friend alone to die. But the more she fought it, the worse it got.

She considered trying to sneak off campus, but it would've been incredibly risky. If she got caught, she'd be sent to the principal. And if she were sent to the principal, her parents would be contacted. Except that the school wouldn't be able to get in touch with them. The only communication Mina had received from her mom and dad in several months was an e-mail telling her they were going to be away for at least another year.

Mina couldn't let the school find that out, though. She just had to keep her secret one more year until she turned eighteen and graduated from high school. Then she would be allowed to live on her own without having to worry about being sent away to foster care. She had to be careful so she could graduate, go to college, and learn every single thing about space, the universe, physics, and how it all fit together. She had to discover a way to get in touch with her friends on the Moon and find out if there were any answers up there about the things her grandfather had told her.

She had already looked for answers down on Earth but had come up short. After her parents were gone for a while, Mina worked up the courage to tear the cottage apart. She searched for evidence that her mom and dad had once had any sort of life before she was born. She had waited a while to begin the search because part of her was scared to know the truth. But after only hearing from her parents every few months via e-mail, Mina's hurt and anger grew so strong that she decided she had to know. Their total disinterest in her life had basically confirmed her suspicions anyway.

Mina had emptied every closet, drawer, nook, and cranny, looking for the albums her mother had told her about, or any old photos or documents that might corroborate her parents' version of the truth. She found nothing, though. The only pictures that existed were the ones she and her family had taken together over the years.

Mina thought it was crazy that her grandfather's tale might be true, but she came to accept it as a partial truth, at least. More true than false. She just couldn't be sure which parts were true.

She'd come to suspect, however, that the truth was somehow connected to her lunar journey. If her real mother was as powerful as her grandfather—or father—had said, then Mina thought this might be the reason she'd been chosen to help save the Moon Travelers years earlier.

There was another part of her grandfather's story that she had thought a lot about too. Papa had said her mother was outraged when Mina was sent home from the Moon and that she still had some role to play there. But if that were true, then why had nobody realized it? From everything Mina had understood about what happened to her and Helen, it was essentially the Moon's own god, *Theia*, who'd been calling the shots. So, why hadn't Theia prevented her from going home? Unless Theia wasn't that powerful—or wasn't really in charge.

The bell rang, and Mina jumped in her seat. A couple of girls sitting behind her laughed, but she ignored them. She grabbed her things and started to head for the door when one of the mean girls whispered loudly so that everyone could hear, "Look, the book-slug is slithering off to the library again!"

Mina paused in the doorway for a second and said, "It's bookworm, Valerie. You'd know that if your IQ were higher than a slug's." Several people in the class laughed at Mina's comment, but she didn't care. Normally, she ignored her class-mates' ridicule, but today she felt too on edge to tolerate anything. Her heart ached too badly for her ailing pup.

Mina took off across the hall, down the stairs, and out of the building. The sky was dark and cloudy, and the wind had a frosty chill that was unusual for the time of year. "Good," Mina thought. "The cold will make it easier to jog home."

She headed for the trail system in the woods behind her school. Here, a thinner trail broke off from the main one before curving around several large hills. At the third hill, an even narrower path split from the curved trail, and this path led down the hill to the gravelly clearing near her cottage. Mina was certain that she and her grandfather had created the narrow path by walking from the cottage up to the trail system so many times over the years.

As Mina worked her way around the first hill, rain began trickling down, gently filtering through the forest's foliage before completing its journey. The wet drops tickled her skin as they rolled down her arms and face. A clap of thunder roared overhead just as Mina made it to the second hill. It was getting harder to see, which meant the storm was gaining strength. The rain fell faster, and black clouds took the place of gray ones, nearly blocking out all the light.

The forest came alive in a symphony of tapping as the rain pelted everything in sight. Mina ran faster, but the rocks and dirt had become so slick that she found it hard to keep her footing. A bright blue flash of lightning exploded above the trees. Out of the corner of her eye, she saw a child scurrying up the hill. She turned her head. But the lightning had already faded, and it was impossible to see through the dark shadows.

"It was probably just a baby deer chasing after its mother," she told herself as she pressed on. Her long, black hair and uniform were soaked, and she had to fight the urge to shiver. She imagined the toasty, warm fire that she and Bonkers would sit in front of once she got home.

Mina had finally reached the far side of the second hill when lightning struck again. For a brief moment, the forest was bathed in light, and during that split-second, Mina spotted something along the trail she'd never seen before. It was a wooden sign nailed to one of the trees, with the words "Steady yourself!" carved into it.

"Okay," thought Mina. "I suppose that's sound advice to someone hiking through a hilly forest." She kept walking, not allowing the sign to distract her from her need to get home safely to Bonkers. She'd almost made it to the beginning of the third hill when another bolt of lightning illuminated the woods around her in bluish white light. The quick spark revealed a second sign nailed to a tree directly across from Mina's face. "Ready yourself!" it declared.

The rolling sound of thunder shook the ground beneath her feet. "Alright, that's a bit weirder," she thought anxiously, but she began to search for a simple explanation. "I'm sure it's just the work of a hippie outdoorsman who wants to offer words of encouragement to the hikers who pass by."

But Mina didn't really believe that. The tingle of electricity in the air had given her goose bumps, and her stomach felt tense with fear. She wanted to sprint home, but she had the sense that she was being watched. Maybe even stalked.

She forced herself to continue walking at the same brisk pace, even though the adrenaline coursing through her had made her legs stiff and her posture awkward. "Please no more lightning. Please no more lightning," she thought over and over as she pushed herself further along the trail.

She reached the spot where a narrow pathway split off down the hill, leading towards her cottage. As she turned to face the path, the forest lit up in brilliant blue light. And that's when she saw it. At the bottom of the hill, right before the clearing, was another tree with a sign attached to it. She held her breath and walked slowly towards it. When she was close enough, she read, "And meet us by the sea!"

CRACK! A lightning bolt struck a tree just a few feet away, splitting it down the middle. Embers of dead wood sprayed towards her, and Mina dashed out of the forest and into the clearing as fast as she could. She picked up the gravel path that led home, but just as she did, another bolt of lightning ripped through the sky. Out of the corner of her eye, she saw the electric blue outline of a man and a dog walking side-by-side.

Mina didn't bother to look closer; she needed to get home fast. She ran to the back of the cottage, but when she reached the door, her heart sank. It was wide open. The light hanging over the kitchen table flickered as it swayed back and forth in the wind. She wasn't sure what to do. She knew it wasn't smart to enter the house when there might be an intruder inside, but she worried that Bonkers was alone and scared. "Did you lock the door this morning or not? Come on, Mina! Think!" she yelled in her head.

Finally, she decided she didn't care. The only thing that mattered was Bonkers. Mina ran through the house, staying fully alert in case someone was waiting to jump out at her. But once she had checked behind every door and inside every closet, she began to relax. She went back to her bedroom to look for Bonkers, who she was sure would be snoozing under his favorite comforter, but when she pulled back the covers, he wasn't there. The sight of the empty bed made Mina feel uneasy. Bonkers had been in such poor shape when she'd left him that it didn't make any sense for him to have wandered off.

She strode through every room and searched every bed, couch cushion, and chair in her tiny house. "Bonkers! Where are you?" she called. She began to worry that when the back-door had flown open, he had gotten scared and hidden from the storm. She looked again in all the closets, behind every door, and under every surface in the house. But her search came up empty. He wasn't anywhere. Mina tried to figure out what could've happened. Bonkers had been so sickly. She didn't think it was possible he could've left the house. She ran back out in the storm. The wind was howling, but the lightning and thunder had died down a little. She looked up and saw a long blanket of dark clouds gliding overhead towards the ocean.

She roamed around the overgrown yard calling for Bonkers. She checked under every bush that surrounded the cottage and investigated every low spot in the grass to see if her sweet friend had come to lie down outside. A flash of light shimmered by the tall trees that stood above the shore. A beam of sunlight had broken through the dark clouds, like a shining finger that was pointing her towards the sea. Mina ignored it. She wasn't ready to accept the supernatural events that seemed to be occurring all around her. To do so was to admit that her dear friend might have truly vanished from the face of the planet.

"BONKERS!" Mina shouted with her hands cupped around her mouth. She listened for a response, but all she heard was a faint coo from a mourning dove. Mina stood in the grass and cried as the dark clouds drifted away, and the sea air blew into the clearing. The sun shone in the clear sky above her, and the flowers, grass, and leaves sparkled vibrantly in the crisp, clean air.

In her heart, Mina knew what she had to do. But doing it was another story. "When you're ready, come and meet us by the sea."

Mina had dreamt of the sea repeatedly during the last several years, but in real life, she hadn't gone anywhere near it since returning from the Moon. The trauma she'd experienced during the tsunami still haunted her. In all of her dreams, a giant wave came to take her away. This wasn't just a nightmare, though. It was a memory. Throughout her early youth, she'd spent much of her time along the water's edge, but it was no longer somewhere she felt safe to go.

She thought of her dream and finding Bonkers' leash in the water. The idea of him being swallowed by the sea was terrifying, but it was also exactly what she needed to build up her courage. If there was any chance that Bonkers might be down there, she was going to go find him. Mina ran back into the kitchen and grabbed at the hook next to the doorframe for Bonkers' leash. But it was gone.

"Of course," she thought sarcastically. She tried to remember if she'd left the leash somewhere else, but she almost never used it. When Bonkers had still been able to walk, she had let him wander the yard freely, sniffing for rabbits in the tall grass.

She ran to check the little, red wagon in the shed, but the leash wasn't there either. "No more stalling," Mina thought. She was certain she could figure out a way to bring Bonkers home with or without the leash. She ran for the trees with her stomach twisting into tighter knots the closer she got. When she reached the clifftop above the sea, she stopped. It was the first time seeing her favorite childhood spot in nearly four years. It looked smaller than she remembered, and sadder too.

Mina surveyed the beach for any sign of her short, furry friend. The dark clouds had moved out over the water, and yellow flashes of lightning threatened the sea from above. She made her way down the battered dunes while looking off into the distance along the beach. But once she reached the shore, she couldn't take her eyes off the water. She worried what might happen if she did.

Choppy waves rushed towards the shore, and Mina stared into the hypnotic ocean. "There's nothing down here except dark waves and sand," she thought. And suddenly something inside of her broke.

"GIVE HIM BACK!" she screamed at the water and the clouds. "He may be old and dying, but he's mine! You had no right to take him! He's mine! HE'S MINE!"

She threw her arms into the air, and the waves grew calm. A cool gust of wind blew against her face. Mina fell to her knees and lowered her head as a beam of light dropped from the clouds. She gazed out across the water and saw the giant ray. It appeared as a spinning cylinder of silver and gold droplets, and in its center, two figures began to form out of the mist and spray.

Mina's heart leapt. "Papa! Bonkers!" she shouted. The fluid-like bodies of her grandfather and Bonkers stared at her from inside the bright, spinning tube. She jumped to her feet and stepped into the waves. But as her feet touched the water, the cylinder vanished, and Mina was left alone by the sea.

CHAPTER 17

THE ANIMALS AND DALE

The morning after Cary's trial, Bob rented a horse and arrived at the Sheep Spa just before lunch. The Sheep Spa looked the same as it always did. It was a sterile, metal building that would've blended in well with the old, abandoned factories Bob had seen decades ago, back on Earth.

He rode to the side of the building to the animals' enclosure. The animals were out of their pen, huddled lifelessly around the scraggily bushes that some of them normally fed off of. When he reached the fence, he dismounted his horse and tied him to a post. A tall fellow came to greet him. "You here to visit Dale?" the man asked.

"Yep, the council sent me. Are you new here?" Bob asked the man.

The man nodded. "Yeah, the council hired new guards last week. I'm surprised they didn't tell you. Or maybe not, right?" the man chuckled in a friendly way, but Bob thought the comment might have been a dig.

Bob asked, "You mind if I poke around? Take a look at the animals for a while?"

The man shrugged. "Suit yourself. Not like the prisoner has anything better to do. You're his only visitor today."

Bob wondered if the guard was being funny. Dale wasn't allowed to have any visitors except for him and Maude. However, he decided to sort it out later. First, he wanted to find out what was making the animals sick.

Bob walked along the outside of the spa to see if he could spot a hole or a crack where Dale had gained access to the livestock. When his search turned up nothing, he went to evaluate the animals. Some looked sickly while others appeared perfectly healthy, though he noticed that none of them were eating.

He walked up to one of the horses and looked at both of its eyes. They seemed glassy and despondent, although Bob knew that was just the way horses looked sometimes. He did the same with a couple of the cows and sheep and a few more horses. When he was examining his fourth horse, he heard a raspy voice call to him from behind. "Baa! You won't figure out anything by looking at their eyes!"

Then another voice began to speak before Bob had a chance to turn around. "Baa! No! No! You aren't looking in the right spot. You're only supposed to check their eyes when they've got a cold or a bad case of death!"

Bob knew right away it was the three-headed sheep, the Spa's infamous mascot, so to speak. When his kids were young, he'd taken them to play with the sheep. At the time he had thought it was a fun idea, like going to the circus or the petting zoo. But once he'd learned how disturbed the sheep were—after hearing them tell Helen a story about watching the rotting corpse of a rabbit for days on end—he realized that maybe it hadn't been so wise to treat the sheep like a kiddy attraction.

Bob turned to face the sheep, waiting for the third one to

take his turn. The sheep blinked at Bob, and Bob stared back. Finally, Bob asked, "Have any of—"

But it turned out the third sheep had just been waiting for a chance to interrupt Bob. He exclaimed, "Go around to the animals' rears and check their other side! The rump is the place to look when they stop eating. Every doctor knows that!"

Bob sighed. "Thank you," he said. "But I'm still, to this day, not a doctor. Remember? We settled the matter years ago when you had me examine that festering boil on your back?"

The first sheep looked aghast and craned his neck to look at his backside. "I see no signs of a festering boil!"

Bob tried to interrupt the second sheep's turn despite knowing better, "I *just* said it was years—"

The second sheep spoke over Bob. "*Boils* are for asses! Why, we've never had a festering boil in our lives! And as you're no doctor, you shouldn't be speaking with such familiarity about our injuries. Real or otherwise!"

The third sheep nodded and said, "Yep, I remember when you popped that thing. I had never seen so much pus before! It oozed for days! Yet as I recall, you got real sick afterwards. A good doctor doesn't lose his lunch after treating a patient. Anyhow, what have you been up to lately, doc?"

The first two sheep glared at the third with their usual expressions of disapproval.

"Well, I'm still not a doctor, mind you, but I've been asked to come and take a look at the animals to see if I can deduce the cause of their ailment. Have any of you been feeling sick lately?"

The first sheep scoffed. "So, you've become some kind of *doctor detective?* Well, I suppose everyone has to do something. The case should be easy enough for you to solve if you have even half a brain."

The second sheep spoke next, "I thought you were mostly

worthless before, but this takes the cake! You haven't even begun looking for clues in the right place. I'd say you should stick to treating patients, but you aren't any good at that either. Hrmph!"

The third sheep said, "It's too late, anyway. We already solved the case. It was the bad man in the factory. He's the one who told the animals to eat the rotten hay. Whispered it to them from behind the wall, he did."

"Hmm," said Bob. "I suspected as much, although I still don't know how in the world he managed to take out the soundproofing in his cell."

The first sheep reacted. "Some crime-solving doctor you are!"

Then the second sheep scolded, "I bet you don't even know the cure for sour hay stomach!"

The third sheep, however, explained what Dale had done. "After the animals got sick, the bad man told them to sneak drinks from the barrel marked 'non-potable water.' He told them it would cure their stomach pains and convinced them it's where the guards hide the medicine. He's a monster, you know? Say, are you the kind of doctor who prescribes executions?"

Bob couldn't help but smile. He'd forgotten how direct the third sheep could be. He found it somewhat charming, but he knew he needed to finish up what he'd come for so he could return to the city in time to meet his friends at John's. "Thank you for your help. I'll take what you've said into consideration and make sure that the bad man in the factory can't hurt the animals anymore. The three of you take care."

The first sheep replied, "Always a pleasure, doc."

The second sheep rolled its eyes and grumbled, "If you even *are* a doctor."

Right before the third sheep took his turn, Bob was able to reply, "I'm not a doctor!"

The third sheep asked, "What do you do for a living then if you aren't a doctor anymore?"

Bob answered, "I became a lawyer a few years back."

The three sheep stared at Bob for a while until finally the third sheep let out a shudder, which seemed to break their spell. Bob backed away, and when it didn't seem like they were going to try and stop him, he turned and began walking briskly towards the factory's side entrance. From over his shoulder, though, he heard the sheep talking loudly amongst themselves.

"Why would he become a lawyer if he was already a doctor?" the first sheep asked.

The second one commented, "Maybe he was tired of doing a piss poor job of saving lives and decided to fully commit to ruining them."

"No. No," the third sheep said. "You both have it wrong, like usual! He's not any of those things he claimed to be. I don't think *he* even knows what he is!"

Bob smiled. "Well, he's not entirely wrong about that," he thought as he entered the factory through the guards' gate. The tall guard who'd greeted him earlier patted him down before escorting him past two more checkpoints. Bob wondered why the council, or likely Goodman, had decided to get rid of the old guards and appoint so many new ones. It wasn't like Dale was some major threat. But then it dawned on him—maybe Goodman did see Dale as a threat. Bob had to admit the thought was concerning, since it most likely meant Goodman had reached the paranoia phase of his authoritarianism.

"I see they sent the lesser of two evils," said Dale as Bob walked through a sliding barn door that led to the tiny visiting area in front of Dale's cell. Bob looked disapprovingly at his gray-haired son, but Dale laughed. "I tease," he said. "It's good to see you, father. Sorry I don't visit more often. I've been busy, you see."

"Yes, it seems you've been *very* busy, Dale, though I can't quite figure out how you managed to pull it off."

"Pull what off?" asked Dale.

"Oh, come now. The three-headed sheep have already filled me in about the 'bad man in the factory.' What I can't decide is how you did away with some of the sound proofing in your cell without anyone noticing."

"Ah, I see. Well, what's a magician without his tricks?" Dale laughed.

Bob scolded him in a serious tone, "Leave the animals alone, Dale."

"Geez! Am I not allowed to converse with *anyone*?"

"No! That wasn't part of the deal you made with your mother. We had our reasons for putting you in a soundproofed cell, and you've proved to us that we made the right choice."

"Oh, I see. Well, I'm not terribly interested in the animals, anyway. They're just a bit of entertainment from time to time," said Dale.

"I'm sure. So, then you won't mind it if we relocate them somewhere away from the Sheep Spa?"

"Nope, not one bit. If anything, you're doing me a favor. I've been trying to get that three-headed sheep to stop talking to me for the longest time. He never shuts up. Sometimes, it even seems like he's talking to nobody at all."

"It's three sheep, Dale—three heads attached to one body. But good. I'm glad that's all settled. Goodbye," Bob said as he began to leave.

"Wait!" called Dale. "Don't you want to spend a few more minutes with your only living son? Well, only living *child*, come to think of it. Hmm?" he asked sweetly.

Bob snickered. "Spend a few more minutes listening while you try and fill my head with your nonsense? No, thank you. Goodbye," he said again as he walked through the sliding barn door.

"I've been thinking, Dad!" Dale called out louder than was necessary, clearly trying to keep his father's attention.

"Never too late to start, Son!" Bob said dismissively while continuing on his way.

"I have some information about Dan that I think could be relevant to what's going on in New Waldoff. I've *heard* things. One of your officers has taken control of the city, right?"

Bob stopped. The last thing he wanted was to get dragged into a conversation with Dale. He knew how manipulative his son could be, and he wasn't interested in being made into a fool by taking Dale's bait.

"Who told you that?" Bob asked, testing Dale to see how willing he was to give up his information. They both knew he wasn't supposed to be having conversations with the guards, but there was no one else around to pass him information.

"You're not the only person who visits me," divulged Dale.

"So, you're telling me you've had other visitors?" Bob asked in disbelief as he walked back towards the cell. "You're not supposed to have other visitors, Dale!"

"Tell that to the guards, then," said Dale, shrugging his shoulders.

"They're already supposed to know that!" Bob yelled, looking over his shoulder at the guard station on the other side of the door.

Dale laughed. "Don't get so worked up. You know you're about a million years old, right? That old ticker can't last forever." Then he narrowed his eyes at Bob's chest. "At least, I doubt it," he said.

Bob ignored Dale. He was extremely upset that his son had been receiving unauthorized visitors, and he hadn't made up his mind about what to do next.

Dale kept talking. "I'm sure the old guards knew about the 'no visitors rule,'" he said. "But I don't think these new ones got the memo. And certainly, you can't blame me for not being the one to spill the beans. But now you've been informed, so there you go." Dale finished his explanation by pretending to tip his imaginary hat to his father—making a show out of his good-natured intentions.

Bob was still angry. "But who in the world would visit *you?*" he asked.

Dale looked hurt, though it was hard to tell whether it was a put-on. "I have friends," he said defensively.

"Who?" Bob asked. "You tried to poison every last Moon Traveler. So, who's left?"

The gray-haired, heavily-jowled Dale stared at his father with a blank expression. But Bob noticed a faint twinkle in his son's eye, and instantly he knew. "Oh my god! I'd almost forgotten about that little she-goblin. She's still around, huh? I'm shocked I haven't seen her in the courtroom yet."

"Betsy keeps a low profile," Dale explained. "She knows what people think of her."

"That she's a lunatic? That she looks like what might happen if a bat swallowed a bag of grapefruits—and has since the day she was left on our doorstep?"

"Tsk. Tsk, father. I never knew looks mattered so much to you. What would mother say?"

Bob shook his head. "You don't seem to appreciate the oddness of that woman, Dale. First of all, nobody even knows where she came from, and she doesn't *look* human. Not to mention the fact that even when she was little, she was nuts, which I assume is why she made such a terrific playmate for you and your brother."

Bob lowered his voice and locked eyes with his son. "But in all seriousness, Dale. There are very few things in this world that have made me question our reality, but *her* existence is one of them."

"I'm sure she'd be pleased to hear that," said Dale with a

smirk. "Anyway, would you like to know what I have to say, now?"

Bob hesitated. The truth was he did actually want to hear what Dale had to say, but it made him nervous too. Dale had been given years to sit and strategize his next move, and Bob didn't want to risk becoming Dale's pawn.

"Fine, Dale," he said, giving in. "But keep it short. You've already taken up enough of my day, and I have more pressing matters to attend to."

Dale looked amused. "I take it you mean all your court cases. Interesting how concerned you are that I'm going to be the one to pull the wool over your eyes when it's obvious some-one's already beaten me to it. Wouldn't you say?"

Bob frowned. "What are you talking about?"

"You've been turned into a stooge. Don't you see? That general of yours—"

"Lieutenant general," Bob corrected him.

This made Dale laugh. "Oh, right. 'Lieutenant general.' But shouldn't we really be addressing him as 'His Grace, Our Supreme Leader, The Prime Minister?' That's his actual title now, right?"

Dale had touched a nerve, and Bob didn't like where any of it was going. "I told you to keep it short, Dale," he chided.

"Fine. How about we try this on for size? Haven't you and Maude wondered why this Goodman fellow took over so quickly? I mean, the cannons you fired at Black Ice Fort had barely cooled before he waltzed in and declared himself top dog with the help of his army buddies. And now you're all just going along with it. *Again*."

"We're not going along with it. We just haven't figured out a plan to counter him yet. You might be surprised how many people support him despite having lived through the nightmare of being drugged, imprisoned, and nearly annihilated by you and your brother. Though, I guess by comparison, Goodman's ways don't seem so bad."

"Until they are," said Dale. "What do you think will happen when Goodman decides he wants to take all the attractive women as his concubines? Or make an army out of the town's children? Or create a class system based on which of his citizens are most loyal to him?"

"We aren't going to let it go that far," Bob objected.

Dale smiled tauntingly. "Really? You did last time."

"We learned our lesson," said Bob firmly.

"I sincerely doubt that, or you would have already stopped him. The two of you let him build a whole city! And now that it's gotten this far, I'd be surprised if it didn't take a lot more than a few silly cannons and some underground resistance to put a stop to it. What you don't understand is that the thing that controls him is *counting* on you to do exactly what you're doing. To dilly-dally around for a while, just like last time. It's studied your every move and has become stronger from the knowledge it's gained."

"'It?' You sound nuts, Dale. Is this Betsy's influence on you?"

"As a matter of fact, Betsy has helped me come to some important realizations. In case you didn't know, she's Goodman's private secretary now. I imagine it's the real reason she's allowed to come and go as she pleases here."

"I don't believe it! Betsy's working for Goodman? What is she? An autocrat groupie?" Bob turned away from Dale in frustration.

Dale replied, "Maybe, but that's not the point. Betsy hears Goodman talking to himself. *A lot.*"

"So? I'm sure he has a lot on his mind these days," said Bob.

"You know who else used to talk to themselves a lot?" asked Dale.

"You?" replied Bob

"No, not me. *Dan.*"

Bob looked back around at his son. "Are you seriously trying to tie your brother to Goodman based on the fact that Dan had a penchant for talking to himself? Lots of people talk to themselves, Dale. Your mother and I do it. So did Helen. Maybe thinking out loud just runs in the family."

"No. Not like this. Dan wasn't just 'thinking out loud.' I would overhear him having entire conversations with someone who wasn't there. I finally asked him about it one time, and he told me he'd always sensed he wasn't alone. I reminded him that he had me, so for the most part, that was true. But he told me it was different than that. He thought he had an angel, or something like it, that followed him around, putting ideas in his head. He said it didn't talk to him but that he could feel it guiding him—that he could feel its thoughts. Dan believed it meant he'd been chosen. That he was special.

"I thought he was crazy. I told him if he didn't knock it off, I would tell you and Maude so you could figure out what was wrong with him. He stopped after that, and I assumed he'd given it up. But later when I went to live with him at the fort, I heard him doing it again behind closed doors. At first, I thought he was talking to that wolf he kept around, but then I'd see the wolf somewhere else, and I knew. I doubt Dan ever stopped talking to it. Whatever *it* is."

Bob had grown even more serious. "Dale, what are you trying to pull here? I get it that you want me to believe this ghost story you're spinning. But why? What does it get you?"

Dale walked all the way up to his cell door and grabbed onto the bars. "Think about it! I don't know this man Goodman from any of those other Moon traveling losers, but I know he chose to be on *your* side last time. You even made him one of your top officers. Why would you have done that if he was such a traitorous jackass?"

Bob snapped, "Watch it, Dale."

Dale laughed. "See! You're even sticking up for him still! After all of this! *Why?*"

"Fine," Bob conceded. "You're right. Goodman was a good soldier and a great officer. I never would have thought he'd be capable of all this."

Dale smiled with satisfaction. "Exactly! He probably wasn't capable of it before. Betsy told me he spends all day in his office. Talking. To nobody. Whatever this thing is that had ahold of Dan's ear has moved on to Goodman."

Bob didn't say anything. He had to think it over for a minute. Dale's theory that some dark angel had been controlling Dan and now Goodman seemed preposterous, yet Bob still didn't know why Dale would be making it up.

"Even if this were true, and I'm not saying it is, I don't understand why it would matter to you. It doesn't change anything in your world. You're never leaving this cell again. You understand that, don't you? That you're going to spend the rest of your life in prison?"

Dale nodded but added, "Betsy has heard some of the things that Goodman's talked about when he's by himself. She thinks he's planning a way to get rid of you and Maude—for good."

Bob shook his head. "No way! Goodman isn't stupid enough to kill us. We may not have the support of the whole city behind us, but we still have plenty of friends, not to mention all the people we've helped over the years. He knows he can't get away with 'offing' his citizens for no reason."

"Right, which is why he would make it look like an accident," Dale said soberly.

For a second, Bob stared at him, like he was trying to solve a puzzle. "You still haven't told me why this matters to you, Dale. And don't try telling me you've developed a soft spot for your dear old mom and dad after all these years. I'm not buying that."

Dale shook his head. "Think about it, Bob. If Goodman gets rid of you two, who's he going to go after next? I'm not doing anyone any good just sitting out here, using up resources all day and night for years to come. With you two gone, I'm guessing he'll find a way to justify getting rid of me next."

"So, you're just trying to save your own skin. Is that it?" Bob asked.

"Yeah, pretty much," confessed Dale.

"Then, what do you think we should do?" asked Bob, hoping the question might lead him to what was really at the heart of Dale's plan.

"What do you mean what should you do? Well gee, Bob. I guess you should go on home to Maude and hold your breath until Goodman finds a way to murder you both. God! Have you gone daft in your old age? You should go back to New Waldoff, gather your supporters, and get out of there as fast as you can. Go somewhere else. Build another city. Do anything but hang around acting like sitting ducks again. *Right?*"

"You know, Dale. If I didn't know better, I'd almost think you cared."

Dale laughed. "No. You've got me all wrong. Caring about other people is what made you and Maude weak."

Now, it was Bob's turn to laugh. "Son, caring has nothing to do with strength or weakness. Caring about others is what makes someone good. I've always found it interesting, though, how so many people view caring as a weakness when it actually takes *more* strength to live your life caring about other people and situations besides yourself."

Dale looked disgusted. "Well, that was a gross little father-son moment. If I'd known you still had that in you, I might have gone ahead and let Goodman do his worst."

Bob nodded. "Yep, there's the psychopath I know so well."

Bob looked like he was about to say something else, but then suddenly a light turned on inside his head. "You said Goodman was going to make it look like an accident."

Dale shrugged. "Yeah, that's what Betsy heard him say. So?"

A shadow of horror spread across Bob's face. He gasped, "The cyakine gas! I have to go!" Then he turned and bolted out the door as fast as he could.

Dale yelled after him. "Cyakine gas? What are you talking about? Who uses cyakine gas?"

But Bob didn't stop, and the last thing Dale heard his father shout as he ran from the makeshift prison was, "I don't have time to explain now! But don't forget, Dale! Leave the animals alone!"

A LITTLE, old stump of a woman with curious features sat at a large, wooden desk in a great big room with tall ceilings and long windows. Throughout the big room, lush, green vines sat in pots or hung at different places along the ceiling. Over the woman's shoulder was a wide, wooden door with pointed, metal spikes that stuck out in perfectly aligned columns. It was one of several décor pieces that Goodman had requested to be hauled over from Black Ice Fort, although very few people knew this fact.

The plump woman was leaning over a stack of papers and didn't appear to notice when a man wearing a police uniform arrived at her office door. "Knock, knock!" said the man from the open doorway.

The woman looked up at him, as if she'd known he was there all along. "Yes? What is it?" she asked coldly.

The man seemed uncomfortable addressing the older

woman. No matter how many times he tried to divert his attention, his eyes kept landing on her warty nose. Finally, to stop his shifting gaze, he looked down at his own hands and said, "Betsy, ma'am, I've come to inform you that the wilted olive tree has taken up jockeying at Little Bo Peep's waterhole."

Betsy rolled her eyes at the ridiculous phrase. "For Pete's sake, Clifford! There's nobody here you have to do that for. You can just spit it out! Bob's gone to the spa on horseback?"

The man looked straight at Betsy's nose again and nodded. "Good! Wait here," she said. "I'll get you the go ahead from the 'PM' and then send you on your way."

Betsy stood up and waddled to the side of the spiky door. Then she lifted a wooden flap which covered a small opening in the wall and spun three metal wheels. Betsy turned the wheels back and forth with focus, and soon there were three loud 'clicks' signaling that the door's locks had disengaged.

The squatty woman pulled on the thick, iron ring that hung from the door. She arched herself backward, as far as a woman of her stature could go, when the door finally gave an inch. This was enough for Betsy to coax it open the rest of the way. Clifford, the man who'd been told to wait, leaned his head to the side to see if he could get a peek at Goodman's private office. It was something all the visitors tended to do since it had been over a year since anyone except Betsy had seen the Prime Minister face-to-face.

The rumors about Goodman's absence from the public eye had begun to spin out of control. There were rumors that Betsy had murdered Goodman to take charge of New Waldoff. There were rumors that Goodman had developed the same deformities as the Moon's first inhabitants and was hiding out of shame. There were even rumors that Goodman had built a spaceship and had flown home to Earth.

Unfortunately for Clifford, it was too dark and hazy to see anything before Betsy pulled the door shut behind her. She walked down a dark, narrow corridor until she reached another door. Then she knocked twice short and once long as she'd been instructed to do. From behind the door, she heard an angry voice bark, "Come in!"

Betsy opened the door to a dark green, smoke-filled room. Goodman was standing behind his desk with his side to Betsy, puffing on a cigar and staring at the wall in front of him. She knew better than to say so, but Goodman's appearance had changed dramatically since his days in the army. His strong muscles had turned to flab, and his long face had become gray and sickly-looking. His skin was bubbled up in places, like he might have some sort of pox, and his previously thick hair was now thin and patchy.

"News?" he asked bluntly.

"Bob's on his way to the Sheep Spa, and the officer's in the atrium, waiting for your orders," Betsy stated in her deep, raspy voice.

"I see," said Goodman, though it seemed like he might be lost in some other world. He paused shortly and then asked, "You know what I've always admired about people?"

Betsy shook her head, even though it wasn't clear whether Goodman could see her in his peripheral vision. "I've always admired how easy it is to manipulate them," he said. "Most will hand over their soul for a pat on the head and a compliment. And it's true with even the least trusting of their lot. All you have to do is tell them they're pretty, smart, or artistic, and they'll gladly make you their god. Want them to do evil deeds on your behalf? Easy! Just give them a reason to hate, and they'll do any wicked thing that you ask. It doesn't even have to be a good reason! Really! And when they need a little convincing, you just have to threaten their safety or the safety of their loved ones, and wham-o! You're right back in business!"

Betsy listened to everything the Prime Minister said while keeping her eyes fixated on the dark crystal that was sitting in the middle of his desk. She could see that it was pulsating with electricity. Goodman turned and caught her staring at it. With a stern look, he picked it up and shoved it in his pocket.

"I notice you're fond of my crystal," said Goodman. "Better not to mention it to anyone, though. Got it?"

Betsy shrugged indifferently but replied, "Yes, sir." Then she asked, "What would you like me to tell the officer in the atrium?"

Goodman groaned. "Tell him to get on with it, of course."

"Okay," she said, turning to go.

"But one more thing, Betsy. You have to stop calling your front office the atrium. I never told you it was okay to cover the whole damned place in those long, ropey plants of yours. And if I find out that you've brought one more of those blasted things in from home, I'm going to murder you and all of your loved ones," Goodman threatened. Then he smiled an evil grin and said, "Ha! See what I did there? But seriously, I'm going to fire you if you don't toss half those plants out right away. They're *everywhere!*"

Betsy looked mad, but she didn't say a word. Instead, she slowly turned and left Goodman's office, closing the door gently behind her. But as she headed towards her own office, she began to fume. "What a dope!" she thought.

She was well aware that persuading, manipulating, and threatening worked well on ordinary humans, but Betsy knew she was no ordinary human. "Besides," she thought, "Goodman may think he's in charge now, but he'll get his soon enough. And then everyone in this stupid town will see who's really in charge!"

This last thought made Betsy smile, and she started to hum an eerie, little tune as she continued her walk down the long, dark hall.

CHAPTER 18

THE CONFRONTATION

Axel flew out of the dark passageway and into the ice tunnels, scanning for any sign of Ragher. However, there was no Ragher to be found, only Fred. He was leaning against one of the walls, watching a scene of a young woman with long, dark hair running through a forest in the rain. As Axel approached him, Fred kept his eyes fixed on the girl.

"Your father is in the void," he told him.

The simple phrase caught Axel by surprise. "You knew?"

"Yes," answered Fred. "The first time you ever went into one of the passageways, Ragher told me you'd eventually learn something that would make you want to tear him apart. I didn't understand what he was talking about then, but I've since lived your story during one of my own journeys through the passageways."

Axel paused. Fred didn't sound like himself. The way he spoke was calmer than before. His speech was plain, but without the dry indifference he'd had when they first entered the tunnels long ago. It was a bit startling, not only because of the noticeable change in the young man, but because Fred sounded almost like a lunar wolf now. His cadence was firm and steady like the sound of a drumbeat while his inflection hinted at a deeper meaning. It was as if there was a chord in his speech that connected to the emotions in his heart, allowing them to reverberate with every syllable he uttered.

Axel wondered if Fred's transition had occurred while he'd been away in the dark, or if it had been more gradual—one that had taken place over such a long span of time that it wasn't easy to recognize until it was complete. Regardless, the transformation was so obvious that it distracted Axel from his anger.

"You seem *different*," he said slowly.

Fred gave a nod and turned his head to Axel. "The poison's been gone for some time. I've lived through thousands of lives and witnessed hundreds of senseless deaths. I've listened to terrible lies being told, and I've had to face many hard truths. I'm not the same person I was before. I know all about your kind, and I know what my purpose is now. Yet still the labyrinth sees fit to keep me here. So, I wait."

Axel's anger towards his father dissipated. He found it difficult to cling to his rage while standing before such an impressive testament to change—and in a man who Axel would've thought incapable of such a metamorphosis, no less.

"Tick, tick, tick…"

The ice walls began to break apart and shift, and Ragher suddenly appeared out of a dark gap between two ice sheets, looking sad but stoic. He rejoined his companions, and the three shuffled along together, out of the way of the moving ice that swept them into the next long tunnel. As they went, Fred spoke, "He's learned the truth, Ragher."

Ragher stared at Axel, who was in front of him. "Oh," was all he said. He wanted to see how Axel would respond once the walls stopped moving. He didn't have to wait that long, though.

Axel seized on the opportunity to tell Ragher how he felt without having to look at him.

"My entire life, I loved Neriti like she was my own mother, so it was no big surprise to find out who she really was. But *you?* And *Tahissi?* Maybe you and Neriti believed you had good intentions, but it was all a huge betrayal! The lies ruined our family and made it so we couldn't even properly defend ourselves against the terror that was plaguing us!"

Ragher asked, "So then, you saw what the dark spirit's minion did to your niece and nephews?"

The ice sheets stopped moving and Axel spun around to face his father. "No!" he shouted. The rage had begun to swell inside of him again. "But I *knew* it had to be that monster. It killed my other parents and sister too. Didn't it?"

"Yes," Ragher answered sadly. "It poisoned and killed them to get to me. I believe the dark spirit suspected our lie almost immediately. But because the monster spared you, your mother insisted we continue with the act. She believed we'd remain safe as long as we stayed the course. And I did as she asked.

"I loved your mother with all my heart. She was the reason I left the ice tunnels all those years ago. I longed to protect her —to die for her, even. I would've done anything for her. But she didn't want me to protect her if it meant sacrificing myself.

"What you need to understand is that she did what she felt was right for our family. Her ultimate goal was to keep us safe *and* together, and she was willing to do whatever it took to achieve that goal. We played a terrible long game—lying to you to keep me hidden while hoping it would all turn out fine. But in the end, we paid dearly for it. We deprived you of any type of normal upbringing or well-adjusted life that you might have otherwise had. And we ruined your sister's chance to live a happy, safe life with her own family by her side."

"EXACTLY!" screamed Axel. "*And* you blamed me for running away when I was confused and needed to figure out my life! When I was at my lowest point ever, you told me I was a disappointment to you. That I didn't live up to *your* expectations! Did you really not see the irony in that?" Axel shouted accusingly.

Ragher said, "I know, Axel. I was angry at myself and your mother for years over what we did, and I redirected a lot of it towards you. Honestly, when I brought you here, I still blamed you for not being the wolf I knew you could be. But I see now that most of that was my fault for not giving you what you really needed—the truth."

Axel breathed hard, as though he were fighting a battle. His head swam with resentment and hurt and terrible sorrow for all the things he knew he would never be able to make right for his sister or himself. "If the dark spirit knew you were hiding, then why didn't you defy Neriti and shift back to your adult form so that you could raise me as your own?"

Ragher hung his head. "Because it wasn't just your mom I was trying to please. When Neriti and I argued over whether I should hide in your place, I fought hard to prevent it from happening. But the truth of the matter is that I wasn't alone all those years I spent in the ice tunnels. There is some sort of being inside the passageways who speaks to me and guides me. She gives me visions like the kind you and Fred have experienced. But she also talks to me directly. She's answered many of the questions I've had over the years, although I still don't know who she is."

Axel had already heard the dark spirit's monster mention the woman, so he wasn't entirely surprised by his father's revelation. "Do you think it's Theia?" he asked with a hint of awe in his voice.

"No, I'm certain it's not Theia. From what I can tell she's an oracle. She knows a great deal about Theia and the dark spirit, and she showed me visions of Neriti's future before I ever met your mother. Although, the majority of those visions never came true."

Fred added, "She's shown me visions of Mina's future and revealed secrets that I don't think anyone else knows. It troubles me how much truth has been hidden. Not just from the travelers, but from the lunar wolves too."

"What truth?" Axel asked sharply.

Fred hesitated. "I can't say. But haven't you seen the darkness that's taking over out there while we remain trapped inside these tunnels? Ragher didn't prevent the dark spirit from taking over when he dragged us here. He only prevented it from overtaking me."

Ragher nodded. "That's true, but it's what the oracle instructed me to do. Just like she told me to go along with Neriti's plan all those years ago."

Ragher turned to his son. "Axel, when your mother came up with the idea for me to hide, I left her for a while and came back to the ice tunnels to seek the oracle's council. I was furious at Neriti for pushing her absurd idea, and I expected the oracle to confirm that I should go ahead and sacrifice myself to the dark spirit so that you and your sister could be raised the way I knew was right. But to my horror, she ordered me to go along with Neriti's plan. I was so strongly set against it that I even dared to argue with the oracle. However, she put me in my place by showing me a terrifying vision of what the future would hold if I disobeyed her."

"Tick…tick…tick."

The tunnels began to rearrange again, and the trio moved silently with the sliding walls, their thoughts as heavy as the solid sheets of ice that skated around them. When the next tunnel formed, Axel asked, "So, this oracle bullied you into following a plan that you knew was bad. But what I still don't understand is why the plan was even necessary in the first place. What did the dark spirit actually want from you?"

Ragher replied, "Originally, I thought he wanted to eat me. During the centuries I was trapped here in the ice tunnels, I watched countless visions of him chasing after Moon Walkers who'd disobeyed him in ancient times. If he got close enough, he would suck out their souls. But it turns out he can't do that anymore."

"Why not?" Axel asked.

"Because he's under a spell," explained Ragher. "He can no longer use a Moon Walker's energy unless he has its permission. Unfortunately, I found this out much too late. It turned out that all he ever wanted was for me to grant him permission to use my energy. He told me he needs it to get revenge on Theia—that the only way he can right some kind of wrong she committed is if he is able to use the Moon Walker energy I have inside of me."

"That doesn't sound right," said Axel suspiciously. "What sort of wrong could Theia have possibly committed against the dark spirit?"

Ragher shook his head. "I don't know. He wouldn't tell me. I went to him right after Tahissi died. I was ready to let him kill me. I didn't care about living anymore. You had abandoned the pack and Neriti had told me about your love for your sister. I'd hit rock bottom, and there was no one to pull me out of it.

"So, I revealed myself to the dark spirit's minion and had it take me to where the spirit resides atop Black Ice Glacier. This is when I found out that all he wanted was my help—that he'd never intended to kill me. The spirit told me that the spell he's under doesn't just keep him from stealing a Moon Walker's energy; it prevents him from physically harming the wolves. However, he found a way around the spell when he created his minion. That's how the spirit was able to go after your adopted family and your niece and nephews—by sending his disgusting pet to do his dirty work. If Neriti had just listened to reason, or if the oracle had…" But Ragher, who'd begun to show his anger, stopped himself.

"What is it?" Axel asked. "If the oracle had what?"

Ragher shook his head, as if to dismiss Axel's question. "The dark spirit told me that until I gave him what he wanted he was going to let his monster continue to torture me and those I loved. I was furious. It was obvious I had more power than I'd ever realized. If I'd just given him what he'd wanted years earlier, it might've prevented him from terrorizing us. The reason he kept sending his minion after the people I cared about was because it was the only control he had over me."

Axel asked, "So you decided to help him go after Theia, then?"

"No," Ragher replied, "because it turned out that I knew something he didn't. The dark spirit wanted to exact revenge against Theia, but I knew that wasn't going to happen because Theia was gone. The oracle had informed me that Theia left around the same time the travelers started to arrive."

"What do you mean 'Theia left?' Theia's the Moon! How can Theia *leave* if she's part of the world we exist in?" Axel demanded.

Ragher looked at Axel, hesitating for a moment, but then Fred answered for him, "She's not the Moon. Theia's a god, but she isn't a part of the Moon the way she claimed to be. That part was just a fairytale, a bedtime story she told the wolves early on so that they would view the world the way she wanted them to."

Axel took a second to think about what Fred was saying. Then he asked, "So you're saying that our god abandoned us, just like the Moon Walkers? Well, where in the hell did she go?!"

"The Moon Walkers didn't abandon you," Fred corrected him. "They're still here."

"Oh, really? They're still here? And how do *you* know

that!?" Axel asked with contempt. It was obvious he didn't like having his own history explained to him by a visitor.

Fred didn't respond, but Ragher said, "Look, Axel, the oracle has been preparing Fred for something big. It's the reason our friend has received so many visions.

"I believe you're about to be given visions that will answer many of these questions you have. The oracle has plans for you as well, although if I'm being honest, this pains me. As your father, I wish it could've been different for you. I wish I could've protected you better when you were young, just like I wish I could protect you now. You deserved a better life—one where you didn't have to be so incredibly tough every second of every day."

Axel sighed. He knew Ragher's words were sincere, but he felt certain he'd never be able to move past all the hurt his parents had caused him—well intentioned or not.

"Here's something else I'd really like to know, Ragher," said Axel. "If the dark spirit was responsible for torturing and killing all these wolves you claim to have loved, then why did you go to work for Dan? Wasn't the dark spirit controlling him?"

Ragher answered, "Because I was trying my best to protect our kind."

"You mean the wolves?" Axel asked.

But before Ragher could answer, the tunnel began to shake. The trio fell to the ground right as a large section of the ice wall collapsed, leaving a gaping hole in its place. Ragher could feel himself being drawn to it.

"I'm sorry, Axel," said Ragher as they stood back up again. "This will have to wait. It seems that the oracle would like to have a word with me. I think I may have said too much." He smiled sadly and began to walk into the darkness.

But before he took another step, Axel stopped him. "It's

calling me too," he lied. "It looks like we're meant to take this passageway together."

Ragher nodded at his son. Then he looked back at Fred. "In case I don't make it out again, I want you to know that I think you've done great, kid. I never expected to see you become the kind of human you've grown into. I guess sometimes the hardest lumps of clay to sculpt take on the best shape in the end."

Fred nodded at Ragher appreciatively and said, "Don't worry, friend. It's not goodbye. I know our paths will meet again." Then he turned his gaze back to the large sheet of ice in front of him to continue watching the dark-haired girl, who was standing by the sea.

It was eerily quiet inside the dark void, and the father and son stood close together in silence, waiting to see what would happen next. Ragher was certain he'd upset the oracle by revealing more than he was supposed to. And Axel had followed Ragher into the darkness to lend his support, not because he saw Ragher as a father figure, or even as a loved one exactly, but because he felt sorry for him. Even though there'd been little in Ragher's story that redeemed him from the terrible lies he'd told, it was obvious to Axel that Ragher wasn't solely responsible for everything that had happened. He understood now that Ragher had been pushed around a great deal during his strange life, and because of this, Axel felt the urge to confront at least one of his father's bullies firsthand.

A vision appeared out of the darkness, surrounding the two wolves. Neriti was laying on the ground in her den with Ragher standing over her. Axel stood next to Ragher in the vision like a ghost watching his mother and father through the veil. "Are you seeing this?" he asked Ragher, unsure whether or not his father would be able to hear him inside the vision.

The Ragher who stood next to Neriti didn't react to Axel's question, but from Axel's other side he heard Ragher's muffled voice. "Yes, I see it. This was right after you and your sister were born. It was the happiest and saddest day of my life."

The Ragher in the vision crouched down next to Neriti, and that's when Axel noticed the two little pups cuddled up against Neriti's chest, sound asleep. Tears slid down Neriti's face, darkening her white fur, and Ragher pushed his head against hers. "You know we don't have to do this," he spoke tenderly to Neriti. "We could still do it my way instead."

Neriti looked lovingly into Ragher's eyes. "No, Ragher. It's too late for that now. Your ice mistress agreed to my plan. If we change things now, we'll have two spirits working against us."

Ragher pushed back. "Maybe not, Riti. The oracle isn't heartless. Maybe I can find a way to persuade her," he said with a hint of desperation.

At first, Neriti didn't respond. She pulled the little ones closer to her and snuggled them for a bit before saying, "No. We have to do this how we planned. It's the only way to keep the dark spirit out of our lives while giving the pups a chance to grow. We can tell them the truth later when the time is right —when they're older."

Ragher shook his head. "No, Neriti. If we're really doing this your way, then you have to promise me that you'll never tell Axel who he really is. I can't bear the thought of him finding out what a coward I am. My greatest hope is that Rothel will teach him how to be a brave wolf. That Axel will never have to be ashamed to know his real father didn't do right by his family."

The vision faded, and a voice sounded through the dark. It was crisp and loud. Axel had never heard such a voice before. He thought it sounded like a voice from another world. "I did not summon you here, wolf!"

Axel replied boldly, "I know, but you're an oracle, so I assumed you knew I was coming."

"An oracle, hmm? I know that's what your father thinks of me. Is this your opinion too?"

Axel answered, "I don't know what to think of you, except what Ragher's told me. All I really know is that you seem to enjoy bossing him around, and I'm not exactly sure what good it's done, except cause a lot of suffering."

The voice spoke to Ragher. "Your son must be very brave to speak to me in this way, a quality he surely gets from his mother." Then the female voice laughed a booming laugh that sent chills down Axel's spine.

But Axel's anger over how the oracle disparaged Ragher was much stronger than the intimidation he felt. He snapped, "What kind of spirit forces someone to do their bidding and then shames them? You want my opinion? I think you're a—"

But the oracle stopped him before he could insult her. "Be careful or I might change my mind and refuse to give you the information you seek."

Axel was having a hard time biting his tongue, but Ragher spoke for him. "Please forgive my son. He hasn't finished processing the difficult visions you've offered him, and he doesn't know your sense of humor, like I do."

"Yes, yes. I know all of this, Ragher, which is why I'm going to give him another shot at this. Instead of allowing you to give him all the answers on your own, I will show him some of the things he wants to know. As long as it's something I'm willing to share. If you'd like, you can explain the visions as we go."

Ragher was stunned. The spirit was paying him a kindness he hadn't expected. "Thank you, oracle," he said humbly.

"Yes, well, he was going to have to know soon enough," she replied. "Now let's begin."

CHAPTER 19

THE OLD WOMAN WHO
REMEMBERED

Maude awoke when she heard the front door close. Bob was off to the Sheep Spa to meet Dale—a trip she was glad she didn't have to make. She put on her robe and walked downstairs to brew some warm tea. Then she took her cup back upstairs to begin work for the day.

She sipped slowly on the steamy liquid while looking over the symbols she'd highlighted the day before. Misshaped triangles and deflated spheres—sometimes merged, sometimes not. None of it made any sense, but she had realized, after spending months counting all the symbols, that these two were the most commonly used throughout the papers she was analyzing.

Each day, Maude grew a little more indifferent about making a breakthrough. All she really wanted was to be with Helen and to spend time with Ruth again. She missed the two terribly and felt as though it had been a cruel twist of fate to lose both of them back-to-back the way she had.

Maude took another sip of her tea, trying to stay awake so she could focus on the papers in front of her. However, the warmth from the warm liquid relaxed her whole body, and soon she couldn't keep her eyes open.

"Well, what's an early nap to an old geezer like me?" she thought. "Might as well rest up if I'm going to be out late again tonight."

She climbed into bed and closed her eyes, and immediately she felt her consciousness drifting away, as though it were riding on top of a cloud. The sensation was peaceful, and it felt good to surrender to it. Soon, a memory came to her as she straddled between the lands of wake and nod. Maude and Ruth were returning from a journey they had taken to visit the wolves after the battle against Dan was over. Ruth had insisted that they call on the remainder of the wolves to thank them for helping the secret army achieve their common goal.

Ruth hated that the travelers who'd united against the twins hadn't done more to prevent the atrocities that were carried out against the wolves. And she was always quick to remind everyone that if they had tried to stop or punish those who'd participated in the massacre, then they wouldn't have found themselves in a situation where they needed a secret army.

The two old women slowed down to rest. Maude's feet and legs were sore, and she felt worn out. But she knew that the trip to the wolves' underground lair had been good for her. Before they'd left, she'd been furious with the whole world. Furious at Helen for sacrificing herself, furious at Ruth for not sharing crucial pieces of the puzzle sooner, and furious at herself for everything else.

Maude realized that she should've done more to stop her sons before things went too far. Even worse, though, she realized that she should've defended the wolves, no matter the consequence. She had convinced herself that their problems were not her own, despite the pity she felt for them. But now she could see how ludicrous this was, especially since she and Bob had been the ones responsible for ushering the humans into the Moon realm to begin with.

"Feeling better, sugar?" Ruth had asked as the two sat

down at the bottom of a hill, their backs leaning against the soft bark of a large hala bush.

"Strangely, I am," replied Maude.

"Nothing strange about it. You was too restless to stay back at base while all them soldiers shuffled around, trying to remember what they'd done with their heads. There ain't nothing you can do to help them right now and ain't nothing they can do to help you neither. You all gonna be dealing with the fallout from what's happened for a while, I suspect."

Maude nodded. "Yes, I suppose you're right, Miss Ruth. But what about you? Won't you be dealing with the fallout too?"

Ruth laughed. "Aww nah, sugar. I'm gonna be right as rain."

Maude wasn't sure what her friend meant by this, but after all the years of knowing Ruth, she'd grown accustomed to just going along with her unusual way of speaking. The two sat in silence for a while until Maude spoke again.

"I'm glad you talked me into this. Honestly, I wasn't sure we'd be able to make it over all these hills and back, but it felt good. And maybe it sounds crazy, but I sort of feel like Helen has been with us the whole time. Kind of like her energy has been walking right beside us."

"That doesn't sound crazy, child. That sounds like love. You and Helen cared for each other very deeply, and not even death can change that. Plus, I suspect part of her is hanging around, trying to help you see things right."

Maude raised an eyebrow. "Trying to help me see things right?"

"Why, yes. You didn't think you had it all figured out now, did you? Helen's on the other side, sugar. So, I reckon she knows more than either of us. Least for the moment, anywho."

Ruth took Maude's hand and said, "Sugar, I'm old and tired. I know we said we was going to stick together on our trip, but I think it best you go ahead and tell one of those strong soldiers to come on back this way and collect my sorry sack of bones. I'm plum tuckered out, and there ain't no way I'm gonna make it back on my own."

Maude was concerned. "I'm not comfortable just leaving you here, Ruth. We aren't that far away from the market. Probably only two or three more hours. Don't you think you could make it a little further?"

Ruth shook her head and clutched her bony legs with both hands. "I just can't do it, Maude. These old knees have been threatening to retire the whole trip, and lordy, I think they've gone and done it now. You go on and bring back a looker to help me out. I'll be right here waiting."

Maude hesitated. "Are you sure?" she asked.

Ruth laughed heartily. "Well, if I ain't, my body sure is. Anyway, I got you this far. I know you can make it the rest of the way on your own," she said, giving Maude a little wink.

"Well, okay," Maude agreed. Before she stood up, though, she put her arm around Ruth and gave her a tight squeeze from the side. "I'll hurry to get help and come right back."

Ruth smiled, and her eyes twinkled. "I know you will, hon. Now, get on with you."

Maude turned and left Ruth, even though she already sensed deep down that it would be the last time she ever saw her friend alive.

The memory faded, and soon Maude began to enter a dreamworld unlike any she'd ever experienced. The colors were more vivid than in the waking world, and Maude felt as though all her senses had come alive at once—like they'd been lying dormant and were now suddenly awake for the first time ever. It took her a moment to adjust to the new world around her, but once she did, she began enjoying her heightened senses.

She walked across a field of grass and felt the wet dew

against the bottoms of her feet. She looked up and saw a dazzling sky with all different colors of light. Shades of blues, pinks, violets, and oranges melted together. Maude thought she might be dreaming of Earth, but something inside her knew that wasn't right.

Soon she began to skip along as she took in the sights. There were tall trees and thick, leafy bushes with beautiful flowers. There were huge boulders, and snow-covered mountains, and hundreds of different kinds of creatures walking and flying about. It was glorious. Maude had never seen so many signs of life, and she wondered if she was witnessing a miracle.

But then, suddenly, something strange happened—she began to grow. She looked down at her feet but realized that they weren't her feet at all. Where her feet should've been, there were two multi-faceted crystals expanding at a fantastic rate. Within seconds, she had grown so large that she was towering above the world, even taller than the tallest mountains she'd been admiring seconds earlier.

The growing stopped, and she looked down again to take in the rest of her ginormous body. Just like her feet, her body was made of dark, shiny prisms. Maude tried lifting her arms and was surprised to find that they moved quite easily. She stretched her hands out in front of her and wiggled her fingers. The smooth mirrored surfaces that made up her long digits caught the sun's rays and sent beams of light back out in every direction—towards the world below and back into outer space.

She took a few steps forward, but then suddenly, she heard a tiny voice calling to her from somewhere near her feet. It spoke to her in a terribly squeaky language that was foreign to her, yet somehow, she understood it. "Oh, ever so giant and merciful one, you have gone and trampled our elven village again. And I fear that some of our elders have perished. We will need your assistance to fix our garden if we are not to starve this winter."

Quite abruptly, all the size that Maude had gained vanished. A loud boom echoed across the ground and sky as her gargantuan crystal-shaped body morphed back into a human-sized one. Back in the grassy field from earlier, Maude found a bluish gray elf-creature standing before her. It appeared to be nude.

She spoke to the little elf, but her voice didn't sound like her own. It was much deeper and much more powerful. "How can I help it if you and your kind continue to build your villages in my favorite spots to roam? I can't be expected to keep track of such matters, and if you try and tell me to be more careful about where I choose to go, I will smite you just like I did your predecessor!"

"But your greatness! If you would only advise us on which spots are your favorites, we would happily find other locations to build our villages," said the elf.

Maude spoke again. "Curse you for trying to tether me to such a contract! The spots I choose as my favorites change daily, as does the weather and my mood. What is today might not be tomorrow. And as your god, I have every right to do as I please!"

"Yes, your merciful greatness. I understand. But please, will you at least restore our crops so that we may feed our families?"

Maude scoffed. "I suppose, though sometimes I feel as if you expect me to be more like a magician than a god."

"Thank you, your majestic excellence. All the elves thank you. The surviving elder elves, the youngest child elves, the—"

"Stop it, Flagstone! Stop talking, or I *will* smite you!"

"It's Flerasone, your most beautiful highness, but you may call me Flagstone if you wish."

"STOP GROVELING!" Maude heard the powerful voice inside of her scream. Then, suddenly, everything went dark like the sun had been extinguished. Maude looked up. Hundreds of gigantic fireballs were falling from the sky above. They raced to the ground and crashed all around them. Maude heard screaming from the creatures near and far, but whatever god she possessed did nothing to stop the terror.

Then, out of nowhere, a large hand made of multi-faceted crystals reached down from high above to scoop up all the frightened creatures. Maude cried out in anger at the large hand, but her screams were ignored. She threw herself on the ground and began to wail and sob like a petulant child.

"Now what in the world are you crying about, sugar?" asked a familiar voice.

Maude pushed herself off the ground and was relieved to see that everything was just like it had been when she first entered the dreamscape. Except now Ruth was there too. Maude rose to her feet and hugged her friend. "Ruth! You came back!" she shouted excitedly.

Ruth smiled sweetly and said, "No, sugar. I didn't come back. Can't you tell by the look of this place? You came here to me."

Maude looked around. "Oh, I see," she said, sounding just like herself again. "Is this heaven, then? Is Helen here too? And what about Dan? Did he make it in? Is he all sorted out now?"

Ruth's smile faded. "Look, Maude. You gotta listen and listen good. We need you to remember now. You've had the power to figure out those symbols for some time, but you're still hanging on to that other world cause part of you is scared. Scared to remember what you know. Well, that's all fine and dandy, I suppose. Memories don't always tell us the nicest things about ourselves, but, hon, that don't matter. It's what you do with those memories that matters.

"Right now, you're hiding from who you were, but that ain't ever gonna get you back to your daughter. You need to face your memories head on. Learn from 'em and move forward. You understand?"

Maude felt weak. Her whole body started to ache just like it did in the waking world, only worse. Maude's eyes clouded over, and she started to shake.

But Ruth put her hand on her friend's shoulder and said in a firm voice, "Knock it off, Maude! You know who you are. Now go *be* her. Just do it better this time around, you hear?"

Ruth's touch stopped Maude from shaking and brought her back into the moment. "I don't know if I can do it, Ruth," she said. "I'm scared. It's like when I was younger, and you used to comfort me. Do you remember that?"

Ruth nodded. "Sure as hay fire I remember! And do you remember what I used to tell you when you were so scared that you might never remember your past?"

Maude smiled. "When we don't remember our past, we gotta work twice as hard to make a better future?"

"Yes, *and?*"

Maude continued, "No matter the situation, we should always try our best because that's how we go on living with ourselves every day."

"That's it, sugar! You're starting to remember. Now go back just a little bit further..." Ruth walked towards Maude until she'd walked right through her, and suddenly Maude felt her mind expanding outward in every direction—growing in size just like her body had done, except it was gaining knowledge instead of mass.

Maude awoke. Her heart was beating fast, but she wasn't frightened anymore. She felt rejuvenated like she'd just awoken from a hundred year's sleep. If she'd bothered to notice the shadows across the floor, she would've realized that it was much later in the day than when she'd fallen asleep—almost dusk. Without even thinking of her usual aches and pains, she jumped out of bed and hovered over her desk, moving her eyes quickly across the papers.

"Oh, my heavens!" she exclaimed. Just as she'd suspected, she was able to read every single symbol of the writings she'd restored. It all made sense to her now. And not only that, but she finally remembered everything from before. After decades of having no idea who she was, it was like a missing piece of her mind had slid back into place, and everything was crystal clear.

Suddenly, the front door flew open, and Maude heard Bob racing up the stairs. She turned around to face the bedroom door. "Bob, you won't believe it! I got my memories back! Plus, I can read all of this now!"

Bob stopped for a second, shocked by Maude's news. But then the fear swept over him again, and he yelled frantically, "Maude, we have to get out of here! Now! Grab anything you ever want to see again and meet me outside! I have to go tell the others!"

Maude frowned. "What are you talking about, Bob? Why do I have to grab everything and meet you outside?" she asked.

"Because Goodman wants us dead. Betsy works for him now. She's his secretary, and apparently, she's been visiting Dale. She told him that she overheard Goodman plotting to kill us. He's going to make it look like an accident. I think he intends to use the cyakine gas!" Bob leaned over and held onto the doorframe as he tried to catch his breath.

"Wait. Dale told you all of this, and you believed him? You know as well as I do, we can't take what he says seriously. What's gotten into you?"

Bob stood up tall again. "Sweetheart, I *do* know that, and I'm skeptical too. Really. But what if he's right? I thought about this all the way home, and honestly, even if he's wrong, I think we have to get out of here. Goodman has put us in a terrible position. If we stay, it will be just like last time when we put up with Dan and Dale's nonsense, even though we knew it was wrong. By not stopping him early on, we allowed Goodman to grow strong. But the good news is we can still leave. We can start fresh. Build a city the way we want—a *new* New Waldoff."

Maude glanced over at her papers. Everything Bob was saying was what she'd been trying to get across to him since Goodman had first come into the picture. But leaving now, just when she'd gotten her memories back, seemed like a lot to manage. Especially, when all she really wanted to do was sit down and analyze everything that had happened during the last several decades.

"I think I might be too old to start fresh, Bob. But I'll go if you think it's best. You better grab the two big tents from the downstairs closet before you run off. I don't think I can carry those out of here on my own. Just leave them on the front walkway."

Bob nodded. "Good idea!" he said excitedly. "And don't worry about being too old. Technically, you're probably younger than me, but I can do all the heavy lifting while we're getting settled again. And you can keep working on your project. Boy, it sure is terrific that you got your memories back! Really terrific! I can't wait to hear everything!"

Maude smiled at her husband, having finally gotten the reaction she'd hoped for. "Okay, Bob. I'll meet you in the street in a little while. Are you heading to the tavern now?"

"Yep. I hope the others are ready for a new challenge. It's going to be hard work, but if it goes the way I hope, then it will all be worth it in the end!" Bob grabbed Maude around the shoulders and gave her a great big hug and a kiss on the cheek. Then he said, "This is going to be great, honey! You'll see. Everything will be much easier after this!"

"I'm sure, darling. Now, run along. If your suspicions are right, we'll need to move fast."

Bob saluted his wife playfully and then turned around and headed down the stairs and out the door, forgetting all about the tents in the closet. "That's okay," she thought. "He can get them when he comes back."

Maude already knew she'd never see the completion of the city Bob spoke of, but she was pleased that the idea of it had breathed some new life into him. She packed some clothes and then shoved as many of the papers as she could fit into two suitcases. "This is it," she thought. After all her years on the Moon, she was off to her final adventure. She smiled as she walked down the stairs and took one last look around the small kitchen and living room. Of all the places she'd ever called home, this one had felt the least like it. Even her booth in the marketplace had been more inviting than this cookie-cutter apartment where she and Bob had been forced to live. "All the better to leave behind," she told herself.

Maude stepped into the street, ready to start her journey. She looked around, searching for a place to wait discreetly until Bob returned. But after a few moments, she felt an uncomfortable tingling up and down her spine. As she watched the people passing along the cobblestone path in front of her home, she suddenly realized that she'd become aware of the energy radiating off each person. It was almost like their insides were oozing out, but instead of guts and bile, it was thought, feeling, and intention spewing forth like a disgusting spray of neuroses.

Maude felt drenched in their energy, as though each person's aura were drowning her in its volume. She held her breath, hoping to fight it by depriving herself of her most essential need. Immediately, the intensity of the sensation dulled, but it was replaced with an alarming clarity that something outrageous and horrifying was about to happen.

Right at that moment, Maude felt her friend, Max, approaching from a block away. She lifted her suitcases up by their handles, holding them on each side for balance as she took off to find him. Seconds later, she spotted Max. He was wearing a long-sleeved flannel shirt and black denim pants. Maude approached him, and once she got closer, he noticed her and said, "Hi there, Maude. Are you on your way to try some stew? Say, what are you carrying those suitcases for?"

But Maude didn't explain. In her mind, she'd been transported back to her days as the leader of the secret army. She ordered, "We have to move *right* now. Do you know where we can get two horses the council won't know about? By *any* means possible, Max."

Max looked worried. "Are you okay, Maude? Where's Bob? I thought you two were coming to the tavern."

But before Maude had the chance to respond, a series of explosions erupted across the city. The ground under their feet trembled, and the two friends looked down the block to where Maude and Bob's home was located. However, there was a huge cloud of smoke pouring through the street and bits of ash rained down all around them, which made it impossible to see more than a few feet ahead.

"Let's go!" Maude yelled. "We've got to find horses. *Now!*"

Max could barely hear Maude over the ringing in his ears. He felt dazed from the explosions, and he looked up to try and get his bearings. Above the rooftops, thick, black smoke filled the sky, and it suddenly occurred to him that the nearby explosions weren't an isolated incident. There was smoke rising up above other parts of the city too. "This doesn't seem like it was an accident, Maude. Did you know this was going to happen?"

Maude shook her head. "Not until about thirty seconds before it did. We have to go!"

Max finally started to come to his senses. "Okay, come on. Follow me. Here, I'll take those," he said grabbing the suitcases out of Maude's hands. Then the two took off together through the maze of cobblestone streets. "A new adventure indeed,"

Maude thought as they moved swiftly. Her restored memories began to race across her mind while she and Max rushed through the city. And soon everything that had happened over the last several decades came into perfect focus. She whispered angrily, "Someone's going to pay for this."

Max turned his head towards her. "What's that, Maude?"

"Nothing," she replied. Her words weren't meant for Max. They weren't even related to their situation exactly.

Everywhere they went, they passed people screaming or crying in the streets. It was pandemonium. But then at times, it would grow oddly quiet as they moved through pockets of the city where there seemed to be nobody at all.

"Stop here!" Maude yelled unexpectedly, startling Max. She darted into a clothing store that seemed to be abandoned and returned with two hooded, black cloaks. "Put this on!" she said, thrusting the larger one at Max. Max did as he was told, and Maude pulled on the one she'd grabbed for herself.

They continued down the cobblestone roads, through the spiderweb of streets that Goodman had designed. Maude wondered if the complicated layout had been cleverly engineered for this very moment. She already knew that the timing of her restored memories was no coincidence. The dark spirit was closer than ever to figuring out the game they were playing, and he would stop at nothing to win. Maude knew there was only one thing left to do. They had to get Mina back.

CHAPTER 20

THE ESCAPE

Bob was halfway to John's tavern when the blasts tore through the city. He leapt forward out of fright before stopping in his tracks. Dust and ash filled the air and caught in his lungs. He coughed and choked on the particles of fine grit that invaded his airways. He knew he had to turn around and find Maude, but his eyes were burning from the black smoke that billowed from the rooftops, pouring into the streets.

"Get it together!" he told himself. He imagined Maude trapped in their apartment under a mountain of debris. He was certain Goodman had targeted them, but why he'd chosen to blow up other parts of the city, Bob didn't understand. However, the madness and magnitude of what Goodman had done terrified him.

He fought his way through the heavy smoke until he reached the end of the block where the air was less dense. There were people running every which way like a colony of ants whose hill had been stomped on.

Bob began to backtrack, although it was difficult to move quickly between all the people and debris. When he finally reached his street, his heart dropped into his stomach. It looked like a bomb had gone off. The front of the long row of two-story, stone apartments was no more. All that remained was the posterior half of the wide building; the remnants of the front half were spilled across the cobblestone in mounds of rubble.

Part of Bob's brain told him it would have been impossible for anyone to survive this sort of blast, but Bob refused to accept this. He climbed frantically over the piles of blown apart building, calling Maude's name. He searched, and yelled, and paused, listening for the sounds of survivors. It was silent, though, and Maude was nowhere to be found.

"You have to keep going," he told himself. He knew if he stopped to think about what had happened—about the fact that the love of his life might actually be dead—he wouldn't be able to go on. When he passed their place, he peeked inside, but there were no signs of life. The second level and stairs were completely obliterated so that he could see all the way through to the building behind theirs.

Bob continued on until he'd looped every block in a five-block radius. Finally, he decided the best thing to do would be to make his way to John's. He knew if Maude had escaped the explosions, she might have gone to the tavern to find him. So, he rushed back in that direction.

When he arrived at the tavern, he ducked down the alleyway behind the building and then climbed the outside staircase to John's loft above the pub. Before he opened the door, he could hear a commotion coming from inside. He entered and found John's small living room packed with at least thirty people, who were all talking at once. John yelled over the raucous, "Alright, listen up! Bob's here now! We're going to bring this meeting to order in just a minute, so settle down!"

The voices in the room quieted a little. John, who was standing on a chair next to his dining table, signaled for Bob to make his way over. Bob crossed the room, nodding at his friends and acquaintances as he passed them. Once he reached John, he saw Jacques sitting at the table in front of a cauldron of brown stew.

"Allo, Bob!" Jacques greeted him.

"Hello, chef. It's good to see you," Bob replied. Then he asked, "Have either of you seen Maude?"

John looked worried. "No, she's not here yet. When's the last time *you* saw her?"

Bob felt a lump rising inside his chest. "I left her back at the apartment. When the explosions went off, I was on my way here to let everyone know they should leave the city. I went and saw Dale this morning. He knew Goodman was up to something. I had no idea it would be this big, though."

John asked, "Have you gone back to the apartment yet?"

Bob hesitated. The thought of losing Maude was threatening to break him again. He grabbed the table hard with one hand to divert the pain that was growing inside him. "Yes," he said grimly, "but there's barely anything left of it."

Jacques stood up. "Oh, mon ami! I am truly sorry. Your Maude, she was a very good woman."

Bob hung his head. "Thank you, Jacques. But I still believe I'm going to find her. Before I left, I told her to pack her things and wait for me in the street. There's a chance she may have gotten out in time."

John put his hand on Bob's shoulder. "I'm sure she did. Maude is a fine lady. One of the best, really. I can't imagine the Moon without her."

Bob looked around the room. "We have to get everyone out of here, John. We're sitting ducks if we stay. I don't think it's any accident this happened the same day we decided to meet. Maude even suggested last night that our apartment might be bugged. I thought she was being ridiculous at first, but I think she might have been right."

John looked like he had suddenly become aware of the

gravity of their situation. "Quiet everybody!" he yelled. "There's been a change of plans. In light of some new information, we're going to need to postpone the meeting. Go home if you're able to. If not—"

Bob interrupted him. "No! It's not safe for us in the city anymore. We have to get out of here tonight. Grab your families and leave New Waldoff. Everyone, go your own way. We'll find each other on the other side of the city walls."

The men and women in the crowd turned to each other and began to murmur, and Bob could tell they were scared. John grabbed ahold of Bob's shoulder and whispered, "Is this really such a good idea? There're only two exits out of the city. If Goodman or the council finds out we're leaving, won't they try to stop us?"

Bob shook his head and spoke to the crowd. "I know it's a terrible situation we're in. *Again.* But think of it this way, after what you've all witnessed this evening, does anyone feel safe staying here, even one more night?

"You'll have to decide what's best for you, of course, but my plan is to go build the city we should've built from the start —one where we have a fair form of government in which everyone has a say. Not this other garbage we've had to put up with *twice* now. If you want what we're offering, then come with us tonight. Otherwise, I wish you the best of luck."

"But how will we get out of the city?" asked a tall lady named Evelyn, a woman Bob and Maude had known since their earliest days on the Moon.

"Bring your tents and supplies with you—anything you need for camping—just like you used after the battle. If the guards ask you where you're going, tell them your house was destroyed and that you plan to camp outside the city until you have somewhere to stay. It's not even much of a lie, really."

This idea seemed to boost the crowd's spirits some. Bob continued, "Try to leave separately. Families can go together, but it will look less suspicious if there isn't a long line of people trying to exit at the same time. Everyone understand?"

Many of the people in the crowd nodded. Bob shouted, "Now go! And tell everyone that you know you can trust to come on!"

People began to leave, and Bob turned back to Jacques and John. "If either of you see Maude, will you let her know I'm looking for her and help her get out of the city?" Bob's fears were still threatening to overtake him, but he steeled himself. "I have an errand to run before I head out. I'll be right behind you, though."

John nodded. "Yes, of course, Bob. I'll even send Egan out to look for Maude while Samuel and I pack our things. I just can't believe it's come to this. I sure wish we had stopped all this foolishness earlier."

Bob shook his head in frustration. "You and me both."

Jacques said, "But I do not understand. Is there really no time to eat? I worked all day on my daube. Surely, it would be okay for everyone to at least have a few spoonfuls? We do not want to voyage on empty stomachs, non?"

"I'm afraid not, friend," replied Bob. "We need to get a move on before the winds start to change out there. It will be much easier to get out of here while there's still bedlam. I have to ask, though. You did know that 'stew' was just a code word for our secret meeting, right?"

Jacques snickered. "Bien sur! Of course! But I wanted to make sure these people know how much better my daube is than that disgusting, watery stew they crave. Daube would have even made a better secret word than *stew*!"

This made Bob smile despite his fear and restlessness. "Stay well, Jacques," he said to the chef. "I look forward to having your culinary skills and lively personality in our new town."

"Yes, well I know that these peasants *here* certainly do not appreciate fine food, so I will join your cause. May I voyage with you, John?"

"Yes, Jacques. You are most welcome. But please, let's do try to be as inconspicuous as possible on our way out of town, shall we?"

Jacques huffed. "Mais, oui! I am always very inconspicuous like a little church mouse. Non?"

John looked at Bob, as though he were asking for backup, but Bob just shrugged with an amused expression. "I better get a move on," he said, becoming serious again. "Best of luck and be careful out there. I don't know what Goodman's endgame is, but it surely won't be in our favor to find out."

Bob headed for the door and down the metal staircase. He traveled across town, keeping his eyes peeled for Maude while surveying the destruction. The terror and excitement on the streets had dissipated, but there were still many people walking around as though they were in shock. Bob suspected that many were, and although he wished he could help them, he knew he had to be careful about who he trusted in this climate.

When he got to the home he was searching for, he began to doubt whether he should go ahead and knock. However, he forced himself to do it. After what he'd witnessed the day before, he suspected Cary might want to escape the city too. But the only way to find out where he and his family were staying, after their shop and home were set on fire, was to ask Margie. He felt anxious, though, because he knew Margie wasn't someone he should trust. But Bob convinced himself he could play it cool.

He knocked twice and waited, but when the door swung open, Bob was suddenly tongue-tied. "Judge Moffit," Bob stammered, unable to hide the surprise in his voice.

The balding judge stood in the doorway, staring out at Bob with a surly expression.

Bob asked, "What are you doing here?"

"I was just about to ask you the same thing," said Moffit laughing condescendingly. "What's the matter? You get tired of that old bat you call a wife? If so, I'm afraid you're a little too late. I've already called dibs on *this* string bean."

Bob felt the urge to grab Moffit around the neck, but just then, Margie appeared in the doorway next to Moffit. "Oh, hi there, Bob. Crazy night, huh? What brings you over?"

Bob knew he couldn't go through with his plan now. Even if Margie didn't suspect anything, he was certain that Moffit would. The man was instinctively paranoid, after all.

"I wanted to make sure your place was intact," he lied. "Maude and I...well, our apartment was completely destroyed. And Maude's missing." Bob's voice cracked. "I thought whoever did this might be targeting the three of us after what happened at the courthouse yesterday."

Margie stared at him sympathetically. "I'm real sorry about Maude. But no, it looks like the two of us escaped this one," she said, motioning towards Moffit. "We just assumed it was some insane accident. Honestly, I hope it was. It would be real awful if there was a bomber on the loose."

Moffit looked at Bob suspiciously and asked, "If you're wife's missing, then why aren't you out *there* looking for her? Seems strange you came *here*."

Bob shook his head, beginning to feel frustrated. "I have been out looking for her, but I thought I'd stop by to confirm that my theory was wrong."

Moffit clearly didn't trust Bob. He looked up at the front of Margie's building and said, "Seems like you shoulda known there was nothing wrong with the place just by looking at it from the outside. What are you *really* after, Bob?"

Margie scolded Moffit, "Honey, his wife is probably dead. Leave the man alone, will ya?"

Bob was trying not to let Moffit get to him, but he couldn't help it. He knew he was fabricating the truth, but it burned him up that Moffit was trying to call him out on it. "Don't be so paranoid, Moffit!" he said. "I'll see you two in the courtroom tomorrow if court's in session."

"Why wouldn't it be?" asked Moffit. "Just a regular Wednesday. The world doesn't need to stop every time there's a slight hiccup. Better to carry on than to stand on your head like an idiot."

Bob backed away. "Okay, judge. See you tomorrow then," he said.

"Damn skippy you will!" said Moffit. Then he slammed the door before Margie and Bob could even say goodbye.

Bob turned and hurried in the direction of the city's far gate. This way would take him back by his apartment, which he hoped would increase his chances of running into Maude. He couldn't waste any more time looking for Cary, and he wished he hadn't ever bothered going to Margie's.

He couldn't believe that Margie and Moffit were an item. Bob had assumed that Margie disliked the judge just as much as he did, and he couldn't help but wonder if their relationship had begun prior to them working together. Either way, he thought it was highly inappropriate, but it didn't matter anymore. All that was important was finding Maude and escaping the ludicrous city.

"Focus, Bob," he told himself. He knew as soon as the others started to make their way out of town, there would only be so much time until Goodman figured out what they were up to. What Bob didn't realize was that Goodman was already well aware of what he and his friends were up to—for it had been part of Goodman's plan all along.

Maude sat behind Max on the back of a black horse as they rode up to the city's far gate. They had gone to the home of some of Max's estranged relatives, or rather to their stables. Max had been under the impression that the barn would be full of horses, but there was only one inside—an old gelding who wasn't in the best of shape, judging by his weak looking coat and ornery disposition.

Nevertheless, Max and Maude were in no position to be choosy, as long as the horse was able to carry them out of town. So, Max saddled him up and then fastened Maude's suitcases over his sides. Then they led him out the back of the stable and away from the house so they wouldn't get caught. Luckily, the sun had set, and the light in the sky was dim.

As they approached the city gate, Max asked, "Are you sure this is a good idea, Maude? Even if *we* don't draw suspicion, I'm pretty sure that your suitcases will."

Maude dismissed Max's doubts. "We've done nothing wrong. Just relax and keep your hood up. Hopefully, they'll think we're doing council business, but if they start to ask questions, let me do the talking."

The black gelding neighed and shifted his weight as they began their descent down the steep ramp that led to the exit. At the bottom was a twelve-foot, iron gate with four guards standing in front of it. Three of the guards chatted casually among themselves while the fourth stood at attention with a laser-like stare that was focused on Max and Maude.

"Whoa there!" he said to them, raising his hand towards the horse's face. "What do you think you're doing, coming down this way? We aren't letting anyone *in* or *out* at the moment. Prime Minister's orders!"

Max quipped, "Do you think there's someone out there trying to get in?"

Maude nudged him in the back and said to the guard, "Good evening, sir. We've been sent on official council business to setup a campsite outside the city. It's for the folks who lost their homes in the explosions. Surely, you've been informed of this already?" Maude asked, but in a much softer voice than usual.

"No, indeed we *haven't* been informed of any such nonsense. Right, guys?"

The men in guards' uniforms who were talking to each other didn't acknowledge him. However, the guard talking to Max and Maude wouldn't be ignored. He raised his voice to the other guards and asked again, "Right, guys?!"

One of the three guards glanced over and said, "Sure. Whatever you say, Neil." Then he snickered and began talking to his pals again.

Maude pushed back. "Obviously, we've arrived before your orders to let us pass, but I insist that you do so anyway. We need to get ahead of the others to begin setting up before it gets too late. There are children who have no home or bed to return to, nowhere to lay their weary heads at this very moment. Do you really want to deprive them of a goodnight's sleep after such a hellish day?"

Neil shook his head. "You aren't getting through here without proper orders. But on the other hand, you know what orders we *do* have? To arrest any old ladies who're trying to break out of here tonight. And from what I can see under that cloak of yours, you look pretty old. Why don't you climb down off your horse and let me take a look at you."

Max began to protest, but Maude put her hand on his shoulder. "It's okay," she assured him. Then she slid off the horse and stood in front of Neil.

"Pull down your hood," he ordered.

Without touching it, Maude's hood suddenly fell. Max held his breath and looked straight ahead at the gate. "So?" asked Maude in a smooth voice. "Are you satisfied?"

Neil said, "Yeah, okay. I guess it was just the dim lighting. I once had the opposite problem picking up a woman in a dark tavern. She looked twenty-something in the shadows, but not so much after we got back to my place."

Max cleared his throat. "Ahem. Can we go now?"

Neil shook his head. "No, I still can't let you through without orders."

Maude pulled her hood back on just as a few families arrived behind them with their camping gear. John and his sons were part of the group, along with Jacques.

"I see," said Maude. "Well, my father isn't going to like this."

Neil laughed. "Oh, really? And why should that concern me?"

Maude replied in a smug tone, "Because I'm the Prime Minister's daughter."

Neil seemed skeptical. "Goodman has a daughter?" he asked. "How come I've never heard of you before?"

Maude laughed. "Why would you think you knew the personal business of your Prime Minister? Do you normally make it a habit to learn about the family members of your leaders?"

Neil looked stumped. "Well, no. But—"

Before he could continue, though, Maude said, "I'm sure my father will be really pleased to know you've called me old *and* a liar, all in one meeting."

It was obvious that Neil was starting to feel in over his head, despite not wanting to give up his control. "I can't let you through without orders, and that's final!" he said, though his voice wavered a little.

But Maude didn't quit. She pointed towards the line of people that was forming behind them. "Do you really think all these people would have shown up here on a whim with their camping gear in tow? Can't your addled brain see that it's more likely the council put together a plan to find these people somewhere to sleep until their homes are reconstructed? Or do you imagine that these poor families are planning some kind of escape? Maybe they're going to go off into the night to build a renegade city that will challenge my father's power?" she asked mockingly.

At this point, one of the chatty guards broke away from his group. "Just let them through, Neil! I'm sure the orders will arrive any minute, but in the meantime, these people are crowding the ramp. If we don't get the orders, we'll go wrangle them up later. It's not like they're going to get very far on foot."

Neil stared angrily at the guard who was undermining him. "But these two have a horse!" he argued.

The other guard rolled his eyes and pushed the lever to open the gate. "Well, whoop-dee-doo! Don't you see how sickly that thing is? They'd be lucky to go a mile before it drops dead. Just look at it!"

The other guards began waving the crowd forward. "Alright, everyone. Mosey along. That's it," the guards spoke as the growing groups of people began to pour through the open gate.

Maude said to Max, "Go on ahead. I'll meet you on the other side in just a second. I want to talk to John." Max nodded and kicked the horse's sides to move him forward.

Several people walked past Maude before John and his sons reached her. "Hello John, Egan, Samuel, and Jacques."

The four men greeted Maude, but Maude noticed that John was looking at her suspiciously. They exited the city, and once they were well clear of the gate, Maude asked, "Did Bob give you the idea to come here?"

Jacques replied, "Mais, oui! You know your husband very well, madame! Bob was how you say, 'the man with the plan.' He told us to bring our tents and such and to get out of the city tout de suite! Right away!

"Tell me, have you thought about what kind of kitchens we

will have in the new city? I do not wish to be shoved into a tiny rattrap of a workspace encore. It is impossible to build master-pieces in such a tiny kitchen. But nobody listened to me when they were building the *novel* Waldoff. They say, 'No, Jacques! You must work with what you are given.' What miserable cows!"

Maude squeezed Jacques' arm. "No. I haven't thought about it yet, Jacques. But I'm sure we can work something out." Then to John, she said, "Listen, I don't think they're going to let Bob leave. Did he tell everyone where to meet after we exit the city?"

John answered, "No. I assumed he had a plan, though."

Maude looked concerned. "I see. Well, we'll have to impro-vise then. I have a feeling there will be a lot of people leaving tonight. If not out of principle, then out of fear."

John nodded, and they walked in silence for a moment before he asked, "Maude, how did you know we were coming?"

"What do you mean?" she asked surprised.

"Well, it sounded like you were already arguing with that guard about getting us through the gates before we'd even showed up."

Maude shrugged and shook her head. "I didn't know you were coming. You must've misunderstood."

John looked at Maude out of the corner of his eye as they continued to walk. "So, I guess then that I also misunderstood seeing you with bright red hair and smooth skin while you were speaking to the guard with your hood down?"

Maude grinned knowingly and said, "Yes, John. I guess you did."

Bob dashed around the corner towards the ramp near the far gate. It had taken him longer to get there than he'd expected. On his way, he had stumbled upon a long row of destroyed homes. Groups of men, women, and children were working together to clear some of the rubble while searching for lost family members who were trapped in the debris. Bob did his best to look past it, to ignore the voice inside of him that told him he should lend a hand, but in the end, he was unable to resist the urge to stop and help.

He spent nearly an hour elbow-to-elbow with the people who lived on this blown apart stretch of street. It was heartbreaking to hear all the stories of missing loved ones, but it also motivated Bob to keep working—even though he knew his chances of escape were getting slimmer the longer he stayed.

Finally, the darkness began to hinder their search. Bob wished he could have run back to his own apartment to fetch some equipment that would've kept the site lit throughout the night, but all of that was gone now, completely obliterated. Before he left, he told several of the people to go to city hall in the morning and remind the council that there should be lots of leftover army equipment stored away somewhere—equipment that could help them with their search.

Bob wished them luck and then hurried down the long row of destruction on his way towards the exit. But then suddenly, he ran into Cary. It turned out that the Dome's had been staying close by with some friends, and when Cary heard the calls for help, he'd gone right away to lend a hand to the search effort.

"Cary!" Bob shouted when he caught sight of him. Cary was hauling several heavy pieces of jagged stone away from a pile of rubble. When he saw his former lawyer, he gave him a cool nod, which surprised Bob. He shrugged it off, though, and continued to approach Cary.

"Hey, can I help you carry some of those?" Bob asked.

"No. I can manage them by myself. You're welcome to grab some of your own."

Bob picked up a few large rocks from the side of a pile and hurried to catch up with his former client.

"I went looking for you," Bob told him. Then in a hushed tone, he said, "After our discussion last night in the tavern, I thought you'd like to know that there's a group leaving New Waldoff. *Tonight*. We're pretty sure Goodman is trying to target us, and so we've decided to build our own city. I think you should come too. You can bring your family if you don't think they'd be opposed to the idea."

Cary dropped the heavy stones he was carrying into a large wagon that had been brought in to help clear away the rubble, and Bob did the same with his.

Cary replied, "You know, Bob. I'm surprised you're making me this offer after leaving things the way we did. It seems like you carry a pretty big grudge towards folks like me and mine."

Bob looked confused. "I do?" he asked. "What gives you that impression?"

Cary scoffed. "You called us a bunch of 'idiot zombies.' Remember?"

Bob thought about it for a moment. The memory of the drunken tirade he'd gone on before Maude came to fetch him was a bit fuzzy, but as it came back to him, he began to look guilty. "I'm sorry, Cary. I didn't mean to say a lot of those things. I think I was still out of my head from the concussion, not to mention the ale. I know you're not an idiot zombie. That was just a terrible choice of words brought on by some leftover frustrations, I suppose."

Cary smiled. "But see, Bob. You just admitted it. You do still have some anger over what happened. And honestly, you have every right to be angry. You might be surprised to know that a lot of us idiot zombies are still angry too."

Bob nodded. "I bet you are, Cary. But the difference is that most of the people on your side don't seem to want to do anything to stop that same kind of crazy situation from repeating itself. Those of us leaving tonight *do.*"

"I'm sure that's true, Bob. But I won't be coming with you."

Bob looked hurt. "I think you should reconsider. If you stay here, it's likely you'll have to go through something terrible again, just like what happened when the twins took over, but probably worse." Bob motioned towards the blown apart street.

Cary shook his head. "It's a firm 'no,' friend. I appreciate that you're trying to help me, but I just can't. It's not who I am. Whether by God or man, I was built to go wherever my people go. Even if that means my own destruction."

The two men stood a second longer, staring at one another until, finally, Bob reached out his hand. The two shook and Bob said, "I think I get it, Cary. You have a good heart. I hope *your people* know that."

Cary smiled. "Thanks, Bob. I wish you and Maude the best. And don't worry, your secret is safe with me."

Bob drew in a breath at the mention of Maude's name. He knew it was time to get going, though. He didn't need to fill Cary in about Maude's disappearance. It was likely the last time he and Cary would ever see each other again anyway, he thought. As Bob turned to run towards the gate, he said, "Take good care of yourself, Cary! And know that you'll always have a home with us if you decide to change your mind!"

Bob was nervous walking down the dark ramp towards the city gate. He could see the lunar surface just outside. He ran his hand over his hair to smooth it down, like he was preparing for a job interview or a first date. He'd almost reached the four men who were guarding the gate when he heard one of them yell, "Nope! Turn yourself around. We've let enough of you through, and we still haven't gotten any orders saying we should. You can go find somewhere else to sleep tonight."

Bob's stomach sank. "Please, gentlemen. You've got to let me through. My wife took the camping gear our friends lent us, and she's already out there. I don't have anywhere else to go."

The guard who'd made the decision to let everyone through earlier laughed. "That's a real sad story you got, mister. I guess you'll just have to go find a nice bed of dirt to lie in with no place to go."

Bob knew the situation looked bleak, but he wasn't willing to give up yet. "Don't you all recognize me? I'm on the council. When Goodman hears—"

The guard named Neil said, "Nope! Don't even start that!"

Then speaking to the guard who'd opened the gate earlier, Neil said, "See what happens when you give 'em an inch, Eli? You know, the four of us are going to be working a double shift because of you! All those people you decided to let through are going to have to be accounted for, and guess who's going to be tasked with that job? The same lame brains who let them through in the first place!"

Bob tried again. "No, really fellas. I *am* on the council. What do I have to do to prove it?"

One of the other guards smirked. "You could show us your official councilman badge. Do you have your badge with you?"

Bob couldn't believe that the council members had badges. "Undoubtedly to get preferential treatment," he thought.

But he replied, "No, of course I don't have my badge! It was in my apartment, and my apartment is currently in teeny tiny pieces all over the city!"

"Oh, that's too bad," said Eli. "Hey guys, maybe we should help him out. What do you say? He looks like a nice enough bloke, even if he's not who he says he is."

The other guards laughed, and right then, Neil moved

around to Bob's back and tightened a handcuff bracelet around one of his wrists.

"Hey! What are you doing?" Bob demanded. He pulled away from Neil, but the other guards rushed to hold him in place as Neil tightened the second handcuff bracelet around Bob's other wrist.

"What in the world did you do that for?" he yelled. "You could have just said *no!*"

Neil faced Bob with a satisfied expression. "We did, remember? You just weren't willing to take 'no' for an answer. But it didn't really make any difference. We were just toying with you. We've been waiting all night for you, Bob. The council ordered us to arrest you on sight. You and your woman. Where is the old bag, anyway?"

Bob was furious. He realized he'd walked right into Goodman's trap. He spat at the guards. "I will never give you Maude! You could torture me for a thousand years, and I'd never tell you where she is." Bob knew this was beside the point since he didn't actually know where Maude was, or that she was even still alive. But he felt the need to lash out, to show them that he wouldn't roll over for them.

Neil shrugged indifferently. "Okay, suit yourself. You're under arrest for conspiracy, and the unlawful use of explosives, as well as the destruction of private property. Anything you say will be used against you. If you seek representation, then I guess you can just go ahead and contact *you!*" Neil said tauntingly.

Bob wasn't listening anymore, though. He'd begun to concentrate on his next move. Only, it was hard playing a mental game of chess when he had no idea where his opponent's pieces were. He knew he was lacking key information that was going to make it nearly impossible to decide what his best options were. He needed to know what Goodman's plan was, and he needed to know fast.

CHAPTER 21

THE TRUTH ABOUT THE WOLVES

Axel was being pulled apart, just like years earlier when the dark spirit had pulled his energy apart on top of Black Ice Fort. He could hear Ragher talking off in the distance, but his voice was muffled like he was speaking to him from behind a closed door.

"After I realized that the dark spirit was unaware of Theia's disappearance, I came up with an idea," Ragher said.

Suddenly, Axel's energy smashed back together, and he found himself on top of Black Ice Glacier, watching Ragher as he confronted the dark spirit. The spirit appeared in the smoky form of a giant, black wolf, standing on its hind legs. Ragher and the spirit were illuminated by several large piles of crystals that glowed in deep red tones.

Ragher yelled up at the spirit, "If I give you what you want, it will be on *my* terms."

The evil spirit glared at Ragher with its demonic, red eyes. His deep voice blasted down from above. "What *terms* do you speak of?"

Ragher paused to think. Then he said, "If I allow you to

use my energy, it will be when Theia is standing before me, just as you are now."

The dark spirit laughed, scornfully. "Why should it matter where she is standing? Is it you wish to warn her first?"

Ragher shook his head. "No, but I won't explain myself any further. I require some time to think this over. I'll return with my answer soon."

The giant, smoky wolf became enraged. "You've wasted my time!" he yelled as his body evaporated into a fine, black mist. "Leave here at once but know this—I will not spare you from whatever torture I see fit until you've returned!"

Then the spirit transformed himself into a dark tornado. He whipped around violently, picking Ragher up and launching him into the darkness. Ragher bounced and skidded across the ground until he came to a stop. Axel watched as his father slowly stood and limped away.

When Axel looked back at the dark spirit, he saw that he had changed himself into a tall, muscular human. Speaking to someone whom Axel couldn't see, the spirit asked, "You've delivered the package to the humans, Gryobe?"

A deep voice answered. "Yes, my lord. It is done."

"Very good. If my plan works, we may not need the Moon Walker to exact my revenge. We'll wait and see how strong the child is before we accept his offer. He's acting suspicious, and I refuse to deal with any more of this drivel. It seems that he's still under the influence of my sister."

The other voice said, "Yes, my master. However, I believe your persuasion has worked on the Moon Walker. He wouldn't have come here today if he still wished to live."

The dark spirit said, "Hmm, possibly. But mortals are so fickle, Gryobe. You can never trust their desire for self-harm. They can be splayed across death's doorstep, dying of thirst and ready to accept their fate. But if you offer them even the tiniest drop of water, instantly an entire oasis of optimism springs forth inside of them. Truly, they find hope in the most pitiful of things. It's horribly pathetic."

"Yes, lord. It's why you should never give thirsty beggars water."

The dark spirit made an annoyed face. "That's not the point, Gryobe. But yes, fine. You should never give beggars anything. It's the only way to teach them not to beg."

Then, without any warning, Axel was pulled into another vision.

"I won't have to give in to him as long as Theia is truly gone," Ragher spoke into the darkness. It took Axel a second to realize he'd been dropped into a different dark passageway inside the ice labyrinth and was listening to Ragher as he spoke to the oracle.

Ragher said, "I'll give the dark spirit my word, but as long as Theia isn't here, I won't have to act on this promise. And in the meantime, the dark spirit will be forced to leave my loved ones alone."

The oracle replied, "No, Ragher. It's important that the dark spirit doesn't know of Theia's absence. He would use it to his advantage and hurt many others besides you and your loved ones."

Ragher lost his temper and began to fume. "My god! Is there nothing you will let me do to ease my suffering?! This pain that you've thrust upon me my entire life? You kept me here against my will for hundreds of years! But for what purpose? I thought it was so I could protect Neriti. You trained me for it with all your visions of the future. You tricked me into falling in love with her before she was even born. I would've done anything to keep her and our family safe! But you've denied me that too! You are no more my friend than the dark spirit. But at least with him, I know where I stand."

Ragher's muffled voice spoke to Axel through the vision. "I was furious with the oracle for preventing me from doing what

I felt was right, *again*. However, once I calmed down, I heeded her warning, because who was I to put so many lives in danger? I didn't return to the dark spirit for many years, and surprisingly, for many years he left us alone. I found out later that it was because he'd turned his attention to Dan, which was partly because of me.

"Despite my obedience to the oracle, the dark spirit found out Theia was gone. He sent his monster, Gryobe, to spy on Neriti and me, and it overheard us discussing what the oracle had revealed about Theia's absence. When Gryobe showed itself, I had to hold your mother back to keep her from attacking it."

Colors seeped through the darkness as another vision appeared around Axel. He heard the ugly creature's voice. "Control your wench, Moon Walker!" Gryobe ordered Ragher.

Ragher jumped on top of Neriti's back, trying to push her to the ground as she struggled to break free from him. She yelled at the monster, "I'm going to rip you to shreds, starting with that filthy white film over your eyes. Then I'm going to tear those disgusting skin-tails from your head and beat you to a bloody pulp before strangling you with them!"

Gryobe laughed mockingly. "Tsk. Tsk, Neriti. I thought you were supposed to be the chosen wolf, destined for greatness among your kind. If you continue to talk like that, the other wolves might realize you're just a foul-mouthed peasant—no better than any of the rest of them."

"Let go of me!" Neriti wailed at Ragher, but he had pushed his whole body down on top of her so she could barely move a muscle.

"No, Neriti. You can't win this fight. It wants you to attack it so it can kill you. I'm certain of it. It's why it's never harmed either of us before. The dark spirit told it not to. But it *will* defend itself."

"I don't care!" screamed Neriti. "It killed our grandchildren! It's tormented us for decades and robbed us of everything precious! I have to kill it. I have to! LET ME GO!"

The rubbery-faced creature howled its deep, monstrous laugh as Ragher continued to hold tightly to Neriti, practically smothering her under his weight.

It spoke again, "What a waste of fur and energy you wolves are. You pick such absurd things to care about. With all the unfair advantages your god has given you, you could've ruled this world. But instead, you allow yourselves to be herded like mindless sheep, never setting foot outside the borders you've been given. No imagination for glory or domination. Such a pity. At least it makes you predictable. My master sensed you might have some valuable information after you visited the off-lands this last time. Guess it's good I've been keeping a close watch on you."

Ragher asked the monster breathlessly, "What do you mean? What unfair advantages has Theia given us?"

The monster snorted. "Are you really this much of a puppet? Or do you just pretend not to know?"

Ragher shook his head. "No, I don't. Why don't you enlighten me?"

The spirit's minion replied, "It is neither my job nor desire to enlighten you. I'm delighted by your ignorance, in fact."

"Then at least tell me why your master doesn't go to the 'off-lands,' as you call them. There's a reason you've never followed me into the tunnels, isn't there?"

Before the monster could reply, Neriti, began to inch her way out from underneath Ragher. "No!" he yelled at her.

But Neriti shot back, "Ragher, I can't breathe!"

Gryobe took this as its cue to leave, but as it did, Axel noticed the white orb by the side of its face begin to glow.

Suddenly, the vision changed again. Ragher narrated, "After the dark spirit learned that Theia was gone, he became obsessed with destruction. He wanted to rid the Moon of all the wolves and humans. And because of what Gryobe overheard me and your mother discussing, he believed he could accomplish this by turning Dan into his human crony.

"You may remember that soon after the travelers arrived, you and Neriti and I went with Ruth to pay Maude a visit. Right away, the males in the room were dismissed so Neriti could talk privately with the two women. During their discussion, Maude was allowed to hold the crystal that Neriti had received at Crystal Crater when she summoned up a vision with the other healers. When Maude held the crystal, her body was possessed by a spirit who relayed a prophecy to Ruth and Neriti.

"This was how Neriti learned that the twins and Helen would someday be born. The voice told her that Helen would come from the light and have the power to bring balance to the moon, whereas the twins would come from the dark.

"Neriti believed that the human twins were our grandchildren, Sangue and Hotep. She'd had visions before they were born that the darkness had plans to steal them and their sister. So, when the spirit possessing Maude told your mother this prophecy, she decided it meant that the dark spirit was going to return Sangue and Hotep in human form through Maude.

"As you know, Neriti also believed that Helen was going to be the reincarnation of your niece, Mawd. She had already had many dreams that she would see Mawd again one day in a different flesh, even before Mawd was killed. So, because of this and what the spirit told her, Neriti sensed that Helen would have special powers and do important things *if* she were allowed to be taught the ways of the lunar wolves."

Axel watched the scene. The lights in Maude and Bob's tiny home dimmed, and a bright light encompassed Maude's body. Axel listened as the loud voice bellowed the prophecy at Ruth and Neriti.

The vision then switched to Neriti talking to Maude and Bob in their living room. Ragher explained, "Neriti shared the prophecy with Maude and Bob after the twins were born. What we didn't know at the time, however, was that the dark spirit believed it was Theia who would come to life in human form as Helen.

"The day that Gryobe eavesdropped on your mother and me, he heard us talking not just about Theia's absence, but about the prophecy that had been shared with Neriti and Ruth. When Gryobe told the dark spirit about the prophecy *and* Theia's absence at the same time, the spirit decided that this must be the reason Theia had gone missing—so that she could secretly try to take control of the Moon as a human. From that day on, the dark spirit became convinced that he was locked in a battle for dominion over the Moon against Theia in the form of Helen, even though it wasn't true.

"After I went to work for Dan, I learned that the spirit was equipping him with powers that would help him carry out the spirit's plan to destroy the Moon realm and Theia. Dan had learned how to become invisible and how to perform some basic mind control by tapping into the dark spirit's energy. The interesting part about this, though, was that the spirit made Dan believe it was Theia's energy he was harnessing.

"Eventually, I realized that the dark spirit had lied to Dan about this because he was certain Dan would try to turn on him if he knew he could steal his energy. And if Dan tried to go after the dark spirit's energy, then the dark spirit would have been forced to kill him, which would've ruined everything he was working towards. As it was, he had Dan firmly under his control and didn't want to jeopardize losing his servant.

"Once I knew that Dan could become invisible, I suggested he should go and listen to what you, Neriti, and the others were teaching Helen—to find out what your motives were. I told him where to find you, but I let your mother know in advance so she could feed Dan lies.

"Neriti decided to use this opportunity to expand on the prophecy in order to keep Helen safe. She knew that Dan wanted Helen dead because he'd already tried to kill her when she was an infant. So, she lied to make it seem as if Helen's fate were tied to her brothers'—that only if the twins *didn't* succeed in taking control of Theia would Helen be able to restore the Moon's balance. She thought Dan would turn his attention towards Theia and leave Helen alone once he heard this. We didn't know then that the dark spirit believed Helen *was* Theia, and that, because of this, the false prophecy only made things more dangerous for Helen.

"Neriti and you told Helen this false version of the prophecy again and again so that Dan would overhear it and leave Helen alone. But Neriti also wanted Helen to believe it too. She thought it would be good for Helen to be wary of her brothers. Yet I fear your mother was wrong to do this. Looking back, I can see how this lie prevented Helen from living her life freely. Just as my presence in your mother's life prevented her from living the life she was destined for. And just like the lies your mother and I told prevented you and Tahissi from living the lives you should've had.

"The false prophecy placed a heavy burden on Helen's shoulders; it made her think that in order to bring balance to the Moon she had to *beat* her brothers. And eventually, this is what made her vulnerable to Dan's terrible cruelty. It's what drove her to face him the day he purged her body from our realm. If your mother and I had only known that the dark spirit believed Theia was inside of Helen, we could have altered the prophecy in a different way to show him it wasn't true."

Axel said angrily, "Or you could have NOT meddled with the prophecy at all. It seems like you and Neriti should have realized what a disastrous impact unintended consequences can have. Why in the world weren't you two being more careful?"

Ragher replied, "Because, Axel. We were desperate to keep everyone safe. We believed we were the only two beings in the entire realm that fully understood how grave the humans and wolves' situation was. Therefore, we felt we had to do whatever we could to stop the dark spirit without getting ourselves killed in the process."

Axel frowned. "When did you finally figure out the dark spirit was targeting Helen?"

Ragher replied, "Not until the very moment Dan erased Helen's body. Helen had shown up at Black Ice Fort unexpectedly. I watched the dark spirit whisper something in Dan's ear. Then Dan disappeared. As soon as he was gone, the dark spirit spoke to me. He told me he was going to take care of Theia once and for all without my help."

A vision of the dark spirit came into view inside a room within Black Ice Fort. Ragher was standing in front of the shapeless, black fog. Its red eyes peered out at him. "You stupid creature! You and your worthless god have thought me a fool this entire time. But I knew where Theia was hiding, and now it's time to end this ridiculous charade. In just a moment, Dan will release Theia from her human body, and I shall feast on her weakened energy, just like I feasted on so many of you Moon Walkers long ago!"

Before Ragher had time to react, a giant wolf head made of black fog emerged from the spirit's side. It was Neriti.

"No!" she screamed. "I will never let you hurt her!"

Ragher cowered against the wall at the sight of his deceased wife appearing out of the dark spirit. "Neriti?" he whispered.

Neriti's giant head nodded at Ragher slightly, but her attention was focused on the spirit. His horrific eyes grew in size as the spirit coiled his smoky fabric tightly, trying to rid himself of Neriti's head like it were a blemish on his body. Neriti howled loudly and began to wrap the spirit's misty particles around her, by pulling in the opposite direction. Ragher realized it had become a tug of war.

Ragher explained the scene. "I was in shock to see Neriti appear from the dark spirit's body, but I knew what she was trying to do. She had come to try and save our granddaughter —to save Mawd in the form of Helen. I knew I had to help, so I ran towards the front of the fort to stop Dan from harming Helen, but it was already too late. Halfway there, I found her. She was furious and scared, roaming the hallways and looking through Dan's torture chambers."

The words Ragher spoke suddenly manifested into a vision. Axel watched as Ragher stood down a dimly lit hallway, staring at Helen. She was running in and out of rooms, crying and screaming at the top of her lungs. Ragher didn't seem to know what to do, but eventually he marched up to the lanky, young woman and ordered her to stop.

Helen was stunned. "You can see me?" she gasped.

But Ragher shook his head. "No. Well, actually yes. But nobody else will be able to. I'm so sorry, Helen. You should never have come here."

Helen looked at Ragher with anger and sadness, like she was on the verge of a complete meltdown. She began to scream again, but Ragher stopped her once more.

"You can't do that here. You can't be here. There's more going on than what Neriti told you. If you stay, you'll be forced to become like Dan or possibly destroyed all together. You have to go back to your parents and wait. You have protection there. However, you mustn't tell anyone of this meeting. It would put Axel in terrible danger."

"But Roger, how do I know I can trust—" Helen began to ask. But suddenly a blood curdling scream erupted throughout the fort. Helen's eyes grew large with terror, and Ragher yelled, "Go!"

Helen turned and ran towards the front of the fort while Ragher galloped back to the room where he'd left the dark spirit fighting Neriti. But before he reached the room, the stone walls in the hallway began to shake, and Axel heard loud footsteps approaching. It was the dark spirit. He had taken the form of a giant man and was tearing through the fort towards Ragher.

"Where is she?" he yelled when he saw Ragher standing in his way—frozen in fear. Ragher tried to think fast, but suddenly Dan appeared out of thin air with a smug grin across his face. "I saw what you did," he said to Ragher tauntingly. "I saw you talking to nobody back there. Only it was Helen, wasn't it? No matter how much time I spend torturing you, you continue to help my enemies. What a waste of torture you are! Maybe it's time I hang your head outside the walls next to the bryobane skulls. What do you say? At least, you'd finally be of some use to me that way."

Axel watched as the dark spirit whispered into Dan's ear, and a twinkle of something sinister flashed across Dan's eyes. "Aw, yes," he said. "I've been given an even better idea. I was going to start testing my new formula on the prisoners soon, but I'll let you perform the tests instead—with my supervision, of course. In the meantime, it's back to solitary for you!"

Ragher began to protest, but the vision faded, leaving Axel and the present day Ragher alone in the dark.

Axel said, "I still don't understand why you went to work for Dan and the dark spirit. There had to have been a better way to keep them in check. Right?"

A new vision appeared around them. Ragher was facing a bright ball of light inside the passageway. From within it, he heard the oracle speaking. "I'd hoped it wouldn't come to this. However, there's too much at stake now that the dark spirit knows Theia is gone. He will try to take over the entire world. You cannot allow this to happen. You must do what he asks of you. I won't lie, Ragher. It will be your hardest test yet. But you must endure it. No matter what wicked things he asks of you, you must do them in order to build his trust. It's the only way you will be able to undermine his plans."

Ragher told the oracle, "I don't think I can do this. I'm not brave enough. I would rather die than allow another creature to be harmed."

"This will be much more than allowing others to be harmed, Ragher. You yourself will be asked to torture and kill. It's regrettable, of course, but it must be done. You need to remember that there are many more lives depending on you than the few you'll be called on to ruin. However, it was your carelessness that caused all of this. By allowing Gryobe to hear your conversation with Neriti, you endangered many, and now this is the price you must pay to make things right."

Axel felt sick to his stomach. He was finally realizing how much of their lives had been orchestrated and controlled, and by a couple of mysterious spirits whom he had never even known existed. He was deeply disturbed by the realization. The freedom he believed he had—believed that they all had—was just an illusion And though he was no warrior, he suddenly felt the desire to fight.

"What about Neriti?" he asked. "All this time, I imagined that she had returned as a ghost when she saved me at the top of the fort. But that's not true. She's trapped inside the dark spirit, isn't she?"

Ragher nodded. "Yes, Axel. I'm afraid so."

Axel was beside himself with rage. "You did this, Ragher! Admit it! You led Dan straight to my mother! You let them murder her so that the dark spirit could feast on her energy!"

Ragher frowned. "No, Axel. I told you before, the dark spirit can't feast on wolves. The decision that led to Neriti's death was one that she made herself. I will explain everything so that you finally understand, and *then* you can make up your mind whatever way you think is best."

Axel's jaw clenched in anger, but he let Ragher speak.

"Your mother and I were barely together after you came back from your year away. I was spending most of my time on the Darkside, just as I had done the several years prior. You probably remember I was gone a lot, but it wasn't on healer business like I told you. Before Tahissi's family was killed, I'd made the decision to keep my distance from the pack. Your mother had been having visions that the dark spirit was planning something horrible. So, I stayed away as much as possible. Often, I would find Gryobe and lead it on a wild goose chase, partly to toy with it, but also to keep it distracted so it was focused on me instead of our family.

"When you returned from your time away, I was furious with you both, so I stayed gone most of the time. But I think that suited Neriti fine. We still loved each other very much, but our relationship had become secondary to all the pain we had caused. It had begun to feel like staying together was equivalent to condoning all the awful decisions we'd made.

"With me gone most of the time, Neriti was able to concentrate on being a mother figure and mentor to you and eventually to Helen too. When the oracle finally gave me my orders to go work for the dark spirit, I met with your mother to tell her what I planned to do. I told her I hoped it would keep you and the others safe and that I loved her and would find a way to pass information to her whenever I could.

"Then I went to the dark spirit and told him I no longer wished to be a wolf and that when Theia returned, I would allow him to use my power against her. My only condition was that I work as Dan's henchman while I waited. The dark spirit loved the idea, and although he kept a close watch on me, it didn't matter because Dan was incapable of keeping his mouth shut. Whatever Dan knew, so did I.

"Like the oracle warned, the tests I was put through to keep their trust were appalling. I was forced to do horrific things to our kind. It darkened my mind in ways I'll never be able to put into words. I only hope that the good I did was enough to outweigh all the bad."

"Like what? What did you do that could possibly outweigh all the bad?" Axel asked with what seemed like genuine curiosity.

"Well, one of the main things was that I continually altered the formulas Dan worked on. Since he forced me to torture his prisoners, I had easy access to the formulas he created to poison the wolves. The gas bombs that he had me deliver to the underground tunnels were meant to wipe out the rest of our kind. However, I changed the formula so that it only took away your voices.

"Dan was livid when he found out you weren't dead, but I told him that it might be Helen's doing. I suggested that maybe she'd gained the power to foil his plans in whatever dimension he'd sent her to. Luckily, he believed this, and for a long time he worried she was spying on him. Whenever the dark spirit wasn't around, he'd talk to her as if she were there listening to him.

"I also changed the formula that Dan used to make Helen invisible, although I've regretted it ever since. When Dan told me he'd perfected the vanishing formula he'd used on Helen as a child, I snuck into his lab and changed it slightly by adding Moon Walker energy. This made it so that whomever the formula was used against gained some of my Moon Walker powers.

"If I'd been able to spend time with Helen alone, I could have taught her how to regain her form. But I knew it was too dangerous to seek her out. What I didn't realize is that the dark spirit knew I had changed the formula. He was counting on me to do it, in fact. He thought this would help him steal Helen's energy—believing, of course, that she was Theia. He assumed that the spell that was cast to prevent him from feasting on the Moon Walkers wouldn't apply to whoever gained Moon Walker powers from the formula. He thought he'd found a loophole in the spell."

"So, you're telling me that the dark spirit can eat Fred and me?!" Axel asked angrily.

Ragher replied, "No. He was wrong. The spell still applies. He can't steal your energy that way. You would have to give him your consent to use your Moon Walker powers. It's why he wasn't able to eat you when you met him on the rooftop at Black Ice Fort. Don't be fooled, though, there are still many terrible things he could do to you that don't involve feasting on your lifeforce."

The oracle spoke, "You can explain the rest later, Ragher. There's more to this than you know, and it's time that you learn your history. To stop the dark spirit, Axel, you'll have to teach the other wolves the truth about where you come from."

Axel asked, "What does that mean? 'Where we come from?'"

"Silence!" boomed the oracle. "You cannot learn by speaking. *Watch instead.*"

Suddenly, all the oxygen in the passageway was gone. Axel gasped for air, but there was none. His lungs burned and threatened to collapse as he tried with all his might to draw a breath and relieve the pain.

Axel's knees buckled, and he fell on his shins. He thought he was about to pass out from the asphyxiation when, finally, the air in the passageway returned. Axel gulped the air into his lungs.

He looked ahead to get his bearings and saw he was standing at the bottom of Crystal Crater. He glanced to his left and found Ragher by his side, looking just as shaken and confused as him. Then, sensing they weren't alone, the father and son turned around to find a woman made of flowing, golden light standing before them, surrounded by hundreds of strange looking beings. The woman was ten times the size of any human, but it was hard to tell if she was, in fact, meant to be a human because her facial features were completely non-existent. Her body was shaped like a woman's, but her skin was made of pure light, and her face was an enigma that was impossible to ignore.

"What is that?" Axel asked his father.

Ragher answered, "I don't know for certain, but she looks familiar. I'm sure I've seen her before. Perhaps in a dream."

Suddenly, Axel felt his mind being overpowered and sensed that the woman was casting some sort of spell on him. The urge he had to walk to her and bask in her light was like nothing he'd ever experienced before. It felt as though the light was magnetic, drawing him in with a promise of serenity.

He forced himself to look away and as his attention shifted, he noticed something strange about the creatures that were standing around. None of them were the same. "Look at these weird things," he said to Ragher. "They don't seem to belong to any one kind. Every single one is a different shape and size."

And indeed, they were. There were large ones and tiny ones, fat ones and thin ones, gray ones that stood upright with pointy ears, and turquoise ones that walked on all fours with no ears at all. "What do you make of this?" Axel asked curiously.

But Ragher didn't reply. He'd been hypnotized by the glow radiating from the golden woman.

"Ragher!" Axel shouted, trying to get his attention. But Ragher still didn't respond.

Finally, Axel yelled, "Turn your gaze, Father! The faceless light siren has sucked you in!"

Upon hearing the word "father," Ragher awoke from the

spell he was under. "Hmm?" he moaned, looking at Axel with a starstruck expression. But then quickly, he sobered to the reality of their situation. "Oh, I see," he said, glancing around at the weird creatures. Then, suddenly, he blurted out, "Oh my god! They're Moon Walkers! The oracle has brought us back to the beginning!"

Right at that moment, the oracle chimed in with her powerful voice. "Yes, Ragher. These are your kind, and that light energy in the form of a faceless woman is Theia. Do you remember this time at all? You were right there at the front of the crowd. See?"

As the oracle spoke, a flicker of light caught both the wolves' attention. They glanced to their side and caught sight of a rainbow-colored creature about the size of a hippopotamus, only it was shaped like a toaster with a retracted head.

Ragher looked back at his son. "Could that really be me?" he asked.

The oracle replied, "Yes, that was you, though none of you Moon Walkers ever held your shape for long. Theia is speaking to you through her light. I thought you might be able to hear her if you listened closely, but it's my fault if you can't. I erased your memory after you came to live in the ice tunnels, which may have severed your ability to communicate through her light."

Ragher's heart quickened. He'd always wondered why he hadn't been able to recall his life before the tunnels, but he'd never thought to question whether it was the oracle's doing. He'd decided long ago that it was likely she'd either created him or found him when he was very young and brought him up as her own. Either of these scenarios he'd been able to stomach, but not this.

"Why would you rob me of my memories?" he demanded angrily.

"Rob you?" the oracle asked in an amused tone. "Nobody

robbed you. You volunteered, Ragher. Turn your attention back to Theia and calm your mind. See if you can remember what was once instinctive to you."

Axel looked at Ragher with a worried expression. "This doesn't feel right, Ragher. Why would Theia captivate the Moon Walkers like this if she's good? Shouldn't she be giving them the choice whether to worship her or not?"

The oracle answered, "It's not Theia's fault that the Moon Walkers worship her, wolf. They were created in her likeness—to shift just as she can. Their love for her is innate because that's how they were designed."

Axel was about to protest when he heard a loud popping sound. He looked at Ragher and saw that his father was suddenly much bigger than before, and he no longer resembled a wolf. Instead, he had shifted into the form of the rainbow-colored, boxy creature that he had been at the time of the vision. And once again, he was fixated on Theia.

"Good, Ragher," the oracle said encouragingly. "You're starting to remember. Now listen quietly."

Axel shielded his eyes from the huge, radiating woman. Something about giving himself over to her felt grotesque. He stared at his paws while Ragher soaked in the light that shone on him from the goddess. However, Axel soon grew restless from trying so hard to avert his gaze. Fearful that he might accidentally give in, he turned his back on Theia. Yet as soon as he twisted around, he realized he'd made a terrible mistake.

Axel's eyes landed on one of the largest crystals in Crystal Crater. It towered over him at twenty feet tall. Normally, the crystal would have been dark, but the light from Theia had flooded into it, causing refracted beams of light to shoot out in all directions.

This time when Theia's light struck Axel's eyes, something strange happened to his conscious mind. His logical self was instantly muted, and all he could think of was *her*. He sat and stared at the glowing crystal for a long time, bathing in the serenity of the warm light. He was transported to a place within himself that was unfamiliar—a place free of anxiety and all burden.

Several minutes elapsed with Axel trapped inside this altered state of consciousness when he began to hear a faint ringing inside his ears. It started off as an angelic sound—a sharp, crisp chime. Then slowly, the high-pitched ringing took on more sounds, as though the bass and treble that followed were being carefully layered on top of the high ringing note. When all the sounds had finally merged, they became decipherable as a woman's voice speaking to him. But not just to him, to all of them.

"I wish it weren't so, but the Moon Walkers who chose to follow my brother have already been changed into their new permanent form. Theo would've continued to use them to torture you, so this is the compromise that was made. None of you will exist as you do now. And I'm sorry to say it, but your memories will have to be erased once you take your new form. It is necessary in order to remove the temptation you would otherwise feel to shift again. I love you all very much, and I promise I will make it up to you by giving you many gifts in your new lives. I will teach you new powers. Better powers, even.

"The last thing is that I need for one of you to step forward and volunteer to stay behind in your current form. Whoever chooses to make this sacrifice will be sent away from the others and taken to a part of the Moon that nobody else can access. It will be a difficult mission, but it is a part of the conditions that have been agreed upon. So I ask, who here is brave enough to accept this challenge?"

Axel didn't have to see what happened next. He could feel it. His father replied to Theia through the energy they were all connected to. "I will go if it pleases my goddess," he said through the light.

Theia's voice spoke again inside of Axel's head, "It pleases me very much, Ragher. Thank you for your sacrifice. You will be blessed on your journey. Now go and follow the lighted path. It will guide you to your new home."

Axel turned to see the clunky shape that had been his father transform into a sleek, four-legged animal with shiny, orange fur. A loud *pop!* rang out as Ragher shifted, and Axel watched the young version of father take off in the direction of a narrow trail that appeared across the ground in soft white light.

Axel looked back at Theia and noticed she was different now. Her face had taken the shape of a wolf's. "It is time, my dearest followers," she spoke through the light, "to do what I've asked and take your new form."

Theia rose up above them, stretching her arms out to each side. Light cascaded like smoke across her entire body, and orbs of light began to form on her fingertips. Her torso bent in half and white fur sprouted all over her as the orbs of light merged together, forming paws at the end of each arm. Theia dropped back to the ground in her new form—a shiny, white wolf. A loud hissing sound rippled across the tops of the Moon Walkers' heads as Theia's paws hit the Moon's surface. Then just like their goddess, each of the different-shaped creatures took the form of a wolf.

Immediately, Theia shifted back into the giant, faceless woman from before. "Perfect!" she praised them. "You have served me well. Now listen to my song. I will sing it to you as you bid a final goodbye to your old lives."

A loud, melancholy tune filled the air around them, and Axel suddenly realized that he needed to awaken from his enchantment. At first, he felt as if he were powerless to pull himself away from Theia's voice, but soon he regained control over himself.

"Father! Father!" he yelled to Ragher who stood transfixed in his large, colorful state. Axel hadn't become comfortable using this word with Ragher, but he would've done anything to break him from his spell.

Axel rammed Ragher with the top of his head. "Stop listening! She's singing that song to make them forget!"

The oracle suddenly spoke again. "Oh, Axel. How clever you are. Theia was never one to waste time. She used that song to steal the Moon Walkers' memories."

Upon hearing the oracle's voice, Ragher slowly began to return to his senses. As he shook himself from the fog, he said, "You know something? I think the dark spirit might be Theia's brother."

The oracle laughed. "Yes. That's right, Ragher. But you're a little behind on your deductions." Then to Axel, she said, "Do you understand why what Fred told you about the Moon Walkers is true?"

Axel nodded. "Yes, I understand. The Moon Walkers never left because some of them became the lunar wolves. They became *us*."

"*And the rest of them?*" the oracle pressed.

Axel growled. "And the rest became the bryobane."

CHAPTER 22

THE PRISONER'S DILEMMA

Bob sat in his dungeon-like prison cell deep under city hall in a fluorescent-lit, stone chamber. A week had passed since his arrest with hardly any human contact, and he was beginning to wonder if Goodman's plan was to let him drift slowly into madness. Being hidden away underground with nobody to talk to and nowhere to go felt a lot like being buried alive. Or at least that was the dark thought that seeped into Bob's head a little more each day.

When Bob was hauled into the police station, the entire place went silent. Many of the officers were women and men who'd served in Bob's army, and most of them seemed genuinely surprised that he'd been brought to them in handcuffs. Bob tried to avoid eye contact the best he could. He was ashamed of his situation, but he also knew he was being set up and wasn't sure how many people were in on it.

While he was being booked, the officer in charge asked him who he'd like to speak to. Bob replied, "I respectfully request to speak to the Prime Minister's secretary."

The man seemed stunned. "You know you only get to

request one person, right? Maybe you'd like to take a minute to think it over?"

But Bob asked, "Why shouldn't I speak to Betsy? We've been acquainted her entire life, and it's not like I can ask anyone else to come visit me without having to worry that you might try to lock them up too."

The officer sighed. "Okay, but I can't promise anything. Goodman will have to approve it. And if he doesn't, well then, you've gone and wasted your request."

Bob nodded. "It's a chance I'll take."

Betsy hadn't shown up during Bob's first week underground. By the third day, he'd decided she must not be coming at all, either because she didn't want to or because Goodman wouldn't allow it. He wasn't sure which was more likely.

Betsy and Bob had never gotten along well, though he'd always tried his best to be kind to her. Days after the twins were born, Bob discovered Betsy on their front doorstep, swaddled in a black, woolen blanket and staring up at him with an unnerving expression. Bob felt guilty for judging a baby so harshly, but he couldn't help it. Betsy looked positively devilish with her crazed eyes and wicked grin. And despite the sheer absurdity of the notion, Bob found himself wondering if the tiny infant was plotting his demise.

Betsy's arrival on their doorstep was especially mysterious because at the time, Maude was the only Moon Traveler who'd ever been pregnant while on the Moon. Therefore, there were only two explanations that would make sense regarding Betsy's existence. One was that a fellow traveler had hidden her expectant condition, and the other was that somehow the baby had come to the Moon from Earth.

Neither seemed likely, though, since at the time, there were only around two thousand travelers on the Moon, and everyone was fully aware of everyone else's business. Or at least so they thought. The mystery sent the population into a frenzy. Overnight, the entire town became amateur sleuths with everyone wanting to be the one to uncover the secret of the mystery child's origin. Nearly every traveler became obsessed with grilling each other for information and asking extremely personal questions to find out who might've become pregnant on the sly.

It got really out of hand, however, when rude and demeaning accusations began to fly about some women's penchant for sexual activity and other women's extra weight—which it was suggested could be due to a "postpartum physique." This is when Bob and Maude decided to put an end to all of it by declaring Betsy a 'miracle orphan' and allowing their neighbors to adopt her.

Their neighbors, the Zuckers, were one of many traveler couples who had desperately wanted children of their own but were unable to conceive. Therefore, they were beyond thrilled to have a baby to love, especially one who they thought might be able to develop and grow, unlike the children who had traveled from Earth.

The husband and wife were warm and loving to Betsy from the very first moment they held the impish-looking infant. And as she grew from a peculiar baby into an even more peculiar child, her adopted parents continued to smother her in unconditional love. They never missed an opportunity to shower her with affection or lavish her with praise, no matter how obvious it was that their efforts were a complete waste of energy. For Betsy never basked in their praise, or soaked in their warmth, let alone returned it. In fact, she never gave any indication whatsoever that she cared the slightest for her parents or their constant doting.

But Betsy's indifference didn't seem to bother the Zuckers. By the time she arrived in their lives, the husband and wife had already stored up so much parental love that they would've been happy to lavish it on a ground hog as long as the ground hog tolerated them treating it like a child. And in many ways, with Betsy, this is exactly what they got—a child who had no natural instinct for the parental-child bond and therefore showed no appreciation for it.

Bob and Maude's decision to allow Betsy to be adopted by a family who lived in such close proximity to their own home was one that Bob eventually came to regret. Maude had thought it would be perfect to have a playmate next door for their twins to grow up with. Yet from the time the twins were big enough to crawl, they were getting into trouble, and Bob noticed that it was *always* worse when Betsy was around.

There'd been the incident of the defiled living room when the three toddlers decided to create a mudpie bakery, the kitchen fire when they'd decided to create an actual bakery, the bathroom explosion and subsequent flood when they'd used the toilet to make witch's brew, and the mystery of the dozens of mutilated insects and worms that kept popping up in all corners of the house. Dan and Betsy had tried to blame this last one on the wolves who visited frequently, but eventually Dale had told the truth. His betrayal, however, had to be punished, so Dan shaved Dale's head while he slept that night.

As they grew, the three friends spent most of their time together, delighting in the despicable plots they carried out. And eventually, over time, their plans became more complex and devious. Then, once they were full-grown, Bob noticed that Betsy had begun to take a secondary role to Dan, allowing him to become the leader of their small group. From then on, Dan acted as the mastermind of their schemes, assigning the parts that Betsy and Dale got to play. This new hierarchy surprised Bob because when the kids were little, Betsy had seemed more like a leader than Dan. And that had proven somewhat of a relief to him and Maude because at least for a little while, they were able to believe that their sons weren't really bad—just under the control of a bad influence.

Back in his cell, Bob thought about the last time he'd ever laid eyes on Betsy. It was right after he and Maude learned that Dan had tried to kill Helen while she was an infant. Betsy was standing outside their front door, waiting for Dale as he left home to go live with Dan on the Darkside. It had made Bob physically ill to watch Dale walk away with the little witch. He'd wanted to run after his son and pull him away from Betsy, tell him he could stay if he promised not to ever go near her or Dan again. But his inner voice had told him not to. Dale had gone along with Dan and Betsy again and again, and when asked about Dan's plot to kill Helen, Dale merely shrugged it off as "typical Dan stuff." Like it was a silly prank instead of attempted murder.

When Bob heard footsteps approaching his drafty, little cell, he didn't bother sitting up or opening his eyes. He was certain it was just one of the guards who came every few hours to confirm that he was still there, or maybe still alive. The heavy clicking footsteps stopped in front of the door to his barred chamber.

"You still breathing in there?" came a raspy, old voice. "I better not have wasted a trip down here. Especially lugging *this* heavy thing," Betsy said huffily.

Bob sat up and faced her. She was wearing her old-fashioned, black dress with the high collar—the only thing Bob had ever seen her wear as an adult. Her hair was pulled into a tight bun, as usual, and her lumpy body was saggier than ever, just like her round face. Bob wouldn't have thought it possible for Betsy to look even more like a wicked troll than she had when she was young, yet somehow her middle-aged years had really helped her nail the look.

"You're here," Bob muttered, more to himself than to Betsy.

"You sent for me, didn't you?" Betsy sneered at him.

Bob nodded and stood. The shackles around his wrists rattled. "Yes, a week ago when I first arrived."

Betsy scoffed. "You're lucky I came at all. Goodman was against it. His plans for you don't involve social visits, assuming that's what this is. I heard you got real mushy with the sergeant who booked you. Told him we'd been best friends our whole lives."

Bob laughed. "I don't believe those were my exact words."

Betsy raised an eyebrow. "No?"

Bob walked to the bars, noticing for the first time a large potted vine by Betsy's feet. "No," he replied. "For one thing, I don't remember us ever being on friendly terms. You spent more time destroying my home than I care to remember. Plus, you worked for Dan all those years he was trying to blow up the Moon. As a rule of thumb, I don't keep friends who assist with plans to exterminate everyone I love."

Betsy smiled fiendishly. "Fair enough. And for the record, I don't keep friends. So, why'd you want to see me, then?"

Bob hesitated. He didn't know how to ask for what he wanted without just coming out and saying it. "I need to know what your boss is planning," he divulged.

Betsy laughed, which sounded remarkably similar to a croaking bullfrog. "And what in the world makes you think I'd give you that information?"

Bob shrugged. "I don't know. A hunch, I guess. I went to see Dale the same day the explosions happened. The same day I got arrested. He told me he thought Goodman was trying to get rid of me and Maude. But I can see now that it was more than that. Did the two of you set me up? Is this Goodman's plan? To keep me locked up for the rest of my life?"

Betsy stared at Bob for a second. Then she said, "Well, lucky for you, Bob, it doesn't really matter what I tell you now. So, here you go, Goodman plans to make you an example. He set everything up so it would look like you and the citizens who escaped the city were working together as political dissidents to overthrow Goodman. When the time's right, you'll be publicly executed to show everyone what happens to those who commit treason. Goodman believes this will solidify his power."

Bob hung his head at the grim news. "But the others got out, then? Maude escaped?"

Betsy snickered. "You still care about her, huh? Dan was sure you'd ditch that old freak after he sent her the aging formula."

"That's not how love works, Betsy. Besides, Maude was *supposed* to age. If anyone's a freak in our relationship, it's me. I've earned a lifetime of wrinkles that refuse to appear. There are days that I *wish* I looked old and dried up. Kind of like you."

Betsy shook her head. "There you go again, Bob. Thinking you have the world all figured out when you're just as clueless as the rest. You think you're the only one immune to caring about looks? Ha! Vanity is just a distraction for the weak-minded. *Real* power has nothing to do with smooth skin and long eyelashes. *Real* power is using strength and violence to control the masses."

"Hmm," said Bob provocatively. "So, it's power you seek, Betsy? Does Goodman know?"

Betsy smiled. "Well, maybe you're not quite as clueless as I thought. Anyway, I brought you a plant."

Bob looked at the potted vine. "Why?" he asked.

Betsy looked perturbed. "Goodman's forcing me to get rid of them. I thought you'd know how to take care of it, seeing as how Maude used to run a plant booth."

Bob ignored the odd gift. "What else can you tell me?"

Betsy frowned. "Rude! You say 'thank you' when someone gives you a gift. It's not like you have any other living creature down here to keep you company. I've brought you a friend!"

"It's a plant, Betsy."

Betsy snapped, "Well, I can take it back if you don't want it." She bent over to pick it up.

But Bob waved her off. "No, leave it. You're right. It's better than being *completely* alone. Can you tell me about the others, though?" he asked, revealing his desperation.

"Goodman is planning to leave them alone for now."

"Why?" asked Bob.

Betsy grinned. "Because he has you, and you're all he really needs to get what he wants."

"Which is what?" Bob said, continuing to press hard for information.

"Your wife."

Bob looked confused. "What does Goodman want with Maude?"

"You really don't know, huh? All these decades together and you still haven't figured it out?"

Bob was getting angry. "Stop screwing with me, Betsy. What is it that you think I haven't figured out?"

Betsy smiled an evil grin. "I think you already know. But if not, I'd hate to spoil the surprise. Anyway, I've outsourced the rest of this conversation to the guards. They'll find out one way or another what you *really* know. Take good care of the plant, Bob."

"Wait, Betsy!" Bob called after her as she spun on her heels and walked to the end of the dimly lit hallway between the empty prison chambers. At the end of the long row, two large men wearing matching, tight shirts were waiting for Betsy. "Go ahead, boys," Betsy said to the men. "You know what to do. Just don't hurt the vine." Then Betsy rounded the corner and was gone.

The men walked towards Bob's cell with menacing expressions. One of them pulled some keys from his pocket and opened the door to Bob's chamber while the other said in a husky voice, "Here's how this is going to go. We'll ask you some questions and you'll tell us everything we want to know. The more you tell us, the less painful it'll be. Got it?"

Bob nodded, but his insides felt as if they'd suddenly become tied together in one big bundle of organs and nerves. And for the first time since he'd arrived in his prison cell, he wondered if he might not make it out alive. The men entered the small chamber as one of them pulled a leather strap from behind his back. The other one asked, "Where are your friends hiding?"

"Hiding?" thought Bob. That meant that the others had done more than just escape. Apparently, they'd also found a way to conceal their whereabouts for the time being. However, this was his last happy thought. The man with the leather strap brought it down like a whip across his shoulder blades with a loud *crack*. Bob let out a scream and fell to the ground. And for the next several minutes he lay there while he was beaten until, finally, he lost consciousness—unable and unwilling to answer any of the guards' questions.

Later on, when he awoke in a pool of his own blood, he thought about Maude and how much he loved her. From the guards' interrogation, it had become clear that Maude's restored memories were somehow valuable to Goodman. Bob wondered how that could possibly be, though, and if he'd ever get to learn the answer.

He thought about his sweet Helen, and everything she'd sacrificed to keep Dan from destroying their world. He thought about the promise he'd made to her in the end—to live his life so that she wouldn't have sacrificed hers in vain. More than ever, he was certain that he hadn't done enough to live up to this promise. After the army disbanded, Bob had thought that staying quiet and biding his time was the noble way to handle the transition of power. He had believed it was inappropriate to interfere when the wave of power had been receding from him and rising towards another.

But now he could see that it had been wrong to keep silent when he was one of the few who had suspected what Goodman was up to. Instead of being stoic and fair, Bob's silence had signaled his own complicity in Goodman's power grab. Bob wished he'd listened to Maude and stood up to Goodman in the early days. The best he could hope for, at this juncture, was to prevent Goodman from getting ahold of Maude and the others.

The men had promised they'd keep coming back, but Bob had already decided to steel himself and wait for the end to come. He would never tell Goodman or his deranged guards all the places that he knew his friends could be hiding. And he felt at peace with this decision as he pictured Helen.

He closed his eyes and began to fall back to sleep, and as he drifted away, he whispered softly into the air, "I love you, Maude. Stay hidden forever and keep yourself safe."

A MONTH HAD PASSED since the night of the terrifying explosions. A month since hundreds of angry and disgruntled New Waldoffians picked up and left the city with little more than a few personal items. John was amazed that their large group had pulled it off, although he suspected there was more to it than Maude was willing to admit.

For so many evacuees to have made it out of New Waldoff, the gates on both sides of the city would've had to remain open for a couple of hours, John thought. Word of their departure had clearly spread across the city, well beyond their circle of friends. Thousands of people had been given the opportunity to choose whether or not they wanted to leave, but John knew that this wasn't even the most miraculous part of it all.

The night they had fled—once he and the other

members of his party were a mile outside of the city—John had turned around and pointed his flashlight back towards New Waldoff. What he saw was a long line of travelers that stretched all the way back to the city—several hundred more people than he had expected to find. The sight was astonishing and invigorating, but it also made him nervous. For he was certain the council would send guards after them as soon as they realized that such a large part of the city's population had fled.

And John was right. Eventually, two bearded men on horseback appeared from out of the darkness at the front of the line. One of the men held a lantern high above their heads and announced, "We've been sent by the council to inform you that you must return now if you ever want to show your faces in New Waldoff again."

Maude, who was again wearing her raised hood, answered, "I think you'll find that none of us here give a damn about your threat, but thanks for making the trip. We'll keep it in mind."

The other guard said, "What do you think you're going to do out here on your own without the protection of the city? Don't you realize there are wolves on the prowl?"

Maude laughed. "If I were you, I'd fear the prowling wolves in *there*. The ones out here don't worry me at all. On the other hand, my constitution is different than yours, which is why I have less to fear from the wolves than someone such as yourself. However, as far as the city's protection is concerned, we have plans to build our own city and are no longer interested in all your pointless protections."

The guards stared at her like she was speaking gibberish. The first said, "Well, it's your funeral. Don't know how you think you're going to survive with such a small group of people. Won't be able to make much of a city either with only twenty men and women, but I guess that ain't our problem no more. Consider yourselves warned!" Then the two men turned their horses and quickly rode away.

John shined his flashlight behind them again to see if the large group from earlier had returned to the city. But he found that, if anything, there were even more people behind them than before. "Twenty people?" John asked. "What in heaven's name was that man talking about?"

Maude lowered her hood and faced him. "Don't worry. He probably just doesn't know how to count. Anyway, I'm glad that's over with. At least we know where we stand now. John, can you and your boys make sure that everyone back there gets the message we just received? Make it crystal clear that this will be their last chance to go back. Anyone who's had a change of heart and wishes to return must do so before the night is over. They won't be allowed back in after that."

John nodded. "Okay, Maude. But have you decided where we're headed? I imagine we'll be asked that question quite a few times."

"Yes," she replied. "Tell them we're going to make camp up in the triple peak mountain valley, just to the west of Old Waldoff. It'll take another day to get there, but we've got to keep moving. We'll be much safer once we've staked claim to the land and set up a perimeter for the new town."

John didn't know why Maude believed this would make them any safer. But he knew it was a good idea to put as much distance between them and New Waldoff as they could, just in case Goodman had a change of heart about letting them leave.

In the month since their escape, John had asked Maude many times over why she thought the guards hadn't forced them to return that night and hadn't come looking for them since. After all, New Waldoff had lost more than ten percent of its population when they'd left, which John was certain had angered Goodman.

But Maude's answer was the same each time. "They probably decided they were better off without us," she told him again and again.

Then one evening, after a long day of work, John and Maude sat on a bench by a sparkling, blue fire, identifying the topics they needed to discuss with the others during their meetings the next day. Maude was saying, "We have to set a limit for the amount of space we create between the houses. We can't give people too much, or we'll quickly run out of room in the valley. We should be able to allot for about ten feet, as long as each family approves the housing sizes we've proposed."

John nodded and added, "At tomorrow's meeting, we need to go over the plans for the government buildings. I know we said we don't want anything too large in terms of offices, but we need to open the floor up for debate over which officials will even have offices. Also, I think we're ready to vote on term limits."

"Yes, I'm glad you reminded me. I'll add that to the agenda. I think that's all we needed to talk about if you want to go get some rest," Maude told him.

John hesitated. "Actually, I was thinking I'd stay out here for a while and enjoy the outdoors. A month in that tent has left me feeling a bit stir crazy."

Maude laughed. "I know what you mean. I'm looking forward to having some space again. I don't know how you soldiers managed all that time on the Darkside. At least our market stalls didn't make us claustrophobic; they were downright airy compared to those tiny tents."

John looked into the distance and asked, "Any news from Max? He's been gone for over a week, right?"

Maude shook her head. "No news. It's been ten days, but I'm not going to worry yet. It won't have been easy for him to get back into the city without drawing suspicion. Hopefully he's managed to stay undercover while he gathers information on Bob."

John sighed, and Maude asked, "Anything the matter?"

"No, it's nothing exactly. I just can't stop wondering why we're being allowed to have our freedom out here. Knowing Goodman, he isn't too happy about our exit. And I don't really trust all the silence. I keep thinking we're going to get ambushed any day now."

Maude turned and looked at John with a serious expression, though John thought he caught a glimpse of something playful in her eyes. "They're not going to find us out here, John. I promise. You don't have anything to worry about right now."

"But how can you be so sure? It's not like we have any reason to trust them."

Maude paused, and then in a cryptic tone, she said, "They can't find what they don't know how to seek."

"What do you mean? It's not exactly like we've hidden ourselves well. And there are plenty of travelers in New Waldoff who know how to track. All they'd have to do is come searching this way, and they'd be bound to find us."

"No, John. Listen to me. I'm telling you this because I need you to make it clear to the others how important it is they stay within the confines of the perimeter we've set up. If Goodman sends his guards to look for us, which I'm sure he's already done, they won't find us. I can't tell you any more than that. You just need to believe that I'm telling you the truth. As long as we stay within the valley, nobody from New Waldoff is going to find us."

John thought about what Maude was saying and then asked, "Does this have anything to do with the way you looked the night we left the city? When you were talking to that guard."

"Yes, it may have something to do with that, but that's all I'm going to say on the matter," Maude replied with a slight grin.

John wrapped his arm around Maude's shoulder as they continued to stare into the fire.

"You know I'm still a married woman," she reminded him.

John laughed. "I know, Maude. I just suddenly have this urge to protect you. I'm not sure why exactly. I love you and Bob, and I would never try to come between you. But while he's gone, I hope you know I'll watch out for you."

Maude looked at John and smiled. "I thank you for that, but I'll be fine. It's the others you should worry about. Those are good people who've had to make some tough decisions. They'll be okay for now, but there will come a day when their lives won't be safe anymore, and then they'll be the ones needing protection. Understand, John?"

John nodded and looked into the fire. "Well, I can certainly believe that. It feels like I've spent most of my time on the Moon protecting myself or others. With the vague promise of a never-ending future that we've been granted, it seems like we've inherited the never-ending burden of having to defend ourselves against total annihilation. I have to say, I wonder sometimes if it's worth it. Back home, I never felt threatened the way I do here."

"Yes, well the most valuable gifts often require the biggest safeguards. Nobody ever tries to take the things that aren't' worth taking."

John squeezed Maude's shoulder. "Yes, I suppose that's right," he said, and for a long while, the two friends sat by the fire, thinking of all that was to come.

CHAPTER 23

THE TALE OF GRYOBE

Fred awaited his final journey through the passageways. He knew his next journey would be his final one because the voice in the void had told him so. The last several times, when he was about to leave the dark passageway, she had reminded him in detail about the mission he was expected to complete once he was released. Then, after her long explanation was finished, she rewarded Fred by confirming how many more times he would be called into the darkness before he was freed.

Ragher and Axel had been gone for what Fred suspected was around a month's time. He'd grown lonely without their company and hoped he might see them again before leaving the tunnels for good. Although the three hadn't always gotten along, Fred had warmed to his companions during the years they'd spent together—sometimes in discussion, but most often in silence.

When they'd entered the ice labyrinth, Fred had believed to his very core that he was nothing like Ragher or Axel. But over time, the thread that connected them became apparent. Each had entered the tunnels as a lost version of themselves with the potential to become much more. While there, they had been forced to face their pasts and expel their inner demons so that they could become who they were meant to be.

"Tick…tick…tick." Fred held his breath every time he heard the large, metal wheels. He hoped it was a signal his friends were returning or that his final journey was about to commence. This time, it was neither. Again.

Fred's heart felt heavy. He understood the importance of the mission that had been placed before him, but there was something that mattered even more to him than the mission— something that kept him yearning for the time he'd be set free.

During all his years in the tunnels, Fred had watched Mina live her life back in her own world. He'd seen her suffer heartbreak when she lost her grandfather and again when she lost her only friend, Bonkers. He'd watched Mina spend lonely nights in solitude, reading over her grandfather's final words and pondering their meaning. He'd observed how she avoided her peers at school and how she pushed away everyone who tried to show an interest in her. His heart ached, as if the pain that Mina felt was his own. Yet simultaneously, he was filled with hope that, one day, they might bring happiness to each other's lives.

"Tick…tick…tick."

Fred's heart skipped a beat. He sensed that his moment had arrived. The tall sheets of ice moved apart, revealing a gap just big enough for him to squeeze through. He looked around at the ice tunnel walls where, for so long, he had watched the images of the past floating by. Fred thought about how he'd never see these walls again, and although this was a relief, he also felt a twinge of sadness. These tunnels had been his entire world—his school, his home, even his temple at times. And it was here he'd found himself during his slow transition into adulthood.

Fred's psyche and constitution had been broken down and

built anew so that he was barely able to identify with the person he'd been when he first entered the moving labyrinth. And because Fred acknowledged all the changes he'd made as positive ones, he couldn't help but feel a fondness for this place that had reared him into what he hoped was an honorable man.

He took his very last, first look into the void that awaited him. It was dark and quiet like usual. His muscles tightened with nervousness over what the oracle might have in store for his final journey through the dark. Barely a second passed before Fred's senses were torn from his position in the stationary abyss to a chaotic scene inside a low-lit tunnel covered in shimmering crystals. Fred stood against one of the walls and watched as dozens of hairless wolves rounded a corner to a dead end where the tunnel had collapsed on itself. Their path ahead was blocked by a solid pile of debris.

Fred scanned the crowd. The strange-looking wolves were showing a mixture of emotions. Some looked terrified while others seemed hopeless. One of their own, a wolf named Thomas, was speaking to them while standing on the massive pile of rubble. He told them that in order to triumph over the bryobane they would have to forfeit their lives. Fred could feel the crowd bending to the wolf's words. He watched the faces of the saggy-skinned wolves transform from fear and despair to pride and acceptance.

Low vibrations began to rumble beneath Fred's feet and along his back which was pushed against the tunnel wall. Soon the vibrations turned into tremors, and Fred knew what would happen next. In several of his previous visions, he'd listened to the story about The Day Theia Shook. Fred, of course, understood that it wasn't *Theia* that shook. It was the Moon. However, what took place in the tunnel was Theia's doing, although Fred was the only one who knew this. Nobody else had ever been given this truth.

The blast rang out and every single wolf and bryobane within two thousand feet of the crystals was blown to kingdom come. In the vision, Fred rose like a spirit floating above the explosion. He glided through the mountain and drifted high above the lunar surface. When he hovered back down, he was thousands of feet beyond the Darkside's border. Yet somehow, there was a large area beneath him glowing dark red. Fred's first thought was that it looked like a pool of blood.

As he neared the spot, he heard a deep voice shout, "What has she done? What the hell has she done? She's going to pay for this! She will suffer like no god has ever suffered before. I will find a way to kill all the wolves and decorate the crystals in that crater of hers *with their HEADS!*"

It was the dark god. He was standing on top of the shiny, red pool in the shape of an enormous bryobane. The dark smoke that formed his body looped around him in ferocious, tight circles. Once Fred was a few feet off the ground, he was able to tell that the red surface wasn't a pool of blood at all. It was a gargantuan crystal that sat inside the ground, fifty feet across in all directions. Instantly, Fred sensed what he was looking at. It was the culmination of crystals the wolves had excavated for the bryobane during their time in captivity. Fred had seen visions from the wolves' perspective of the tall piles of jewels that had been hauled from the mines during the day. And he'd seen how the piles had miraculously vanished every night.

Just like the wolves, Fred had wondered what happened to the crystals after the bryobane hauled them away, but now it made sense. He knew the dark god had ruled over the bryobane—who were formerly the Moon Walkers that had chosen to follow him. Under his control, the bryobane had melted the crystals and poured them into the large pit where they'd hardened once they cooled. Fred could see it in his mind's eye and wondered if the oracle was showing him what had occurred, like a vision within a vision. However, he still had no idea why the dark spirit would want such a large crystal.

As he thought it over, he noticed something moving in the corner of his eye. Standing in the shadows beyond the giant crystal was a bryobane. He was holding the end of a rope which was looped around the neck of a frightened, hairless wolf. Fred recognized the wolf from previous visions. It was Gertie, the sister of Thomas.

Thomas and Gertie had been the youngest of a long line of rebellious siblings. Yet from an early age, Gertie had shown that she didn't have the same unruly spirit as the rest of her family. She'd always preferred to play it safe rather than breaking the rules or causing trouble. Unfortunately, just like her brothers and sisters who came before her, she had been called on to make the ultimate sacrifice.

Fred watched as the dark spirit paced to and fro over the shimmering, red gemstone. Then, suddenly, he stopped and looked directly at Fred with his freakish, red eyes. "I see my sister has sent one of her blasted spies!" he yelled. "I think it's time I had my *own* assistant. Alas, if Theia won't play fair, then why should I?!"

The spirit stormed towards Gertie and the bryobane. The kind wolf wasn't able to see the dark god, but she cowered under his terrifying gaze, as if she knew her fate had just been sealed.

The dark god stopped right in front of them. "Bring me my prisoner!" he hissed at the bryobane.

The hideous bryobane with jiggly, gray skin walked out onto the crystal's smooth surface, dragging Gertie behind him. The dark god, in his monstrous bryobane form, snatched the rope from the creature's hands, and Gertie whimpered—terrified by the invisible force that was suddenly pulling her forward. The bryobane, however, being the mindless brute that it was, growled at the large god for tearing the rope from its hands.

The dark god bent down and roared in the bryobane's face. Then he grabbed him around the neck and hoisted him into the air. "You think you're worth something to me because you're the last of your kind? Imbecile! I don't need *any* of you anymore!" The dark god shook the bryobane violently while howling in delight.

Crack! The beast's neck splintered like a twig. Gertie, who'd been watching the scene while hunched down on all fours, seized on this moment to make her escape. She turned around to sprint away, but she wasn't fast enough. The frightening god reached out its long, smoky arm and tore her off the ground. A maniacal grin spread across the god's giant bryobane face as he brought Gertie and the lifeless bryobane close to his mouth. He clenched his tiny playthings tightly in both hands, like he might be about to gobble them down. A second later, he let out a bone-chilling scream and he, Gertie, and the deceased bryobane vanished beneath the surface of the dark red crystal.

Fred moved closer to the crystal's edge and looked below its surface. Deep down inside, he saw Gertie struggling to get free from the spirit's grip. But, of course, she was no match for the evil god. He thrust his hands inside his victims' bodies with ease and began pushing the creatures together. Electric blue sparks ignited and flew from both the wolf and bryobane's skin. And soon, Gertie and the dead bryobane's bodies were melding together as the little, blue sparks turned into bursting, orange flames.

Gertie wailed in agony as she watched her and the bryobane's bodies consume one another. The dark god's hideous laughter blasted through the red crystal, which caused the dirt and rock around the gem to quake and tremble.

Fred was so engrossed by the terrifying scene below that he barely noticed the ground move beneath his feet. A large, orange fireball had grown around the incinerated bodies so all that was left of the two creatures were their heads—staring upwards, as though making one last attempt to escape their hellish damnation. Soon, each head was devoured by the inferno, and right as they were absorbed, the dark god pulled his arms out of the fireball and soared back to the crystal's surface.

Fred leapt away from the edge of the crystal, unsure about what the dark god would do next. The flickering light from the fireball below shone hundreds of feet past the crystal's borders, illuminating the area that surrounded them in a crimson red radiance. The dark god moaned loudly as his black smoky body unraveled from its bryobane form. It billowed outward until it was covering the surface of the huge crystal inside the ground. A loud, striking whistle cut through the air as the dense smoke began to make waves up and down over the red gemstone. The whistling grew louder and sharper like a banshee's cry. It stabbed at Fred's ears, and he covered them with his hands in a futile attempt to drown out the noise.

Through the thick fog, he saw the spirit's wavy, dark form thrashing across the crystal's surface like a black, smoky sea. Deep within the crystal, the fireball began to radiate so brightly that its light blended with the spirit's smoke. And just as Fred thought his eardrums might rupture from the piercing whistle, the crystal exploded into thousands of shards. Tiny fragments of glass burst into the air before crashing back down to the lunar surface like dark red hail.

The dark god took a living form again along the edge of the empty pit where the crystal had been. This time, though, he chose the shape of a giant head with rubbery skin, large bulbous eyes, sharp teeth, and two long antennas that hung down on both sides of its face.

From out of the smoking pit, the monster known as Gryobe emerged. Just like the form the dark god had taken, Gryobe was covered in rubbery skin, with large eyes coated in white film, pointy teeth, and two long antennas capped by orbs. One dark and smoky and the other bright white. The dark god let out a wicked laugh. "Yes, monster! YES! Speak to me!"

Gryobe trembled several times but managed to ask in the same deep voice Fred had heard so many times, "How do you wish me to serve you?"

The dark spirit answered, "You're a blessed, monster. You have been created to serve a mighty god. I will give you many important tasks, indeed. My name is Theo, but you shall address me as *master.* Understood?"

Gryobe replied, "Yes, master."

"Finally!" Theo exclaimed giddily. "An intelligent creature to work with. You may be worth more than a million bryobane if you follow my orders. If not, I will do things to you that I'm sure you will find much more objectionable than the pain you've just suffered. You are part bryobane and part wolf, but your nature comes from me. You must do your utmost not to listen to the part of yourself that is wolf. It will be useful to you in the ways of deception, but you must not allow it to affect your decisions."

"Yes, master," Gryobe replied again.

"Good. Now let's go kill some wolves!"

The vision faded, and once again Fred found himself back inside the passageway. He felt appalled by what he'd just witnessed, but before he could find the words to express himself, the oracle spoke to him. "It was important for you to see not just the cruelty that Theo is capable of, but the madness too. You must not underestimate him or the lengths he'll go to in order to win. And as you know, his idea of *winning* is very different than any traditional sense of the term."

"But how was Theo able to see me if that vision happened in the past? This wasn't the first time he's looked right at me, but I'd always just assumed it was a coincidence before."

"Theo is a god, and his power is strong. He's always been able to see some aspects of the present, past, and future, as though they were happening simultaneously. The fact that you're now part Moon Walker makes his ability to sense you even greater. The Moon Walkers were made for Theia and Theo to rule over, but Theo's interest in them has always been more nefarious than that of a benevolent god. He saw them, not as subjects, but as tools to carry out his evil deeds. You must remember that you're an even bigger target to him now than you were before. Do you understand?"

Fred nodded. "I do."

"Good. Then it's time for you to go free," said the oracle.

"Before I go," Fred spoke cautiously, "there's something that's been troubling me."

"What?" asked the oracle.

"I've noticed worrisome similarities between Ragher and myself, and I'd like to know how my journey will be different than his," replied Fred. "From what I can tell, you created the conditions for Ragher to fall in love with Neriti by showing him hundreds of scenes from her life. Just like you've shown me hundreds of scenes from Mina's life during my own time in the tunnels. Are you putting me on the same path that you put him on? Setting me up to ruin Mina's future the way Ragher mistakenly ruined Neriti's?"

The oracle responded, "No, Fred. You're free to believe what you want, but Ragher's purpose wasn't to protect Neriti. His purpose was to test Theia. If you recall the visions I've shown you, you should be able to see how this was the case. Can you not?"

Fred let out a sigh of relief. "Yes, I think I can."

"Good. Now do you remember your mission? You must first—"

Fred stopped her. "I remember. I've thought of almost nothing else since you first told me."

The oracle replied, "That's good. You will need an infinite amount of determination to get through the trials that await you."

Fred asked, "Am I right to assume you will tell Ragher and Axel everything you've shared with me, including Theia's whereabouts?"

The oracle didn't answer at first, but then she replied, "No. I've given you different visions than the others, ones with more depth and explanation. It isn't necessary for Ragher or Axel to know everything in order to leave here and fulfill their duties. I don't plan to tell them what happened to Theia. It would put too many people in danger if it became common knowledge. Plus, it would jeopardize your mission."

Fred posed, "But don't you think there's been enough lying? I understand it can serve a purpose. That it *has* served a purpose at times. But what I've witnessed again and again in the visions you've shown me is how harmful these lies can be. And it's not just you. Nearly everyone in the realm has lied or been lied to from the very beginning. It's caused chaos and terrible pain. Don't you think at some point it might be better to tell the truth instead?"

The voice didn't respond. Fred waited in the dark silence for a long while until finally he said, "I can see that my question is unwelcome. I don't pretend to know all that you do. However, you've given me the privilege of knowing more than any of the other creatures in the Moon realm. So, I speak from my own experience when I say that it's been quite freeing to understand how this world works, as well as my purpose in it. I think it would benefit the others if they were allowed to know the truth too."

The voice replied, "What you speak from is your own perspective. No two truths are alike. They each have their own flavor depending on which creature and set of circumstances you're referencing. I've found it's much easier to help others if I don't give them all the details they desire."

Fred wanted to reply that he thought the oracle did this to control others, not to help them. But he knew better than to anger her, especially when he was about to be granted his freedom. "I'm ready to go now," he said.

The darkness began to fade as the ground beneath him shook. Light broke through a wall that had suddenly appeared in front of him. Fred shielded his eyes. It always took him a moment to adjust to the light when he was freed from the passages, but this time the light was even more intense. Fred crawled through the hole that'd opened before him and stepped out into the world again. He looked behind him to see where he'd come from, but much to his dismay, he found nothing there. No wall, or mountain, or rock, even. There was just air.

A short distance away, he saw the domed entrance where he'd followed Axel down into the ice tunnels years earlier. He thought of Axel and Ragher for a moment and wondered if the oracle would free them soon, too. In some respects, Fred felt guilty for leaving them. After spending so much time together, he'd come to think of them as a team. However, the oracle had warned him that once he was freed, he would have no time to spare. There was nothing he could do to help his friends now, anyway. They each had their own separate journey waiting for them.

He paused one more moment to soak in the bright light of the strange, quiet space. Then he steeled himself and walked back into the Darkside. He wasn't the young man he'd been when he'd left it years ago. He had grown more than any other period in his life—in size, of course, but in spirit too. Fred was ready to face challenges that he never would have dreamed of before. He no longer thought it silly to risk his own life for the good of others. Instead, he believed it to be an honorable act and one that he hoped would someday make him worthy of the woman he loved.

It was mid-day in the valley, and Maude and John were taking full advantage of the overhead sun by pushing the building crew to make haste. "Jim, James, and Jacques! You three come over here and help me hold my side of the frame while Margot and Janice screw the adjoining sides together," instructed John.

Maude and a few other crew members were holding up a one-story metal frame for the side of a small house. John and the three men lifted their side so that one of the ends of their frame butted against the framing that Maude and her team were steadying. The two ends pushed together formed a corner. The crew was in the beginning stages of building their second house. However, fourteen additional houses had already been built in their new valley home. John's sons, Egan and Samuel, had each been put in charge of their own building crews along with a few other men and women who had previous experience doing construction.

John and Maude stood elbow-to-elbow as they attempted to align the frame properly. John looked up towards the top of the valley's west side and asked. "Does anyone know if the ore team has returned from the mines yet?"

Jacques responded, "It would be unusual for them to return this early. Non?"

Maude shook her head. "No. They voted to change their schedule yesterday. Part of the team should be hauling back their early finds from this morning. They're hoping the new routine will make them more efficient."

Maude could tell Jacques wasn't listening to her answer, though. Instead, he was staring off into the distance through squinted eyes. Suddenly, he exclaimed, "Mon dieu! There's a strange looking man watching us from up there! A spy! C'est de l'espionnage!"

He let go of his part of the frame and pointed towards the long, gradual slope that ran between the valley's mountain peaks. The others turned in the direction Jacques was pointing, and a few of them let out loud gasps. John, however, kept his cool. "You stay here with the others," he told Maude. "I'm going to call down the slope to Egan and Samuel so they can accompany me to meet this stranger.

Maude replied, "Nope, I'm going with you, John. Jacques, grab ahold of your end again. Janice and Margot, keep screwing the frame together. We aren't going to let some dark-haired stranger keep us from getting our work done."

John scowled. "You know, it would be a lot easier to keep you safe if you'd stop putting yourself in harm's way."

Maude laughed. "I told you I don't need you to keep me safe, John. I know what I look like, but appearances can be deceiving. Seems like someone in your line of work would realize that better than most."

John snickered. "You don't have to tell me that, Maude. Your appearance might be the most deceptive one I've ever come across."

Maude gave him a half-cocked smile that showed partial amusement, yet also seemed to suggest that she wanted him to keep his mouth shut about such things in front of the others. John ran down the slope to where Samuel and Egan were working with their respective crews. Maude heard John call to them, "Come up here and join me, lads! I need your help with something!"

But before John had a chance to walk back up the hill with his sons, Maude took off towards the dark-haired man who was descending down the slope towards them. Moments later, John caught up to her with his sons lagging just behind. Struggling to catch his breath, John said, "For heaven's sake, woman! Can't you even wait two seconds for us to escort you? I know you've got your special powers, but there're others to worry about if this man means to do us harm."

Maude smiled. "Oh, don't go getting your knickers in a twist. I knew you all would catch up. Three strapping men such as yourselves can surely climb faster than my old lady joints will allow."

Samuel reached John's side and asked, "What's all this about, father? Do we know this man?"

John replied, "No, that's why I called you and Egan to join us. I think it will be good for him to see he's outmatched in strength."

Egan asked from the other side, "But what if he's brought more men with him?"

John didn't say anything as they got within ear shot of the stranger.

Suddenly, Maude stopped in her tracks and grabbed ahold of John's arm with one hand while laying the other across her heart. John turned to her with a worried expression. "Are you okay, Maude? You aren't having a heart attack, are you? We can wait here and let the man come to us if you want."

But Maude didn't look at John. She was staring straight ahead at the man. "Oh, my word! Fred! You've grown up, and *then* some!"

John looked back at the man who stood a few feet in front of them. "Fred? You mean the first angel-child from Earth that Ruth predicted? This is *that* Fred?"

Fred smiled. His dark eyes shined brightly at them. "It's good to see you, Maude," he greeted her. "I'm sorry I don't recognize the rest of you, but to answer your question, yes. I am *that* Fred."

John and his sons looked at each other confused. "Well how in the bloody hell did you manage to get so big then? And where on the Moon have you been all this time, lad?" John asked.

Fred looked at Maude knowingly but then replied to John, "I went to explore the underground tunnels after the battle was over, but I got trapped down there. I spent years wandering through a labyrinth. Sometimes it felt like I might never find my way out. As far as getting bigger, the tunnels don't seem to prevent travelers from aging the way the Moon's surface does. So, here I am. All grown up, I suppose. Though to be honest, I haven't looked in a mirror in quite a few years."

John looked at Maude who was grinning happily at Fred. Then he looked back at Fred and asked, "Well, that still doesn't explain how you ended up *here*. Did you go to the city first? Did they tell you where to find us?"

Fred looked at John seriously. "No. They don't know you're here yet, but they will. During my journey through the tunnels, I made a powerful friend. She's given me some important information to share with you all."

"Powerful friend? In the tunnels? What in the devil are you talking about?"

Fred ignored the question, though. Instead, he looked at Maude and asked, "I don't mean to trouble you, but it's taken me a long time to get here, and I'm still getting used to being out in the open again after spending so long underground. Is there somewhere I could rest for a while?"

"Of course!" Maude answered. "Come with me, Fred. I'll take you to my tent so you can have some time to yourself while you adjust."

She grabbed Fred by the arm and began dragging him down the slope, back towards the metal homes in the lower part of the valley. John and his sons turned and walked behind them, and over Maude's shoulder, John whispered in a hushed voice, "Maude, are you sure we can trust this fellow? If I remember correctly, he was a bit of a sly one."

But Maude shook her head and responded loudly enough for them all to hear, "Look at him, John. You can see he's grown up since then. Besides, we need all the help we can get building these houses, and Fred will make a fine helper. You, Sam, and Egan should go back to work and let the others know that more help has arrived."

John began to protest, but Maude cut him off. "I'll see you back at the work site in a few minutes," she said firmly.

John sighed, but he and his sons did as Maude said and began to head back to their separate worksites.

When they were far enough away, Maude stopped walking and turned to Fred. "I knew you'd come back, eventually. It really is wonderful to see you, Fred."

Maude looked down the hill at the men departing. Then she wrapped her arms around Fred and pulled him in for a hug while whispering in his ear, "Did she tell you it's almost time?"

Fred nodded, tickling his cheek against the wisps of white hair that hung along the sides of Maude's face. Softly, he whispered back to her, "Yes. It's almost time. But first, I have a message for you."

CHAPTER 24

THE LAST PASSAGEWAY

Axel was practicing what the oracle had been working hard to teach him. "I'm not *half* Moon Walker," he told himself. "I'm a wolf. Once upon a time, we were all Moon Walkers. I can do this."

"Pop!" Axel willed himself to change into a ferocious looking wolf, but it didn't exactly turn out the way he'd planned. His torso and head were the same size as before, but his legs and tail had grown much larger. The result was that his head and body were suddenly light as a feather while the rest of him felt like he had giant tree trunks instead of legs. *"Pop!"* He changed back into his normal form.

Axel and Ragher continued their way through the ever-shifting ice labyrinth. Fred was gone, and a few months had passed since the father and son learned the truth about the wolves' history. Since then, Axel had been called into the dark passageways three separate times, and he only had one more journey left to make into the void. Ragher, on the other hand, hadn't been summoned at all. He told himself that this was okay, though. He knew the oracle was preparing Axel for something important.

"Have you found out what the oracle wants you to do once you're set free?" Ragher asked as his son prepared to shift again. He'd been doing his best not to pry whenever Axel returned from the passageways, but he was beginning to sense that he didn't have much time left with him. While Axel had been working on changing his form over the last several months, Ragher had been readying himself to say goodbye to the son he was finally free to love the way he'd always wanted to. The thought of never seeing Axel again weighed heavily on his mind, but even worse was the thought that he might never know what became of him.

Unfortunately for Ragher, Axel wasn't in the mood to talk. His inability to master the innate gift that he hadn't even known existed until a few months ago was frustrating him to the point of anger. "It doesn't matter what my mission is! I'll never be able to do what that woman in the passageways expects of me if I can't get this simple *trick* down. If only Neriti had taught me the ancient healing ritual. I'm nearly certain the healers were using Moon Walker magic when they changed into Earth creatures during that ceremony."

Suddenly, there was another loud *"pop,"* and Axel transformed into a lunar wolf with a head so large that it bent his neck to the ground. Quickly, he shifted back again and yelled at the top of his lungs, "Damn it!"

Ragher, who'd been reluctant to comment too much on Axel's training, ignored the outburst. He said, "Your mother chose not to teach you the ritual because she worried you'd be too good at it. She believed it might reveal you as the son of a Moon Walker. It was all part of the web of lies she kept telling." Immediately, Ragher regretted his choice of words. His feelings for Neriti were complicated because of everything they'd been through, but he hadn't intended to talk badly about Axel's mother to him.

Axel stopped trying to shift and turned his attention to

Ragher. "But why did you allow her to continue with the lies? You've let too many people make your decisions for you. I understand you didn't always feel like you had a choice in the matter, but what was the worst that could've happened? You were already willing to sacrifice yourself to Theo."

Ragher sighed. "You're right, Axel. I wish I could go back and change a lot of things, to be honest. But at the time, I was trying to make Neriti happy. And I felt I had to satisfy the oracle's demands. But really what it all boils down to is that I loved your mother so deeply I chose her path despite knowing it was wrong. Her lies were my lies because I wanted her to be mine."

Axel didn't say anything. It pained him to hear Ragher express regret over the decisions that had cost their family so dearly. Just like his father, he wished he could go back and make different choices, ones that he believed might have made his life happier.

"I need to ask you something," Axel said after they'd walked silently through several more tunnels. "Since we've been here, I've longed for, yet dreaded the vision that would show me how Neriti died and what role you played in her death. You began to tell me the story before, but I've been too afraid to ask you to finish it. However, I need to know the truth now before I leave this place. Were you the one who told Dan where to find her? Did you help them kill my mother?"

Ragher stared at Axel with sad eyes. "Yes and no. I created the circumstances that led to your mother's death, but it wasn't intentional. I had no way of knowing what would happen."

"How is that possible? Either you told Dan where she was, or you didn't," Axel said in frustration.

"You have to understand," Ragher explained. "Neriti designed a *setup*. It was all part of your mother's plan to kill Gryobe. Neriti and I had been communicating secretly back and forth through your mother's friend, Imgu.

"When Dan declared war on the wolves, I knew we needed to be able to get messages back and forth, so Imgu met with me at a hidden location every couple of weeks. The first message she delivered was that Neriti had become aware of a giant target on her back. She'd sent you away to transport as many wolves to the underground tunnels as possible because she couldn't stand the thought of anything happening to you. And she knew that if you fought the travelers, you'd be killed.

"However, sending you away wasn't enough assurance for her that you'd be safe. Neriti believed there was a possibility that Gryobe would track you down. Therefore, she decided that our best option was to assassinate the monster."

"So what happened?" asked Axel. "It killed her?"

"No. At the time, Dan was pumping me for information about which parts of the Moon the different packs were located and where all their hiding spots were. I was only telling him about the sites that had been previously occupied, but after his followers racked up a few failed ambushes, Dan became irate. He told me either I was going to get the next location right, or he was going to let his followers kill me.

"I knew he wouldn't actually do that. Theo wouldn't allow it, but I'd also seen the lengths he could go to when he wanted to be cruel. Torture isn't even the right word for it. It was primeval. Truly barbaric stuff.

"I decided I'd use the opportunity to give Neriti what she wanted. Using Imgu as our go between, we decided on a location. I gave the location to Dan, but I also told him I thought the wolves were moving around to keep from being discovered. I suggested he send Gryobe to the location first so that the thing could confirm whether the wolves were there and then report back to Dan before he sent the travelers to ambush the wolves again.

"Dan took the bait, or so I thought. He sent Gryobe the next day to check out the area. But much to my surprise, no more than twenty minutes after Gryobe left, Dan threw a rope around my neck and told me to track the monster. I didn't understand why at first. If he'd wanted to check out the site on his own, why had he bothered to send Gryobe alone?"

Axel looked horrified. "Oh my god. He knew it was a trap!"

Ragher's expression turned grim. In barely a whisper, he said, "Yes. He knew."

"So Gryobe and Dan both killed my mother?"

Ragher shook his head. "No. When we got there, Gryobe was barely alive. Neriti and the other wolves had attacked it successfully. The monster was lying on the ground with its dark antenna severed, and the healers were gathered around it performing a ceremony. They were trying to free the spirit of a wolf that they believed was trapped inside the other antenna's orb.

"They were so engrossed in the ceremony that they didn't hear us approaching. When we got closer, I tried to warn them, but Dan knocked me out. It turned out that Dan had sent word for the travelers to meet him there. They'd been hiding less than a mile away, waiting for his signal. When I awoke, I was tied up and lying next to Neriti. The others were already dead —slaughtered. But your mom still had a moment left. I rocked myself back and forth so I could get close to her, and then I pushed our noses together as she took her final breaths.

"I waited with my eyes closed and my face next to hers. I was expecting Dan to kill me too. I understood that he knew I'd betrayed him, and I didn't care. I wanted to die. I wanted to be with Neriti and Tahissi. But Dan didn't do anything or say anything to me for a long time. He walked around the field of dead wolves, talking and laughing with the other travelers while smoking his cigar.

"After the travelers got on their horses and rode away, Dan sat down on a rock near where your mother and I lay and began speaking to me. I still remember every word he said. 'You did me a huge favor. It's not every day you get to kill two beasts with one stone. I needed that thing out of my life for good, but you know how the loud voice feels about his pet. *Gryobe, you obey so much better than Dan. Gryobe, you're always a step ahead of Dan. Gryobe, it's so wonderful that you can see me. Dan never gets how upset I am because he doesn't see me glaring at him with my angry eyes.* What a suck up that thing was! But thanks to you, I don't have to worry about that loser ever again.'

"Dan told me he'd followed me to my rendezvous with Imgu, or 'that lady wolf,' as he put it, which is how he found out about our plan. He said I'd done all his dirty work for him by getting rid of Theo's minion *and* serving up the wolves to the travelers who 'were long overdue for an easy kill.' He said the best part was that he got to kill your mother himself. Apparently, Dan had harbored a personal vendetta against her for decades. He told me that she'd been a thorn in his side since he was a kid because of the prophecy she'd revealed to his parents. Through laughter, he told me I'd wiped out a whole 'beast battalion' by double-crossing him.

"If I hadn't been so beaten down, I would've ripped off my binds and torn his throat out right then. But I retreated inside my thoughts, instead, thinking of you and your sister and Neriti. I imagined the life we might've had if it hadn't been for all the darkness that plagued us. I thought about how Neriti could've been the awe-inspiring healer that she was in all those visions I saw of her before we first met. I thought about all the roads Tahissi might have taken if she'd been able to live her life free from the secrecy that surrounded us. And I thought about how you could've become a true healer like your mother. You and Neriti could've gone out together and served others the way I know she would've liked to if we hadn't had to hide all those years. And—"

"Please stop," Axel pleaded. His heart ached so badly, he

thought it might stop beating all together. "I don't think I can stand to hear any more. Just tell me how it ended," he said quietly.

Ragher nodded, though he appeared to be lost in his memories still. "I understand," he said distractedly before continuing, "So, I let my mind wallow in self-pity while Dan dragged me back to the fort. He brought Neriti's body with us, which at the time, I believed was for the purpose of torturing me, or possibly because he wanted to keep it as a prize.

"When we got back, Dan locked me in the dungeon with the other wolf prisoners. He told Theo what happened to Gryobe and explained that I'd set up the ambush. He told him he'd tried to stop the other wolves from killing Gryobe, but Theo already knew the truth—that Dan was also responsible for the thing's death.

"The next few weeks were terrifying. Theo punished everyone with nightmares that I can't even describe to this day. The punishment was worse than death or physical torture. I thought I'd completely lost my mind. I heard and saw things— horrible creatures performing wicked acts, doing unspeakable things to me and to each other. I've never known for sure whether any of it was real or not. It certainly felt real at the time, even more real than waking life if that's possible. But when I came to my senses again, I told myself it was all a dream, not because I thought that was true, but because it was the only way I could move past the terrible nightmares. Even now, I'm still scared to close my eyes for long."

Axel looked concerned. "Why didn't you try to escape afterwards? If you knew he was capable of torturing you like that, why didn't you flee?"

Ragher shook his head. "Don't you understand, Axel? There's nowhere in the realm we can escape the gods, except for here in the ice tunnels. And if I'd come here, the oracle would've just sent me back out *there* again. More than ever, I had to do what that awful god ordered me to do. Of course, I didn't know for sure that he was a god back then, but I always suspected it.

"All the head healers and leaders knew of the dark spirit's existence. But many believed he was Theia's alternate personality—the dark side of Theia that punished the bad wolves. I was the one who told your mother about the dark spirit and Gryobe. However, we decided not to reveal the truth about who they really were because we worried it would create panic if the rest of the wolves knew that their worst fears were even more dreadful than they'd imagined."

Axel interrupted, "But my god, Ragher! All the lies! I just keep wondering how much better off we'd all be if everyone had told the truth this whole time."

Ragher nodded. "I know. I've wondered that too."

"Can you tell me how Neriti got trapped inside the dark spirit's energy field?" Axel asked.

"I don't know," Ragher answered. "I can only guess that it might have had something to do with Dan bringing Neriti's body back to Black Ice Fort. But, even then, I still don't know how it was possible."

Suddenly, the ice walls next to them broke apart, and a dark passageway opened up between them. Axel could feel it calling to him. He looked at his father, and for the first time since arriving in the tunnels, he felt sad at the thought of leaving Ragher.

Ragher, however, didn't give Axel the chance to think about it for long. "I guess this is it, son. I know you aren't comfortable with me calling you that, but it might be the last chance I ever get to say it. I'm sorry I wasn't brave enough to be a real father to you. I've done a whole lot of things I regret, but the one thing I don't regret is finally being honest with you. I know it doesn't make up for lost time or for all the pain I've caused, but I'm glad the truth is out in the open now and that you know I love you. Even if I was the absolute worst excuse for a father ever."

Axel peered into the void. He felt torn between his father and his freedom. He knew staying wasn't an option, but he hated to leave Ragher all alone with the oracle. Especially since he had no idea what the oracle planned to do with Ragher. Axel hadn't exactly grown to love Ragher as a father, but he was filled with sympathy for the wolf he'd once considered his closest friend.

He looked at Ragher and said, "You did the best you could under the circumstances. I want you to know that I no longer hate you. The truth has even helped me to understand your point of view some. I don't know that I can ever forgive you and Neriti for what you put our family through, but even so, I hope this isn't our last time together."

Axel forced himself to move into the passageway, but before he'd fully committed, he turned back to Ragher and pushed his brow against his father's for one quick second. Then he broke away and allowed the passageway to swallow him.

Once Axel was alone in the darkness, his chest began to heave, like he couldn't get enough air. He took deep breaths as he tried to fight it, but soon he was sobbing harder than he ever had. It was a complete and unexpected release of emotion—a mourning for everything he'd missed as a fatherless child and for all that could've been if their lives had been different.

The moment was also a marker like a stake thrust into the timeline of Axel's life. It signified the exact moment when he chose to move beyond all the pain his parents had caused him. Axel decided that to live a better life, it was time to leave his feelings of anger and resentment in the past and give himself the opportunity to heal.

.   .   .

AXEL WASN'T certain how long he'd spent in the dark passageway. After he took the time to confront his feelings, he fell into a deep, dreamless sleep. Upon waking, he felt disoriented. He couldn't remember at first where he was, but then when it came to him, he felt anxious that he'd allowed himself to become so vulnerable. Axel didn't trust the oracle, and it disturbed him to think of her watching over him as he slept.

"Oracle?" he called into the stale, muffled air.

But there was no response. Axel walked further into the passageway.

"Anyone there?" he asked. "Oh, creepy, bodiless woman?" Axel called to the oracle in a sing-song voice. "Are you here? Or are you off tormenting some other sad sack?"

Still, no response. Axel kept walking, hoping that his movement would get the oracle's attention. He was ready to get things started so he could face whatever vision she had in store for him and then move on.

He saw something up ahead. A white shadow. "Hello?" Axel called to it. But again, there was no reply. He moved in its direction and soon realized that the shadow was drifting towards him, levitating off the ground. Axel stopped. His voice caught in his throat, and his blood ran cold. The hovering, white spirit coming towards him was a ghostly version of Neriti with hollowed out eyes and a ghoulish expression.

"Neriti? Mom? Is that you?" Axel asked as the specter drew near.

Axel started to turn away, worried that the lifeless figure was about to grab him when suddenly something appeared behind it. Two glowing red eyes. "Theo!" cried Axel.

The dark god appeared out of the void as his shadowy figure separated from the darkness around it. Rising high into the air, Theo spread out in the shape of a fifty-foot tall man ready to crash down on top of them.

Axel looked at his mother. She was no longer hovering

above the ground, and her eyes had reappeared in their sockets. She stared at Axel in terror, like she knew what was about to happen to them. And just before the horrible god-monster lowered his foot to crush them, she shouted, "Axel, please! *Do something!*"

Without giving it a second's thought, Axel's bravery took charge. A deafening *"pop"* rang out as Axel transformed into a huge, metal wolf twice as big as Theo. With no time to spare, Axel grabbed the giant god in his mouth and flung him across the dark expanse and out of sight.

Axel's heart was beating wildly, and his mind felt like a whirlwind of adrenaline. He looked down to search for the tiny version of his mother, but she wasn't there. He shifted back into his regular-sized body, but there was still no sign of Neriti.

From all around him came the sound of clapping. "Well done, Axel! Well done," said the oracle. "Sometimes it takes a bit of practical use to teach a creature how to shift. I must admit, though, that was quite a show. I dare say you're even better at shifting than Ragher. Good for you! Just remember to hold on to the feeling you just had. That determination is what you'll need to use every time you want to change on command."

Axel snarled at the oracle. "That was a dirty trick! I thought I was going to die! Are there no limits to your deceitfulness?"

The oracle laughed. "So ungrateful. I teach you how to use your gift and you scold me for it? Tsk. Tsk. Well, I suppose you'll show me some appreciation soon enough. Now that you've mastered your shifts, you're going to go out there and lead what's left of the wolves into a war against Theo. The only way your kind will ever be free is if you succeed at destroying him."

"How do I even know that's true? It seems to me we'll still be beholden to you and Theia *if* she ever returns. That doesn't exactly make us free. Maybe instead, I'll lead the wolves to the other side of the Moon. To a faraway corner where none of this insanity can follow us."

The oracle laughed. "That's cute that you think such a corner exists. However, if you need me to guarantee your freedom, then I'll oblige. Theo knows this world wasn't promised to him. Yet he's prepared to do everything he has to in order to take it for his own, even if that means destroying it first. He won't stop until he's become the one and only god of this realm. You and your allies can't allow that to happen if you wish to survive."

"So then, that's what all of this has been about? I'm to take my father's place as your puppet. And you'll rule the rest of my life the same way you did his?" Axel asked defiantly.

"You do not want to test me, Axel. I'm giving you these orders so that you may protect what's left of your kind. If you don't obey, then you will certainly become an extinct species, soon."

"And what about Ragher? Why isn't *he* here now? Why don't you send *him* to lead the last of the Moon Walkers? Hasn't he earned that right after all this time he's spent as your lap dog?"

The oracle responded in a tone of suppressed anger, "I have other plans for Ragher. But that's nothing you need to concern yourself with."

Axel scoffed. "Nothing I need to concern myself with? *Really?* First, you give my father orders that ruin our lives and prevent our family from ever being happy. Then you have the nerve to bark orders at me, and in the very next breath, tell me not to be concerned about the well-being of the father you deprived me of!? Who the hell are you? Seriously! I want to know!"

The oracle laughed mockingly. "Ha! You mortal creatures get so hung up on definitions. I *am* whatever you want me to be. I am a seer in the darkness. A protector of the eternal. A goddess of memory. Your lifespans have always been your biggest weakness. They create terrible neuroses for all those who're inflicted with them.

"Instead of enjoying the infinitesimally small gift of existence you've been given, you walk around with your constant obsessions. Counting *everything*. Assigning meaning to *everything*. Trying to make sense out of *everything*. So that every last drop of your lives can fit into neat little packages that make no sense at all except in the context of your own tiny little thread of life. None of that's real, though. True reality is confusion and chaos. All your definitions are worthless against the backdrop of eternity."

Axel blinked at the darkness. "What in the world are you talking about? How does that answer my question?"

The oracle sighed. "There is no answer to your question. Does that answer your question?"

Axel was angry, but he didn't press any further. It was obvious that the oracle didn't want to tell him the truth—that she was only toying with him.

"Can I go now?" he asked.

The oracle didn't say another word. The ground shook, and a dark path rose up, leading to the outside. Axel started the short climb. Then right before he reached the exit, he paused. He could feel the presence of his father like an invisible chord that tugged at his heart, reminding him what he was leaving behind.

It hurt Axel to leave Ragher trapped in the tunnels at the oracle's mercy, especially since he'd secretly made the decision to disobey her orders. But Axel knew that he couldn't let his feelings prevent him from following through with his resolution. Unlike his father, he wasn't going to allow the oracle to boss him around. Unlike his father, he was going to do what he knew was right.

CHAPTER 25

THE PRISONER TRANSFER

Betsy had spent all morning riding to the Sheep Spa, accompanied by an exceptionally tall guard with tan skin, blonde hair, and noticeably large muscles. She had orders from Goodman tucked tightly under her arm. Orders that gave her permission to take Dale from the Sheep Spa back to New Waldoff.

The hunky guard followed Betsy's lead, steering his horse slowly down the steep path to the base of the mountain near the gloomy factory. When they reached the animal enclosure, the traveling companions dismounted and tied their horses to the metal fence. A guard came out to meet them, and Betsy pulled down the hood of her riding cloak to make eye contact with him.

"What's this?" he asked, looking at his clipboard. "I don't see you on today's schedule."

Betsy responded curtly, "Since when am I not allowed to come and go as I please? That schedule of yours is just a courtesy we paid you to make you feel like your job out here in the middle of nowhere is important. I see that it's worked.

However, I have a newsflash for your schedule. Here! Take a look!" Betsy shoved Goodman's orders at the guard's chest.

The guard stared at Betsy, as though he wanted to give her a piece of his mind, but he took the papers and read them. "You're transferring him? But why?"

Betsy quipped, "Oh, did the Prime Minister not provide you with an explanation on the orders he wrote? Hmm. I guess he didn't realize you were going to require more details. I'll just go back and tell him that Guard…oh sorry, I don't know your name. Well, anyhow, I'll go back and tell him that 'Guard No-Name' has questioned his authority and would like for him to provide more information about the transfer he's requested."

The guard looked at Betsy in disgust and handed back her papers. "Go ahead and take him," he said through gritted teeth. Betsy smiled wickedly and waved to the guard she'd brought with her to come on. She stopped to show Goodman's orders at all the check points, and by the time they'd reached Dale's side of the factory, he was standing at the door with a big grin plastered across his face.

"Well, happy birthday to me! Now, what have I done to deserve a visit from the wicked witch of Waldoff and her meat clown escort?"

Betsy snorted. "Grab your things, Dale. It's time to go."

Dale patted his chest and pants and looked around, as though he might have forgotten something. Then he replied, "Think I'm all packed. Let's hit the road, Bets!"

One of the Sheep Spa guards pushed past Betsy and opened Dale's cell. Betsy's escort, who was at least a foot taller than Dale, moved towards him with a pair of shackles and motioned for Dale to put his wrists together.

Dale stuck out his bottom lip and asked, "Is this really necessary, Auntie Betsy? I promise to be a good boy on the way to the ice cream parlor."

Betsy rolled her eyes. "You're still a prisoner for now, Dale. This is non-negotiable until we've taken you to see Goodman."

Dale looked at the guard who was already putting the large metal cuffs on him. "Go easy there, Goliath. Can I call you that? You might be used to your gorilla-like strength, but I have tender wrists. See? They're bold, yet fragile. I've been told they're the wrists of a nobleman."

Betsy said, "Alright, come on you two. We've got a long journey back, and Goodman's expecting us before nightfall."

Clip-clop. Clip-clop. Later that day, Betsy rode through the gate onto the cobblestone path at the far side of the city. The guard who'd escorted her to the Sheep Spa rode behind her with Dale sitting in front of him. Guard Neil greeted Betsy as they entered. "Good evening, Betsy. I didn't realize you'd left the city. What business were you on?"

Before Betsy could respond, though, Neil's attention shifted towards Dale and his shackled wrists. "Oh, I see. Goodman has plans for him, then, I take it?"

Betsy replied tersely, "That's none of your business, Neil. You wouldn't want Goodman thinking you've been sticking your nose where it doesn't belong, would you?"

Neil looked up at Betsy's warty face, and stammered, "N-no, of course not, Betsy. I didn't mean to pry. I appreciate you smoothing things over with Goodman after…well, you know, after those traitorous heathens abandoned New Waldoff on the night of the explosions. I swear I haven't forgotten about that! And neither have the other guards. Especially since *they* were the ones who went and let the cowards through, even though I told them it was a bad idea!"

Betsy frowned. "Such a brown noser, Neil. Just don't let it happen again. Okay?"

Neil nodded and backed away to let Betsy and the guard

pass. "Yes, ma'am. We've put several measures in place to prevent anything like that from ever happening again. Just like you ordered! No one leaves New Waldoff without the proper documents from now on!"

"Good man," said Betsy before nudging her horse forward.

Neil saluted Betsy as she rode up the ramp with Dale and the guard following right behind.

BOB SAT IN HIS CELL, hunched over the vine that Betsy had given him weeks earlier. It had been the only time she'd paid him a visit, although the guards had come to visit many times since, just like they promised. Bob found it nearly impossible to keep track of time in his dark, underground cell. Yet he was fairly certain that the prison guards who checked on him did so about every eight hours. And using this imprecise estimate, Bob had calculated that he'd been imprisoned for over three months.

Unlike the guards who checked on him, the guards who beat him didn't follow a routine. They came twice a day, once a day, every two days, or sometimes every three or four. Bob assumed they did this in order to inflict psychological torture. Knowing his tormenters could show up at any second, or not at all, kept Bob in a heightened state of anxiety at all times.

During the first few sessions, the guards had questioned him and whipped him for long periods. Eventually though, they had found a way to become more efficient at their job. Now, they no longer bothered asking him questions. They entered Bob's chamber quietly, took out their pipes, or metal lined straps, or wooden canes, and got right to business. It was painful, and traumatic, and scarring. Bob screamed and begged for mercy every single time.

The most recent beatings took less time than the first ones had, but Bob felt sure that if they'd lasted any longer, the guards would've killed him with their updated choice of weapons. As it was, Bob was knocked unconscious relatively quickly almost every time. But when he did manage to stay awake, one of the guards would remind him, "You're doing this to yourself, mate. Tell us where your wench and the other traitors have gone, and maybe the boss will let us go easy on you."

This statement was the only relief Bob ever garnered from the cruel set of circumstances he endured. He knew it meant that Maude and his friends were still out there, and there was still hope they'd be able to hang onto their freedom permanently. He thought about it constantly and wondered how they'd managed to go undetected for so long. It became a perplexing mystery that provided him with hours of preoccupation—a welcome distraction from the chronic pain he suffered due to his injuries.

Bob's body had begun to feel like all the stolen time had finally caught up to it. His bones had become brittle, his skin had thinned out, his joints and tendons ached as though they belonged to a man his actual age. Bob was forced to lean slightly forward whenever he sat because the lacerations on his back were never given enough time to fully heal. And it was agony to position himself any other way.

The vine Betsy had brought him had grown twenty feet since her visit. At first, Bob thought the gift had been random, but the longer it grew in length, the more he believed it was actually part of a mind game she was playing with him. Every day his despair grew a little more, just like the vine. At times, he found it difficult not to imagine how much better it would be if he went ahead and ended it all. And here Betsy had given him the perfect gift by which to accomplish this task if he did choose to slip away into the darkness—a vine stronger than the sturdiest rope. However, it was for precisely this reason that Bob decided not to give up. He refused to allow the little witch-goblin to weaken his resolve so easily. He would tough it out until the very end, or at least he would resist the temptation to do himself in with every ounce of bravery he had.

Bob had been in a trance for several hours, hovering over his vine, and allowing his mind to wander when he heard multiple footsteps approaching. His heart skipped a beat. Rarely had he heard so many footsteps during his time in prison, and he worried what it might mean. Was it another prisoner being brought in? One of his friends, perhaps? Or maybe even Maude?

He listened closely. They were still on the path down the long corridor that led to his chamber's hallway. Bob wished he could stick his head through the bars to see what was happening. He knew if they passed by, then it was likely they were throwing someone new into a cell. He wanted to call out to whoever was there and ask them to reveal themselves, but he knew it was too dangerous. It wasn't long, though, before he began to recognize one of the voices.

"Beautiful place you got here, Betsy, but when are we going to ditch the charade? These cuffs are chafing pretty bad, and meat clown's charm is beginning to wear off. I think he might be thick in the head. Seems like he doesn't know who he's dealing with. No offense, meat clown, but you need to remember you'll be working for *me* soon."

When Bob realized it was Dale, his head began to spin. He needed to figure out why they'd brought Dale to the prison. Was this another attempt to get to him? Clearly, they'd overestimated Bob's affection for his son if that were true.

A few seconds later, Dale was hauled in front of his cell by the biggest guard Bob had ever seen. "That must be *meat clown*," he thought. Betsy was there too, although Bob couldn't see her because she was wearing a black robe with the hood draped over her head to hide her face. Bob couldn't help but smile at the sight. Betsy trying to disguise herself under a robe was like a pineapple trying to disguise itself under a napkin. Their bizarre shapes were always going to give them away.

"What's going on?" Dale asked angrily upon seeing his father on the other side of the barred door. "Why'd you bring me to see *him*?"

The giant guard answered Dale while Betsy unlocked the door to Bob's chamber. "You're not here to *see* him. You're here to take his place. Goodman ordered a prisoner swap. This is your new home."

Bob was shocked. Why in the world would Goodman order him to swap places with Dale? Unless that wasn't really what was going on. He began to panic. What if Goodman had finally decided that he was useless? That he had no valuable information to offer?

"Oh my god. This is it. He's going to kill me," thought Bob. "Then he's going to turn his attention to Dale. He'll torture him for a while to see if he has anything useful to share, but eventually, he'll kill him too. And he'll keep on killing until he's sure he's neutralized every last threat to his power."

Bob was about to ask Betsy to confirm his theory when Dale yelled, "Betsy! You better let me in on your plan right this second if you want me to let you live after I get out of here! This isn't funny. Tell meat clown to get his paws off me! I want answers *now!*"

Betsy didn't move or respond, though. Instead, the giant guard picked Dale up by the waist and tossed him effortlessly into the prison cell. Then before Dale could stand again, the guard clutched Bob firmly by his wrist and yanked him through to the other side of the chamber, slamming the door shut behind him.

Betsy went to lock it, but Dale tried to stop her by shoving his hands through the bars and grabbing at her fingers.

However, the large guard grabbed ahold of Dale's wrist tightly and uncuffed him from his shackles while Betsy finished locking the door. The guard turned to Bob, who was watching in stunned silence as the scene unfolded. Using Bob's stupor as an opportunity, the guard quickly transferred Dale's cuffs to Bob's wrists.

Dale, who was becoming desperate, decided to focus on Bob. "Father! You have to listen to me! Something's gone horribly wrong. This witch was supposed to release me after I told you all those things back at the Sheep Spa. She promised that Goodman was going to appoint me to the council. I don't know what they're planning, but I'm starting to get a really bad feeling."

Bob looked Dale in the eye and said, "You're right Dale. Something has gone horribly wrong, but maybe for once in your life, you could take ownership for your part in it. Good luck to you, son. It looks like we're both going to need it."

As soon as Bob was through speaking, the guard pulled out a piece of cloth from his back pocket and shoved it towards Bob's face. Bob leaned away from him, but the guard moved in closer. And in one quick motion, he pulled a dark brown prisoner hood over Bob's head so he couldn't see.

Dale laughed. "Looks like you're going to need it more than me, Pops!" he said tauntingly.

The guard grabbed one of Bob's shackled arms and dragged him down the corridor, away from his cell. Betsy, however, stayed behind for a moment to speak to Dale alone. She pulled down her hood so she could look at him. With a mysterious smile, she said, "Sorry it had to come to this, Dale. But never forget you're just a loose end to Goodman and his people. Soon, you're going to have to make a choice about which side of this fight you really want to be on. Choose *wisely*, or it will be the last choice you ever get to make."

Dale balked. "What the hell does that mean, Betsy? You *are*

Goodman's people. We had a deal! A *DEAL*, you ugly, old troll! Get me out of here, or I swear I'll kill every last vine in this whole wretched world! Starting with the one right here!"

But Betsy ignored Dale's tantrum and walked coolly down the corridor towards the larger hallway. When she reached the end, she stopped and said to him over her shoulder, "A deal, Dale? *Really?* What's a deal among liars and swindlers like us? But I wish you good luck. Your father was right. You're going to need it."

CLIP-CLOP. Betsy and the guard approached the near side gate. Each rode on their own horse with Bob on a separate one too. His hands had been fastened to the saddle, and the large guard had used a rope to secure Bob's horse to his, in order to keep the horse and Bob moving along beside them.

Bob had asked repeatedly about the hood over his head with no response until, finally, the guard said in exasperation, "Don't you know these folks think you're a monster? You and your simpleton friends set off bombs all across their city and then fled. If these people see your face, they're going to tear you off your horse and rip you to shreds. So quit with the yakking and count your blessings that Goodman told us to give you a disguise. 'Cause if a mob attacks, there ain't no way I'm putting myself between *it* and *you*."

Bob stayed quiet after his scolding. He supposed it was a good sign that Goodman hadn't wanted him ripped to shreds by an angry mob, even though he was well aware that the only reason an angry mob would want to do that was because Goodman had orchestrated all the events surrounding the explosions.

Eventually, the group of three descended down a long slope, and Bob heard a woman speaking to Betsy and the large guard. "Back so soon, Betsy? You two have been busy today!"

Betsy replied in her raspy voice, "Yes, yes. We went through the far gate on our way back into the city but had to pick up an extra horse to carry this guy out to the Sheep Spa tonight. Can't afford to exhaust the horses under the weight of two large men."

The woman said, "I see. Well, it sure is nice of Goodman to put someone in Dale's place. I'd hate for those poor guards over there to be out of a job. I heard several of their families lost their homes during the explosions. Don't know if it's true or not. The way people talk about it, you'd think everyone in New Waldoff had lost their home in the explosions."

Bob tensed up, certain he'd finally figured out Goodman's plan. Goodman had told everyone that Bob and the others were responsible for the explosions, but really it was Goodman who'd chosen which homes, businesses, and people were destroyed in the blasts. He'd purposely targeted the homes of the guards' families because he knew that, eventually, they'd be the ones responsible for looking after him at the Sheep Spa.

Bob suspected that Goodman was hoping the news of Bob's transfer would reach his friends and that they'd then come to rescue him at the spa—a location that they'd probably assume was an easier target than New Waldoff. However, they wouldn't know that the armed guards would be waiting for the attack. But not just waiting for the attack. Waiting to exact revenge for their families.

"That has to be it," he thought. Goodman was transferring him to the Sheep Spa to set a trap and dangle him as the bait. He had to find a way to get a message to Maude, to tell her not to risk the rescue attempt. But how?

Betsy and the woman continued to chat for a few more seconds. Then the guard pushed the lever to open the gate, and their caravan slowly exited the city. After riding along in silence for thirty minutes, Bob asked, "Now that we're out of the city, wouldn't it be alright to take my hood off? We could go a lot faster if you'd let me steer my own horse."

But neither Betsy nor the guard bothered to answer him. A few more minutes passed before they began to angle down a steep slope. Bob leaned back to keep his balance, wondering where they might be going. He knew they shouldn't be headed down without having gone up first. Or at least that were true if they really were on their way to the Sheep Spa.

Being kept in the dark was taking a terrible toll on Bob. It emphasized the lack of control he had over his own fate, and it awoke the trauma that had snowballed inside of him during the months he'd been tortured. He was about to tell the others that he knew they weren't headed to the Sheep Spa when he heard the guard ask Betsy, "What do you think? Has he behaved well enough? Should we let him have his freedom?"

Betsy replied, "Yes, I think so. He's suffered long enough."

"Whoa there!" the guard called out, and Bob felt his horse come to a stop as the hood was pulled from his head. Bob squinted his eyes and looked at his captors, but instead of finding Betsy and the large guard, he found a tall, dark-haired man and a much younger version of his wife staring back at him. Bob leaned backwards in his saddle, surprised and a little frightened by what he saw. "What in the devil!" he exclaimed, not quite sure whether to believe his own eyes. "Who are you?" he demanded.

Maude smiled lovingly and explained, "That's Fred, Bob. He's been trapped inside an ice tunnel labyrinth the last nine years with Axel and Roger, or *Ragher*, as you might remember he used to be called. Fred's able to change his appearance because Ragher fed him a formula similar to the one Dan used on Helen and Axel. And he's older now because being stuck down in the ice tunnels aged him."

Bob hadn't finished processing what Maude had told him

yet, but he couldn't stop himself from asking, "And you? How do you look so…so…so *young*?"

Maude laughed. Her gray hair and wrinkles had been replaced by a bright red braid that hung over her shoulder and white porcelain skin that was smoother than Bob had ever seen it before. She knew it was a lot for her husband to take in all at once, and she tried to be patient while his brain caught up. "Don't worry," she said teasing. "Once we make it to the valley, it will all go back to the way you like it. I don't want to scare the others. John caught a glimpse of me this way, and I can tell he's still spooked. Or possibly in love. Probably, he thinks I'm a sorceress. If he only knew the truth, he'd realize I'm even more damned than he suspects."

Fred reached for Bob's chains to set him free, and Bob examined him closely. He could see that this man was, in fact, an older version of Fred. He had the same features, only they were more refined now. It was his eyes, however, that showed the most change. They weren't aloof or jaded the way they'd looked when Bob had met with him after the battle. They conveyed something deeper. Bob couldn't pinpoint it exactly, but he thought that "stoic" might be the best word to describe it.

Bob looked at Maude questioningly, but Maude smiled and tilted her head towards Fred, as if to encourage Bob to address Fred directly with whatever was on his mind. Bob cleared his throat and asked, "Fred, were you able to see Axel while you were down in the tunnels? And Ragher? He didn't cause any trouble?"

Fred shook his head. "No, Ragher isn't what we all thought. But, yes, I was able to see Axel for the same reason I'm able to change my shape. Like Maude mentioned, I drank a formula. I'm part Moon Walker now."

"I see," said Bob, carefully trying to fit all the pieces together. "And Maude?" he asked his wife. "You're a Moon

Walker too, then? Is that what you remembered that horrible night…the last time…the last time I saw you?" Bob's voice cracked, and he looked away for a moment, trying to hold back the flood of emotion threatening to overtake him.

Maude positioned herself right next to Bob so they were facing each other atop their horses. She raised her hand to his face and rested her palm gently on his cheek. Gazing into his eyes, she said, "I'm so sorry we couldn't get to you sooner, sweetheart. I had a heck of a time convincing John to let me come after you at all. But to be fair, he didn't really understand how it was safe because we couldn't tell him we were going to change our bodies."

Bob nodded and looked deeply into Maude's eyes. "Yeah, that was risky, Maude. I'm not sure you should've come. Goodman was only after me because he wants *you*. There's something about your memories that he thinks will be useful to him."

Maude continued to smile. "Yes, but it's not my memories he's after. It's my identity. He thinks I'm Theia, Bob."

Bob laughed. "Well, that's the most ridiculous thing I've ever heard. Why in the world would he think *that?*"

Maude's eyes twinkled at him. "Because it's true."

Bob's head jerked back like Maude's words had slapped him in the face. "What? But how?" he asked. "You're a human! And Theia is supposed to be *the Moon!*"

Maude looked at Fred and then back at Bob. "There's too much to explain right now. I know it's confusing, but I promise I'll tell you the whole story later. Right now, you need to hear what Fred has to say. It's much more urgent."

Bob asked incredulously, "More urgent than you being a Moon goddess?!"

Maude gave her husband a look and said, "Yes. At this particular moment, it is. Fred's come up with a plan to get Mina back, but it's going to take some of your expertise."

"Get Mina back? But that's impossible! We don't even know that she returned to Earth. And even if she did, how would we track her, let alone get her back?"

Fred replied, "It's not actually as complicated as all that. I know a way we can find her if you're willing to help."

Bob thought about it for a moment and then said, "Well, after everything you just risked for me, I don't see how I could possibly say no. Of course I'll help you. What do we do first?"

CHAPTER 26

MAUDE'S CONFESSION

When they reached the valley, Bob received a hero's welcome. His friends and acquaintances who'd heeded his order to flee New Waldoff on the night of the explosions lined up to greet him, along with the several hundred others who'd fled the city that night. It was an emotional sight—teary folks thanking Bob for having the courage to warn them before it was too late.

A close friend of Bob's named Sal, who'd been one of the officers not to follow Goodman's lead, walked right up to Bob and gave him a hug. "This is long overdue," she told him. "If all of those people back in New Waldoff had listened to you and Maude from the beginning, then maybe none of these terrible events would've ever occurred."

As Bob continued down the row of people stretched out on both sides, he noticed several different people staring at the fresh scars on his arms. Yet when he locked eyes with them, he could tell it wasn't pity they felt for him. It was admiration. And for the first time ever, Bob felt comfortable being a leader. It wasn't because of all the adoration he was being shown, though. It was because he finally felt like he had earned his place among the people he'd spent a lifetime serving.

John was also happy to see Bob. He waited at the end of the line, and when Bob got close, John stuck out his hand. But Bob pulled his friend in for a hug. "I heard you looked after Maude while I was gone," he said as he let go of him.

John smiled sheepishly. "Well, I tried to. That's for certain. But I think she might've been looking out for me more than the other way around. You know, Maude's the whole reason we got out of the city safely." Then John looked around to see who was nearby, before leaning in and whispering, "Maybe you already know it, but I think Maude might be part fairy or elf. Don't go mentioning it to her, though. She's a bit touchy on the subject."

Bob just laughed. "Okay, John, but later you'll have to let me try whatever new ale it is you've been drinking."

As soon as the welcome party broke up, Bob, Maude, and Fred took off to the top of the valley, leaving the others to continue their work building the new city. Before they left, however, there was a landslide of questions about what they were up to. But Bob put everyone's minds at ease by telling them he'd come up with an idea on how to power the city by harnessing energy from the sun.

Then as a distraction, he set them to the task of coming up with names for the city they were building. This got people talking about something else for the time being, but Bob knew it would only buy them so much time. They'd have to complete their work quickly if they didn't want the questions to start again.

Fred, Maude, and Bob worked non-stop for a week before they finally finished building the machine Bob designed. Once Fred explained how he knew where to find Mina, Bob became intrigued—obsessed even—with the new invention. It was unlike anything he'd ever worked on, and it was just the type of challenge he'd been craving for so long.

One time when Fred disappeared to grab some materials, Bob asked Maude a question he'd been thinking of ever since she'd told him all about her restored memories. "Maude, if you're Theia, then who was Helen communicating with all that time after she decided to sacrifice herself? She seemed certain that Theia was the one she was connected to, the one guiding her and giving her the powers she had."

Maude stopped what she was doing and sat down. Looking nervously up at her husband, she said. "It wasn't me, Bob. It was Helen. Helen gained some of my powers when she was born. Then when Dan changed her with that awful formula, it began to open her mind to the powers she'd always had. But without any explanation as to why she suddenly had these new powers, she drew on what the wolves had taught her in order to understand it. She believed that Theia was the *Great Energy,* and so she assumed her newfound powers were part of that energy.

"However, what the wolves believed is what I taught them, which basically amounted to fairytales. That's something I regret now. Many times, I've failed to protect the creatures of this realm. But I thought that this time, if I made them love me like I was the very planet they lived on, then maybe they'd obey all the things I taught them. Like staying away from the bryobane and worshipping me the way I wanted to be worshiped."

Bob asked, "The way you wanted to be worshipped?"

Maude looked a bit embarrassed. "Yes. To be honest, I was never a goddess who enjoyed one-on-one attention from my subjects. I never wanted to be needed, *just loved.* What I found was that by creating space between me and the wolves, it gave me the freedom I required to love the wolves in return. I began to actually want to spend time with them.

"For a while, I appeared to them in many different forms. I pretended to be what they had been—the Moon Walkers. I didn't want the wolves to treat me as their god, I wanted them to treat me like I was also a mortal. I told them that I brought messages from Theia, and I offered them special gifts in the form of spells and rituals so they could harness energy through the crystals.

"I made up stories to tell them about how the Moon Walkers created them *and* the bryobane. It was another way to put some distance between me and them so that I didn't feel so burdened being their creator. I also made up the story about how I was attacked by the Earth long ago because I wanted them to feel sympathy for me the way I felt sympathy for them. But also, I knew that if they thought I was too weak to give them things, then they wouldn't ask for much.

"After a while, the stories I told them began to take on a life of their own. I realized that the wolves were repeating the stories to each other every night before they went to sleep. Sometimes they even acted them out. Many times, the stories were even bigger and more exciting than what I'd originally told them, and I loved hearing all the new versions that the wolves came up with. It was fascinating to see their imaginations at work.

"But after a while, I grew bored with pretending to be different Moon Walkers, and I decided I needed my space again. I told the wolves that the Moon Walkers didn't have enough energy to continue living on the planet. But I left the door open for a possible return, in case I decided to visit them again one day.

"For thousands of years, I let the stories I'd told the wolves continue to transform while watching the wolves worship me from afar, the way I preferred. There were lots of times I could've stepped in to help them, of course, but I didn't want to get sucked back into being a full-time goddess. I'd accepted that this was a better way to do things.

"Only one time did I make an exception in all those millennia—when I set up the circumstances that led to the annihilation of the bryobane. But even that decision had less to do with helping the wolves and more to do with punishing Theo for enslaving some of my subjects. I realize now that most of the decisions I made were just plain selfish, and I'm ashamed of myself for not doing more to help those who depended on me."

Maude leaned over and hid her face in her knees. Bob sat beside her and put his arm around her. "I'm not ashamed of you. You may have been a lousy god, but you're an amazing wife. I feel lucky that our fates crossed the way they did. Not many men get to say they're married to a goddess and actually *mean* it," he said smiling.

Maude looked at him. "But fate had nothing to do with it, Bob. Don't you see? *I* was the one who brought you here. When I was desperate to recover my memories, I looked across to the Earth and summoned you here. *All of you.* I opened up the portal that brought you. I was trying to get the Earth to send me a sign that would help me remember what had happened. But instead, I forced it to send you. Accidentally."

Bob thought for a second and then replied, "Well, since you didn't really intend to do it, I'd say there was still some fate involved."

Maude smiled at Bob. "That's sweet, honey."

Bob looked at her suspiciously. "You aren't implying I'm simple, are you? Now that you've remembered you're a god, you aren't going to walk around acting all superior, right?"

"Didn't I already do that?" Maude laughed.

"Hmm. That's a good point," replied Bob. "It was easier to stomach, though, when I thought it was just an act."

Maude laughed again and changed the subject. "I'm glad

those folks down there honored you the way they did. You've done more for the Moon Travelers than any of us. You've always been a hero to them, whether they recognized it or not. And I think you might be a tiny bit right about fate. You were the perfect person to travel through the portal first. I don't know that anyone else could've done as well as you have while dealing with all the nonsense of this realm. The twins, the wolf killers, my brother, Betsy, Goodman. *Me*, even. You may not be a god, but you sure have the patience of one, although truthfully, I've never known any of us to have much patience."

Bob asked, "How many gods are there?"

Maude bit her lip. "I'm not sure. I've been here for so long there's no way to know. It's a family business, though."

"I see," said Bob. "Are there other gods like you that have become humans? Or any who've married humans?"

Maude nodded. "Yes. It happens a lot, actually. There are quite a few demi-gods, like our kids, wandering around different realms out there. Most of the time, they never meet their god parents—or even know that one of their parents *is* a god or goddess. Problems have arisen in the past with the demi-god children challenging the gods, which is often why the truth about their divine-like status is withheld."

Bob looked upset. "That doesn't seem right, though. Does it? To allow a child to be born and then abandon it, just because they don't want to risk being challenged? Wouldn't it be better if the gods took responsibility for their children and taught them how to use their powers to help others?"

Maude laughed uncomfortably. "Not all of us are so noble, Bob. But it's nice of you to think of us that way."

"Well, you're noble, Maude. You've always done the right thing. At least since I've known you, anyway."

Maude rested her head on Bob's shoulder. "Maybe. But I had amnesia. I didn't really know any other way to be. You and Ruth were the ones who helped me to walk the noble path. It was the two of you who showed me the right way to be human."

Right then, Fred returned, hauling several sheets of metal. "Oh, I see how it is," he said with a smile. "The old geezers send the young man to get supplies so they can sit down on the job while he's gone."

"Who're you calling an old geezer?" asked Maude. "Bob and I may be old in Earth years, but in god years I'm as youthful as a sprite. And in Moon years, Bob's still the same twenty-something year old stud he's always been. Isn't that right, darling?" she asked, sitting up straight and putting her hand on Bob's shoulder.

Bob stood and took Maude's hand, pulling her to her feet. "To be honest, I *have* been feeling rejuvenated since you two broke me out of prison." Then in an old man voice he said to Fred, "Thank ya for bringing up those materials there, sonny! Now, let's get to building ourselves one of them new-fangled machines!"

Fred laughed, and then he and Bob spread out the sheets of metal so they could begin cutting them into the pieces they needed. The three worked around the clock to construct the large machine. The base was made into a raised metal surface with several wide pipes of varying widths and lengths that stuck upwards through the top of it. Fred and Maude were in charge of welding the pieces together, and they recruited John, Jacques, and Sal to help them construct some of the larger parts. Bob was in charge of the wiring, of course, which ran from the base of the machine into the two bodysuits and headsets that he and the others had fastened together using metal and cloth.

The medium-sized tower that sat in the center of the platform was topped with an adjustable cone-shaped pointer designed to shoot a highly concentrated beam of protons across a long distance. And to make this easier, the entire machine was built at the top of the valley so that the beam could be projected directly into Crystal Crater over on the Darkside.

Once the finishing touches were completed, Maude, Fred, and Bob stood in front of their shiny invention, marveling at what they'd accomplished together.

"Well, I guess we should test it out," announced Bob.

"Will it have enough energy stored up already?" Fred asked.

"Plenty," Bob replied. "This baby started soaking up the sun's rays the first day we began working on it. By now, it should run for a full day without any problem."

Maude instructed, "Well, go ahead and turn it on then. You should start training me on how to use it right away. Soon as the folks down there hear the engine whirring, they're going to come around asking questions. We might as well begin trying to find Mina before they figure out this is more than just an energy generator."

Suddenly, without any warning, a loud *boom* echoed across the sky, like the sound of cannon fire erupting in the distance. Maude walked several feet to the top of the valley, between the two larger peaks and looked out to discover something she'd never seen on the Moon before. A storm. Dark black clouds filled with yellow bolts of lightning drifted high above the plains and on up towards where they stood in the mountain valley.

Bob and Fred joined Maude. "A storm?" Fred asked in disbelief. "How in the world could a storm manifest on the Moon?" But when he looked to his friends for an answer, they were both giving him a raised eyebrow, which Fred took to mean, "You're hanging out on the Moon with a goddess and a man whose body hasn't aged in sixty-years. You're really going to question a storm?"

The wind picked up, and the tie holding Maude's hair back

was ripped away so that her long flowing locks flew wildly behind her. The three companions turned away from the clouds to shield themselves from the intensifying gusts. "Come on," Maude called loudly to Bob. "Start walking me through the controls. That way, when this thing blows over, I'll be up to speed on what I have to do to project you and Fred through the beam."

The couple moved together down the slope, towards the metal platform, but before they reached it, a giant blast of air shot out of the sky above them. Fred, who'd stayed behind at the top of the valley, watched as Maude and Bob were torn apart and thrown to the ground in opposite directions. He sprinted down the slope to help, but before he got to them, another gust of wind came blasting out of the sky. The tower that held the cone shaped pointer was lifted off the platform and tossed into the air before landing twenty feet away.

Bob and Maude slowly returned to their feet. Bob yelled, "We need to take cover until the storm passes! We can fix the beam projector later!"

Maude looked at Fred with a serious expression as he came closer. "Bob wants to go back down and take shelter with the others, but I'm of a different mind. To find Mina, we're going to need both of you in those bodysuits while I run things. It'll take too long if I'm not here to help you."

Fred looked at Maude with a knowing expression. "Yeah, okay." Then to Bob, he said, "She's right. It's important that we do this now."

Bob was confused. "Why? Can't we just wait out the storm down there and return together afterwards? What am I missing?"

Maude looked at Bob with a mixture of guilt and sadness. "No, Bob. There's something I should have told you. I've been too scared to say it out loud, but I guess I better do it now. I don't have much time left here. Before Fred left the ice tunnels, he was told that my time as a human would come to an end soon. It's something I've sensed for a while now. Even before I got my memories back, I could feel a big change coming."

The clouds slid through the opening at the top of the valley, blanketing everything around them in a cool, dense fog. Bob felt the electricity in the air tingling against his skin, but he barely noticed it. All he could think of was how his heart had just been ripped right out of his chest.

"When were you planning to tell me this, Maude? We've been together for over a week! Or did you think you would just slip away into the night? Disappear without even telling me?"

Maude shook her head. The moisture from the clouds clung to her skin and clothes. "It's been hard for me to talk about it, Bob. I don't want to leave you, but I don't have a choice. Just like I didn't have a choice when I came here. I'm being called home. Back to my own realm."

Lightning sparks lit up the fog around them, and a clap of thunder crashed over their heads. Fred, who sensed he was watching a private matter unfold, backed away slowly, but Maude grabbed his arm. "No, Fred. We're doing this *now*. We have to find Mina!" But Fred put his hands up in front of him and took a few more steps backwards, disappearing into the clouds.

Bob yelled, "So Fred and I don't even get a say in this? You know you're going to get us electrocuted out here! Maybe that doesn't matter to a goddess, but it certainly matters to us humans! Stop being so selfish, Maude!"

Tears filled Maude's eyes, but she didn't say a word. Instead, she walked over to the cone-shaped pointer lying on the ground, checking it to make sure the wires were still attached. Then she pulled it off the fallen tower and walked back to Bob. "Show me how to work it," she said in a pleading tone. "We can fight about how selfish I am later. But right now, we're going to help Fred find Mina. We messed everything up when we sent her away, and now we're going to fix it."

It took Bob a moment to speak to Maude, but finally he said in a sad voice, "Push the button here to warm up the beam and then this other one to turn it on. Once the meter hits this line, you push the red button. That will project us through the beam."

Bob pointed to a green line that was part of a small display on the base side of the cone. "But it doesn't matter, Maude. It's not going to work until the clouds have moved past us. We need to be able to see which direction we're pointing it."

Maude nodded. "And we will. How long are these wires?" she asked, looking up towards the top of the peak that was nearest to them.

Bob followed her gaze. "No! You're not going up there. You don't even know if there's cloud cover up there or not."

Maude looked at Bob seriously. "Yes, I *do*. And there isn't. Now, can I make it up there with this thing or am I going to run out of chord first?"

Bob looked worried but said, "No, I spooled the wire around the platform. It can be pulled out through the hole where the tower used to be. But, Maude, I spooled all that wire under the metal platform to give it a boost of electric charge from the solar energy that was stored up. I don't think it will work for very long outside of the platform."

"That's fine. There's electricity in the clouds, too. That should help some with the charge. We're just going to have to take our chances for now. Hopefully, the two of you will have great luck finding her, and we won't need too much energy. Now, go put on your bodysuits. We're doing this!"

Maude did a half turn with the pointer in both hands, but Bob grabbed her arm. "Bob—" she began to protest.

But Bob brought her in close and kissed her passionately

before she could speak. "I'm going to say something now, Maude," he told her as he pulled away. "From the very first moment I met you, I knew you were the most hardheaded person I'd ever met, which is still just as true today as it was then. I want you to know, though, that it's one of the things I love most about you. I'm thankful I've gotten to spend my life with you. I don't know what it means when you say you're being called home because I thought *I* was your home and that we'd always be in this together.

"Back on Earth, time was confusing. The hardest trials seemed to take forever, whereas savoring the best moments felt like trying to hold onto water in the middle of a raging river. For a while after arriving here, I believed that this place was promising something better—an eternity to spend with the ones I loved. Then when Helen died, I realized that wasn't true. But the one thing I took solace in was that I would always have you. Please, Maude. Please don't go. But if you really can't stay, then at least let me come with you."

The fog had thickened and enveloped the couple inside their own pocket of mist. Tiny sparks of lightning twinkled around them, and in addition to the droplets that slid down their skin, Maude could see tears beginning to glide down Bob's face. She set the metal cone on the ground and wrapped her arms around him tightly.

"I love you, Bob. But there's nothing I can do or say to make this moment any easier for either of us. I haven't been given a choice any more than you have. I do know, however, that you have more life to live here. Some of it will be sad and lonely, but some of it will be beautiful and amazing too.

"I'm so sorry I can't take you where I'm going, but I'll watch over you when I'm gone. I want you to promise me, though, that you won't mourn me the way you might have if I'd been just an ordinary human. You and I got to live a long life together, longer than most couples get. There's no reason to lament over any of it. In many ways we were fortunate, even though we faced our fair share of tragedy."

Maude stared into Bob's eyes. "Before I go, will you let me do this one last thing? You know how high the stakes are, and you know what it will mean if we don't find her. Let me help you. Please," she said softly as she cupped her hands on the sides of Bob's face.

Bob wrapped his fingers around Maude's tiny wrists and pulled her hands to his lips. Then he kissed her palms and said, "Okay, Maude. We can try."

She smiled at him lovingly and picked up the cone. Bob said, "Let me carry that to the top of the peak."

Maude shook her head. "No," she said as her hair turned bright red again, and her skin smoothed out in front of his eyes. "I can manage like this. Find Fred and get your bodysuits on. I'll whistle down to you when it's ready to go."

Maude turned and began to climb the sloped peak in front of her, taking her time and watching her footing. She was careful to make sure not to pull the wires too fast in case they snagged. The wind blew harder the higher she climbed, but soon she had made it past the clouds to the highest part of the mountain.

From the top, Maude could see for miles, all the way to the dark curtain that hung over the Darkside. She pushed the button to warm up the beam and then situated herself so she was facing Crystal Crater. She knew the spot well. It had been a sort of home before she'd become human. She'd been able to shapeshift and interact with the Moon Walkers there. Then after she'd decided to take a hands-off approach with the wolves, it's where she'd told them to journey to on their pilgrimage. Having them come to Crystal Crater once a year had allowed her to take note of how her subjects were doing without having to get too bogged down in what she had believed were their mundane lives.

Maude held the projector steady against her chest to gauge how much strength it would take to keep it there for long. She could tell right away that she was going to have to find something to balance it rather than holding it herself the whole time. She leaned over to set it down when, suddenly, she felt a stabbing pain in her chest. A loud clap of thunder rolled across the sky, and Maude fell to her knees, with her hands clutched over her heart.

"No," she pleaded, as though speaking to the wind. "Fred said there'd be more time. I thought I'd get to help them find her first."

Everything around her grew bright as a shining beam of light fell from the sky. She looked up. "Please," she whispered, fighting against the pain that was radiating through her chest.

"Please don't take me yet. I didn't get to say goodbye." But the light grew stronger until it became blinding, leaving her no choice. Maude closed her eyes and surrendered to it. Then just as she'd arrived in human form years earlier, she departed— vanishing with the light.

CHAPTER 27
AXEL'S MISSION

Seventy-one. This was the number of wolves remaining after Dan was defeated at Black Ice Fort. Seventy-one wolves who experienced the trauma of watching their great packs whittled into near extinction. Seventy-one wolves tasked with passing on the memories and traditions of their ancestors. Seventy-one wolves in charge of reimagining a future that they knew wasn't promised to them.

While the travelers came together to figure out what to do after Dan was killed, the wolves banded together to determine their own path forward. Some wolves insisted that they should move to the other side of the Moon, as far away from the humans as possible. Others wanted to continue living underground, which they insisted was the only place they'd ever be safe. About half of the wolves wanted to go back to the way they'd lived before, reclaiming the lands that they and their ancestors had inhabited for generations.

Unlike the humans, the wolves didn't feel the need to come to a consensus. They had always lived separately in packs, and so they chose to split up and form three new packs based on their preference.

The first trip Axel made after he left the ice tunnels was to visit the wolf pack who'd chosen to go underground. He had expected a kind welcome, but when he arrived inside their lair, he was astonished by how many traps there were to keep intruders out. He had to tiptoe and maneuver his way around dozens of tripwires, nets, and metal devices in order to reach the deep network of tunnels that they occupied.

Before Axel left the ice tunnels, he had seen visions of all three wolf packs, and therefore, he knew of the underground pack's paranoia. However, what he encountered went well beyond a rational concern for safety. Instead, Axel was able to see quite plainly that the pack's obsession with protecting themselves had metastasized so severely that they had turned their living space into a self-made prison.

Unintentionally, the underground wolves had eroded their own freedoms. They lived their lives inside the tunnels, believing that the enemy was still after them, when in reality nobody had given them much thought the last nine years. Because these wolves had allowed the trauma of their past to dictate their future, they were living life only to survive, not to flourish.

Axel knew right away he needed to do something. It took some convincing, but after spending several weeks telling the underground pack about his experiences in the ice tunnels, Axel was given permission to demonstrate to the wolves how to summon their Moon Walker powers. During many sessions of trial and error, he developed methods by which to teach the wolves. Using meditation and focus, Axel showed the pack members how to use their power to speak again. Then once the wolves were reconnected to their voices, he taught them how to shift.

Axel enjoyed his time with the wolves immensely. He found it deeply satisfying, teaching his friends how to access their powers. And while doing so, he discovered something he hadn't realized he'd been missing—the joy of living within a pack. After the other wolves found their voices again, they would sit and tell stories before bed about ancient times. Axel knew that most of these stories had been fabricated by Theia, but he made the choice not to spoil this part for his friends. Storytelling had been such an important part of the lunar wolves' traditions that he couldn't justify ruining it for the others. In Axel's mind, it was just as much a part of who they were as their Moon Walker side.

Axel's plan was to get the pack to follow him aboveground in his first step at reuniting the packs. But when he revealed his desire to the underground wolves, they refused. Their leader, who was Imgu's daughter, Elu, was the one who gave him their answer. "We are grateful to you for coming here and sharing your truth with us, Axel. However, we've made our decision to live underground. We believe there are more terrible things to come, and so to preserve our ways and protect our kind, we are choosing to stay here until it is safe again."

Axel protested, "But Elu, what if it's *never* safe? Do you really want the pack to spend the rest of eternity living down here? Never getting to see the stars or feel the fresh air?"

Elu smiled. "We enjoy our lives down here, Axel. We don't feel sorry about our existence, though it seems you feel sorry for us. We like it here. Up there was our home before, but these tunnels have also been our home for many years. Most of us have spent far more time down here than we have above. I would think you could relate to this after all the years that you yourself spent down here, as well as in the cold tunnels you've spoken of."

Axel frowned and looked around at all of the wolves who were watching their exchange. He sighed. "No. Not really. I didn't hate the tunnels, but I had no desire to stay. I longed to leave them so I could find freedom again."

Elu laughed. "I suppose you think we aren't free because

we live underground? But freedom is having the choice to do what you want. Is it not?"

Axel relented. "Yes, I guess that's true."

"Well, this is what we've chosen for ourselves, and we're happy. Really, Axel. We are."

Axel knew there was nothing left he could say. He didn't try to change the underground wolves' minds after that. He stayed for a few more days so that the pack wouldn't think he was leaving them on bad terms. Then he bid everyone farewell and took off to find the other two packs.

It was a tough decision, choosing which one to visit first. He considered journeying across the Moon to find the wolves who lived farthest away, in a remote location at the southern tip of the Moon's axis. But after his experience with the underground pack, Axel sensed he might have difficulty convincing the pack to return to their ancestral lands. So, he decided to visit the closer pack first in order to recruit a few of the other "aboveground" wolves into going on the journey with him. He hoped these wolves might help persuade the southern wolves to reunite with them.

The northern pack, who'd settled in the former valley home of the once largest wolf pack, were happy to send some of their members to visit the southern pack. However, they weren't interested in trying to convince the southern pack to reunite with them. Instead, they sent a few wolves with Axel to see how the southern wolves were living and to find out if it was worth establishing some type of trade route with them.

It took several weeks for Axel and the four wolves he traveled with to reach the smaller, southern wolf pack. And once they did, Axel and the others stayed for several months. It was here on the south side of the Moon that Axel was reacquainted with the tiny pack he'd led before the battle against Dan took place. The two younger male wolves in the group were ecstatic to see him. They ran to him and greeted him, as if he were their long-lost, older brother. The two female wolves—the widowed mothers of the younger two wolves—were also pleased to see Axel, though they were more formal with their greetings.

The southern wolves had made their home in a large, shallow crater that had its own tunnel system. The tunnels began in the walls at the bottom of the crater and ran deep underneath the ground, like the subterranean tunnels on the Darkside. Just like Axel had done during his visit with the first two packs, he told stories of his time in the ice tunnels while also teaching the pack how to speak again and how to shift. The wolf pack, in turn, showed Axel the unusual crystals they'd found deep under their crater. The crystals looked as if they'd been painted in an explosion of neon colors, and they were more multi-faceted and oddly shaped than Axel had ever seen before.

Once the wolves regained their ability to speak, several of them told Axel and the other visiting wolves a strange tale about creatures that lived under their crater. They explained how during certain parts of the year, when the sun wasn't visible from the southern part of the moon and the lunar surface was lit only by earthlight, there were beings that came out of the tunnels to play.

The story went that the creatures walked upright like the travelers and the bryobane, but they were much smaller. They had squeaky voices and their own language. And they each wore their own glowing crystal which seemed to have something to do with why they were able to leave the tunnels at all. The southern wolves told Axel and the others that the little creatures liked to cause mischief but that mostly they were harmless. The wolves said that over time they'd realized that the creatures weren't actually bad. Just silly.

The wolves laughed as they told the stories of the little creatures, which made Axel happy. He enjoyed the fables that the southern wolves told. He thought it was great that they were continuing the wolves' ancient tradition of storytelling, and even better that it was new stories that everyone understood were make-believe, instead of the old stories that were lies.

After many months in the south, Axel began to pressure the southern wolves to journey back to the valley with him and the others so they could form a larger pack. He told them how he'd been commanded to lead them into battle against Theia's brother—the evil god, Theo. But he also promised that he would never follow through with what had been ordered. He explained how his intention was to combine their forces into a neutral pack. From now on, if they helped anyone, they would help everyone. If they refused to help one group of humans, they refused to help them all. Axel had decided that the best way to maintain peace and prosperity was for the wolves to mind their own business and not get involved in the humans' wars or politics.

However, once he was finished explaining all of this to the southern wolves, he was, again, rebuffed. This time, it wasn't that the pack was scared of the humans like the underground pack. It was that they loved their new home and didn't want to leave it.

Axel was frustrated. For several days after the wolves announced their decision to stay in the south, he sat and listened to them tell their funny stories while he stewed over what to do next. At one point, he began to watch a play that some of the older pups put on, pretending to be the fabled creatures. Axel thought it was fun to see how much the pups enjoyed their antics, but after a while he left the play and went on a long walk around the crater's rim and beyond.

He climbed to the top of a large hill and sat for a long time, looking up into space. Several shooting stars passed over head, and Axel watched the Earth rise above the horizon as the sun set. He noticed that there appeared to be beams of green light up above him, moving around in gently rolling waves. It was majestic and peaceful, and Axel lost himself in it for a while.

When he emerged from his spell, he had made a decision. Even if he couldn't unite the packs, he would continue his mission of neutrality. He realized that he didn't need the wolves to band together in order to defy the humans' requests. In fact, it might be easier this way, he thought—less wolves to fight over whether or not they acquiesced to the travelers going forward.

Axel understood, now, that his determination to unite the packs stemmed from the part of him that was nervous about disobeying the oracle. She'd ordered him to bring all the wolves together under his leadership, so allowing them to stay separate like they were meant he was defying her on all levels.

He returned to the others who were winding down for the night. Many had retired into the tunnels to sleep, but there were a few who remained outdoors, enjoying the darkness that had been brought on by the recent sunset.

Axel wandered over to a small group of wolves, who were staring up at the same wavy green lights he'd been watching earlier. A male wolf on the edge of the group noticed him and said, "Good night for a visit."

Axel nodded at the wolf politely but said, "I'm too tired to visit. I think I'll pack it in. I'm going to begin the journey back north in the morning." Now that Axel had made his decision not to bring the packs back together, he felt a sense of relief and was ready to leave.

The male wolf looked back at the green lights and said, "We'll be sorry to see you go, but you're always welcome to return whenever you'd like."

Axel bowed to the wolf and then moved to a spot a little ways off from the groups who had gathered to star gaze. He lay down on his side and drifted into a restless sleep. His body felt tired and ready to relax, but his mind couldn't get itself into the correct rhythm. It kept stirring excitedly and jolting him out of his slumber. Eventually, he drifted into a deeper sleep, but he kept dreaming that he was standing by a blue and purple fire and that the warm flames were reaching out to engulf him.

After a while, it grew quiet around him as the other wolves went inside the tunnels or fell asleep outside. Finally, he was able to enter into the deepest level of sleep where everything ceased to exist. His breathing spaced out, and he began to snore lightly. He could've easily slept for several hours even *with* the incessant tapping on his forehead. But when one of the gray creatures grabbed ahold of Axel's tail and yanked it, like she was ringing a church bell, Axel's eyelids flew wide open.

"Ouch!" he cried out in pain as he quickly sat up and tried to get his bearings. Four small, elf-like creatures, who were each wearing a glowing, multicolored crystal—and nothing else—stood in front of him, staring up at his face.

Axel gasped, "Oh my god! You're real! I thought you were just some made up story!"

The smallest of the elves spoke to him in an excruciatingly squeaky voice, "What were you thinking? You've really gone and screwed things up now, moon dog!"

The fattest of the elves nodded and said, "Yep. Yep. She's going to stuff your guts into a cryotrap for sure! Yep. Yep."

Then the taller, lankier elf creature said, "She's going to make you into crystal soup. Yum! Yum!"

Axel had had enough with all the elves' ridiculous jibber jabbering. He interrupted them before they could continue. "What are you all talking about? *Who* is going to stuff my guts into a trap and make me into soup?"

The rosy cheeked elf who hadn't spoken yet said, "The loud voiced empress! Ruler of the Moon! Her Royal Highness!"

Axel thought he understood now. "You mean the oracle? Does the loud voiced empress you're referring to speak to you from a dark void?"

The plump elven creature replied, "Sure. Sure. She speaks to us in the dark, but she used to speak to us everywhere before the *others* came."

"Others?" asked Axel.

"Yes. Yes," replied the sweet-faced elf. "The others don't like us, so we were banished. And you'll be banished, too, if you don't get out of here and do what the empress ordered you to do!"

Axel looked around to see if the other wolves had been disturbed by all the noise. But the few who'd remained outside were still asleep. However, Axel suspected this might not be the case for long when he noticed that there were another couple dozen elves roaming about. They were chirping squeakily and dancing with excitement all across the crater floor, and he spotted a few who were sprinkling something on the sleeping wolves.

"What are they doing?" he asked the four elves.

The elves giggled like little kids who were playing a prank. "They're peppering them with the gas dust! Oh boy, oh boy! Better take cover when it starts to work! It's going to get loud and smelly soon!" exclaimed the littlest elf between laughing fits.

Axel understood now why the wolves had called the elves mischievous. "Okay, you can go back and tell your empress, *her royal highness of the moon*, that I'm not going to unite the wolf packs like she commanded. Tell her I've decided we're going to be neutral. The wolves are tired of being pushed around. And we're going to do what's best for *us* since we're the only ones looking out for our best interest."

The little gray creatures looked at each other with worried expressions, but then all at once, they burst out laughing.

"Yum! Yum! He's gonna make some delicious soup for the empress!" said the lanky elf. Then they all doubled over with laughter, patting each other on their little backs and wiping away tears.

Axel didn't have the patience to deal with such nonsense. Now that he was certain he wouldn't get any more sleep if he stayed, he decided to begin his journey back to the valley early. He knew that if he went slow enough the others would catch up if they decided to return to the valley too.

Before he walked away from the laughing elf quartet, he said, "You can tell her if she wants to find me, I'll be right out in the open for all to see. Not hiding away in some lightless underground void, barking orders at my subordinates."

But the elves only responded by making loud slurping sounds, as though they were thoroughly enjoying the imaginary soup they believed Axel would soon become.

CHAPTER 28

FINDING MINA

The storm had disappeared. Fred and Bob sat on the edge of the metal platform, staring up at the top of the valley. The men had gotten dressed in their bodysuits and waited. But when nothing happened, and Maude didn't return, Fred offered to go check on her. He followed the trail of wires up the slope, but the second he saw the cone-shaped pointer, he knew. For a moment, he looked out over the Moon's landscape and thought about where she was.

Breaking the news to Bob wasn't easy. Fred had walked the pointer back down the hill with the wires dragging behind it. "She's gone, Bob," he said, feeling heartbroken for his friend.

Bob stared at him with a blank expression, as though Fred's words didn't make sense. But then as the meaning hit him, he darted up the peak. He searched all over the top of the mountain, calling for his beloved wife, even though he knew she was really gone. The storm hadn't been an anomaly; it had come for her. The bright light that had appeared seconds before the clouds vanished was the sky reaching down to take her back. He knew the stories of her arrival and understood that it all made sense.

The two men sat silently on the edge of the platform for a long time before Fred finally spoke. "You know, if you want to take some time to process everything, I wouldn't blame you. It's already evening. We could just put this on hold for a few days."

But Bob shook his head and stood up, as though Fred's words had lit a fire inside of him. "No. This is how Maude wanted it. She spent the last few days of her life building this machine, and I'll be damned if we aren't going to use it, just like she wanted us to."

Fred stood also. "Do you want me to go get John to help us? You know we can't both go unless we have another set of hands to operate the beam."

Bob thought for a second and replied, "No. I don't want to get anyone else involved in this if we can help it. You wear the suit, and I'll hold the beam. I think if I take a minute to get used to where the buttons are without looking at them, then I can wear the headset. I'll take out the wires so I'm not projected, but at least I'll be able to see and hear whatever you do."

The two men got to work, and within half of an hour, they were ready to begin. Fred looked at Bob with some trepidation. "You're sure this is going to work, right?"

Bob looked down at the headset he was holding. "Yeah. It'll work. We'll need to hurry, though. I'm not sure what the long-term effects of the beam protons will be—if any. Also, to be on the safe side you should probably resist touching anyone while you're in your projected state. I don't know what the outcome would be if you did."

Fred frowned. "Is this supposed to be a pep talk? Because I've got to tell you, you're starting to give me second thoughts here."

Bob brushed away Fred's concerns. "You'll be fine. We'll get you in and out as quickly as we can. And I'll be here, talking you through it the whole time. Put your headset on and let's go find her."

IT WAS A COLD JANUARY DAY. The wind whistled through the leafless trees and pierced the knit scarf around Mina's neck. She strode across campus bundled in a thick, woolen coat with her hands shoved deep into her pockets for warmth. The old, ivy-covered brick and stone buildings had become a home to her during the past four years.

Since she had arrived at school, Mina hadn't traveled home to her cottage at all. Her parents were still somewhere off on their over-extended trip to Africa, and each year she heard from them a little less. The last time they'd corresponded was to inform her that they'd paid her last tuition bill but were expecting her to get a job and earn her own living as soon as she graduated. Mina wasn't expecting them to show up for her college graduation any more than she'd expected them to show up to her high school one four years earlier.

She had stopped thinking of them as her parents long ago. Even if her grandfather had never told her that they weren't her real parents, their lack of involvement in her life during the last several years would have made her wonder. As far as she was concerned, blood was the only thing that made them family now. And even that was questionable.

What kept Mina going most days were memories of Bonkers, her grandfather, and her time on the Moon. She still believed that if she were able to find a way to communicate with the people she'd met on the Moon, then maybe she would get some answers about who she was and where she belonged. After all, her grandfather had told her that her search for answers would lead her to her future.

She had chosen courses in college that would help her learn what she assumed she needed to know in order to begin working on interdimensional communication. She was careful, however, not to talk too much about her belief that this was possible. She'd learned early on that most of the men in her classes didn't take her seriously, and she knew it would only get worse for her if they figured out what she was after.

Interdimensional communication was considered fringe theory, mostly because it hadn't even been proven yet that other dimensions existed. Sometimes, Mina wished she could clue everyone in so she could get some of her classmates to collaborate with her on her research. But she knew it was more likely she'd get booted out of school, or worse, sent off to a mental institution.

As usual, Mina made it to class with plenty of time to spare. She walked in and sat down at a row in the middle of the classroom by herself. She glanced at the professor, who was sitting at the front of the room, reading a magazine. He didn't appear to be much older than the students, but Mina knew he was one of the smartest scientists in his field.

Professor Dodgson had graduated from high school by the time he was ten and completed his doctorate in quantum physics at fifteen. He had worked at the forefront of quantum mechanics for almost two decades, and if anyone could teach Mina everything there was to know about the subject, it was him. She felt butterflies in her stomach as he stood from his chair to start class. Finally, her chance to discover more about her past and future had arrived.

FRED AND BOB had been searching for Mina for over twelve hours. They'd seen a hundred variations of a college campus, and Fred had approached far too many dark-haired, young women to keep track of. "I think we're right where we need to be now. Keep your eyes peeled for her," Bob said encouragingly.

Fred was doing his best to humor Bob, but he was worn out from the search and feared that Bob wasn't going to let him stop until they found her. "Alright. But I'm the one doing all the walking. If we don't find her this time, I'm going to need to rest for a while. Okay?"

"Hmm," said Bob pensively. "I guess that's okay but only for a little bit. We really need to keep going. Now that Maude's gone, it's even more important that we find Mina."

Fred knew it was true that they needed to find her quickly, but he sensed that Bob had thrown himself into their project because it bought him more time before he had to face the reality of losing Maude. That would have been fine if it hadn't meant Fred having to do all the hard work for hours on end. He'd begun to think of himself as a hamster trapped in a wheel, with no way out.

Suddenly, Bob blurted, "Look! That woman walking down the path. That looks just like her. Older, sure. But I think that's her."

Fred was pretty sure Bob had said these same words at least twenty times already, but he checked anyway. Hovering over the scene from above, he floated towards the young woman. Dark hair, check. But he needed to see her face before he'd know for sure. Fred dropped down to the grass a few feet in front of her. The woman's hair was covering her face, and she was leaning forward with her hands shoved into her pockets. He noticed her shiver inside her coat, and as she passed him, a cool breeze swept between them and blew back her dark strands.

Fred's heart leapt. It *was* Mina. He walked towards her, ready to say something, but Bob stopped him. "I haven't projected you yet, Fred. The energy on the beam is getting low. I don't know how much longer it's going to last before we have to recharge it. I think you should follow her while I monitor the energy level. If there's still the same level of juice left in a few minutes, I'll send you down. I'd hate for you to disappear on her before having the chance to explain everything."

Fred nodded. He realized he felt nervous. He'd been waiting for this moment for such a long time, but now that it was here, he didn't know how to act or what to say. He followed Mina as she walked along the curved paths that ran past fountains and through greenspaces between the old, brick buildings.

When Mina reached her building, she slipped in behind another student, who was halfway holding the door open. As soon as she was in, it slammed shut. Fred asked, "What do I do now? I can't open the door on my own until you project me, right?"

Bob suggested, "Maybe you could try to sneak in behind someone else, like Mina did."

Fred stood by the door and waited a few minutes for the next person to come along.

"You know this would've been a lot easier if I could just float through things like a ghost," Fred commented.

"Well technically, you can," Bob told him. "But I don't think it's a good idea since we don't know how your energy will affect this world and vice versa."

Fred asked, "What's the worst that could happen, though?"

"You don't want to know. It's pretty bad," replied Bob.

"Try me."

"Well, you could break the boundaries of time and space in Mina's world. And then your consciousness would meld with the material you're walking through, causing you and it to be pulled into some sort of interdimensional black hole that theoretically exists, but also doesn't exist."

Fred muttered, "I thought you said it was bad."

Bob laughed. Then he said with excitement, "Look! Here comes someone. Follow them!"

Fred moved out of the man's way, careful not to let the swinging door touch any part of him before rushing through the entrance after the man. The door slammed shut behind him, sending shivers down his spine. He hoped he'd be able to find Mina quickly, mostly because he wanted to see her, but also because he now had a terrible fear of touching anything.

"How's that energy meter looking, Bob?" Fred asked as he moved down the long, fifties-style hallways with green and white, speckled flooring. Everything seemed shiny. There were glass cases built into the walls where science and engineering awards were on display. Fred glanced at them in between peeking through the slit window of every door he passed— searching for Mina.

After a few moments, Bob replied, "I think there's still plenty of energy left. The meter hasn't dropped in the last thirty minutes. I've calculated that we'll have about two hours left once we turn the projector back on."

Just as Bob said these words, Fred looked through one of the door windows and caught sight of Mina. She was sitting in the middle of a tiered classroom, watching eagerly as her professor began class. "Well, I guess it's now or never. Fire it up, Bob. I'm going in."

Bob pushed the button and Fred could hear the steady hum of the proton beam which he assumed was a sound that was penetrating his headset back on the Moon. "Alright," said Bob giving him the go-ahead. "Whenever you're ready."

Fred felt a knot growing inside his stomach, but he tried to remind himself that despite having watched Mina the last few years in the tunnels, he actually *knew* her. She wasn't some celebrity he'd seen on television. They had a relationship from when she'd saved him before. "You can do this," he told himself. "She saved you. Now it's time to save her."

Fred threw open the door harder than he'd meant to and charged into the room. Mina was turned around, handing some papers to a guy in the row behind her. Fred heard the professor make a joke about the door opening on its own, since he wasn't able to see Fred. "Well, I guess we have one more joining us today. Maybe our spirited friend could close the door next time also," he quipped.

Fred went and sat down next to Mina. She had grown into a beautiful young woman with long, black hair that was disheveled in the most perfect way. Fred thought of Mina's messy locks as a representation of her wildly independent spirit.

He held his breath, longing to say something, but he didn't know how to get her attention without embarrassing her. Luckily, Bob guided Fred to a piece of scrap paper and a pencil nub that was underneath the chair next to him. He leaned away from Mina, grabbed the pencil and paper, and began to write the first thing that came to mind. "Long time no see."

He tore off the little note and pushed it in front of Mina, but to his surprise, she flicked it away. Fred knew, however, that Mina had no idea it was him, and therefore didn't allow himself to get discouraged. He listened to the professor for a minute to see if he could come up with another idea. The man was going on and on about something called quantum theory, a subject that seemed rather odd to Fred. So, he decided to write, "Do you think this guy really knows what he's talking about?"

Mina looked at the note this time but then shoved it back to him. Bob laughed. "You're going to have to try something else, Fred. She's telling you she's not interested."

But Fred didn't give up. He watched Mina out of the corner of his eye. She was listening to the professor intently while taking notes, although for the life of him, Fred couldn't understand why she cared so much about all this boring talk. He wrote another note to try to get her attention, "This sounds like a bunch of mumbo jumbo if you ask me."

This got Mina's attention but not in the way he'd hoped. In a huff, she picked up her things and moved down the row away from him. Fred knew he was running out of chances before she lost her cool and the whole thing blew up in his face. He had to show her it was him somehow. He followed her and wrote, "I'm serious. I think this guy is just making stuff up as he goes. I mean, really! Ghost particles? Back on Theia we just call them Moon Walkers."

Mina glanced at the note and then turned to him. She looked into his eyes with a surprised expression but there was something else there, too. Something that made Fred's heart skip a beat. In that instant, it felt like a connection between them had snapped back into place. Fred smiled at her, worrying that she might be able to see straight into his heart and see how much he cared for her.

The professor asked, "Is everything okay, miss?"

Mina turned back towards her teacher. Fred watched Mina bite her lip and nod her head. He spoke to her. "It's good to see you, Mina. Sorry to surprise you like this, but I really need to talk to you. Preferably alone."

Mina looked nervous. She whispered back, "I can't just leave in the middle of class. I need to take notes so I don't miss anything."

Fred said firmly, "No, it has to be now. This is important. You have no idea how hard it was to find you. Get the notes from one of these bozos." Fred pointed around the room at Mina's classmates.

Mina shook her head. "No, I can't walk out. The professor would torment me the rest of the semester. It's bad enough being the only woman in most of my classes. I already get the wrong kind of attention from practically everyone."

Fred looked up at the professor and then back at Mina. "Hey, I know. Why don't you tell him you're going to the Moon? That'll get a big laugh from all these clowns and then you won't have to worry anymore about what they think."

Mina sighed. "I'm not going to tell him I'm going to the Moon, Fred."

"Why not?" Fred asked.

Mina began to say, "Because I can't just—"

But the professor interrupted, "Are you sure you're okay, miss? Do you need to be excused?

Mina was horrified. She glared at Fred but responded, "No…I mean, yes. I mean, I do need to be excused to go to the restmoon. I mean, the restroom! Sorry! It's been a weird day."

Some of the students snickered. "I see," said the professor with a raised eyebrow.

Mina stood up and motioned to Fred to follow her out of the room. Fred commented, "Well, that way worked too, I guess. But my way would've gotten a bigger laugh. Just saying."

When they reached the hall, Mina shut the door behind them and asked, "What are you doing here, Fred? You can't just barge into my class after all these years and expect me to drop what I'm doing."

Fred felt disappointed that Mina wasn't more excited to see him. He looked back at the class still going on behind Mina and said, "Actually, I think that's exactly what I just did. I thought you would be happier to see me, though."

Mina relaxed a little. "You're right, Fred. I'm sorry. I was embarrassed back there, but I am happy to see you." She reached out to hug him, but he backed away.

Mina looked at him with a bruised expression, but he quickly explained, "No, you don't understand. I'm not actually on Earth with you right now. I'm still on the Moon. Bob found a way to project me in a pseudo-physical form onto Earth. It means I can interact with objects, but we're not certain yet what effect it would have on people. Oh, and I should've mentioned. You're the only one on Earth who can interface with me."

Mina's jaw went slack. "Are you telling me that nobody else in that classroom could see or hear you?" she asked in disbelief.

Fred smiled. "Yeah, sorry about that."

"But the professor spoke to you when you came in!" Mina protested.

Fred shrugged. "He was just making a stupid joke. You know, like your 'restmoon' one."

Mina put her hand to her forehead. "Well, I guess I'm just going to have to drop this course now since I can never show my face in there again, which means I can forget about graduating altogether, I suppose!"

Fred nodded, "Sure, sure. Graduate. Don't graduate. None of that really matters right now, though."

Mina was furious. "And why is that?"

The light in Fred's face suddenly dimmed, and his eyes filled with tears. "Because Maude died last night, Mina. I've come to tell you—you have to come back."

"Oh my god!" she exclaimed, placing her hand over her heart. "I'm so sorry, Fred. How is Bob doing? Is he okay?"

Fred nodded. "Yeah, sort of. He's the one who pushed us to keep going today. Maude really wanted us to find you before she was gone, but it just didn't work out that way. Oh, and Bob can see and hear you too, by the way. He's wearing a headset. But without Maude there to control the machine, he had to stay behind to work it."

"Hi Bob," Mina said as she looked towards the ceiling. "I'm very sorry about Maude."

Fred smiled. "He appreciates your sympathy. Look, Mina,

we need to go somewhere we can talk. I have lots of things I have to tell you before we start the extraction."

"The extraction?" Mina asked. "That sounds like some kind of terrifying medical procedure. I'm guessing you mean sending me back to the Moon, though?"

"Yes. You *have* to come back. I'm sorry to be so blunt, but it's not safe for you here. You were never supposed to return in the first place."

Mina's heart skipped a beat. Fred's words matched what her grandfather had told her just before he died. For whatever reason, she wasn't supposed to have returned to Earth. And it made sense, because the years since her return had, in many ways, felt like one long, horrible dream. Her existence had seemed like only a shadow of the one she'd known before.

She looked back at her classroom, realizing she didn't need to be there after all. What she'd been searching for all these years had finally come to her. There was no point in fighting it. "Okay, Fred. I'll grab my things. I know somewhere we can go."

THIRTY MINUTES after Mina and Fred left the college campus, they were sitting on a nearly empty train, headed back to her hometown. At the beginning of the ride, they talked, laughed, and reminisced. Then slowly, Fred began to tell Mina about his time in the ice tunnels and what he'd learned. In hushed voices, they discussed Fred's revelations and all the repercussions that these revelations entailed, including why Mina needed to return to the Moon. It wasn't exactly what she had been expecting, but it did explain everything—from her parents' disappearance, to her grandfather's deathbed confessions, to the horrible day by the sea when Bonkers vanished. It also explained Mina's dreams.

On a few occasions, Fred reached over to touch Mina while

explaining the most difficult parts of his story, but one of them always stopped him, fearful over what the consequences would be. Mina felt somewhat relieved that Fred couldn't follow through with his desire to physically console her. She had gone so long without any kind of human intimacy that she wasn't sure she was ready to unlock that side of herself again.

The pain of losing everything that had ever mattered to her had made her tougher than she would've ever thought possible. She had built a fortress around herself to keep others from getting to know her. She told herself it was to keep her secrets hidden, but it had been more than just that. It had been to prevent anyone from ever having power over her heart again. She wasn't willing to risk being vulnerable because she knew it might lead to terrible pain.

However, after spending an hour listening to Fred fit together the puzzle pieces of her confusing life, something inside of her began to change. As she watched Fred's clumsy attempts to reach out and touch her, her heart softened towards him. Mina began to imagine that he *could* touch her and thought about what it might be like to have his warm fingers gently press against her knee or forearm.

To her surprise, the thought of this made her skin tingle with longing, and after a while, she realized that not only did she wish Fred could touch her, she yearned for it. The idea of his forbidden caress had stoked a desire in her that she had never felt before. It wasn't just repressed sexual tension, however. It was an intense desire to be held and loved by someone who had been through many of the same odd experiences as herself, someone who understood what it was like to feel all alone.

Halfway through the train ride, their eyes suddenly locked, and a strained silence full of palpable tension ensued. Mina's face flushed, and Fred looked awkwardly out the window. A minute later, he told Mina that Bob was going to turn the projector off to conserve energy. He told her he would stay close, though, and meet up with her again once the train ride was over.

After Fred disappeared, Mina watched the world race by, feeling an odd mixture of emotions. She felt anger and mistrust due to all the lies she'd been told, melancholy for the world she was leaving behind, and excitement about the adventure she was about to undertake.

She understood what Bob and Fred were expecting her to do, but the idea of it terrified her. Practically every dream she'd had during the last nine years had ended the same way—being swallowed by a wave. Now it all felt like a warning that had been leading up to this very day. To travel back to the Moon, Mina was going to have to face her biggest nightmare. She was going to have to return to the sea.

CHAPTER 29

THE STRANGE GOODBYE

Mina got off the train, looped her bag over her shoulder, and stood on the platform looking for Fred. Soon the small crowd of travelers had dispersed, and yet there was still no sign of him. So, she decided to begin the long walk back to her cottage, alone.

It had been nearly four years since she'd returned to her childhood home. She'd thought of it often during her time in college, but the idea of going back had been too painful to seriously consider. Mina knew that visiting the cottage would feel like a blatant reminder of everything she'd lost.

Once she reached the grassy path that led to the cottage, Mina began to worry that maybe she had dreamt Fred. She'd been certain he would be there waiting on her when she deboarded the train. But now, almost two hours had passed since he disappeared, and Mina couldn't help but dwell on how strange the whole experience had been—her friend from the Moon showing up out of nowhere like an imaginary friend coming to her rescue.

Slowly, she walked towards the cottage. The last thing she wanted was to be there by herself again, and she thought about turning around. But when she was just a few feet away from the little clearing that ran alongside the house, Fred appeared from out of the blue, right by her side. Mina wanted to throw her arms around him, thankful he was there, but she held back, knowing it was too dangerous.

Fred smiled at her. He could tell she was nervous. "It's going to be okay. I'm here, and I'm going to help you get through this."

Mina gave him a little nod and glanced towards the cottage. "Can we go inside for a minute before we head down to the water? Do you think there's enough time?"

Fred nodded. "Sure. I'll follow you."

Mina led the way through the back door. The cottage seemed even smaller than she remembered. She didn't think she'd grown any since leaving for college, but her memories of the place had somehow made it seem grander than it actually was. It didn't help that all the furniture was covered in white sheets—a reminder that when she'd left, she'd already known she was unlikely to return soon.

"Charming," said Fred as they moved through the kitchen into the living room. "I especially like all the lumpy ghosts."

Mina laughed. "My grandfather and I used to sit on that sofa, reading stories and watching old movies for hours on end. When I came back from the Moon, I worried I didn't have much time left with him. His mind had been sick pretty much my entire life. But he actually seemed better than ever. I thought my return might have been the reason why. Like it cheered him up so much that it made him better. But that seems silly now. I was still such a child, really."

Fred wanted desperately to comfort her. He reached towards her but quickly pulled his arm away again. "That's not silly, Mina," he said. "I'm sure it cheered him up, and who knows? Maybe it *did* make him better."

Mina didn't say anything. She walked by her grandfather's

room and peeked in. The bed was neatly made, just like it had been since he died. As she wandered into her own room, she noticed that the house smelled like dust and damp ashes. Fred walked behind her but stopped in the doorway. Mina tried to turn on her bedside lamp, but nothing happened. "Of course," she said in frustration. "With nobody living here, I'm sure the electric bills weren't being paid."

Fred nodded. "Yeah. Probably something like that. Do you want to leave?"

Mina looked around at her vanity and her bed and her old books. Then she said, "You know, I used to have the strangest dreams after my grandfather died. You were in a few of them. You would be right out there." Mina pointed out her window. "Only you were always trapped in the middle of a giant wheel. You'd try to speak but your face was covered by ice. It was horrible. I would try to help you, but every single time I was—"

"Swallowed by a large wave," Fred finished her sentence.

Mina looked surprised. "Yeah. How did you know?"

Fred shrugged. "I don't think they were dreams. Not for me, anyway. I had the same vision several times while I was down in the ice tunnels. That's when I first realized I had to find you. Even before I learned about all the rest of it."

Mina smiled and swept her fingertips across the top of her old comforter. "Okay. I think I'm ready now. At least as ready as I'll ever be."

Fred nodded, and they walked back down the hallway to the kitchen. Mina laughed as they opened the backdoor to the cottage. "You know, I think I only ever used the front door to this place once or twice. I'm not even sure I remember where it is."

As Mina stepped out into the grass, the sky grew dark, and a terrible shiver ran through her. Fred looked up at the clouds and then back at her. "It's going to be okay. Remember, I'll be here with you," he told her. "I'll stay by your side as long as I can."

Mina couldn't take her eyes off the sky, but she nodded to let Fred know she'd heard him. And together they walked towards the tall trees that stood like giants above the sea. Once they'd climbed down to the shore, Fred walked all the way to where the water was rolling gently across the sand. He looked back at her, as if he were trying to show her that nothing bad was going to happen. Mina thought of the time when she had stood right where Fred was standing, looking back at Bonkers reassuringly. It was right before the sea came and took her away.

Mina didn't want to go any further, but she knew Fred and Bob were counting on her. Plus, she had no desire to stay, especially after everything Fred had revealed.

She walked to where he stood facing her. "What do we do now?" she asked.

Fred looked towards the water. "I suppose we take a swim. I think that once you go far enough, the rest will happen on its own."

Mina heard everything he said, but she had begun to feel lightheaded and dizzy. She could feel her fear taking over as the adrenaline began to course through her. Without thinking, she reached for Fred's arm to steady herself, but he pulled away fast. "You can't, Mina. I'm sorry. I'd love nothing more than to carry you through this, but I don't want anything bad to happen."

Fred's words helped to ground her some. She confessed, "I'm scared to go in the water, Fred. I haven't dared go in since before all this started. In all of my dreams, I get swept away by the ocean. What if I go in there, and I don't make it out again?"

Fred thought about Mina's concerns for a moment and then said, "Do you remember when you helped me through the small tunnel, right after Axel and his pack saved us from the well?"

Mina nodded.

"I'm going to stay right by your side the whole time and hum, just like you did for me then. And you can hum back whenever you need to take your mind off your fear. Okay?"

Fred's dark brown eyes looked so confident, like he was certain his plan would work. Mina didn't know if it was such a good idea, but she knew that Fred was doing his best to help her, and it wasn't like she had a better idea. "Okay," she said. "I'll try."

Fred began to hum as he walked into the water, and Mina slowly followed him, inch by inch. She harmonized with his tune, just like he had done long ago in the tiny tunnel they had crawled through together. Strangely, Mina found that the humming did put her mind at ease, and soon she and Fred were swimming along next to one another, humming and smiling at each other as they went. Mina imagined that they were dolphins gliding through the ocean and enjoying the cool water against their skin.

When the giant, glass pathway crashed into the sea, it didn't even startle her, like it had years before. Of course, she had known it was going to happen this time, but it wasn't just that. Mina was actually enjoying her time in the water, something she hadn't expected, or even thought possible. The dark clouds overhead disappeared, leaving only the bright blue sky above them. Mina glanced at the curved, glass pathway and then raised her eyebrows at Fred as if to say, "Want to race?"

Fred responded by taking off at full speed through the water. He reached the bridge first, but when he looked back at Mina swimming towards him, he knew he'd made a mistake. Leaving her behind had broken whatever spell the humming had put her under. Her face said it all—she was anxious and scared. Fred began to hum again as he pulled himself onto the sloped glass surface. He motioned towards Mina to encourage her along, but she looked dazed. Fred began to worry, wondering if she'd be able to go through with it.

A few seconds later, however, she pulled herself onto the glass surface and carefully, they began to climb. Fred stopped humming once he realized it was no longer having any effect. "Are you okay?" he asked.

Mina replied, "Yeah. Sorry. This is just a lot. The humming helped for a while, but I think I'd like to stay alert for this next part, if that's okay."

"Of course," Fred agreed.

The two climbed the long, arched walkway in silence for a while until Fred decided to tell Mina the story of how he and Maude had broken Bob out of jail. He tried to tell the story in a funny way to help her relax, but he realized after a few minutes that she wasn't listening when he asked, "Can you imagine what it would be like having to listen to Dale talk for four hours straight while sitting on a horse in front of you? I don't know why I didn't think to gag him. I *did* think once or twice about knocking him out cold."

Mina didn't laugh. Fred looked back at her and saw that she didn't look right. Her eyes were rolling around strangely, and she'd started to sway back and forth. Fred glanced towards the water below them and realized they were several hundred feet from the surface. "No, no, no, Mina! Stay with me!" he yelled. But she didn't seem to hear him. She began to fall sideways off the path, and with no other choice, Fred grabbed her wrist and pulled her towards him.

He let go as fast as he could once Mina was safe again, kneeling on the glass bridge. "Mina! Mina! Look at me! Are you okay?"

Mina took a few deep breaths. "I think so. I'm just...I'm feeling woozy. And the higher we climb, the worse it seems to be getting. I don't know what's wrong with me. This didn't happen last time."

Fred felt scared. He didn't know what he'd do if Mina wasn't able to keep going. And to make matters worse, Bob had already warned him that the energy meter was critically low. He bent down and looked at where he'd grabbed Mina's wrist. It was bright red and swollen, as though it had been burned. "Does that hurt?" he asked.

Mina looked at the spot. "It's okay. It stings pretty bad, but I'll take it over the alternative." She smiled sweetly. "Thank you, Fred."

Fred nodded seriously. "Mina, I'm going to disappear soon. I don't know when, but I'll be waiting for you on the other side when you arrive. Just remember what I told you. It may take a long time to get through this but promise me you won't give up. I'm positive you'll make it back to the Moon realm if you keep going."

Mina nodded. "Okay, Fred. I promise. I won't give up."

They continued to climb while Fred asked Mina questions about her life to keep her talking. He heard all about her college studies and the time she'd spent alone after her parents left. Much of it he already knew from watching her life while he was in the ice tunnels, but he enjoyed hearing all of it from her perspective. Plus, he hadn't told Mina about all the time he'd spent spying on her. He realized it might sound creepy, and he worried it would scare her off if she knew that the one thing that kept him going during his many years inside the labyrinth was knowing he'd get to see her again one day.

Eventually, Fred noticed his body was beginning to fade. He wished he could continue on Mina's journey with her, but he also understood that once she reached the top of the pathway, she'd be on her own no matter what. "I'm going now, Mina. I won't be able to see or hear you again while the machine recharges, but I'll find you as soon as you're back."

He looked down and saw that Mina was clutching her wrist. Instantly, he could tell something wasn't right. The hand below her injured wrist was nearly transparent. "Mina, why didn't you say some—"

But before Fred had time to finish his question, he vanished into thin air. Mina raised her hand so it was right in front of her face. "It's going to be alright," she told herself. She knew it was bad, though. She hadn't told Fred, because she was certain there was nothing he could do about it, and she didn't want him to feel bad about saving her life.

She looked at the path stretching high up in front of her. "Okay, Mina," she said. "We've done this before, and you've faced worse than this since then. Just keep it together." She took a couple of steps, and then a couple more, and she kept the cycle going until she'd picked a stride that felt comfortable.

She climbed for what seemed like it could have been minutes or hours. Her mind had wandered in far too many directions to tell. But eventually, she reached the top of the curved glass walkway, where it glowed neon blue. Mina searched for the hole that she'd stumbled upon abruptly on her first journey, but this time, she was able to spot it before she'd almost walked through it. "Here we go," she thought as she took a deep breath and pulled herself up.

Mina wasn't sure what to expect. Fred had told her that once she reached the top of the bridge, everything would be different than last time. She'd done her best to prepare herself for the unexpected, however, she was extremely alarmed to find herself falling headfirst. Instead of inching her way onto a platform in outer space, she tumbled end over end until she landed in a dark, cozy space.

Judging by her equilibrium, she was pretty sure she was upside down, wedged between a bunch of cardboard boxes. The boxes smelled sweet and musty, like mildew. She pushed her one good hand against the ground and pulled her feet to the floor, bringing herself back up into a standing position. Mina felt around until she found a door handle. She turned it, and the door suddenly flew open as Mina and the boxes tumbled out of a closet, into a dark bedroom.

Mina caught herself before she hit the ground. Then she straightened up and looked around the room. There was a desk in front of her with a computer sitting on top of it. To her right was a small bed with a woman and man lying wrapped around each other, asleep. Mina looked for another door to sneak out of but realized that she was going to have to walk past the bed to reach it. Quietly she tiptoed towards the door. The woman, who had her face buried in the man's chest, pulled away and looked up at Mina dreamily. Mina gasped and then covered her mouth. It was *her.* The woman lying in the bed was Mina.

The alternate version of her rolled away, repositioning herself towards the wall. The man, still asleep, turned so that he was lying flat on his back. "Oh my god!" thought Mina. "That's Professor Dodgson!"

Her heart began to beat so fast that she could barely breathe. "Oh my god! I slept with my professor!"

She ran for the door and opened it, quickly slamming it shut behind her. Suddenly, she was back in her own bedroom inside the cottage. She turned around and walked towards the living room. But before she reached it, she heard the sound of familiar voices. Right away, she knew that it was her parents, her grandfather, and herself. They were talking to each other and laughing. She peeked her head into the living room and saw the whole family sitting around the coffee table, playing a boardgame. Bonkers was there too, wagging his tail happily as he ate popcorn off the ground.

Mina looked closely and saw something unexpected. The Mina sitting atop of the ottoman was an older version of herself than the one who'd existed when her grandfather died and her parents abandoned her. And this detail darkened the happy scene.

Mina couldn't help but dislike the other version of herself, for she knew that the other Mina had lived a much easier life than she had. Although Mina understood that in some ways it was better to know the truth, it was still painful to see how happy this other version of her family was. She stepped away from the living room and walked through her grandfather's bedroom door.

Again, she was transported to another place and time. Only here, Mina felt as though she were being stretched thin like a rubber band. She'd walked directly from her cottage into one of her high school classrooms. But in this version of reality, everything was elongated and warped. It looked as if the entire world had been pulled into a fun house mirror. Mina could see herself sitting at her desk, reading a book while the girls who sat behind her taunted her mercilessly. They laughed about what a freak she was and made jokes about her nerdy personality. Mina moved into the hallway, although she felt like she was walking through molasses, and the more she tried to hurry, the harder it was to move. She found the door to the girl's bathroom and walked through it, into the backseat of a moving car.

In this world, everything was back to normal, although the roof of the car seemed a bit compressed. There was a man and a woman sitting in the front, but Mina moved across the backseat to the opposite door, without stopping to see who they were. However, as she slid, she caught sight of her professor in the rearview mirror. She jerked her head towards the passenger's seat and saw that, indeed, *she* was the woman sitting there.

"Do we really have to go to this thing? You're not even planning on working at the school after this semester," she said. The Mina in the front seat turned her head, and she could see that this alternate version of herself looked to be about ten years older.

Dodgson replied, "I know, darling. I assure you I don't want to go either, but if I ever want to ask these people for funding again, then it's important I continue to show an interest in the program. You know how this works."

The older Mina sighed. "I know. I just hate leaving her overnight with my parents. If grandfather were still around—"

Suddenly, a car from the other lane swerved in front of them, and before the younger Mina had time to react, she was thrown through the door of the car. Mina closed her eyes and braced for impact, but when nothing happened, she opened them again. She was standing in front of the restroom at the public library—the one she and Bonkers had visited almost every weekend for years.

Still trembling from the experience she'd just had, Mina straightened up and took a few slow breaths to calm down. Then she moved towards the door to the backroom where the magazines and copy machines were. When she got there, however, she found that not only was the door locked, but it wasn't a normal door. It was about a foot and a half shorter than any regular-sized door she'd ever seen. She looked up and noticed that the ceiling was also lower than it should've been. In fact, she was able to reach up and touch it with her fingers.

Mina forced herself to look at her other hand. It ached terribly, although not much had changed since the glass pathway. She could still see it, even if it were a bit more faded than before. She headed to the front of the building and walked through the exit, praying that this would be the final door she would have to go through. But nothing happened. She was just outside the library. Her body tensed with worry as dark thoughts flooded her head. "Calm down," she told herself. "It's going to be okay. Just keep going."

Fred had told her that no matter what, she had to keep finding doors to walk through. "Maybe I need to try a different building," she thought. She walked across the street and tried to open the door to a restaurant, but just like the door to the back room of the library, it was shorter than normal and locked. Mina peeked inside the window and saw people sitting at tables. "Okay, *that's* strange," she said out loud.

Trying her best not to panic, she moved on to the next building which housed several art studios. Mina tried all the outer facing doors, but just like the others, they were locked. Unable to keep the panic at bay any longer, Mina began to run through the city, turning every doorknob and jiggling every handle that she passed. "The whole town can't be locked!" Mina shouted in anger.

Her head felt oddly heavy and unbalanced, like someone was pushing her to the ground. Her heart pounded in her chest, and she knew what she had to do next. She headed for her cottage. She made her way through the city streets, across several forest trails, and into the clearing by the sea.

As she walked to the backdoor, she heard someone moving around in the front yard. She crept along the side of the house, and when she'd almost reached the front, she heard two people talking softly, though they were arguing back and forth. It was her parents. She peered around the corner while hiding behind a thick clump of purple flowered vines that wound along the side of the cottage. Her parents were standing face-to-face with her father pointed in her direction.

He looked older than she'd ever seen him. In a loud whisper, he said, "She can't just stay in that room by herself every single day. She needs to get out and play, go on walks, enjoy the fresh air for crying out loud!"

Her mother was harder to hear, but Mina thought she heard the words, "I don't think we should push her yet. She needs some more time to heal before we shove her out of the nest."

Mina's father grumbled, "I don't think she's healing by spending all her time locked away by herself. She should be out meeting people her own age, getting her mind off her troubles for a while."

Mina had no idea what they were talking about, but she was ready to leave. It was obvious she had stumbled into one more strange, alternate version of her life, and she didn't care to know the shape of it. She just wanted to escape from this "existential crisis maze" as quickly as possible.

She stepped backwards, but as she did, her father looked right at her and began walking towards her. She held her breath, preparing for the weirdest confrontation of her life, but when he rounded the corner of the house, he kept going. She watched him from behind as he went around to the back of the house. "He can't see me," she thought.

She walked to the rear of the cottage and opened the back-door, hoping this would be the one to send her on. But alas, she entered the kitchen where her dad was standing, staring into the fridge. He let out a sigh as she walked past him, into the living room and down the hallway to her bedroom.

When she reached the door, she saw that there was a girl with long, dark hair sitting on the end of her bed. The girl's back was turned to her, and she was facing the window. "Who in the world is *that?*" Mina wondered, though in the back of her mind, she was already beginning to suspect.

The girl began to hum a familiar tune. It sounded distant and a bit eerie coming from this child who Mina didn't recognize, even though she was sitting inside Mina's bedroom, as though it were her own. Mina listened to the melody closely for a moment, and soon she recognized it as the same tune she had sung to make the wings fly her to the Moon, once upon a time.

"Okay, Mina," she thought. "It's no big deal if there's a strange, little girl humming in your bedroom. It's not your concern. You just have to keep going!"

Mina pushed through the doorway, willing it, with all her

might, to be the one to send her on. But again, all that happened was that she entered her old bedroom. The little girl turned around and looked at Mina with dark, familiar eyes. Then with a knowing smile, she said, "I've been waiting for you."

HOURS HAD PASSED since Fred disappeared from the glass pathway and returned to his own reality on the Moon. He and Bob had been monitoring Mina's whereabouts as best they could with the location device that Bob had set up to ping Mina once they found her. Using the device, they were able to tell whenever she moved from one splintered dimension to the next. However, Fred had grown extremely concerned after it became apparent that Mina had stopped moving. She was no longer jumping between realities. As far as they could tell, Mina had been in the same place for hours.

Finally, after obsessing over it nonstop for the better part of an hour, Fred asked Bob the question that kept going through his head, "Do you think she's still alive?"

Bob shrugged. "Yeah, I think so. But I have no idea how we're going to pull her out if she's stuck. Most of this goes way beyond my understanding of how the universe works."

Fred's heart ached, but he nodded. "We knew there were risks involved. She knew it too. I guess we just try to find a solution if there's one to be found. I just hope…I just…*Damn it!* Do you think it's because I grabbed her? Do you think the proton projection might have erased her? Could the effects of my touch have spread to her whole body?"

Bob moved towards Fred. "Don't do this to yourself. We don't know what's happened yet. Maybe she's okay."

Fred began to pace, looking up at the sky as though it

might give him some sort of answer. He knew what he'd been told in the ice tunnels, and he'd believed it. He'd believed that Mina would be able to return to the Moon realm. But now, he was beginning to doubt everything. What if he'd been lied to just like all the other creatures in the realm had been lied to so many times? What if it had all been a trick to hurt Mina, and he'd played along with it like a fool?

Fred continued to stay lost in thought like this for a long time until, suddenly, Bob let out a gasp. "Oh my god! She's made it! She's across the barrier!"

"Wait! Are you sure?" Fred asked as he ran to Bob's side to check the location device. "Oh my god! She's here! I've got to go find her. Is that okay? Can I take one of the horses?"

Bob smiled at Fred but with a hint of sadness. "Of course. Just don't get distracted. Find her and bring her here fast. The powers Maude used to hide this place disappeared when she did, but I'm working on something else," Bob said as he tapped his temple. "We don't want Goodman to find us, though, in the meantime. You'll have to be extra careful not to lead them back here."

Fred nodded. "Got it! Thanks, Bob!" he yelled as he tore off his headset and ran down the hill to grab one of the horses.

Fred rode for many miles over the lunar terrain until he reached the spot where he and Mina had both first arrived on the Moon many years earlier. Then he spun around on his horse until he caught sight of a woman with dark hair walking towards the old city. He took off in her direction.

When he was within fifty feet, he pulled his horse to a stop, got off, and ran to her. Mina turned to face him with an affectionate smile. But as he walked the last few steps towards her, he noticed she was holding her arm behind her back.

"Are you okay?" he asked.

Sheepishly, she brought her arm out in front of her, for Fred to see. Her hand was even more transparent than before, and her wrist was colored in dark shades of crimson and purple from where he'd grabbed her.

"It's okay," she reassured him. "But I think I can kiss my lifelong dream of becoming a puppeteer goodbye," she said with a grin.

Fred smiled back. "Would it be okay if I hug you now?"

Mina looked at him and bit her lip. The tingling she'd felt on the train suddenly came rushing back. She nodded, and Fred wrapped his arms around her tenderly.

"I want you to know," he said, "I never stopped thinking about you after you left. I've spent almost every single day of the last nine years hoping I'd see you again. I think that, somehow, we're connected, Mina. I think that's why your dreams and my visions were the same. I think it means we're supposed to be together."

He stood up straight while continuing to hold her around the waist. He stared passionately into her eyes and touched the side of her face gently with the back of his hand. He'd dreamt of this moment for so long. He turned his gaze to her soft, red lips and closed his eyes. He leaned in to kiss her, but before he could, Mina exclaimed, "Wait, Fred! There's something I have to tell you!"

"What is it?" he asked, pulling away, worried that she was about to reject him.

Mina replied, "While I was trying to leave, I saw something strange. Well actually, I saw *a lot* of strange things. But there was one in particular that really stood out."

"Which was?"

Mina bit her lip again nervously but forced herself to spit it out. "I don't know exactly how to say this. But I think I have a daughter."

CHAPTER 30

BETSY'S SURPRISE

A week had passed since the unauthorized prisoner swap. Betsy was furious when she found out what had happened, but she'd kept her cool to prevent anyone from knowing she wasn't the one behind it. After she learned about the transfer, she sent word to the guards at the Sheep Spa, ordering them to keep quiet on the matter and continue to man their posts until further notice. She needed to keep anyone from finding out that Bob had been freed, especially Goodman.

Late in the afternoon, on the seventh day after Bob's escape, a guard from the underground prison came storming into Betsy's office. Betsy banged her fist on her desk the second he came in. She'd grown impatient with the guards over the last week as they continued to use her as their official complaint box whenever Dale stepped out of line.

"What is it now? I told you all to gag him if he won't shut up! I'm not your mother. Figure out a way to handle him on your own!"

The guard looked confused by Betsy's outburst. "Begging your pardon, ma'am, but I'm not here about Dale."

Betsy relaxed a little. "Oh. Then, what is it?" she demanded.

The guard replied, "It's that other prisoner. The one with the metal face cover. We think he has something he's trying to tell us. Either that or he's dying. It's hard to tell for sure, but he hasn't given us any trouble before. We thought we better get your permission, though, before we take his cover off."

"Ah, so the little weasel is finally ready to talk," she said with a wicked grin. "That's good news, Hanz. I'll come with you. I want to hear what he has to say."

WHEN THEY REACHED the prisoner's cell, the guards entered first. Betsy followed them in and watched as they unlocked the metal plate that fit across the prisoner's mouth and nose with just two tiny pin holes for his nostrils to breathe through. The young man let out a loud gasp for air as the plate was unhinged from his face.

Betsy mustered up the sweetest smile she could manage, though it made her look like a crazed jack-o-lantern. "I've been told you have something to say?" she asked.

The man nodded. "I have information about the escapees' whereabouts. I can tell you where to find them if you let me go."

Betsy laughed and turned to her side, as if she might leave. "Is that all you have to tell me?" she asked. "Tsk tsk. Surely, you don't think we haven't figured out there whereabouts ourselves by now. After all this time? No deal, darling. Boys, rough the little dumpling up before you put his mask back on. I think he needs a better appreciation for the severity of his situation."

The man pleaded, "Wait! That's not all. I have information about Maude. I saw something. Something unusual that I think you might want to hear."

Betsy turned back to look at him. She raised her dark black brow and leaned her head towards him like a crow eyeing its lunch. "Give us a minute," she said to the guards.

Once the guards had left the cell, she asked, "Okay, what is it? This better be good or I promise I'll have you disposed of in the most terrifying way possible. Your skin will be shredded and ripped from your bones!"

The man shuddered. "When we were leaving New Wald-off, the guard at the gate stopped us. He said they were looking for an old woman. Maude stood face-to-face with him, but he didn't seem to realize she was an old woman. And when I glanced back at her, I swear she had bright, red hair and smooth skin, just like when she was younger."

A light in Betsy's beady, black eyes suddenly flickered on. "Hmm. You may have just saved your own skin, Max." Betsy ran to the cell door and yelled to the guards, "Bring the prisoner to my office and wait with him until I arrive. And bring Dale too. I have an announcement for everyone!"

Betsy left and hurried to her office, grabbing a large object from her desk that she hid behind her back. She turned the metal wheels to unlock the big, wooden door and then opened it to the dark hallway that led to Goodman's office. When she reached his door, she flung it open without knocking.

Goodman looked grotesque. His skin was dark gray and parts of it were peeling off. His eyes were crazed and there was barely any of his dark hair remaining. "What's the meaning of this?" he demanded. "You can't just come in here unannounced! I'm doing important prime minister work! Get out!"

Betsy looked at the glowing, dark crystal on his desk. Then a big grin spread across her face as she raised a cartoonishly large mallet above her head. Goodman stood up and reached towards her. "Noooo!" he cried as she smashed the large hammer down on his desk, breaking the crystal into tiny fragments.

A dark black smoke sprayed out of the crystal shards, and Betsy declared giddily, "It's okay, Father! I've received confirmation about what we suspected all along! Theia has been trapped inside of Maude this whole time. You don't have to hide in the crystal any longer. It's time for you to take your rightful place in the light!"

Goodman, who looked horrified by the scene that was playing out in front of him, suddenly realized what was happening. His eyes locked on Betsy, and she nodded at him evilly. Then the black smoke pulled together to form a dark, humanoid shape, and all at once, it flew into Goodman's body through his mouth.

Betsy giggled like a little girl as she watched Theo take control of Goodman's body. Right away, Goodman's face transformed so that it no longer looked grotesque like before. It did, however, seem to have a dark, other-worldly aura around it. In his deep voice, Theo said, "That certainly took longer than I was hoping. How in my name could it possibly have taken you this long to figure that out?"

Betsy frowned and said, "I'm not even a full god! Why didn't *you* figure it out sooner?"

"Never mind," said Theo. "I take it you've captured Theia, then? I want her brought in front of me immediately!"

Betsy looked nervous all of a sudden. "Well, not exactly. I wanted to bring the news of her identity to you before all the capturing business. I'm positive that it will be easy to apprehend her, though. I have a prisoner waiting in my office, who can take us to her."

Theo was livid. "You mean to tell me that you set me free without bringing her in first? What an imbecile! This will never work until Theia is entirely under my control! I knew I should've chosen a human woman to have my child. You've been such a disappointment! You never get *anything* right!"

Betsy had a vicious look in her eyes, like she wanted to

wrap her hands around Goodman's neck. "I'm going to take care of it. I've already set the wheels in motion. You just need to trust—"

Suddenly, Goodman's eyes popped out of their sockets, and the dark gas that had entered through his mouth a moment earlier began to seep out of the two gaping holes in his skull.

"BETSSSSY! I TOLD YOU!" screamed Theo as Goodman's whole body turned to dust, and the black smoke evaporated into thin air.

"Oh, crap!" Betsy exclaimed as she watched her father get swept away—presumably, back to Black Ice Glacier. "Okay," she said to herself, attempting to stay calm. "I guess we'll just have to go with plan B."

She walked back down the hallway into her office and found the guards waiting there with Max and Dale. She shoved the spiky door shut and then began to hobble back and forth in front of them with a stone-cold expression.

"I'm your new boss, effective immediately! Anyone who has a problem with that shall be arrested and thrown into prison. Do you understand?" she asked forcefully.

One of the guards raised his hand. "What is it, Chuck?" asked Betsy.

"Umm, what happened to Prime Minister Goodman?"

Betsy frowned. "The job was too much for him, so he's left me in charge. This is the only time I will ever answer that question, though. So spread the word and make sure that everyone understands that I will not be disobeyed. I have a penchant for enjoying others' pain, and I will unleash terror for the sake of keeping things orderly."

The guards looked at each other, as if deciding what to do, but then after a few seconds, they began to salute Betsy, one by one.

"Good," she said. "Your first order of business is to leave these two prisoners with me and go arrest the council. I want each member in their own prison cell by the end of the day. They are to be brought in on charges of conspiracy against Prime Minister Goodman, and I will be the one to question them. Got it?"

The guards replied, "Yes, ma'am!" Then they saluted Betsy one more time and left.

The moment the guards were gone, Dale said, "Well, Bets, I gotta say, I didn't think you had it in you. What I'd like to know, though, is where you see me fitting into this grand scheme of yours."

Without missing a beat, Betsy replied, "You work for me now, Dale. It shouldn't be too hard for you to manage since you spent most of your life working for that idiot brother of yours. Take Max here and have him show you where the escapees are hiding out. There's a war coming, and *we're* going to be the ones to strike first."

RAGHER HAD BEEN WANDERING around the ice tunnels alone for several weeks with no sign that the oracle wanted to see him. He'd reached a low point. He missed Axel and Fred. It had been decades since he'd been by himself for so long, and he wondered if he would ever see the outside of the tunnels again. Being ignored felt like torture, and Ragher had come to resent his keeper—this spirit he'd obeyed his entire life, even though doing so had made his life miserable.

"Tick…tick…tick." Finally, the ice sheets moved aside, revealing the dark passageway he yearned to see. Ragher entered the void more boldly than ever, ready to tell the oracle exactly how he felt. The walls closed behind him, but before the voice could speak, Ragher said, "I've decided I no longer answer to you. Kill me if you must. I don't wish to be alive if it means being bound to your orders. They've caused me and the ones I love nothing but pain. Show me mercy and end my suffering now!"

The oracle replied, "I am sorry you feel this way, Ragher. I never gave orders with the intention of inflicting pain on you or your loved ones. But your wish will be granted soon enough. I have one last mission for you, and then you shall be free of me forever."

"No!" shouted Ragher. "I will not obey you! Do your worst, but I am done with you!"

The voice spoke. "You will obey me. I know this because I, too, have a child and know what it's like to want to keep them safe. Your mission is the only thing that will prevent Axel and the last of the wolves from being exterminated."

Ragher screamed into the darkness. "Why do you insist on tormenting me? Have I not kept your secret well? Have I not done everything you've ever asked of me? And yet you insist on spinning every last second of my life into a tragedy. Why do you torture me this way?"

The oracle didn't respond right away, but then she laughed. "You Moon Walkers always were theatrical. I tell you that you've almost reached the end, just like you've asked for, and yet you make such a big show of it. Well bravo, Ragher. But let's get on with it, shall we?"

Ragher hated the oracle, but he knew he had no choice but to hear her out, *again*. "What must I do to protect my son?"

"Your son has decided to defy me. He was supposed to lead the wolves into battle against Theo and the humans who are aligning themselves with him and his daughter. But instead, Axel has decided to stay neutral, whatever *that's* supposed to mean. I've always thought of neutrality as a coward's bargain, and Axel didn't strike me as a coward, so this development was surprising.

"You must make it right. Luckily, you'll finally get to do what you've always wanted by sacrificing yourself to Theo."

"I didn't *want* to sacrifice myself to Theo. I wanted to protect my family."

"Right," said the voice. "And this is how you're going to do that. Visit your son one last time. Tell him that you know there's a war coming. Tell him you're going to go to Theo to ask him to let the wolves remain neutral. But then, when you're face-to-face with Theo, I want you to do whatever it takes to get the dark god to kill you. By doing so, you will pull Axel and the others into the fight. It's the only way to protect the Moon realm from falling to the dark god."

Ragher asked, "But how can I know that any of this will keep Axel safe? He'll still have to fight Theo after I die."

The voice answered, "You don't, but I give you my word that I will send my own child to fight by his side. And if they win, they'll inherit the realm. Together."

Ragher thought about it for a moment. His mind and body were worn out, emotionally exhausted after years of going along with the oracle's grand schemes. He wanted to be done with it all, but his heart kept nudging him—reminding him how high the stakes were. Ragher had little to no legacy except for his son, and he wouldn't allow any harm to come to Axel. However, he wasn't willing to throw his entire life away without one condition, at least. He replied, "Fine. I'll do it. But before I go, I have one demand."

"What is it?" asked the oracle.

"When this is all over, and the wolves prevail, I want you to send Neriti back. Allow her to live the life she never got to have—the one I ruined when you sent me to her."

"How very noble, Ragher," said the oracle. "Alright, then. It's a deal."

ABOUT THE AUTHOR

K.E. spends most of her time with her family, including her husband, growing humans, and full-sized pets. When she is not dreaming, writing, or editing, she is asleep. Or she is possibly outside on an adventure with her growing humans and pets.

If you enjoyed reading *The Lunar Wolves*, please consider leaving a review. Reviews are the backbone of an author's success, and it always means a great deal to get readers' feedback. Thank you for your support!

The Gods of Time, book three of The Moon Travelers Trilogy, is available now. K.E. also has a new series coming out in 2024 and a prequel to the Moon Travelers Trilogy planned for shortly after.

Follow K.E. on Facebook, Instagram, Twitter, and Threads @davenportwriter. Or visit her website to sign up for the monthly newsletter.

www.kedavenport.com

www.ingramcontent.com/pod-product-compliance
Lightning Source LLC
Chambersburg PA
CBHW060943190726
48286CB00005B/1408